D1561726

There once was a time when honor was more precious than the blood spilled to earn it.

What They Said About SHADES OF GRAY

"It is a book that I think could have the impact ... of a *Gone With the Wind*."
— *Jonathan A. Noyalas*
Director for Civil War Studies, Lord Fairfax Community College

"A fine addition to anyone's library of historical novels." *– J.E.B. Stuart, V*

"A beautiful story with a timeless message. It touched my heart and soul."
– Catherine Bennett

"Exciting, intense, romantic, and thrilling from start to finish. The most balanced book on the War Between the States I have ever read."
— *Bob O'Connor, Civil War Author*

"Andrea and Hunter are like a Virginian, Civil War-era Elizabeth and Mr. Darcy."
– Literarily

"Not since reading *Gone With the Wind* have I enjoyed a book so much."
– Sarah Winch

"[James'] work stands out among the best of the historical novelists, and is a worthy addition to the Civil War fiction line-up. Huzzah!" *– Scott Mingus, Civil War Blogger*

"The book took my breath away. Honestly, you will not sleep."
– Bookworm's Dinner Blog

"I think it is the best Civil War fiction book since *Cold Mountain*."
– James D. Bibb, SCV Trimble Camp 1836

Noble Cause

A Novel of Love and War

An epic tale of honor, faith, and
courage under the Southern Cross

By Jessica James

Patriot Press
Gettysburg, Pa.

150th Anniversary of the Civil War
Commemorative Edition

PUBLISHED BY PATRIOT PRESS

Gettysburg, Pa.

www.patriotpressbooks.com

Noble Cause

ISBN 978-0-9796000-4-3

LCCN 2011920167

May 2011

USA

0 9 8 7 6 5 4 3 2 1

Edited by Wendy Jo Dymond
Cover design by Cathi Stevenson, Book Cover Express

*"To all those intrepid souls who now rest
beneath the soil they held dearer than self.*

*There are some who have not forgotten you
—who will never forget. To you and to
them this book is sincerely dedicated.*

Chapter 1

"But one of them would make war rather than let the nation survive; and the other would accept war rather than let it perish. And the war came."
— Abraham Lincoln

Northern Virginia
1862

A piercing bugle blast preceded the sound of galloping horses by mere seconds. Captain Alexander Hunter tore his eyes away from the horse and rider he pursued and focused on the Federal cavalry unit now pursuing *him*.

Blast it. Tricked again.

This was not the first time the large black steed with its agile rider had been spotted in advance of a Union assault—but Hunter swore today would be the last. Signaling his men to scatter, he spurred his mount toward the forest where his foe had disappeared. His band of warriors took off in every direction, their escape aided by a roiling mass of dark-bellied clouds that launched their own assault. With the storm as an ally, Hunter knew the Federal cavalry would not long sustain the chase. He worried not for the welfare of his men, who were familiar enough with the land to evade the enemy no matter what the weather. He cared only to find the Yank who led him into the trap and see him punished.

Punished severely.

Hunter lowered his hand to one of the revolvers at his hip. *Damn that scoundrel.* The timely arrival of Union reinforcements over the past few months could no longer be considered a mere coincidence. It was time for this cunning adversary to pay for the disruptions he'd caused.

Hunter guided his mare through the underbrush and around fallen trees, but entertained little hope of finding his antagonist. The rider possessed a habit of appearing, only to disappear into thin air. Even today, when he'd thought the elusive character within his grasp, Hunter had instead found himself in another trap.

The distinctive sound of running water replaced the hushed patter of rain and called Hunter from his thoughts. "How about a drink, ol' girl?" He urged his mare forward, leaning low over the saddle to avoid tree limbs, then jerked on the reins at the sight of a youth crouched on the opposite bank gulping water by the handful. Hunter's gaze shifted to the horse hungrily grazing on green shoots at the water's edge. Enormous and coal black, its chest glistened from being ridden hard.

Hunter reached for his revolver and blinked to make sure the fading daylight was not playing tricks on his vision. The scout was smaller and younger than he expected. He cocked his weapon and shouted across the fast-moving stream, "Don't move!"

Startled, the youth stood and challenged him. "What do you want?" he asked, holding nothing but dripping water.

Hunter's confusion intensified as he stared at his opponent. Dressed in an oversized coat, slouch hat pulled low, and baggy trousers, the boy looked harmless enough. *Can this really be the Union scout I've been chasing?*

One more glance at the horse answered his question. Few such horses existed in this part of the country, certainly none of such quality that had not already been confiscated by one or the other of the armies. This was no guiltless civilian. This was a Yankee. And a cunning one at that.

"I think you know what I want. It appears we've spent the last week watching each other, and still have not been introduced."

He urged his mare down the bank to a sandbar, but hesitated. The creek was not wide, but the swift-running current and slippery rocks made fording here treacherous.

"If I may offer you some advice, sir?"

"Begging your pardon, son, but I don't think you're in any position to offer advice."

"So it appears," the youth replied, "but this is not a safe place to cross. If you go right down there—" He pointed downstream, but Hunter, blinking in disbelief at his audacity, interrupted.

"Thanks for the advice," he sneered, urging his horse forward in the ice-cold water, "but I'll not go back without the scoundrel who's been reporting my movements to the Yanks."

Hunter attempted to keep his eye on the enemy while guiding his mount through the maze of rocks in the streambed. About halfway across, he saw the youth bolt to his grazing horse and gather the reins. Reacting instinctively he fired a shot, causing his mare to lose her footing and plunge to her knees. The panicked animal struggled a moment before bounding up with a great surge of strength, knocking Hunter off balance. As he tried to regain control, the mare lunged again, this time unseating him and sending him sailing backward. Hunter felt himself falling, seemingly in slow motion, until there came a skull-cracking thud and a blinding flash of light. Then nothing.

ℋ ℋ ℋ

Andrea Evans waited breathlessly, fearing a trick, before leaping into the cold water. The Rebel floated face up, yet the red froth swirling around him told her his injuries were serious. She grabbed him beneath his arms and backed toward the bank, slipping, falling, spitting mouthfuls of water as she fought the current and struggled with the man's weight. By the time she dragged him onto land, her legs trembled from exhaustion and her lungs screamed for air.

"Dammit, I told you not to cross there," she groaned between teeth chattering from the cold. Leaning down to get a closer look at his injury, she shook her head. "Now what am I to do with you?"

Without warning the man's eyes flew open, and his hands grabbed her arms like a pair of steel vises. "The question is, what am I to do with you?" he snarled, rolling her onto her back. He straddled her, pinning her to the ground with the strength of an angry bull.

Andrea clenched her teeth and studied her dreaded foe. He did not speak; his eyes did the talking—and what they said drove through her like a ramrod. "I should have left you to die," she spat, regretting her impulsive decision to rescue him.

"It's your undoing that you did not."

As the soldier scrutinized her face, Andrea began to kick, push, and squirm beneath him in a violent but futile attempt to escape. Pushing with all her remaining strength, Andrea grimaced at the uselessness of the effort against his powerful arms. Resigned to her fate, she relaxed and looked up into eyes that now appeared glazed and unfocused. She felt his grip loosen, watched him blink and sway before groaning and collapsing to one side. Andrea remained on her back for only a moment, sucking in air and listening to the chaotic pounding of her heart. Then she rolled out of his grasp and stared at the unconscious form.

She knew this was the notorious Captain Hunter, a man the North feared as a calculating guerilla leader and the South glorified as a knight. He was a legend for his ability to keep the Federal army on constant alert and in a continuous state of panic. His unorthodox methods of warfare left Union troops wondering when to expect him—and dreading what to expect.

Even unconscious he appeared a formidable image of strength and power, making Andrea fear that the muscular frame beside her would rebound with the force and vitality for which he was so well known. She crawled another arm's reach away, but not before catching a glimpse of the gash, still seeping blood, from beneath a mass of brown, wavy hair. She closed her eyes to quell the chill of fear inching its way up her spine. She had never been so terrified in her life— terrified he might awake and terrified he might be dead. Although death had surrounded her for months, she never anticipated actually being the *cause* of it.

A voice in the woods behind her jolted Andrea from her thoughts. She swore at herself for losing another opportunity to escape.

"The gunshot came from over here," yelled someone with a distinct Southern drawl.

Lantern light reflected off the leaves, casting shadows on her and her unconscious companion.

"Over here! I found the Cap'n's horse," another voice shouted.

Andrea held her breath. With no sign of her horse, she slipped into the darkness, hoping the soldiers were too busy searching for their leader to hear.

"Over here! I found him!"

Light flooded an area not forty yards downstream and a dozen Rebels descended from the tree line. Andrea decided it was time to run, and run she did, cutting away from the bank and into the temporary safety of the trees. More concerned with speed now than caution, she sprinted through the woods, pushing blindly through the profuse underbrush into the awful blackness beyond. Yet the trees tried to stop her, their branches snagging her clothes and holding her in their gasp. Long, prickly limbs appeared out of nowhere to tear at her cloths and lacerate her skin. She whimpered at their savagery, but fear of capture inspired her legs to move faster.

Pain seared through her when her ankle twisted on a fallen limb, and she dropped flat on her face—but only for a moment. She scrambled to her feet, or tried to anyway, half-crawling, half-running a few steps until a tangle of vines stopped her. Disengaging herself with frenzied urgency, Andrea ran again, but only a short distance more. She could go no farther, certain her lungs would burst from the exertion, or the pain in her ankle would cause her to collapse.

Andrea leaned against a tree, clenching the spasm in her side and trying to gulp in air quietly. When a twig snapped, she froze. *Just my imagination.* She let her breath out slowly. *Or maybe a fox or a deer.*

Standing still like the trees around her, Andrea grimaced as something warm trickled down her cheek and into her mouth. The metallic taste of blood gave her the urge to spit, but she swallowed instead when another noise came, closer still than the last. She held her breath and clutched a limb with shaking hands. *Someone is coming.* She listened to them shuffle through the underbrush, then stop. Andrea crouched and waited, her heart pounding like a locomotive in her ears. She reached into her boot for a derringer, but realized it was use-less, soaked from her swim. *Dammit.* Her only other weapon, a Colt .44, was still on her saddle. The words of Colonel Jonathan Jordan suddenly raced into her mind: *War is no game.*

Those were the last words he had spoken to her before she left with his dispatch two days earlier with orders not to delay. Those were the words he spoke every time he saw her. She closed her eyes while fighting the hopelessness consuming her. When she opened them, the veil of clouds parted, throwing a sharp beam of light through the dense canopy above. Andrea held her breath and peered around the tree, spotting the outline of her feared predator. Her heart lurched at the sight of the four-legged creature, all but invisible in the darkness.

"Justus," she whispered.

Mounting her horse soundlessly, she did not take time to contemplate the close bond they shared or the significance of his name: *Just us.* She urged him forward and prayed they had time to escape the danger surrounding them.

Chapter 2

"Fondly do we hope, fervently do we pray, that this mighty scourge of war may speedily pass away."
– Abraham Lincoln

A pounding headache woke Hunter just after dawn. For a moment he believed he had foolishly indulged in some of his men's bad whiskey, but pressing his fingertips to the back of his head, he real-ized his mistake. A bump the size of a lead ball caused him to wince and swear simultaneously.

Hunter took a deep breath and struggled to sit up, his skull throbbing in perfect tempo with his heart. He collapsed against the pillow and flung his arm across his eyes to escape the penetrating rays of the sun pouring in through an open window. Hazy images of the Yank he had chased drifted into his mind like clouds scudding across the sky. But when he tried to concentrate, they dis-persed and dissolved into an unrecognizable haze.

Falling back into a restless slumber, Hunter floated down a river of dreams. Water swirled around him, lulling him into a sleep from which he feared he might never rise and was powerless to stop. But as he drifted, hands reached for him and dragged him toward the bank. The water and the person seemed to be in a duel over his body, each pulling in opposite directions. After a long struggle the current lost its battle and Hunter lay on the riverbank, safe from the water's grip. He opened his eyes and reached up to touch the face of his rescuer leaning over him—

"Cap'n, you awake?"

"Damn it, Malone!" The worried gaze of one of his men came into focus just inches from his face. He put his hand to his head as another wave of pounding pain ensued.

"I'm sorry, Cap'n. Jus' checkin' to make sure you was all right. Heard you groaning in your sleep."

Hunter closed his eyes and tried to bring back the image that seemed close enough to touch seconds ago. His rescuer's face was gone. Was he dreaming, or had someone pulled him from the water? If so, then who?

"How did I get here?"

"We brought you back by wagon."

"Where did you *find* me?" Hunter grew impatient at his inability to remember the chain of events.

"Cap'n, like we told you last night, you was lying near the bank."

Hunter shook his head, trying again to clear the cobwebs. "Any sign of anyone else?"

"Only one other set of footprints," Malone answered. "And those of a horse. A big darn horse from the looks."

A vague image began to form in Hunter's mind, causing him to close his eyes and concentrate. He pictured the horse, ambling along the other side of the creek as it pulled up clumps of grass. It was a big horse, the black horse they had been chasing. Like the winged Pegasus, it flew into his memory just as it had appeared before him yesterday, soaring across the landscape as effortlessly as a gale of wind. Then it disappeared, replaced by the image of the youth standing startled by the water's edge. "And what of the rider?"

"Don't know. None of us saw him once we scattered. We did find this, though." Malone walked over to a nightstand and picked up a scrap of paper. "Could be the scout's. We found it on the bank near where we found you."

Hunter squinted at the piece of paper the private handed him, closing one eye so he would only see one image. After much concentration, the blurry words came into focus.

Headquarters Jordan's Battalion
Guards, Pickets and Patrols: Pass the holder, Andrew Sinclair, at all places and at all times, with or without the countersign.
By order of Col. Jonathan P. Jordan
Officer Commanding

Hunter closed his eyes, then opened them and gazed out the window, trying to recall more details of the previous day's encounter.

"Doc's on his way from the Talbert's." Malone's tone conveyed grave concern.

"I don't need a bloody doctor," Hunter snapped, easing himself to a sitting position. After resting on the edge of the bed for a moment, he stood and stared at Malone.

"I want that blasted scout caught if we have to walk through Yankee blood to the knees!" He waved a fist in the air and grimaced at the ensuing pain. "I want him in *my* hands if we have to hunt down and kill every last mother's son-of-them to find him! Do you *hear* me?"

There was no need to pose the final question. For one thing, Malone had already started backing out the door to fetch the doctor. For another, it would have been difficult to believe that anyone within a ten-mile radius had not heard his thunderous declaration.

Hunter stood in the middle of the room, swaying and cursing the enemy with every throb of his head, until a rousing revelation came to him. He once thought that he pursued a specter, so cleverly had the scout eluded him in the past. But now he knew he was dealing with someone of flesh and blood—a mere mortal that, to his own detriment, appeared to possess more compassion than common sense.

H H H

Miles away from her ill-fated encounter with the Confederate officer, Andrea's heart had still not stopped its violent thumping. She urged Justus on through the dark, knowing every hoof beat bore her closer to the place she'd called home since the age of twelve. Her cousin Catherine lived not twenty miles away among the rolling hills and green meadows of northern Virginia. Familiar territory and friendly faces were not far away.

The pain in Andrea's sprained ankle brought her back to the present, the swelled tissue seeming determined to burst its way out of her boot. She pulled Justus to a walk and removed her foot from the stirrup. *I'm sure his head is hurting worse than my ankle.* Leaning down to pat Justus' neck, she tried to ignore the grip of fear engulfing her. Hunter was a legend here. His name alone was enough to cause terror in the Federal ranks, as much for what he didn't do as for what he did. His tactic of forcing the enemy to watch, wait, and wonder when he would strike strained their resources, and their nerves, more than an outright battle.

Andrea shivered, remembering the Rebel leader's eyes and tight grip upon her. The cat-and-mouse game she had played the past few weeks was a dangerous, and perhaps a foolish, one. But she detested the Confederates' stubborn pride, their unmitigated arrogance at having carried the war so far.

The sound of a train whistle floated across the night breeze, halting her reveries. Urging Justus forward off the trail, she rode to a large oak that stood like a guardian to a well-concealed ford. Andrea threw her leg over the saddle and dismounted with a suppressed groan when her weight landed on her ankle. She knew she would have to walk from here, the brush being too thick and the tree limbs too low to ride any farther.

"Come on, boy," she said to Justus, leaning on him heavily while she hopped alongside. "Your turn to take it easy."

Andrea dreaded the short walk to the river, more so for the profusion of spider webs crisscrossing her path than the pain in her ankle. She shivered at the contact of the invisible threads. "I'd rather face an enemy battery than walk through these," she muttered to herself as she clawed another strand from her face and fought her sense of unreasonable panic. "Make that an enemy battery at close range," she whimpered, slapping at the sticky traps more fretfully and stifling the scream that arose in her throat from her irrational fear. "An enemy battery at close range commanded by Captain Hunter," she sobbed, fumbling to clear the way ahead of her while smacking at biting insects that had begun to light on every pore and scratch of her skin in a feeding frenzy.

Andrea at last heard water lapping at the riverbank. Hopping on one leg to the water's edge, she paused to take in the sight of the majestic Potomac. When the moon peeked from behind a cloud, Andrea slid down the bank to a strip of gravel and gazed at her reflection.

Memories of her early years of pampered elegance caused Andrea to suppress a laugh. If only her father could see her now. But the mere thought of Charles Monroe made her smile disappear. She threw a rock into the water and watched the image disperse in waves. Yes, the aristocratic child of the South was gone. Sometimes she wondered if that child had ever really existed.

Andrea limped back to Justus and allowed him to take a quick drink, before splashing across and up the opposite bank. They had not traveled far before Andrea smelled the unmistakable odor of the encampment, and her lips curved into a smile. She took a deep breath. She was home.

Not long after came the expected challenge. "Stop, rider! Who goes there?"

"A friend. A courier seeking Colonel Jonathan Jordan."

"Dismount and proceed with the countersign."

Andrea groaned at the thought of dismounting and reached into her pocket for her pass. She and Justus both jumped in surprise when a soldier, not attached to the voice up ahead, appeared from the shadows beside them.

"Boonie? Is that you, you dang fool Yankee?" She continued to fumble in her coat for the pass.

"Sinclair?" he answered, calling her by the name she used in camp. "Colonel's been snapping at the bit waiting fer word from you. Dang gum it, where ya been?"

"Got detoured." Andrea continued riding while the sentry walked along beside. She had a sinking feeling in her stomach when she realized her pass was gone.

"You on picket duty?" She tried not to sound distressed as she searched through other pockets in the dark.

"Just got relieved. Heard a rider come splashing across the river like there weren't no war, and thought it might be you," the lanky soldier said.

The woods opened up into a large, sloping meadow that lay dotted with white tents and dying campfires. Andrea frowned at his cynical comment while taking in the scene of the sprawling camp. A few men lounged around a smoking pile of coals, likely those fresh off picket duty. But for the most part, the camp appeared silent and dark.

"Colonel told me to fetch him no matter what time you got in," Boonie said. "Probably fixing to have you arrested for desertion."

"Tattoo has sounded?" Andrea asked incredulously, not knowing the lateness of the hour.

"Yea, about *two* hours ago." Boonie shook his head in exasperation.

The realization that it was now past midnight, combined with the excitement of her hairs-breadth escape, served to increase Andrea's exhaustion. "Is it really necessary to wake—" She turned to Boonie, but he had already disappeared into the maze of tents.

Doggone it, Boonie. Why you always gotta follow orders so exact?

Andrea waited for the Colonel, and he finally appeared, looking disheveled and a bit annoyed at being awakened so late. He wore his coat, but his suspenders hung down below as if he had dressed too quickly to bother with them.

"Sinclair. It's late," he barked, barely looking at her. "Come with me."

Andrea winked at Boonie, then bravely attempted to follow the Colonel without limping. When she entered a tent behind him, he turned, threw his arms around her, and kissed her on the cheek. "Thank goodness, Andrea, you're safe! We heard there was trouble near Mount Gilead." He held her by the arms and took a step back. "And from the looks of you, you were in it. Are you all right?"

"Other than a few scratches and a sore ankle, I'm fine." Andrea smiled to reassure him. "Much better off than Captain Hunter, I'm sure."

Colonel Jordan had turned to light a second lamp. At the mention of the Confederate captain's name, he stopped and whirled back to face her. "You tangled with Hunter?"

"You could say ... we met." Andrea hobbled over to the nearest chair and lowered herself into it. "Can you help me get this boot off?"

Colonel Jordan's soft brown eyes appeared to change from concern to apprehension, and the tone of his voice became laced with alarm. "What's wrong with your ankle?" He stared at the obvious swelling of her boot.

Andrea watched his eyes flick up to her ripped pants and scan her torn and ragged coat. She knew, even without a mirror, that if she had escaped from a den of tigers, she could look no worse.

"If it was Hunter after you," he said, raising his gaze to meet hers, "it appears like he darn near succeeded."

"Now, J.J.," Andrea said, making light of her injury by calling him the pet name only she and his wife were privy to. "You know 'darn near' doesn't count in time of war."

Andrea thought her comment was cause enough for a good laugh, but "J.J." ignored it and knelt down to examine her ankle.

"Blazes, Andrea, how long has it been like this? We're going to have to cut your boot off."

Andrea gripped the side of the chair, her knuckles white, and put her head back as the throbbing intensified. "It's only a sprain," she said through gritted teeth.

"And a ruined pair of boots." He did not bother to hide the sarcasm in his voice as the leather fell apart under his knife.

Andrea shrugged and drew in a sharp breath as she gazed at her cousin's husband. Having lived with them for five years, Andrea considered J.J. more like a dear brother than a commanding officer. Obviously a man of courage and conviction, she esteemed him even more for his remarkable gentleness—a trait she had never before witnessed in the male species. With striking good looks and warm, brown eyes, he had an easy-going manner that made everyone feel instantly at home.

Even his men admired and respected him, both for his calm demeanor in camp and his steady nerve under fire. If they could only see him when in the company of his wife. She took a deep, exasperated breath. Sometimes the love J.J. and Catherine shared scared her. It seemed foolish to care for someone so, to depend on someone so desperately. Her mother had married for money and power alone. The adoration and esteem Catherine bestowed upon J.J., and that he returned tenfold, confused her.

"How does that feel?" He looked up, tearing Andrea from her thoughts.

"Much better." She leaned back in the chair, resting her gaze on her ankle that had swelled to more than twice its normal size.

"Hopefully the swelling won't get any worse," he said as he wrapped a bandage around it. "I should have someone take a look at it in the morning . . . and this." J.J. grabbed her arm and narrowed his eyes at one of the deeper gashes. "Now, tell me what happened."

Andrea chewed the inside of her cheek, took a deep breath, and closed her eyes for a moment to gather her thoughts. J.J. must have seen how fatigued she was.

"Never mind. You must be famished and exhausted. Hunter is no doubt long gone by now. You can tell me in the morning."

Andrea smiled. "More tired than hungry—or too tired to eat. I'm not sure which."

"You can sleep here." J.J. nodded toward his cot. "I'll find quarters elsewhere."

"No, no. I'll sleep outside." Andrea stood to leave, but her eyes never left the cot. Though small, it appeared considerably more comfortable than the ground.

"That's an order." J.J. blew out the lamp to end the conversation. "I'll see you in the morning."

Chapter 3

"That man will fight us every day and every hour till the end of the war."
— General James Longstreet, speaking of General U.S. Grant

"Rise and shine, sleepyhead." J.J. opened the tent flap, allowing a stream of sunlight to gush in and fill every corner. "Please tell me you didn't sleep with one boot on," he said, holding a steaming cup of coffee in one hand and a pair of shiny boots in the other.

Andrea blinked at the sudden brightness. "I guess I was more tired than I realized. It's been awhile since I slept in a bed."

J.J. winced. "I would hardly call that a bed." He stared at his wife's cousin sitting on the edge of his cot, elbows on her knees and face in her hands, trying to wipe away the sleep that remained. Her blonde hair lay tangled with twigs and leaves like the mane of an unbroken horse. Her pants were torn and muddy. The picture she presented was one of determination and a strong will, two traits equally at fault for leading her into frequent trouble.

"You must stop this." He handed her the cup of coffee. "It's getting too dangerous."

"Now is hardly the time for ease and comfort." Andrea gave him a look that indicated she did not think he was being rational. "The Union is at stake—"

J.J. shook his head and put his hands up to stop her. She pushed his patience, and his nerves, to the limit. The decision to allow her into camp had been a source of much regret from the start. But in his defense, he had been given little choice. She had enlisted the aid of his wife to stand against him, and between them, they had worn him down. With much reluctance he had allowed her to carry messages back and forth to Catherine, a distance of some twenty miles. At the beginning of the war, the idea seemed harmless enough. He rather enjoyed the frequent communications from his wife. But that was back when everyone assumed the Confederacy would be defeated in a single battle, when the conflict's duration was prophesied to be short, and the Union's success was considered to be certain.

Although he could not recall the exact circumstances, somewhere along the line she had been asked to deliver a message to an outpost close by—then another and another. And now here she was, entrenched in a war that had no end in sight, her heart and soul enlisted in such a way it seemed impossible to remove her. Every officer in this part of the state knew of the kid called "Sinclair." They knew of his familiarity with the countryside and the swiftness of his horse. And though they assumed he was too young to enlist, they heard he was fearless.

What they don't know is that "he" is a "she" who has more courage than sense. And that it's entirely up to me to keep her out of trouble.

"You were supposed to be back two days ago," J.J. said, shaking his head. "I cannot allow this to continue."

"I came close to finding the headquarters." Andrea took a sip of coffee and did not bother to specify whose headquarters. "I could not just *leave*."

"You see?" J.J.'s voice grew loud. "I sent you to deliver dispatches to General Nelson. There was no mention of finding any headquarters in those orders."

Andrea let out her breath in rude exasperation. "We must not stop now. We need only to match his cleverness and cunning."

"You disobeyed my orders. I cannot allow insubordination in my ranks."

"J.J.—"

"Don't *J.J.* me. I'm your commanding officer."

"Colonel Jordan," she began again. "You cannot expect me to ride into enemy territory with my eyes closed. Hunter's men cause chaos in our ranks, and every Command sent after him is destroyed."

"That has nothing to do with you," he snapped.

"But, sir, I ride alone. I have been able to move around his Command unnoticed. I have given you valuable information about his movements, have I not?"

J.J. stared at her unblinking, knowing she was right. "That is not the question."

"But if we found his headquarters we could stop—"

"You are a courier, at best. Not a spy. Not a scout. Do you understand? You are to deliver dispatches, not gather intelligence on the enemy's strength and movements."

Andrea nodded, but defiance remained in her eyes when she turned away, making it obvious the furtive headquarters of Captain Hunter had become an obsession.

"Andrea, the man is satanically clever," J.J. said, trying to reason with her. "He knows what we are doing—and even what we intend to do—yet no one can tell where he'll be, when he'll be there, or what he'll do—"

"I can play his game." She swung around to face him. "He operates un-molested, robbing with impunity, picking up supplies from our troops as he desires, and greeting and accepting invitations from citizens with the popularity of a king. If you would authorize it, I could find his headquarters."

"Yes, that would work splendidly," J.J. said sarcastically. "That is if Hunter didn't capture you, which he probably would, and then decided to spare your life, which he probably wouldn't."

"You worry overly much."

J.J. studied the uncompromising look on her face and decided to change the subject. "How's the ankle?"

"Much better." Andrea sounded none too sincere as she limped over to the chair.

J.J. knelt down, took off the bandage, and checked the swelling. "It's still swollen. You should try to stay off it. Why don't you head back to our place and rest for a few days?"

Andrea nodded somewhat willingly in response to the invitation, then sank deeper into the chair.

"Now, tell me about last night." J.J. stood and crossed his arms.

After propping her foot on a chest, Andrea wrapped and rewrapped the bandage in an obvious effort to stall for time. J.J. surmised she had planned to think her story through before being questioned. That plan, he concluded, had not been implemented and was now too late to enact.

When he began tapping his foot, she gazed up with a forced smile. "On my way to deliver your dispatch, I noticed a couple of Hunter's men hanging around on the outskirts of town." She stared out over her toes. "So I found one of our patrols and told them they might want to take a look." Andrea paused for a moment to catch her breath . . . or figure out how she was going to con-tinue her account. "I guess they pretty much scattered the riders."

"You're sure it was Hunter's men you saw?"

Andrea shrugged and focused her attention on a single button on J.J.'s coat rather than his eyes. "Pretty sure."

"But that's not everything. How did you sprain your ankle?"

Andrea gulped. "Oh yes, my ankle. I, uh, sprained my ankle when . . ."

"Come on, Andrea, the truth." J.J. continued to stare at her, focusing on every word and concentrating on any possible slip-ups.

"All right, that's not quite the end of the story. Justus needed a drink and so did I, so we stopped along Swift Run. Unfortunately, Captain Hunter had the same idea."

"You were *that* close when the Union patrol attacked?" His eyes grilled her, letting her know he had deduced the part of the story she had neglected to tell—that she had acted as a decoy to divert Hunter's attention from the alerted patrol. "What did you do then?"

"Well, the good thing is, he was on one side of the stream and I was on the other. You know how Swift Run is … it's kind of … well … swift …"

"Yes, I know how it is," J.J. snapped, agitated at her ramblings. "What happened next?"

Andrea sighed. "Unluckily for him, but happily for me, his horse fell and he fell, and I was able to get away." Finishing the sentence, Andrea clapped her hands together and stood.

J.J. stared at her back, knowing he could probably find a shade of truth in her story. Yet he knew Andrea well enough to recognize she had a way of taking an acorn of fact and turning it into a great oak of a fable. "You still have not told me how you sprained your ankle, Andrea. What are you hiding?"

"Blazes, why do you have to know me so well?" Andrea hobbled to the far side of the tent while biting one of her fingernails.

"You said the good news is he was on the other side of the creek and he fell off his horse," J.J. started for her. "What, pray tell, is the bad news?"

"The bad news … " Andrea bit her lip. "The bad news is, I … Well, he struck his head when he fell."

"And?"

"And I thought he might drown."

A long pause ensued before J.J. prompted her again. "And?"

"So I jumped into the water and dragged him out."

Andrea mumbled the last part of the sentence, but J.J. heard her just the same. He threw back his head and laughed—until he saw the look on her face. Then his expression instantly lost all hint of humor. "You are joking, right?"

"No, I'm not joking." Andrea threw her hands up in exasperation. "He hit his head, and I thought I could at least get him out of the water. But by the time I did, his men were swarming around. They heard the gunshot I suppose—"

"*Gunshot?*" J.J.'s voice grew thunderous.

Andrea took an exasperated breath. "Well, yes. He fired a shot—"

"At *you?*"

She winced at the shrillness of his voice. "Yes, but no need for alarm. His aim was amiss."

"It's your logic that is amiss!" J.J. yelled. "There's a war going on everywhere except between *your* ears! Do you think Captain Hunter would pull *you* out of the water?"

When she did not answer, J.J. took her by the arms and shook her. "War is not a game! How many times do I have to tell you that? War means fighting and fighting means killing."

"There are better ways for a man to die than drowning in a blasted stream," Andrea responded defiantly. "If he'd been bleeding to death on a battlefield, that would be different."

"No, Andrea, it's not different." J.J. ran his hand through his hair in agitation. "This war cares not how men die, or where they die, but what they died *for*. Brave men are taken every day by disease, by infection, by malnutrition. Is that fair?"

"But I do not wish to be an instrument of death," she responded, her chin starting to quiver.

"Then you may as well stop putting yourself and others in danger!"

When Andrea turned away, he could not resist placing a hand on her shoulder. "I'm only telling you this because you're like a sister to me," he said tenderly, unable to stay angry. "You know that, don't you?"

"Excuse me, sir." An aide stuck his head inside. "Rider just came in."

J.J. hurried outside to accept the dispatch. When he re-entered the tent a few moments later, concern lined his forehead. "I'm afraid I may need a favor." He read the message again and frowned, hating what he was about to ask.

Andrea tested her ankle gingerly. "Of course. Anything."

"This," he said holding up an envelope, "needs to be in Harmony as soon as possible. Since you're heading in that direction to visit Catherine, I thought perhaps you could take it."

Andrea nodded. "I'm at your service."

Walking over to his desk, J.J. began to write his orders. "I wouldn't ask you, but there's been some ... complications." When he heard Andrea clear her throat, he paused and raised his eyes. "Yes?"

"I'm just curious as to what kind of contact you need in Richmond." She stared vacantly at the floor while stroking brambles out of her hair with her fingertips.

J.J. started to answer, then stopped when he realized she was not curious at all. She only wanted to confirm what she thought she had heard take place outside the tent a few moments earlier. He leaned forward over the desk. "You were eavesdropping?"

"I could not help but overhear." Andrea shrugged.

J.J. stared at her intently, rubbing his bearded chin. "No. Impossible." He waved his hand in the air. "Forget you heard it." He bent back down over his paperwork.

"What do they need?" Andrea gazed up at him with bright, curious eyes.

15

J.J. put down his pen and sat back in his chair. "They need someone in the city ... someone who can keep their eyes open. A contact, nothing more."

"I am perfect for the job."

"No." He stood and began pacing back and forth, stroking his beard thoughtfully.

"But I was schooled in Richmond. I know every inch of it." Andrea put her hand on his arm. "I'm so grateful you and Catherine sent me there for a year. What better way to pay you back?"

J.J. frowned at her attempt to persuade him. "But you are reckless. And you would be by yourself behind enemy lines."

"I can take care of myself. I always have."

"Frankly, we had not thought of the possibility of using a woman." He rubbed his chin again while looking her up and down. "You would have to act and look the part of a lady. You would have to be discreet ... And frankly, I believe you are about as capable of either one as I would be at getting a camel through the eye of a needle."

Andrea laughed. "Oh, I can act like a lady. Though I should hesitate, I suppose, to trade in this nice outfit for an impractical gown."

J.J. gazed at her dirty, ripped clothing, and they both laughed. "And sweep every Confederate soldier who sees you off his feet, no doubt." He watched her smile fade at the necessity of being in such close proximity to Rebels, but then her eyes began to glow again. J.J. regretted getting her hopes up. He was not sure it was a good idea to consider sending her into the very heart of the Confederacy, away from all Union defenses. But on the other hand, she would be under another officer's eyes, not gallivanting through the countryside like she did now. And Richmond had one other promising feature—no Hunter.

"You can trust me with such an enterprise," Andrea said with conviction.

J.J. stared at the disheveled being before him with a frown. Somewhere, perhaps, amid the tousled hair, muddy face, and messy clothes was a refined young lady, one with the upbringing to fit in among the Southern aristocrats. She had, after all, been raised as one of them, and possessed all the inherent poise and deportment that noble breeding creates.

Andrea limped over and put her hands on J.J.'s arms. "Don't hold yesterday against me. I can do this."

"Yes, well, all this does bear bringing up one more thing."

Andrea looked up sharply. "What do you mean?"

"It's time to let someone else ... get involved."

J.J. waited a moment for his words to sink in, and it was not long before the green eyes turned turbulent again. "No! You cannot let someone else know who I am ... *what* I am!"

"Listen, Andrea. The colonel I have in mind is a great friend of mine. We went to West Point together. I've been debating telling him about you for a long time anyway—in case something should happen to me. And now I know it's the right thing to do."

When Andrea opened her mouth to argue, J.J. stopped her. "Listen, you can do it my way or you can go stay with Catherine for the rest of the war. I've had enough of this."

He watched Andrea bite the side of her cheek and nod, accepting she was powerless to protest. "Good." J.J. gave her shoulder a brotherly squeeze in an effort to relieve the tension. You'll be delivering this dispatch to the officer I am talking about—Colonel Daniel Delaney. I'll include a letter of introduction with this message."

He sat back down and began writing again.

"What will I do with Justus?" Andrea stared into space as if already planning her trip.

"*If* you go, you can leave him with Catherine. He'll be safe. Heaven knows no one in their right mind would try to ride him." They both laughed. "It's better you leave him behind, anyway," J.J. said, thinking of how the enemy must be on the lookout for such an animal now. "That horse stands out like soot on a snowdrift."

"It sounds like you've got it all figured out." Andrea tested her ankle again while holding onto the back of a chair.

"I've not made any decision yet." J.J.'s voice grew stern. "I said I'll consider it. I also need to discuss it with Colonel Delaney. He oversees any information coming out of Richmond."

Andrea slipped on her jacket and appeared to ignore his last comment.

"I've explained everything here to Colonel Delaney." He handed her the letter. "Give him my regards."

"I will." Andrea frowned, making it clear the thought of another officer knowing her identity was distasteful to her.

"And here," he said, handing her another envelope. "This is for Catherine. Give her my regards as well." J.J. was grateful Andrea ignored the way his voice cracked at the mere mention of his wife's name.

"I won't let you down, Colonel."

"Good. Now give me a hug." J.J. became all business again. "The boys will give you something to eat before you leave. I've got to ride out to the pickets, so I can't see you off. Are you sure your ankle is all right and you got enough sleep?"

Andrea nodded. "Another cup of coffee and I'll be wide awake. And thank you ... for everything."

J.J. nodded, uncomfortable with saying goodbye. "We'll talk about the Richmond proposal when you return. That is, if you're sure you want to go through with it." Andrea did not bother to respond with anything more than a look of resolute determination.

"Be careful, Andrea." J.J. felt suddenly apprehensive about letting her go. "For all we know, Hunter's men are between here and Harmony."

Andrea shrugged carelessly but, again, did not answer.

He reached out for her arm and stopped her when they stepped outside the tent. "Sinclair—"

"Yes?" She looked up questioningly.

"War is no game. Don't test the depth of the river with both feet. All right?"

"I won't, Colonel." Andrea winked at him before turning and limping toward a group of his men standing around a fire. J.J. watched them greet each other with sound pats on the back.

"Sinclair, you crazy cuss," he heard one of them say. "I dreamt I heard that beast of yours come thundering into camp, and land sakes, here you are. Just like a damn, bad omen!"

J.J. cringed at the none-to-delicate camp language she endured and shook his head. The men all adored her, protected her like she was their little brother—especially Private Boone. Yet they knew nothing about her. She was good at keeping her thoughts, or her past at least, to herself. Gracious sakes, she didn't even share her pain with him. Yet, from what he knew about the atrocities she had witnessed as the daughter of a slave owner, she carried enough of it around for all of them.

Watching her limp away with the group of raucous men toward a cook fire, J.J. wondered what would happen if they knew her true identity. What would they think if they found out the spirited, affable Sinclair was really a fragile young lady carrying so much hurt inside she could barely feel anymore? That the brave courier who rode in and out of camp was really so afraid of feeling emotion that she pretended to feel nothing at all?

If only she would find someone to sweep her off her feet, penetrate that icy fortress she built to shield her soul from everything and everyone. J.J. sighed at the thought. Highly unlikely she would find such a person in the middle of a war. Perfectly implausible dressed like *that*.

Staring at the group while they bantered back and forth, J.J. said another silent prayer for her safety. Heaven knows she needed someone to look out for her. With nothing to live for and her country to die for, she needed protection from her own worst enemy.

Herself.

Chapter 4

"Why do men fight who were born to be brothers?"
— General James Longstreet

Colonel Daniel Delaney leaned forward, arms crossed over the pommel of his saddle, waiting for his men to get into marching formation. *Used to ride here*, he thought, gazing out across the rolling hills. *Used to hunt with the Denning brothers not twenty miles distant. Now we're shooting at each other.*

He jerked his head around at the sound of one of his men cursing and the shrill whinny of a nervous horse. On the heels of the audible disturbance came a blur of motion that whirled to a stop in front of him, causing his mount to take a hasty step backward.

"What is the meaning of this?" Delaney yelled to the intruder as he fought to bring his mare under control. "Who do you think you are?"

His gaze darted to the road, searching for the pickets who should have halted the rider. He realized they had been pulled and were already in formation, preparing for the march.

"I apologize, sir," a soft, out-of-breath voice, answered. "Colonel Jordan sent me. I'm looking for Colonel Delaney."

"You have found him," he responded gruffly. "What is the communication?"

Delaney stared at the newcomer's horse, unable to suppress his astonishment. A deep-chested brute with legs wide as tree trunks, the stallion's rump appeared to possess the power of a locomotive. With nostrils flaring and lathered top to bottom, the animal continued prancing, intent it seemed on preventing its hooves from coming in contact with Mother Earth. Delaney's eyes drifted upward to the rider who sat casually astride the beast.

"My letter of introduction," the youth said, handing over the document.

Delaney took the letter from the rider's hand and scanned it, then lifted his gaze to watch the black horse occupy itself by doing pivots, first one way and then the other. He flicked his eyes up to the rider. "You—are—Sinclair?" Long and lean, the figure before him resembled a farm boy, the oversized clothes giving no sign of the femininity that, according to the letter, lay beneath.

"I am," came the loud, somewhat defiant response.

Delaney blinked in obvious surprise but quickly erased all emotion from his face. "Pleased to meet you. You come highly recommended by a well-respected friend."

"On my way here I ran into some men I believe are Hunter's." She nodded in the direction of the nearby train depot, ignoring the comment. "They appear to be planning some mischief."

Delaney motioned over her shoulder for his bugler to signal the men, then turned his attention back to her. "You think it was Hunter's men?" He frowned with concern when the rider nodded in affirmation.

"I dismounted in a glade of trees to tighten my girth, and overheard one of his scouts. They are planning to derail the train."

"Then we must make haste." Clucking to his horse to move forward, Delaney grasped the rider's hand. "It's an honor to make your acquaintance. Can I impose on you to deliver a communication for me?" He pulled a pad out of his coat and scribbled with a lead pencil. "I've spread myself rather thin." He talked while writing. "I need to get word to General Mathis. He's in Wheatland, not far from here."

"That is *south* of here—"

"Yes," Delaney said, glancing up at the tinge of fear he heard in her voice. "But not far. And he's north of it." He handed her the piece of paper.

"Sir, my pass ... I'm afraid I—"

"Oh, yes, of course," Delaney started scribbling again. "Sinclair, right? Perhaps we can meet again under more pleasant circumstances."

The rider hesitantly met his gaze. "Yes, perhaps." She glanced at the pass with an expression that resembled relief, then gave the massive horse a light jab with her spurs and galloped away.

♃ ♃ ♃

Not far away sat Captain Hunter, holding his steel-gray mare in check with one hand while she pranced and strained at the bit like an over-anxious racehorse.

Hunter smiled out of the corner of his mouth as he surveyed the damage his men had wreaked. Even he could not have envisioned a more thorough job of devastation in such a short amount of time by so few. The ties had been removed from a twenty-foot stretch, and the rails, heated from the wood, had been crossed and bent like huge bowties around nearby trees. His gaze shifted to the curve in the tracks that would give the engineer little time to react when he noticed the destruction, and then to the downhill grade that would prevent the train from stopping even when he did. Hunter expected a bountiful yield from the harvest they were about to reap in rations, supplies—and greenbacks.

Hunter's mare tossed her head and pawed the ground in obvious revolt at being restrained. Even without its daunting rider, the large-boned warhorse was an imposing animal. Appropriately named "Dixie," she had a reputation for lunging and baring her teeth at the slightest provocation.

"Looks like we're about ready, Captain," a lieutenant with a cigar clasped between his teeth reported, keeping his distance from the unruly horse. "Nothing to do but wait for the train."

Hunter nodded but did not reply. The jovial group he gazed upon appeared more like a band of gleeful schoolboys than a force of ruthless warriors. They milled around the burning ties, laughing and slapping each other on the back as if attending a celebratory bonfire. Yet Hunter knew, as did the enemy, they could fight as fearlessly as any set of men on earth. Though not one of them was a trained soldier, none had needed much schooling. A high sense of honor and love of country served as the impelling principle for their service to the Confederacy, while the adventure and romance of serving with Hunter compelled them to fight like demons.

Hunter gave a silent signal and the group and their horses disappeared into a small grove of trees by the tracks. The men made themselves comfortable on the carpet of pine needles, though they remained ready for action with reins looped over their arms. Some laid down to grab a few minutes of sleep, while others sat around in groups talking in low tones. Hunter sank down under a tree at the edge of the gathering to nurse his aching head, but his eyes remained vigilant, scrutinizing everyone and everything.

What he saw before him was a gathering of some of his best, strange collection though it was. Ranging in maturity from boys of but fifteen summers to those well silvered over with the frost of age, the conglomeration proved he robbed proportionately from cradle to grave for his recruits—as well as from every segment of Virginia society and culture. Sprawled around him were store clerks and farmers, wealthy landowners and millers, a mingling of traits and lineage and social status that bore out equally on the battlefield. *Dissimilar, yet united,* Hunter mused, *for all possess a common bond: the desire to defend their native soil.*

And young or old, rich or poor, his followers had something else in common—they were too reckless and too wild for the discipline and monotony of the regular army. Hunter's perilous style of warfare suited this group of men perfectly. The detached nature of his command and the mystical nature of its commander added to the appeal of its outlaw allure.

Truth be told, Hunter thought, these men would not know how to pitch a tent if they were handed one or how to execute a lateral oblique if they were ordered to. The only strategic movement they understood was "split up," a command rarely ever ordered with more than a wave of his hand, because each man knew instinctively when to initiate the action. Their camp was the saddle, and their homeland was the battlefield.

When not on active duty, this gallant band of men protected themselves by disappearing into the homes of Virginian families equally devoted to the cause of Southern independence. It was on the generosity of these families the cavaliers relied for meals, and as a result, kings were neither better fed nor more reverentially treated.

Hunter's musings ended when the unwelcome bugle call of Union cavalry fell upon his ears. In fact, the sound of the approaching train and the sound of the approaching enemy reached the group at the same instant.

All eyes fell upon Hunter. After a loud curse, he gave the order to mount up. "Meet at Ebenezer," he yelled as his men began to scatter.

Blazes, how did they know? The image of a young, skinny kid skirted across his mind as he turned his mare south. Urging her faster, he damned the Yankees for stealing his chance to provide the ailing Confederate army with needed supplies, and for robbing his men of their just reward for service.

$$\mathcal{H} \ \mathcal{H} \ \mathcal{H}$$

Hunter leaned his shoulder into the doorjam of the church and studied his men. Some were occupied with writing letters to sweethearts while others were engaged with playing cards. But all displayed on their faces disappointment over the failed raid. The result of the disrupted foray was more serious than just the loss of spoils. The effect on morale could no longer be tolerated.

Turning over the day's events in his mind, Hunter remembered something one of his scouts had reported to Lieutenant Carter. He walked around the side of the church with deadly purpose, scouring the yard until he found the face for which he searched.

"Twiggy, gotta minute?" Hunter paused to light his pipe.

"Why sure, Cap'n. What's on yer mind?"

"That boy you saw today," he paused, searching for the right words. "What'd he look like?"

"Like I told Lieutenant Carter, Cap'n, jus looked like some farm boy," he replied in a slow Southern drawl. "Figgered he was one of yer new recruits."

"Well, did you notice anything at all unusual about him?"

"Naw, not really." Twiggy rubbed his whiskers, pondering the question.

Hunter let out a sign of relief. "Thanks. That's all I wanted to know." He turned and started to walk away.

"Well, of caws, thar was that haws."

Hunter froze and felt the hair on the back of his neck begin to rise. "That horse?" He did not turn around. He did not need to. He knew what Twiggy was going to say next, and his hands clenched into tight fists.

"Yea." The rebel scout spit and wiped his mouth with the back of a dirty coat sleeve. "Big black thing, it was. Prettiest darn piece of haws flesh I've seen fer quite awhile."

Hunter let out an oath with the breath he did not even realize he'd been holding, then stomped away, not uttering another word until he reached Dixie. "Mount up!"

From all around the churchyard, loafing—and startled—Rebels leaped from where they rested. Spurs, belts and pistols clattered as they were hurriedly gathered. Bridles and saddles flew from tree limbs, bushes, and fence rails, as a few dozen men scrambled to follow the order without delay.

✚ ✚ ✚

After delivering the dispatch, Andrea rode a short distance before coming to two conclusions: Justus needed a rest, and Catherine would have to wait a little while longer for her message from J.J.

Pulling her canteen from her saddle, she plopped down on a sun-warmed rock and mulled over the day's events. She pushed from her thoughts the image of the Confederate scout she had encountered, and dwelled instead on the handsome figure of Colonel Delaney. Then she closed her eyes and tried to clear her mind of that vision as well. She did not have the time or the inclination to deliberate upon the officer's superb martial bearing or how she felt about it.

Laying her head back on the rock, Andrea realized how physically exhausted she was. The few hours of sleep the night before had done little good, especially with the excitement and danger she had undergone today. The heat of the rock soaked into her like a warm embrace, and the low sun made her drowsy. *Maybe I'll just close my eyes a few minutes,* she thought, eyeing the terrain around her. She was on a small knoll, with a few trees shielding her from the vision of anyone coming across the fields below. If she needed cover, she had only to ride up the hill behind her where larger boulders offered protection. *Who would find me here anyway?*

Andrea awoke later sensing something was amiss. Finding Justus nearby, she began to tighten his girth when she heard a loud crack that sounded like a horse kicking a stall door. That peculiar sound was followed almost instantaneously by a strange *thwack* of something striking a rock near her. She stared drowsily at the rock and then shifted her gaze to a cloud of dust traveling like a fast-moving thunderhead down below. She continued to watch for a moment, too stunned to move. The approaching horsemen rode in distinct columns of four. *It cannot be Hunter,* she thought. *His men ride in a come-as-you-may order.*

Barely awake, she stood contemplating the possibility that it was indeed Hunter's men attempting to appear like a Union scouting party to confuse her. Another bullet whizzed by her head, convincing her that the possibility was in all probability a certainty. *Stay calm,* she told herself as she scrambled and clawed her way over the rocks. She jumped on Justus without bothering to tighten the saddle and headed up the hill full tilt. *War is no game, Andrea.* Those words replayed in her mind again as the image of J.J. scolding her appeared before her eyes.

Her saddle began to slip, her heart to pound. Not knowing where she was heading, Andrea slowed Justus down as the terrain became more difficult. Glancing back over her shoulder once, she saw the riders had started up the incline and were gaining on her. She tried to choke back her fear, but the litany of what she had done and should not have done continued to run through her mind. Had she not delivered that last dispatch she would be at Catherine's by now. Had she not rested . . . Had she kept riding . . . Had she . . . "Oh, blast it!"

A bugle blaring in front of her caused Andrea to lift her head in surprise. About twenty yards up the hill sat Colonel Delaney wearing a careless smile. Turning in his stirrups, he yelled a command to a small detachment of men before heading straight down the hill at a reckless gallop. "Careful, boys. It's Alex again. And I think he's mad."

A few of Delaney's men dismounted and saluted the approaching force with a crackle of carbines. Andrea slid from Justus and slumped to the ground behind a boulder, her legs trembling too much to bear weight. With her head between her knees, she listened to the fury down below, knowing beyond a doubt the skirmish would not last long. Hunter would scatter his men, recognizing it was useless to fight on such ground; and Delaney would pull back, knowing the obvious danger of pursuing rebels skilled in the art of ambush. The notes of the Union bugle recalling the cavalry troopers soon confirmed her belief.

Within minutes she heard the sound of a horse's hooves striking the rocks as it approached from below. Too tired to move, she closed her eyes and prayed it was not one of the enemy.

"Thanks for being our decoy. I owe you one."

Andrea smiled at the sound of Daniel Delaney's voice, but was too weary to set the record straight on who was in debt to whom.

Delaney crossed his hands over his pommel and gazed down at her. "You look a bit worn. How about joining us at camp? It's not far from here." Dismounting and extending a gauntleted hand, he helped Andrea to her feet.

"I appreciate the invitation, Colonel, but I'm already behind schedule. I should get moving."

"Nonsense." He cut her off. "You can't possibly be thinking about riding out now. It's too dangerous with Hunter's men around, and I would feel responsible." His voice was persuasive and filled with brotherly compassion. "Anyway, a hot meal and a good night's sleep will do you good."

Andrea preferred to move on, but her exhausted body told her she should rest. Coupled with the fact that her ankle throbbed and she was too tired to come up with a rebuttal, she nodded her head.

"Are you injured?" Delaney's tone was laced with concern at her limping gait.

"Only a sprain. I'm all right."

Without giving her a chance to mount by herself, Delaney lifted her into the saddle and then climbed on his own horse. "Wherever did you get that beast?" he asked, after they had ridden a short distance.

"I've had him since he was a foal." Andrea did not bother to say more, did not believe it necessary to tell him she had stolen him from her father's stable in South Carolina.

"Does he know how to walk?"

"This *is* his walk," she replied nonchalantly. "He has two other gaits. Fast and faster."

Andrea smiled shyly at Delaney's look of surprise, and then they both began to laugh. From that moment on, Andrea felt at ease with Daniel Delaney, and understood why J.J. cherished him as a friend.

When they retired after dinner to a large table under a tree, Andrea studied the colonel's face in the firelight. Dark complexioned and strikingly handsome, he possessed eyes that appeared audacious and mirthful, not grave and stern like when she had first hailed him. He had a distinct gentleness about him that made her feel safe, and a courteousness that conveyed a man with firm upbringing. And though he appeared strong and commanding in his role as an officer, there was something reckless and boyish in the way his blue eyes twinkled that was both fascinating and attractive.

It was late before the other men retired, but despite her weariness, Andrea waited until the last one had departed. "I understand you are looking for a contact in Richmond," she said casually, as though she'd not been burning to ask the question all night.

Daniel stared at her, showing surprise at first, but then he acquired the same thoughtful gaze J.J. had. He cocked his head to the side. "Colonel Jordan told you about Richmond?"

Andrea grinned. "N-not exactly. I ... overheard a conversation."

Daniel put his head back and laughed. "Ah-ha. I see." He winked at her, but gave Andrea little time to analyze the look. Leaning forward, elbows on his knees, he became all business. With his blue eyes assessing her, he asked in a hushed tone, "You would be interested in such a position?"

Andrea nodded earnestly. "I was born in South Carolina and schooled in Richmond."

"I did not detect your accent."

"I was tutored in speech and diction befoe the wah, suh. But I declayah, talking like this comes natchral enough."

Daniel laughed and leaned back. "It would be extremely dangerous nonetheless."

"I understand."

"Colonel Jordan is comfortable with you accepting the assignment?"

25

Andrea began to answer yes, but stopped mid-breath when she looked into Daniel's honest eyes. "N-not exactly. I believe he wished to confer with you first."

"Well, I'll have to think about it." He stood up and brushed off his coat. "Colonel Jordan implied he had something to discuss with me, but it will have to wait. At any rate, it's late. You must be exhausted."

Andrea sighed and nodded.

"Next time you'll have to tell me about yourself. I fear I bored you with talk about me and my men all night," he said, helping her to her feet.

"I was not bored in the least." Andrea looked up and met his gaze. "As for me—it's a long story."

Daniel placed his hands on her shoulders. "It's funny," he said in a soft, serious tone, "but I feel like I've known you all my life, Sinclair. Yet I know nothing at all about you, not even your real name."

His words caught Andrea off guard. A part of her felt bewildered, ready to run. Yet another part found comfort in his eyes, a feeling she could tell this man anything—and perhaps everything. She cleared her throat and tried to suppress the emotions raging within her. "I think I'd better say good night, Colonel."

"Yes, of course." Daniel led her toward a row of tents. "I apologize for keeping you up so late. I know you've had a long day."

"Actually, there is one more thing I'd like to ask you."

"Of course." Daniel stepped closer. "What would you like to know?"

"When I, when *we*, were being attacked, you called the Confederate officer by his given name, Alex. Are you acquainted?" Even in the dim light from the campfires she saw a shadow fall across his face.

"Yes, I know him very well." His voice was almost a whisper, and he averted his gaze. When he looked back, a somberness that had not been there before filled his eyes. "But that's the way of this war, is it not?" He said nothing more, just tipped his hat respectfully and disappeared into the darkness.

Andrea wrapped herself in her blanket and laid down, but instead of falling instantly to dreamland as she had anticipated, she lay awake thinking about the gallant Colonel Delaney. She recalled how he made her laugh and how comfortable she felt in his company. Although she lived, ate, and slept around men every day, they were simply friends and comrades, nothing more. But this one's indescribable charm made him somehow different. He seemed so gentle, kind, tenderhearted—the complete opposite of the infamous Captain Hunter. Andrea shuddered at the thought. Yet when she did finally drift off to sleep, it was Captain Hunter's piercing gray eyes she saw in her dreams, not Colonel Delaney's sparking blue ones.

Chapter 5

"For if destruction be our lot, we must ourselves be its author.
... We must live through all time, or die of suicide."
— Abraham Lincoln

Andrea's visit with her cousin was a pleasant one, though it did not last long. Anxious to get back in the saddle after only one day, she rode well into the night to return to J.J.'s camp. It seemed she had no sooner laid her head down before Boonie was shaking her awake. She stared drowsily at the rose-colored sky that revealed a new day had already begun.

"You gonna sleep all day, boy?"

Andrea groaned. "Darn it, Boonie, I ain't slept but a few hours in the last week."

"Tell yer problems to Jordan. He wants to see you."

Andrea closed her eyes and tried to remember what she may have done to aggravate J.J. Unable to think of anything, she sat up. "What for?"

"Dunno and didn't ask. I'm a soldier, not yer mother."

Andrea hurried and dusted off her pants as best she could. Maybe he had something to tell her about Richmond. Or maybe he had changed his mind. She quickened her limping pace toward headquarters without a backward glance.

ℋ ℋ ℋ

"Sinclair." J.J. frowned with anxiety when he saw her. "This is Captain Warren. He's here under orders to request you for special service detail."

Andrea nodded in the direction of the officer and then turned her attention back to J.J.

"And I have told him I cannot allow it. You are too valuable here."

J.J. knew if given the opportunity, Andrea would seize it, and he would never be able to rein her in. There would always be another assignment, each more dangerous than the last. When Andrea looked at him with evident surprise at his response, he took satisfaction in the fact he had avoided lighting her volatile temper. Had he just said "no," he would have had a fight on his hands.

"General Whittington is asking a favor, not giving an order," the captain said to Andrea. "But he did say he wants you."

"He is not available." J.J. sat down at a table and began writing a dispatch, making it appear time was of the essence. "He will be on his way forthwith to Centreville. For me."

The captain stood for a moment and then, apparently realizing any further attempts would be futile without a direct order, turned to leave. "As you wish, sir."

Andrea flopped down on the cot. "What do you suppose *that* was all about?"

J.J. did not bother to answer other than to grunt something under his breath that suggested extreme annoyance.

"I think I'm getting old, J.J.," Andrea groaned. She put her hand on her head and stretched out her legs. "Everything hurts."

J.J. stopped writing and looked up. "Does that mean you're ready to stop this foolish game?"

Andrea sat straight up. "No."

"I thought not. I need you take a dispatch to General Lawson." J.J. tried not to appear nervous as he put the finishing touches on the communication. "He's in Centreville. Report directly back to me with his response."

Andrea stood up and grabbed for the dispatch, but he held onto it.

"After you deliver the message, head back through Hopewell Gap. I'll be in the vicinity of Monroe's Mill. Do you understand?"

Andrea nodded. "Yes, sir."

"It's dangerous out there, Andrea. This area is not all behind our lines."

Andrea gazed at him as if he had told her nothing more significant than that it might rain, then stood and saluted him. "Yes, sir!"

J.J. frowned at her theatrics. "Come here. Give me a hug. How's the ankle?"

"Oh, it's fine," Andrea said. "And don't worry, I'll be careful."

J.J. sighed loudly at her futile attempt to hide her limp and the offhand way she spoke. She made the pledge to use caution with little reflection, and knowing Andrea, she would violate it with as little hesitation.

"I'll see you at Monroe's Mill." He followed her outside and watched her saddle and mount. "Remember—"

"I've got it, Colonel." Andrea sounded more than a little exasperated as she hauled on the reins to keep Justus under control. "Centreville and hence to Hopewell Gap."

J.J. shook his head as she rode away, feeling guilty he had to lie. He knew what the general wanted her for, and he knew he would not be at Hopewell Gap when she returned. No one would be. His regiment was heading down to Thoroughfare Gap—so was the general, and so were a lot of Rebels.

He wanted to keep her as far away from that dangerous part of the country as he could.

Chapter 6

"Boldness has genius, power and magic in it."
– Goethe

They moved through the darkness without making a sound. So stealthy were their movements and so ominous their silent shadows, Hunter knew a legion of specters rising from their graves could not look more menacing. Even the horses appeared of another world tonight, seeming to float upon the swirling mist among trees that stood like sentinels guarding a numinous world.

Dressed inconspicuously and mounted on his favorite steed, Hunter rode in front of his band seeking some game to flush. His men were hungry for battle, and as their leader, he felt it his manifest duty to feed them.

Halting the group about fifty feet from a country farmhouse, Hunter listened to the strains of music coming from within while silently studying the scene. The sight of four horses tied out front, Union officers' mounts most likely from the accoutrements they carried, brought a smile to his face. Riding forward with one other man, Hunter dismounted and banged on the door with the butt of his revolver. When a young lady answered, he positioned himself in the shadows so she could not identify the color of his uniform.

"Pardon the interruption, miss," he said in a smooth, low voice, tipping his hat courteously. "Any officers in the house are requested back at camp immediately."

Within a heartbeat of his last word, four men dressed in Union attire pushed their way past the lady. "What do you say? What is the meaning of this?"

By this time Hunter had pressed himself against the wall, out of sight of the four standing in the doorway. Their focus was therefore intent on Lieutenant Carter, who leaned nonchalantly against the porch post with a well-chewed cigar hanging from his mouth.

"Who sent you?" asked one of the officers, stepping through the door with the others following close at his heels. "What is the meaning of this? Is there trouble?"

When they were all on the porch, Carter nodded his head toward the doorway. "Ask *him.*"

Hunter appeared from the shadows behind them, blocking any retreat back into the house. "Indeed there is trouble. Do you know of Hunter?"

"Yes," one proclaimed. "Have we caught the infernal plundering pirate?"

"No," Hunter replied, a satirical smile spreading across his lips, "but he has caught you."

He raised his gun to eye level and cocked it to reinforce his statement. The four men stood dumbstruck before raising their hands in surrender.

"You cannot be Hunter," one of the men finally spoke. "We heard he was in our front, being pursued by our advance guard."

"I believe that was this morning," Hunter said, relieving the man of his gun and saber. "While the hounds were sleeping—or socializing—the fox was on the move."

"But this is an insult," he roared. "You Rebels do not fight fair!"

Carter put his gun to the man's head. "If I were in your boots, I'd be more humiliated than insulted." He snarled the words with the cigar still clenched firmly between his teeth.

Hunter ignored the conversation, intent instead in pulling documents from one of the officer's pockets. "How far to your camp?" he asked without raising his eyes from the communication he held.

No one answered until Carter's gun flashed up again. "'Bout two miles outside Chantilly, there's a schoolhouse."

"How many?" Hunter raised his eyes from the dispatch and then lowered them again.

"I'll wager we outnumber you. You don't stand a chance." The officer speaking squinted into the darkness, trying to count the shadows that remained concealed in the cloak of night.

"You may indeed outnumber us," Hunter said, "but I do not intend to give your men time to count noses in the dark." He gave the officer a cold smile as he glanced over the letter he held: "*Our picket post was attacked by Hunter's men this morning. The confounded raiders appeared out of nowhere and disappeared in the same direction ...*"

Hunter stuffed the dispatch into his coat, and spoke into the darkness. "Anyone need to make any trades?" Four or five of his men bounded up to the porch and promptly swapped boots, hats, and even coats with the officers, while others grabbed saddles, bridles, and horses.

"I hope you are proud of this thievery," one of the Federal officers said.

Hunter leaned against the porch post watching the procedure. "It's called trading," he said in a voice full of indifference.

"Trading?" the man bellowed, looking down at the tattered boots he now wore. "What are we trading?"

"In your case," Hunter said, staring at the pompous Federal colonel, "your boots for your life."

Turning away from the prisoners, Hunter yelled into the yard. "Max and Larson, escort these gentlemen to Richmond, please." Then he tipped his hat respectfully toward the prisoners, mounted his horse, and melted into the darkness with the remaining dauntless souls of his command.

Twenty-two men, along with their horses, disappeared without a sound on the dust-covered road, as if they had never been there at all.

✻ ✻ ✻

Hunter and his men moved forward with some caution, yet they were unaware of any imminent danger. It was known from captured dispatches that some outposts had been alerted of their presence, but Hunter planned to accomplish his objective and be gone before they had time to organize any major assault.

"Might be getting a bit dangerous to git all the way over to Gainesville," Carter said, riding up beside him. "With the storm that's coming and all." A clap of thunder in the distance seemed to emphasize his concern.

"We cannot turn back now." Hunter continued to stare straight ahead. "They have some horses well suited for us."

Hunter relied entirely on the Yankees to supply his men with quality horseflesh, and with good reason. Each man needed at least two mounts, and most had three due to the lively chases that often commenced on their excursions. He deemed no effort too large relative to the collection and welfare of horses. His men could fight on empty stomachs; in fact, he had come to learn they fought better that way. But horses must be acquired, fed, and rested at any cost and at any sacrifice.

A loud report of gunfire suddenly shot through the midnight air.

"Looks like we're outgunned, outmanned and outnumbered, Captain," one of his point riders reported as he came galloping back. "Appears to be at least a regiment of cavalry."

"Then it appears this is our lucky night," Hunter said with characteristic coolness. "If each man here fights like ten, I am confident our odds will be almost even. Are you with me, men?" He did not wait for an answer before issuing the necessary orders as calmly as if discussing the weather, and then offered one last piece of advice. "Men, they do not know how many we are. Make them think we are many."

Despite not knowing what lay before them, Hunter's renegades followed him through the darkness. In a maneuver that was certainly more bold than wise, they rushed forward, a small band of men making enough noise for thrice their number.

But it did not take long for Hunter to discover that what lay before him was more than a regiment of cavalry. Expecting Stuart and fearing Hunter, the Federal outposts had been strengthened to prepare for the worst. Hunter faced a unit of cavalry positioned only as bait. Additional infantry sat waiting to ambush them from behind the walls of an old barn not a hundred rods distant.

Yet as fate would have it, the Yankees opened fire before Hunter's men were even in range, providing him with ample warning of the danger. Seeing the unevenness of the numbers and the unfairness in their positions, Hunter found a way to extricate his Command from the perilous situation. With characteristic courage and coolness, he yelled four words in a loud, booming voice. *"Bring up the artillery!"*

Yankees poured out of the building like so many ants spilling from an agitated anthill, while God Almighty seemed to simultaneously heed his call. For at that moment the brewing storm hit, shaking the ground with claps of thunder and lashing the sky with brilliant bursts of lightning. To the Yankees, the very heavens appeared to be in league with Hunter. The artillery hurled from the sky that night was evidence of yet another weapon in the Confederate wizard's arsenal.

ℋ ℋ ℋ

Lieutenant Carter watched Hunter pace sullenly while he and the rest of the men waited out the storm in a thicket of cedars. He knew they were not done yet. With one plan thwarted, Hunter would simply feel obligated to try another. And indeed, it wasn't long until Hunter ordered Carter to take charge of the group and meet up with a regiment already in place at Thoroughfare Gap.

"Keep an eye out, Carter," Hunter said before galloping away. "I can feel it in my bones. There's a battle near and soon."

Carter put his head down against the wind-driven rain and reflected on his commander. Had he met Hunter anywhere but on the battlefield, he would have thought him a gentleman of quality and breeding. He had a noble air about him, a manner and tone that instantly riveted attention. Whether giving orders on the field of battle or merely conversing with his men, there was something in his voice that was irrefutably authoritative.

But in battle Hunter had no equal. The admiration he inspired in his comrades and the fear he aroused in his foes caused him to be adored or despised in legendary proportions. The gallant Hunter or the devil Hunter—it was all a matter of geography. But in Virginia, where he was considered the epitome of Southern honor and chivalry, it was just plain "Hunter," a name itself equated to divine royalty.

The veneration was well deserved. Carter knew no heart burned more brightly with the fire of patriotism nor with more intrepid resolve than Hunter's. It was obvious in the way he fought, fearlessly exposing himself to the enemy's fire. He led by example, his invincible form forever seen where the carnage was greatest, ever ready to risk his own life on behalf of the sacred soil he cherished.

Even without a military background, Carter mused, Hunter had quickly taught the Yankee high-ups an important lesson. A captured dispatch had said it best: *"Trying to use a large, well-armed force to catch a small band of horsemen on their native soil is a bit like trying to catch a field mouse with a bear trap."*

He's taught me a lesson too, Carter thought. There's not a man alive who knows more about what to do and where, nor when and how to do it than Alexander Hunter.

Carter's mind flicked back to the present when one of the men rode up beside him.

"Cap'n Hunter's hanging back in case of pursuit, I reckon," Gus Dorsey commented.

Carter nodded and smiled. "Knowing the Captain, he's back there trying to *encourage* one."

Chapter 7

"The veil of night is no disguise,
No screen from thy all-searching eyes;
Thy hand can seize thy foes as soon
Through midnight shades as blazing noon."
— Psalms 139:5

Andrea rode forward, so bone weary and wet she could barely keep her eyes open. The storm had come fast, at first just a breath of wind stirring the leaves, then a rush of hot air followed by torrential rain and lightning. The wind on the mountain path had rivaled the thunder with its roaring for a time, but all had quieted now. Only an occasional tree limb broke the silence, writhing and groaning against another as if in excruciating pain. The cold rain from the storm had passed too, replaced by a slight drizzle and thick mist that seemed to rise up from the ground to swallow everything in its path.

Andrea tried desperately to make headway, hoping the fact that she had gone beyond the call of duty would somehow appease J.J.'s wrath when she returned late. This shortcut through Thoroughfare Gap, according to her crude map, would help her make better time. She had heard rumors Hunter had been heading in this direction, but assumed, if true, she was ahead of him. Surely he had been delayed, if not entirely cut off by all the Union troops she had passed.

But just thinking about the possibility that Hunter might be lying in wait made the woods unexpectedly frightening, and caused Andrea's imagination began to run wild. Suddenly every drop of rain falling from a leaf, every whisper of wind, every snapping twig became her feared predator.

She tried to penetrate the gloom and mist that reached out endlessly in front of her, but could see nothing. Muted moonbeams transformed trees into menacing-looking figures, creating a haunting trail of fright. Even Justus seemed nervous, shying at ordinary limbs that, in the darkness, appeared as ghostly arms.

A sudden, death-filled scream in the woods from some small animal accosted by an owl or fox nearly threw Andrea out of the saddle in fright. The scream grew louder, then died away. Andrea pulled Justus to a halt and listened over the sound of her pounding heart. Only hushed and oppressive silence remained, yet she could not shake the presentiment of impending danger. Andrea comforted herself with the thought that it would soon be dawn. She could get her bearings and head north toward the mill where she was supposed to have met J.J. Her head began nodding in her weariness, and she thought once again of sleep. *Lord, my Savior, get me through this and I promise I'll—*

The click of a trigger hammer from out of the heavy stillness resounded like a thunderclap. Andrea sat up, jarred wide-awake.

"What is your business?" A low, sinister voice spoke from the darkness, not fifty paces ahead of her. The voice rang with the resonance of one accustomed to giving orders, a familiar, deep voice that carried a distinct air of authority.

At first Andrea saw nothing, though her eyes searched frantically the dark path before her. Then, as if by command, the mist swirled and parted, revealing a horse and rider from within its protective folds. Hunter held bridle reins in one hand, revolver in the other.

Andrea did not answer at first, but sought a way to escape. To her right appeared a steep, rocky bank; to her left a yawning void that dropped off abruptly. *Dare I take the chance and run?* Despite the darkness and the mist, she feared Hunter's legendary trigger finger would be quicker than her ability to disappear. It seemed reasonable to assume he would shoot first and find out if it was justified later.

Andrea swallowed hard in an effort to drown the hive of bees buzzing and vibrating in her chest. Her voice, hoarse with weariness and cold, finally responded, "A courier with the ...Virginia." Andrea hoped he did not notice her deliberate attempt to mumble the name of a regiment. She prayed that with the fog, he had not yet seen the color of her horse, that he had merely hailed the sound of an approaching rider.

"Where is your escort?" he asked after a long silence.

Andrea's heart fluttered. "M-my horse is fresh. They could not keep up."

"Proceed with your hands in the air."

Hunter sounded utterly calm, but Andrea was not sure that meant he believed her. Filled with dread, she had no choice but to obey. He sat in silence, one firm hand on his unruly mount, the other aiming his gun with deadly precision. Distorted by the mist, the horse and rider appeared supernatural, forcing Andrea to remind herself they were but flesh and blood like her.

Behold my hands and my feet, for a spirit hath not flesh and bone. Andrea strove to drive the Bible verse from her mind and concentrate on extricating herself from her blunder. "I'm looking for my unit, suh," she said, still twenty paces out, straining to keep her voice calm.

"You can ride forward with me," he responded. "This mountain is crawling with Yanks."

Ah, there is help nearby. Closing her eyes, she said a quick prayer. *Preserve me, dear Lord, for in you I take refuge.*

"I believe there is Union cavalry behind me," she said then, trying to put some urgency in her voice. "I passed a scouting party on patrol."

"No fear. My men are dug in ahead."

Just fifteen paces away now. Hunter would soon be able to distinguish the color and size of her horse. Perhaps he already had. Fourteen … thirteen … twelve … Andrea closed her eyes momentarily and took a deep breath. *For whosoever shall call upon the name of the Lord shall be saved.*

"Sir, behind you!" Andrea pointed over his shoulder, pretending to spot an unseen foe. Wheeling Justus off the path, she plunged down the bank and crashed into the woods with the sound of gunfire echoing behind her.

"Forward the Fifth! Forward the Fifth New York!" she yelled, choosing a regiment she knew Hunter would not wish to meet. This ruse seemed to work. She heard a muffled curse and the sound of hoofbeats fading away behind her.

Andrea dismounted and leaned against a tree to catch her breath, then sank to the ground as the night returned to nerve-racking stillness. She watched and waited and listened, but her own heart thumping in her ears was the only sound she heard. Resting her head on her knees, she closed her eyes in utter exhaustion.

Just as she got her heartbeat back to normal, the distinct shuffling of approaching horses and the sound of muffled voices fell upon her ears. Instinctively she held her breath and waited.

Has he come back with reinforcements? She listened, then stood and carefully slid her gun from its holster on the saddle. Her nerves twitched with fear as she sank noiselessly to the wet ground, her fingers grasping the handle of the gun for comfort. Listening intently, she heard at least two horses moving back and forth over the trail she had left. The riders appeared to be trying to discern from where the gunshots had come. They began talking, revealing distinctly northern accents.

In fact, she recognized one of the voices.

Chapter 8

*"My religious belief teaches me to feel as safe in battle as in bed.
God has fixed the time for my death. I do not concern myself about that."*
– General Thomas J. "Stonewall" Jackson

Pacing on a rocky eminence near Thoroughfare Gap at dawn, J.J. searched for signs of a lone rider. If Andrea had gone through Hopewell Gap as instructed, she should have ridden in behind him by now. Even with a few hours rest at the mill where he'd left a man to advise her of the change of plans—she should have been here. He had expected her yesterday afternoon for heaven sakes!

An aide rode up and saluted. "Anything?" J.J. asked, mounting his horse.

"No sign of Sinclair at Monroe's Mill yet, sir."

J.J. rubbed his beard and gazed heavenward. *Where in the hell could she be?* He'd received a report that Hunter had crossed the mountains last night. Who knew where he was *now?*

"There was that storm sir," the private offered.

J.J. nodded, but he knew Andrea feared neither darkness nor storm. Mother Nature may have slowed her travels, but it would never have stopped her. She would have continued right on no matter what the conditions.

J.J. heard one of his men yelling and turned to see him pointing in the opposite direction he'd been looking. The gaze of a half-dozen men followed his, riveted on the movements of a lone horse and rider galloping through the pass less than a hundred yards away. He closed his eyes in prayer. *Thank you, Lord. Disobeyed orders—again—but at least she's safe.*

His feeling of relief turned to utter disbelief in a split second. The angry bark of a fieldpiece filled the air, and in a moment, the woods across the gap erupted in full song, spewing forth a steady stream of fire. J.J. watched the explosion of smoke and flame, incredulous at first, as if it were a dream—and then in complete horror when reality set in. Every man with him instinctively leaned forward with squinting eyes, each one realizing that the gunpowder blasting from those weapons was focused on one lone figure.

"Land's sake!" J.J. cried, urging his horse forward and standing high in his stirrups. He looked at the stricken faces around him and realized they were thinking the same hopeless thought. What chance had flesh and blood to survive that hellfire?

"To horse, men!" He turned to a courier by his side. "Alert the sharpshooters in the mill. Tell them to pick off as many as they can!" There was no need for the order. Guns already barked, and spurts of fire erupted from the mill in reply to the voluminous display of weaponry on the opposite ridge. To add to the spectacle, the sun now poured down a crimson light, tinting the smoke so that it appeared almost bloody.

J.J. waited, somehow expecting the horse and rider to reappear from the haze. Much as he tried to conjure up the image, he saw nothing but the continuous belching and spattering of guns. The peaceful valley of a few moments ago smoldered in a sea of smoke as seconds ticked slowly by.

Suddenly there appeared from within the smoke some movement—hard for him to discern at first, but yes, it was a horse. The men around him gave a collective, involuntary moan at the sight of the riderless animal until someone with a spyglass pointed. "By Jupiter, there he is!"

J.J. saw Andrea appear as if by magic, leaning low over Justus' back. He cursed and applauded her foolishness all at once. He had often seen her perform the same trick, throwing one leg over the side of her mount and bunching into a ball with all her weight in one stirrup. How many times had she fooled him, laughing when he thought she'd been thrown from her mount? J.J. continued to hold his breath, fearing any moment the horse would go tumbling, especially after she turned her head toward the enemy and gave them a mocking salute.

"Fletcher, ride down to Broad Run and intercept Sinclair before he heads to Hopewell Gap. Looks like he might finally be following my orders."

J.J. still heard the popping of gunfire as the Confederates realized the rider had not fallen, but Andrea was well out of range by now.

The sound of firing suddenly increased again, and his gaze shifted farther up the hill. With the aid of his spyglass, J.J. watched men in blue descending on the Confederates from behind. Forgetting about Andrea for a moment, he ordered his men forward. They now had the Rebels pinned in on three sides with only one direction for escape.

H H H

Captain Hunter put his hand in the air to signal a cease-fire. "Confound that scoundrel!"

The horse and rider were well out of range now, no sense in wasting ammunition. They'd lost their chance once again, despite the fact they'd waited on this ridge all night for just such an opportunity.

Hunter stared in disbelief, as did the rest of his men, at the feat just pulled off before their very eyes. It seemed impossible that a mere boy could rush with such recklessness through the very gates of hell with only his fortitude as a shield. A prettier piece of daring and audacity even Hunter had not yet achieved.

"Hell of a rider there," Lieutenant Carter said, chewing thoughtfully on his cigar. "Got no fear or no sense."

Hunter did not answer at first. He continued to stare at the familiar horse tearing through the valley with long strides, its rider sitting effortlessly as if the gauntlet through which he had just ridden was a sporting event. "I rather believe the latter," he said with disgust, turning to his horse and motioning for his men to follow. "They'll be coming soon. Let's go, men."

No sooner did he utter the words than heavy fire rained down from behind him. He realized then that the rider had been a decoy, giving the Union troops time to move in behind him and determine the location of his guns. By firing at the galloping target had done nothing but show the Yankees their exact position.

"The devil with you! You are *mine*!" Hunter waved his fist at the figure, now only a dot in the distance. The trick inspired him with a rage for revenge, but he knew he must concentrate on getting his men to safety. He had only a small piece of real estate to use for his escape—and come hell or high water, he had every intention of making his withdrawal a costly one for the enemy.

H H H

When Andrea finally cantered into the Union encampment behind the guide, she tried to act as though nothing of importance had transpired. "Nice and clear up here, boys," she said to a group of men standing around Justus. "Strangest thing. A bit of a fog suddenly rolled in down below."

Some of the men gazed with a sense of admiring awe as their eyes traced the path of her recent flight. "Sinclair, you crazy fool," one of them yelled. "By gravy, you must be the luckiest sonbitch I ever seen!"

"I thought you was food for powder, sure," another said incredulously.

"Kicked up a little dust is all," Andrea joked. It was well known that Virginia roads were either dust or mud, depending on the season, and the dry version was not what clung to her at the moment. She was covered in a spattered layer of juicy earth, accumulated from the bed of fathomless mire through which she had galloped.

Andrea looked up to see J.J. stomping toward her, and gave him an exaggerated salute despite clear signs he was not in a joking mood.

"Follow me, Sinclair." J.J. turned and tramped away without the waste of any more words. Andrea heard the men behind her talking in hushed tones as she limped after him. Now that she was out of danger, her ankle throbbed and her legs trembled. She was dizzy with pain by the time she reached the stone mill that J.J. occupied.

"Damnation! Are you trying to get yourself killed, or does it just appear that way?" J.J.'s breath came in gasps as he patted the perspiration off his head with a handkerchief. The pop, pop, pop of gunfire from the upper floors of the mill echoed through the room as sharpshooters continued to find targets.

"For the love of liberty, if you wish to commit suicide, I will supply the gun," he roared. "You needn't provide target practice for the enemy!"

"Obviously they are in need of practice," Andrea replied matter-of-factly. She loosened a drying clod of dirt from her arm and watched it explode into little pellets as it hit the floor.

"Where have you been?" J.J. bellowed, his voice booming over the din. "From what I witnessed, your tardiness isn't due to your horse being lame or your spurs being broke."

Andrea almost smiled at the use of the two most familiar excuses used by cavalrymen, but decided by his expression that humor was not his intent. "I was ... detained."

"Did you forget my orders?"

This question stumped Andrea for a moment because she rarely ever committed his orders to memory—therefore she could not have forgotten one. "No," she replied honestly. "I did not forget your orders."

"Did I not tell you to come through the other pass?"

"Oh-h yes . . . but this one was faster—"

"Faster? For what? Dispatching you to your heavenly creator?"

J.J. paced up and down, stopping only long enough to pour himself a drink, which he emptied with a shaking hand.

"A little early for that isn't it?" Andrea stared at the empty glass, thinking she would not mind having one herself.

"You did not answer my question." J.J. slammed the glass down. "Do you believe yourself immune to death or are you trying to get yourself killed?"

Andrea shrugged. She had never seen J.J. quite like this. Although it was common practice for her to seek forgiveness rather than permission, J.J. did not seem predisposed to either one today.

"Is your affection for danger so great that you must amuse yourself with it? I believe you would jump off the face of a cliff with the intention—and the hope—of growing wings on the way down!"

"J.J." Andrea sighed heavily again as she pulled out a chair and sat down. "Duty is ours, the consequences are God's. If a bullet finds me, it will be according to the order of Providence."

"It will be according to whether you have any sense or not! Holy Jerusalem! I would have thought your horse's life, at least, had a little value to you."

"Please, Colonel," Andrea said, chafing at his tone and manner. "Perhaps from your vantage point you could not see, but the incline was too steep. They were content with firing over my head."

"Oh, you have that right." He walked over and pulled off her hat. "They were indeed shooting over your head!" He pointed to a ragged bullet hole she had not known was there. "Why do you seem to get the most enjoyment out of

39

life when you are within an ace of losing it?"

Andrea stared uneasily at the hat as she spoke, but did not allow her voice to betray her. "I only did what I thought was best, considering the—"

"Did it ever occur to you *not* to think? To just follow orders? Was your mission not clear? Were my orders not implicit?" Must you persist in your obstinate refusal to obey?"

"You evidently did not follow your own orders, Colonel," Andrea said as sulfur smoke, sinking down from the upper floors, began to fill the room. "I am apparently not the only one to have taken the wrong pass."

"I never *intended* to be at Hopewell. I intended to keep *you* away from this Gap and the enemy, and thereby out of trouble!"

Andrea blinked in disbelief, realizing for the first time he did not trust her.

"Blazes," J.J. said, running his hand through his hair. "I'm going to have every blasted officer on this side of the Bull Run Mountains demanding my report on this."

"I believe you'd be less likely to criticize my actions were I a man," Andrea countered, her voice rising in anger.

"You'd be imprisoned for insubordination if you were a man! And if you still carry any notions about going to Richmond," he said, standing directly in front of her now as if she couldn't hear his yelling from across the room, "then I can't help but fear the voice of reason has entirely abandoned you."

Andrea's gaze jerked back to his and she rose to her feet, but he held out his hand for her to be silent. "My scouts tell me Hunter squeezed through our lines and has returned to wherever he came from, so there's no use deliberating over it now. You are dismissed."

"Sir, with all due respect—"

"I *said* you are dismissed."

When Andrea turned to exit, she nearly collided with an officer striding through the door. "Ah, there you are, boy. Never saw anything like it. How about you, Colonel?" Colonel Dayton dragged Andrea back into the room by her shoulder. "Did you ever see anything like it?"

"Can't say I ever have," J.J. said. "Seems to me only a fool or a madman would attempt extinction in such a manner."

"Colonel, surely you mean dis-tinction," the officer exclaimed. "Why, I can't begin to fathom how this young man got through that pass, knowing darn well those hills were full of Rebs. Then to have Delaney move in behind—mercy but it was incredible. Splendid piece of work turning the tables on Hunter himself. Wouldn't have believed it if I hadn't seen it with my own eyes."

"I've ... not had time to be briefed on the full account," J.J. said, staring at Andrea.

"What's your name anyway, son?"

"Sinclair, sir," Andrea answered, her gaze locked on the floor.

"Well that was well done, Sinclair." Dayton slapped her on the back so hard she stepped forward to remain standing. "Devilish clever!" He turned to leave, and Andrea turned to follow.

"Sinclair!" Andrea stopped at the sound of J.J.'s voice, but did not turn and did not answer. "Get some sleep and then report back to me. Get something to eat too. You can't live on mudpies."

Andrea departed the room with the relief of one who has escaped the scene of a scalping. Heading for a quiet spot near the stream, she wrapped herself in a discarded blanket, laid her weary body down on the cold, wet ground, and fell instantly asleep.

Chapter 9

"The same canteen, my soldier friend, the same canteen,
There's never a bond, old friend, like this!
We have drunk from the same canteen."
— "We Have Drunk From the Same Canteen," Civil War Song

When Andrea awoke a few hours later, the inside of her mouth felt like it was caked with mud, and her throat itched as if ants had taken up residence there. She coughed and spit, trying to force herself into consciousness. Looking down at her clothes she remembered her earlier ride, and the events the night before—and her meeting with J.J.

Rising stiffly from the wet ground, she heard the familiar hum of shouted jests floating in the breeze from somewhere downstream. She limped to the creek and splashed the sleep from her eyes, gasping when the cold mountain water hit her face. Cupping her numb hands, she drank, then stood as a voice behind her beckoned.

"You awake, Sinclair?"

She turned to see Boonie making his way down the bank.

"My eyes is open ain't they?" Andrea wiped the water off her face with her coat sleeve.

"That don't necessarily mean you're awake." Boonie stared hard at her. "Guess you seen we got a regular powwow going on here." He nodded toward the mill.

Andrea turned her stiff neck. Tethered in front of the millhouse were a dozen horses, obviously those of officers and their aides. "What the plague is going on?" She tried to sound interested, but for all she knew or cared they were up there drinking wine, smoking big, fat cigars, and discussing world politics.

"What's going on?" Boonie looked dumbfounded. "They're here about your little escapade near's I can tell. They say Jordan's fit to be tied."

Andrea looked back to the mill, but simply shrugged at his remark. "You don't say." She sat down and tried to detach her boot from her swollen ankle.

"You don't say?" Boonie's voice got louder. "Is that all you got to say?"

"Well, as to the Jordan part, I was fully aware 'cause he's already given me jaw about it," Andrea said. "As to the other, I doubt my little escapade was of enough consequence to draw the attention of all those officers."

"Well, they ain't here for nothin'," Boonie said. "I heard tell a dispatch came in from the division commander and your name was in it."

Andrea did not answer. Camp rumors no doubt. Once something like that got told, it took wings and flew. But her mind was no longer on the officers or what they were there for. Instead she thought of how she should have had the sense to remove her boot before going to sleep. Her ankle had swollen tight against the leather again, and she knew J.J. would never consent to giving her another pair if she had to cut this one off.

"We're gettin' a card game goin'," Boonie said. "Wanna lose some money?"

"In a minute." Andrea wrestled again with her boot and grimaced at the slow progress she made.

Boonie walked over and gently helped her pull it off. "Still bothering you, huh?"

"A little," Andrea croaked, when he pulled her to her feet. She held onto his coat for balance, half-walking, half-hopping toward a circle of soldiers.

"That was sho 'nuf some ride this mornin', Sinclair," a man named Leroy said in a voice louder than necessary. "If that warn't some tall fun to watch, then I'm no judge."

"Colonel Jordan didn't think it was too fun to watch." Andrea sat down and banged her boot on a rock, sending clods of dried mud flying.

"You about scared the bejeezes out of him," Boonie said, shuffling a deck of cards. "You can't hardly blame him, plumb crazy as it was."

Andrea frowned at her friend for taking the colonel's side, but did not bother to defend herself. She was still exhausted from the excitement of the previous day's events.

"You could've knocked the colonel over with a lick of spit before you come riding through that smoke," Leroy said. "He thought you was headin' to the boneyard sure."

"Yea, I thought you had your passport to paradise," one of the others said.

"Passport to paradise or permit to purgatory, one or the other." Boonie's voice was full of sarcasm as he began to deal.

Andrea shifted her gaze to Boonie. "I look forward to the former and I'm already in the *latter*."

"All right, break it up you two. By George, you look like you got a bad case of locked bowels, Sinclair." Leroy pulled a canteen out from behind a rock. "Have a drink."

Andrea gazed around at the circle of flushed faces. All, with the exception of Boonie, appeared to be in sparkling good spirits. "You boys intoxicated on patriotism or bad whiskey?"

"Bad whishkey!" Jasper Clemons, the youngest of the group, yelled.

"Blazes, keep your voices down." Andrea hit him in the knee and reached for the canteen.

"Did you see all of them officers up at the mill?" Jasper pointed in case she hadn't. "They're thick as flies on a goddamn warm carcass!"

Andrea frowned and considered getting beastly drunk along with her comrades. If nothing else, a couple good belts would give her the good night's sleep she desperately needed. She took a long draw on the canteen, closing her eyes as the fluid hit her throat.

"Easy with that! You don't want to get stumblin' drunk." Leroy grabbed the canteen. "I'll be bound, I don't even think you're old enough to drink. How old are you anyways?"

"Old enough to get shot at, Leroy," was her blunt reply, which sent the rest of the men into fits of laughter once again.

"Da'gone right. And don't you go worrying about how old he is," Boonie said. But then he paused and stared at Andrea, a quizzical look on his face. "But how old are you anyhows?"

Andrea bit her cheek. "Seventeen." Again the group erupted into laughter.

"Now that's some moonshine! Next thing you'll be telling us you're a *girl*!"

Andrea stood up as if challenge Jasper to a fight over the comment, but Boonie pulled her back down.

"I do declare, Sinclair, had you been pursuing Satan this morning you'd of caught him sure," Jasper said, trying to change the subject.

"That's funny," Andrea answered soberly, "cause the only thing I caught so far is *hell*."

This pronouncement sent the soldiers into more hoots of thigh-slapping laughter until a booming voice from the mill quieted them.

"Sinclair!" All eyes turned to Colonel Jordan, who stood motioning impatiently for Andrea.

"Guess he did tell me to come back when I woke up," Andrea said.

"Blazes, Sinclair!" Boonie shook his head

Andrea hurriedly pulled on her boot, wincing as it squeezed around her ankle. Seeing that J.J. had disappeared from the porch, she pointed to the canteen. "Give me another slug of that. Need to clear the cobwebs from my throat so's I can talk loud and clear in front of all them fuss and feathers."

"Don't give him that," Boonie warned. "It puts the devil in him."

"Don't need no whiskey to put the devil in Sinclair." Leroy laughed.

The liquor made its circuit and stopped in front of Andrea again. Putting her head back, she closed her eyes and gulped.

"Easy with that!" Boonie grabbed the canteen from her grasp.

Andrea stood up gingerly and brushed off her coat. "How do I look, gentlemen?"

"Like you rode through the gates of hell and didn't get enough sleep afterwards," Boonie said.

Frowning at Boonie while bowing grandly as if responding to a summons to be honored by the king, she turned and limped toward the mill.

Chapter 10

"We fail more often by timidity than over daring."
— David Grayson.

W hen she arrived at the mill, Andrea was greeted with stern indifference by Colonel Jordan's orderly, a straight-faced, glum sort of man. She gave him an exaggerated salute, thinking perhaps she could get him to smile—but the door opened before he did, and then closed before she would have had time to see it anyway.

She found herself in the same room she had earlier met with Colonel Jordan, which was now in deep shadow. Blinking in the dim light, her gaze fell on J.J. sitting stiffly behind a table amidst stratified layers of smoke. Out of the corner of her eye she saw at least three other officers in the room. Then the effects of the alcohol began to kick in.

"At ease," J.J. said without looking up. "Sinclair. I believe you've met Colonel Dayton. And this is Colonel Blake. And you know Colonel Delaney."

Andrea had not noticed Daniel standing by the window with his back to her, but at the sound of his name he turned around and nodded politely. Andrea did not think the greeting very courteous and began to have a distinct sense of trouble. She attempted to stand with soldierly erectness, but her ankle

44

throbbed and her body ached, and her mind was becoming too soothed by the alcohol to really care about decorum.

J.J. cleared his throat. "You understand why you are here, do you not? It's to all of our benefit that we learn the facts of what occurred during your recent ... excursion. I understand now there were some extenuating circumstances that led you to come through this pass."

Daniel stepped forward. "I explained you were diverted to Gainesville."

"And he explained to me that you came across his regiment in the Gap and devised this scheme to act as a decoy," J.J. continued. "Do I understand the scenario correctly so far?"

"Well, I'm not sure I would characterize it exactly—"

"From what I can gather," he interrupted, apparently not interested in her opinion at all, "you told Colonel Delaney it would be unwise and dangerous for his men to proceed through the Gap, but that if you went through first, you would be able to draw the Rebels out."

Daniel stepped forward and looked directly into Andrea's eyes as if warning her not to speak. "I explained it was entirely my fault. I accept full responsibility."

J.J. ignored him as well and continued. "I'm still a little confused about why you would attempt such a foolish scheme." He leaned over the table. "Perhaps you can enlighten us."

Andrea bit the inside of her cheek, and then cleared her throat. "Colonel Delaney has no fault in the matter, sir."

"How so?"

"I told him I was going through with or without him. That I could serve as a diversion—"

"And he did not try to stop you?"

"Um-m, yes, sir, he did."

"And you did not listen to him?"

"I thought it a good opportunity to use the enemy's tactics and surprise them from the rear," Andrea said, looking at the floor.

"And you did not listen to him?" J.J. repeated, louder this time, in case she had not heard.

"I *listened*," she replied, her voice rising just a little too. "I did not *obey* if that is what you are asking." Andrea came to the conclusion that she should not have taken that final slug of whiskey, because it no longer felt warm and welcoming in her veins. In fact, it felt like it was no longer welcome in her body at all. She imagined herself throwing up in front of these men of great prominence and rank, and the thought made her stomach lurch. And then she heard a voice in her head—Boonie's voice—telling his buddies in his calm, deliberate Northern drawl what he thought of Sinclair getting physically ill during an interrogation.

"Now there's a spectacle won't be equaled in quite some time, boys."

Andrea's mind began to race and a surge of queasiness began to overtake her. *It can't be the whiskey making me sick,* she thought. *Perhaps it's the cigar smoke. Yes, that's it, those vile cigars. Or the after effects of the sulfur smoke hanging in the air from the sharpshooters. Or maybe it's the fact I've not eaten since . . .*

Andrea shifted her weight again. She could not remember the last time she'd eaten. Swallowing hard to make sure she could still move things in that direction, she looked around the room. Everyone was staring at her, so she guessed it was her turn to speak. Problem was, she had not been paying attention to the question. She looked blankly at J.J., but he did not offer any help.

How dare he act like he's a—a darn colonel or something! He's just J.J.

But "just J.J." just sat there drumming his fingers on the desk, glaring at her with his head cocked to one side, waiting for her to respond. Andrea cleared her throat and elaborated on the last question she remembered being asked, hoping they had not proceeded too far in her mental absence. "I knew I was late getting back to Hopewell Gap where I was supposed to meet up with you. I'd made up my mind I was going through, with or without Colonel Delaney."

Colonel Jordan leafed through some papers on the table. "There were reinforcements being brought up. You were aware of that?"

"Yes, Colonel Delaney told me that. B-but I feared our chance would be lost by then."

"And let me see," J.J. said, looking up and leaning forward, "what rank have you that gives you the authority to make such decisions?"

Andrea rolled her eyes but succeeded in suppressing a verbal response other than, "none sir." She had never been through a grilling of this nature before and was fairly certain she would not be desirous of doing it again—at least not on an empty stomach full of whiskey.

J.J. let out his breath in exasperation. "Let's go back to the beginning. How did you know there were Confederates in those hills?"

Andrea looked over at Daniel, who turned his back on her and continued his watch out the window. From what she could tell the view offered nothing more than a cavern of darkening shadows, but he seemed intent on studying them nonetheless.

Andrea cleared her throat nervously. "I knew ... I mean, that is to say, I had reason to believe that a Virginia regiment and Hunter's command were there, at the very least."

J.J. looked up sharply. "On what did you base your information?"

Andrea shifted her weight onto her sore ankle in the hopes the throbbing pain it produced would take her mind off the excruciating ordeal she faced. Daniel had not asked nearly so many questions.

"On what did you base your information?" he repeated louder. "Colonel Delaney tells me you were confronted in the Gap. Supposedly by one of Hunter's command?"

"Yes." Andrea tried to sound calm. "It was one of Hunter's command."

"How did you know it was someone from Hunter's command?"

Andrea sighed. There was no way out of it now. "Because—" She paused, then tried again while staring at the floor. "Because I know—"

"Yes, you know?" J.J. leaned forward.

"Because I know what Captain Hunter looks like." Andrea finished as quietly as she could yet it was apparent everyone in the room heard her.

"The devil you say!" Daniel strode toward her, his cavalry boots and spurs echoing loudly in the room. "It was *Hunter* you met in the pass?"

J.J. came to his feet, his hands tightly fisted and trembling. "Let's make sure I have this right. You knew Hunter was there ready to strike, yet contrary to every sensible deduction that could be drawn from the laws of nature, the decrees of mankind, or the edicts of our heavenly Father, you decided to create a *diversion*?"

Andrea let her gaze drift to the window and pretended she was somewhere else—a tactic she often used when she was somewhere she did not wish to be. The sound of J.J.'s fist hitting the table returned her attention to the present.

"A commanding officer told you not to go!"

Andrea jumped and refocused her attention on him. "That is correct, sir. Colonel Delaney told me he was concerned for my safety. He said I should wait for the reinforcements to come up."

"And your response?"

"I told him . . ." She took a deep breath and glanced at Daniel. He leaned casually against the windowsill now with his arms and legs crossed, his eyebrows raised as if waiting with great anticipation to hear her answer himself. His pose told her he thought her in too deep for him to save now.

"I do not recall my exact words," she mumbled.

J.J.'s glare then fell upon Daniel, who gazed sternly at Andrea. "I believe your exact words were, 'Come with me or get out of the way.'"

Andrea rolled her eyes at his brutal honesty. "Colonel Delaney did everything in his power to follow military regulations," Andrea admitted, looking up at J.J.

"And you did everything in your power not to," he responded. The room fell silent, and then J.J. cleared his throat. "Gentlemen, if you will excuse us, I'd like to speak to Sinclair alone.

After the door closed, J.J. stood staring broodingly at her for a few long, uncomfortable moments. "It seems to be the consensus of the other officers that the success of the expedition outweighed the risk and disobedience."

"Sir?"

"We've got prisoners ... three of them from Hunter's command, plus one killed. That's quite a loss for him."

Andrea stood stunned and speechless for a moment. "Killed? *Dead?*"

"What other kind of *killed* is there?" J.J. yelled. "How many times do I have to tell you this is not a game?"

"I know it's not a game," Andrea responded angrily, limping as she paced the room. "I guess I just thought we would *stop* them, not *kill* them."

"Dash it, girl! Those men are fighting for their lives. Their honor! This is their homeland! They would rather die on it than '*stop!*'"

Andrea sat and put her aching head in her hands. She couldn't think about this right now.

J.J. cleared his throat. "Anyway, somewhat to my surprise and not at all to my understanding, Colonel Delaney has taken your side."

Andrea looked up at him sharply. "He needn't have. I accept full—"

"I know that. But it made me realize how much he believes in you. And for that reason, and after cool reflection, I've decided to let you go ahead with Richmond."

Andrea looked up to see if he was joking, and when she saw he was not, leaped to her feet—one foot anyway—and hopped over to him. "But you said today—"

"May not a man change his mind?"

"J.J., I won't let you down. I promise," Andrea said, hugging him.

"You have Colonel Delaney to thank. I respect his opinion. And for some reason he believes you have some sense hiding somewhere in that head of yours."

Andrea blushed. "Will that be all?"

"No. One more thing."

She looked up when she heard the seriousness of his tone.

"Hunter's men, the prisoners, were very vocal about you."

"About me?"

"The little kid with the big backbone on the black horse to be precise." J.J. paused to make sure she was listening. "And they said you are as good as dead if Hunter ever gets his hands on you."

Andrea bit her cheek, then shrugged. "We'll have to make sure that doesn't happen, won't we?"

"I'm not sure you understand the seriousness of the matter." J.J.'s voice grew louder. "This from a man who does not threaten in vain."

Andrea nodded. "Will that be all?"

J.J. decided not to further waste his breath. "Yes," he growled. "That will be all."

Andrea turned to leave with her lips curved in a smile, but when she reached the door, she paused with her hand on the latch. "That's not why you're sending me to Richmond, I hope." She forced a laugh, and looked back at him over her shoulder. "To protect me from Hunter."

The room fell silent, but the silence spoke louder than words. The sound of the slamming door echoing through the Union camp warned everyone in earshot to steer clear of Sinclair. He was no longer in the best of moods.

H H H

Colonel Delaney stepped from the shadows of the picket line, stopping Andrea as she stormed toward Justus. "It's a little late for a ride, is it not, Sinclair?"

"I'm not afraid of the dark and was not aware I was under a curfew." Andrea picked up her saddle and threw it over Justus' back a little harder than she should have, causing him to jump sideways.

"Where are you going?" Daniel asked, sidestepping the prancing horse.

"To hell in a handbasket," was the immediate retort. Though she said it under her breath, Daniel heard it nonetheless.

"You can't just come and go as you please," he said forcefully. "Soldiers have to have a little discipline."

"In case you haven't noticed," Andrea replied, limping to the other side of her horse to untangle the cinch, "I'm not a soldier. At least I'm not treated as a soldier."

"Perhaps if you acted with a little more restraint and obeyed orders you would be. Subordination, no less than valor, is the duty of a warrior." Daniel winced when Andrea let out a string of curses from the far side of the horse, her hands pulling and slapping at the leather as she worked to untangle it. Justus continued sidestepping and snorting, trying to avoid her wrath. "These hills are still full of Rebels," he said, changing tactics.

"Good." Andrea came back from around the horse but did not stop her work. "Perhaps one of them would be kind enough to shoot me. That torment could not be nearly as agonizing as that through which I just passed." Cursing again as she strove to buckle the cinch of the saddle with fingers that bungled the job, Andrea added a few more sentences—all richly punctuated with profanity—when her toe was almost stamped upon by her jumpy horse.

"You're tired," Daniel said, touching her arm. "Stay here the night."

Andrea stopped, took a deep breath, and leaned her head into her horse's neck for a moment as if to gather strength. "You and Colonel Jordan have it all figured out, don't you?"

"I don't know what you mean."

"Sending me to Richmond. To protect me from Hunter."

Daniel cleared his throat. "That's what Colonel Jordan told you?" He laid his hand on Justus' rump to calm him.

"No." Andrea wheeled around to face him. "That's what he did *not* tell me!"

Daniel met her gaze but did not speak.

"It *was* all your idea, wasn't it?" Andrea glared at him accusingly. "Jordan wasn't going to let me go until you talked him into it."

"I thought you wanted to go to Richmond."

"I did. I do!" Andrea turned back to her horse. "I don't want to be exiled there so you and Jordan can be rid of me."

"It's not like that." Daniel put his hand on her arm and led her deeper into the shadows. "Look, I was with the prisoners when they were being interrogated. Hunter means business."

"Oh, hang him!" Andrea said, freeing herself from his grasp and walking away. "I don't fear Hunter."

"Then you do need protection," Daniel said grabbing her arm and pulling her to a stop. "Because you should!"

"You know him so well as to believe I should fear him?" Andrea's eyes probed his.

"I know he's a soldier fighting for what he believes in. That's reason enough to fear him."

"We're all fighting for what we believe in," she countered.

Daniel let out an exasperated breath. "You don't understand. He's as devoted to his men as they are to him. There'll be blood to pay for the one he lost—and the three he's missing."

Andrea stood staring into Daniel's eyes as if contemplating what she saw there. "I'll stay the night," she finally said, turning back to Justus and removing his saddle. "And I'll take the offer of Richmond under consideration."

Daniel shook his head in bewilderment. Now he knew why Colonel Jordan said he had his hands full. This was a woman with no little spirit—even now when he knew she was fighting exhaustion. "Is it so hard to believe we're doing this because we're concerned about you?"

Andrea stopped what she was doing but did not turn around. "Your concern is misplaced. I'd rather have your trust."

Daniel put his hand on her shoulder from directly behind her. "Perhaps you should try trusting us first." He watched her take a deep, quivering breath, and was astounded when she turned and looked up at him with woeful eyes as if he had said something that hurt her.

Instinctively he wrapped his arms around her to comfort her and she responded by burying her head against his shoulder as if in desperate need. Daniel drew her even closer then, surprised at her softness and fragile vulnerability.

She pulled away after only a few moments and stared at the ground as if confused. "I think I'd better say good night, Colonel Delaney." Removing the saddle and placing it on the ground, she turned and started walking toward the mill.

"It's Daniel. I wish you wouldn't be so formal when we're alone."

Andrea stopped, looked back over her shoulder, and smiled. "Well then, good night—Daniel."

"That sounds better. Good night—Andrea."

Chapter 11

"Madness in great ones must not unwatch'd go."
— Hamlet, *Shakespeare*

The camp lay wrapped in deep silence a little before dawn when Daniel stumbled onto the wide wooden porch of the mill and stretched. Drawing in a deep breath of the fresh, cool air, he pulled his suspenders over his shoulders and started down the steps. The flickering light from a campfire caught his eye, followed by the sight of a solitary figure silhouetted against the flames.

Daniel could tell upon his approach her mind was miles away. She seemed to be staring into the fire in deep—and private—reflection. "Sinclair," he said in case anyone was about. "You get any sleep?"

Startled, Andrea looked up and shrugged. "Yes, sir. A little."

Daniel pulled a pot of coffee off the fire, cursing under his breath when he burned his fingers, and poured the warm liquid into a battered tin cup. He wondered why she sat up awake when she looked so dreadfully tired. "Well, I'm glad to see someone's up keeping the coffee hot," he said teasingly. Andrea nodded slightly, but her gaze remained locked on the fire.

Glancing up at the sky, as all soldiers do when they know they have a ride ahead of them, Daniel smiled when he saw a few stars. *Good. No rain—for a little while anyway.*

"I ah, need a guide," he said, taking a sip of coffee and grimacing at its strength. "Was going to wake up Logan, but since you're up—if you're willing."

He did not have time to finish. Andrea jumped to her feet, took a final gulp of coffee, dumped the rest, and limped quickly to the picket line.

"I didn't even tell you where I'm going," Daniel said after catching up.

"Doesn't matter," Andrea answered. "I don't like sitting around camp."

Yes, I've noticed that, he thought as he spread a map on his horse's rump and lit a match. "I'm heading here."

Andrea nodded, barely giving the map a glance. "I'm familiar. Let's go."

After refolding the map, Daniel gave her a leg up on her prancing beast, then swung into his own saddle with easy grace. Riding a few paces behind the silent figure, he watched her drift into the night with the ease of one familiar with its depths.

Daniel remained silent, but noticed Andrea took her business seriously, constantly scanning the terrain and studying the ground. Instead of following the road as he assumed she would, she soon directed him into a grove of pines. He followed her by sound, not sight, for under the cover of the trees he could barely see his hand in front of his face.

After a few miles, Andrea reined in Justus while pulling a spyglass from her saddle. When she finished looking at the horizon, she handed it to Daniel, then circled her prancing horse back into the shadows of the trees.

Pointing the spyglass in the same direction, Daniel saw the image of shadowy horsemen about a mile away, standing in bold relief against the sun rising behind them. He watched in disbelief as they came row after row over a hill, the Southern Cross fluttering proudly in their midst.

"I saw tracks when we crossed the road a ways back." Andrea's voice was low and hushed. "Their advance must have come through right before us. I figure about two hundred cavalry and at least one fieldpiece. What thinks you?"

"That looks about right," Daniel said, a bit overwhelmed at her ability to summarize numbers so quickly. He wondered what have happened if he'd brought Logan as a guide. *No doubt we would have run directly into them.*

The first stirrings of the birds began announcing morning's birth as the two sat under the cover of trees, watching their foe advance westerly. The landscape began to reflect the soft pinkish hue of the dawning sun, but neither had time to appreciate the view. "Doesn't look like Hunter's men," Andrea said, turning her experienced eye back to the horizon. "Could be Stuart."

"And they're heading straight toward Salem," Daniel replied.

Andrea nodded. "I have the fastest horse," she stated with authority. "I'll head to Salem to warn Dayton while you go gather your men. We may be able to flank them yet."

Daniel turned and looked into green eyes that appeared to gleam with mad impatience. "Capital plan, that. But I don't think Colonel Jordan will approve."

"It matters not," Andrea said bluntly. "We have no choice."

Daniel now heard the distinctive rattle of sabers clanking against saddle fittings.

"Can't be Hunter with those sabers." Andrea moved Justus back to the edge of the tree line to scan the scene again.

Daniel circled his horse in the shadows, mulling over her plan. "I know of your readiness to undertake danger, but you can't keep pushing Colonel Jordan like this," he said at length, trying to keep a firm hand on his suddenly unruly mount. "You can't keep on with this complete disregard for military regulations and orders."

"It's not a question of danger, but duty," Andrea retorted in a hushed voice. "I'm doing no more than my duty—and no one can expect me to do less."

When Daniel did not reply, she leaned forward in her saddle, causing the leather to creak. "Do you have a better plan, Colonel Delaney?" She appeared calm and confident as she gazed at him. "If you do, I'll gladly yield mine to yours."

Daniel looked from her to the spectral parade of gray-clad horsemen and back. "No."

"Then I'll see you in Salem." Andrea did not wait for him to change his mind.

"Caution will be the order of the day," Daniel yelled in a hushed voice. But she had apparently already thrown caution to the wind. Her horse disappeared into the shadowy landscape in the blink of an eye, and in another moment even the sound of hooves had faded. Daniel stared into the treeline and shook his head. *That girl would fan the flames of hell—and then charge through them—simply for the thrill of the ride.*

◈ ◈ ◈

J.J. listened with half-closed eyes to the sound of Daniel's pacing. Suddenly the door burst open.

"I have a report from one of my scouts," Colonel Dayton said, throwing his hat on a chair.

"About Sinclair?" Daniel asked, stepping forward.

"Yes, it seems your scout, Sinclair, was seen trailing the enemy closely." He paused and cleared his throat. "So closely in fact that my man lost sight of him."

"He *what?*" Daniel's fists tightened by his side.

"Apparently he was riding north of the enemy column. When the Confederates made the unexpected turn away from Salem toward Middleburg, my scout says Sinclair just kind of got mixed up in their line."

Daniel and J.J. looked at each other and simultaneously exhaled. Daniel even put his hand to his head as if he felt a sudden rush of pain.

"There's no need for worry," Dayton insisted, sitting down and pulling a pipe out of a drawer. "He says Sinclair just sort of blended in with the enemy. There was no alarm."

"Was Sinclair on the black horse?" J.J.'s voice did not mask the concern he felt at the fact that she had once again thrown caution, and all else, aside.

"No. He ran into some of my men on patrol and borrowed one of theirs."

J.J. glanced at Daniel again and knew they were both thinking the same thing: Justus would still have been fresh. That she had used some foresight in anticipating the Rebel cavalry would be on the lookout for a big, black horse, did little to ease their anxiety.

After the general excused himself, Daniel and J.J. remained in his office, one gazing out the window, the other pacing restlessly back and forth. "I fear she will do something foolish," Daniel said.

"In all likelihood she already has." His friend did not try to hide his apprehension.

"Why does she do it, John? What possesses her?"

J.J. stopped pacing for a moment. "I've tried, with little success, to find that out myself. All I can determine is she has a recollection of wrongs suffered and a desire to set them right."

"It must end," Daniel said. "She's not eaten and hardly slept for two days."

J.J. turned to face him. "Land's sakes, man! You should know by now she doesn't have to eat or sleep. She feeds on danger and thrives on risk. And I swear to you," he added through gritted teeth, "if she makes it back alive, I'll kill her with my own two hands."

"Not if I get to her first," Daniel said, watching raindrops gathering in intensity on the glass.

By the time the full report came up from the scouts, the officers discovered they had even more to worry about. The column Sinclair had fallen in with was Stuart's. But the report said Hunter and his men were expected to join up with them by nightfall. Whether Sinclair knew that detail, they had no way of knowing. But it was clear if she did not get out by dark, she may not get out at all, because she would be in the midst of two of the most dangerous, ruthless, quick-striking forces in the entire Confederate army.

ℋ ℋ ℋ

Andrea sat huddled by a smoky fire in the pouring rain with her tired and soaked new comrades. The storm, which moved in quickly, had been a blessing. Riding with their heads down against the onslaught, the Confederates took no notice of the new rider in their ranks, and the rain slicker she now wore helped her blend in.

Andrea's gaze shifted from the fire to the men around her. There were some in their prime; some well past. All looked like they had not eaten for quite some time and that sleep had been scarcer than food. They obviously suffered from the wet and cold, yet all looked ready to fight. Andrea remembered she also had not eaten for quite some time and concluded that the prospects of getting a meal here looked slim. Furthermore, she was exhausted from the lack of sleep of the past two days and scolded herself for not resting when she had the chance last night.

So far, no one appeared to suspect her. Most, she surmised, were too miserable to even notice her. But her walk through the encampment had done little to uncover any intelligence of where this cavalry unit might be heading next.

Sitting on a log turned on its end, Andrea faintly heard the door of the farmhouse behind her slam shut. She was unaware of anyone approaching until she felt a strong hand squeezing her shoulder with the strength of a bear. It was apparently a friendly gesture, but she knew she would not forget the power in that hand as long as she lived.

"At ease, men," a deep, ringing voice said, as the men around her began to struggle to their feet. "Just came down to invite you up to the porch if you'd like. Get out of the rain for a spell."

Andrea felt a tingle of fear run the length of her spine. She knew by the devoted looks on the faces around her that the man behind her was General J.E.B. Stuart. She tried to keep from breathing in short gasps as Stuart continued making small talk with the men, his hand still resting on her shoulder.

"Might take you up on that, Gen'ral," one said.

"There's a barn down the road a piece too, if any of you boys want to hunker down there for the night. We'll be moving out at dawn."

A courier appeared with a dispatch, and Stuart went down on one knee by the smoky fire to read it. As he stood, Andrea turned her head away to avoid meeting his gaze. Seeming not to notice, he nodded to the group of men, patted her on the shoulder again as though she were an old friend, and headed back toward the house.

Andrea followed the others, and after a little nudging, found a small space to sit down at the edge of the porch. The spot was barely shielded from the rain, but she appreciated being out of the mud. Just as she settled in, the sound of heavy footsteps and jingling spurs jolted her like a lightning bolt.

She knew without looking that it was him, sensed his presence even before his indomitable figure came into view. Perhaps the current that ran through the others on the porch caused the reaction. Or perhaps it was the way he walked into her view, his form imposing and commanding as he followed one of Stuart's aides to the house. Striding toward the porch with the bearing of a warrior, he removed his gloves while tramping up the steps with neither a look to the left or the right. Men instantly clamored out of his way, making a path that appeared to move before him like the parting sea. Although he had said not a word, everyone seemed to know he meant business.

Andrea herself was spellbound, only turning away when she unintention-
ally made direct eye contact with the cigar-smoking lieutenant who followed
close behind. A sudden apprehension of death stirred in Andrea's soul when
she glanced into those fighting eyes.

"Captain Hunter!" Stuart's voice boomed from within as the door opened.
"You're late. Out looking for that elusive fox of yours?" The gallant Stuart
laughed loudly as if he thought his friend's misfortunes a rather good joke.

"He's got more holes than a prairie dog," Hunter answered, not sounding
amused.

"I've no doubt you'll sniff him out, my boy. Don't you worry; he'll come
out of his den into the jaws of Hunter yet."

Andrea heard Hunter remove his rain slicker, and soon after, the sound of
rustling papers. There ensued a short silence as Stuart apparently read an in-
tercepted dispatch, followed by a deep, booming laugh. "Captain Hunter, your
name has become well known to the Union ranks, you devil. They don't seem
to know which way to turn."

"Your name is mentioned as well. I can't take all the credit for their panic."

"Ha!" Stuart's voice boomed. "This Yankee officer says here, 'I'd rather face
a full division of Jackson in my front than a dozen of Hunter's men in my rear.'
The Yankees have gotten a good deal of education at your hands—and paid
high tuition fees to boot!"

Andrea heard Stuart's spurs clanking across the room and the sound of
a deep chuckle. "You've made quite a name for yourself—highly deserved I
might add."

"I don't feel deserving. Not after yesterday."

Andrea cringed and hoped no one noticed.

Stuart's voice grew grave. "I heard you lost a lieutenant."

For a few minutes the conversation was spoken in low tones, making it
unintelligible to Andrea. Not long after, a rider galloped up on a lathered horse
and slid to a stop in front of the steps. Sweat began to drip down Andrea's shirt
despite the growing cold.

"Capt'n Hunter in here?" The young man did not wait for an answer. He
proceeded up the steps two at a time, knocked once on the door, and entered.
The group on the porch grew quiet in anticipation of what was to come. They
did not have to listen hard. The voices inside carried well.

"What have you, Gus?" Hunter asked.

"Sir, I have reason to believe there is a Yankee in our midst."

Andrea stopped breathing altogether. She listened and waited in silent suspense

"Go on, boy!" Stuart boomed.

"I watched a rider following the column earlier. He didn't reappear. This is the only place he could be."

"You're sure?" Captain Hunter's voice carried as he walked to the door. The sound of his approaching spurs caused convulsive chills down Andrea's spine.

"I'm sure, sir. I stayed out to make certain."

The men stomped out the door and onto the porch. "Inform all the pickets, no one in or out of this camp without our expressed consent," Hunter said to one of his men. Then Stuart yelled to one of his. "Secure this camp! Make it so tight the ghost of Caesar cannot escape us!"

Stuart and Hunter walked off the porch still talking and gesturing, each warrior looking formidable and impressive in his own way, together creating an image that made Andrea's blood run cold.

Dropping off the side of the porch, Andrea leaned against the house in a deep shadow created by the chimney. Perhaps Stuart was right, she thought, the hunted fox may be forced into the vengeful jaws of Hunter yet. She shivered with inexplicable dread, then took a few deep breaths and willed herself to calmness. *Think. Think.* She forced her weary brain not to panic as she paced back and forth in the shadows.

First, she would need a horse, a fast one, a mount that could be depended upon to be fresh. She could not risk her escape on a steed already fatigued from hard riding. She scanned the yard where horses were tied hither and yon. None looked especially fleet; most appeared wet and miserable.

The realization of which horse she needed to find—and take—brought a smile to her face. The comprehension of the difficulty of getting her hands on it made the edges of her lips tremble.

And the smile disappeared.

Chapter 12

"When the mouse laughs at the cat, there is a hole nearby."
— Chinese Proverb

Trying to move without raising any suspicion, Andrea walked toward the barn, sticking her hands in her pockets and whistling under her breath when soldiers were near. When she got close to the building, she picked up her step to indicate urgency.

A camp guard stopped her, sounding more tired than commanding. "What's your business?"

"Get out of the way, man," she said, her voice full of impatience. "Captain Hunter ordered me to get his horse."

"Cap'n Hunter? He's already on his haws."

"I know that. He needs his second. The other tripped in the dark and is lame. Hurry, man! He said he needs a fresh horse!"

The picket walked over to a sleeping soldier and nudged him with his gun. "Dodge, git up and fetch the Cap'n a haws."

The man sat up sleepily. "He's got Fleetson."

"Well, saddle up Stump. It'll take but five minutes."

"No," Andrea yelled a little louder than she intended. "I haven't that many seconds to spare. Just show me the horse. The captain's already got his saddle."

"He's that bay on the end of the picket line," the man who had been sleeping said. "Two white socks and a blaze. You one of Stuart's boys?"

"Yea," Andrea said over her shoulder as she untied the horse and headed away from the barn.

Andrea paid no heed to the pain in her ankle. She walked fast, practically dragging the animal called Stump behind her. "Stump," she whispered to him. "What kind of lowlife name is that for the horse of a cavalryman? Sounds like you should be pulling a hay wagon."

Scrutinizing the horse in the shadows, Andrea saw he was nearly the size and build of Justus, but he moved lethargically, and with a name like Stump ... well, she would soon find out.

The men guarding the rear entrance stared at Andrea suspiciously so she continued walking, deciding to try her luck at the farm's main entrance. With both sides of the lane bordered by four-foot stone walls, she would have only two directions to worry about a confrontation. "Stump" would have to be relied upon to outrun anything she came across.

"Why couldn't your name be Lightning or Blitz, for heaven sakes," she mumbled while attaching the thick, hemp lead rope to the horse's halter for

58

reins. She mounted by hopping on him from the bed of an empty hay wagon. "Or Dazzle even, or—"

The moment Andrea touched his back, Stump became a different horse. Perhaps he did not like her comment about pulling hay wagons. Possibly he thought humans should not ride without saddles. Or maybe he was simply taking on the characteristics of an ornery Rebel. In any event, he hopped and skipped and pranced, first in one direction and then another, with a sudden rebellious temper. Andrea used every ounce of her strength and skill to move him toward the gate.

"Halt." A sentinel stepped out in front of her and grabbed the makeshift reins. "Where you think yer going?"

"Egads, man! Captain Hunter is clamoring for this horse, and I've got to get it to him!" Andrea tried to sound authoritative, but she was already out of breath.

"No one can pass through this gate without the expressed consent of Cap'n Hunter or Gen'ril Stuart," the whiskered old man barked, repeating the commander's order word for word.

"Captain Hunter gave his consent when he ordered me to get this horse," Andrea yelled. "He's down that lane right now, sitting on a dead lame horse, probably watching that spy get away while you're holding me up. Why are you carrying your gun that way anyhow? That's no way for a soldier to stand duty. What's your name?"

"Pass on." The man stepped aside.

Andrea kicked the horse, her spurs gouging into his sides, urging him in a southward direction. But even with the aid of spurs, the ornery animal did not seem to know in what direction to travel. He continued instead to prance and spin within the confines of the stone walls.

After what seemed like miles, but was certainly much less, the horse settled into a reasonably straight path. Reaching down to pat his neck, Andrea took a deep sigh of relief—just before all of the blood rushed out of her heart and pooled into a large coagulated glob in the pit of her stomach.

At first all she saw was a tall figure silhouetted in the faint starlight along the road. But then the reflected gleam of his Colt revolver, held low by his thigh, caught her eye, followed by the distinct click of its hammer reaching her ears. Mounted on a dark bay tonight instead of the gray, Andrea fathomed she could actually feel, rather than see, his eyes upon her. The sensation his vengeful stare produced unnerved her more than the gun.

Andrea pulled the horse to a stop while contemplating her options. Concealment was impossible at this point, and flight all but hopeless. In an effort to mask the fact that her insides had distilled to jelly, she drew her gun. The act of defiance did little good. Attempting to control her mount with one hand was not a realistic proposition.

"Ah-ha, Stuart was right. My fox has finally left the henhouse," Hunter said coolly, seeming to enjoy her struggle with his horse. "And I see you've met Stump. Interesting choice."

Andrea would have answered had she not been so intent on staying on her mount while he reared, circled, and pranced in sheer rebelliousness. But she was rather glad for his antics. It gave her time to seek a way out.

"You've got two commands of cavalry behind you and *me* in front of you," Hunter said as if reading her mind. "I'd say you've set a pretty good trap for yourself—on a stolen horse no less."

He smiled with a kind of contented look that brought to Andrea's mind the image of a vulture preparing to feed on a carcass that is not quite dead.

"Perhaps I have," she said, pretending a calm she did not feel. "As for the horse, he carries the U.S. brand. Indeed he was stolen by *someone*."

Her voice did not falter. Yet Andrea could not suppress the urge to glance at the sky with the hope that God would furnish a lightning bolt to strike Hunter down, or perhaps a squadron of angels to carry her away. And then she worried, just a little, that these were the only two possibilities for escape that appeared feasible to her at the moment.

"All the angels in heaven cannot save you now," Hunter said, again seeming to divine her thoughts. He continued watching her struggle with his horse for a moment with a look of vague surprise mixed with anger. "I lost a good man yesterday," he said then as if to remind her of it. "And woe to the hand that shed that costly blood."

Andrea shuddered—not so much at his words, but at the odious tone in which he said them. Numbness began to set in now, numbness and fear. And the glob in her stomach started to congeal in her veins. "It was not my intention. Nor was it my bullet that took his life."

"It was not your intention or your gun, yet still he is gone. A costly sacrifice of a man who would have served his country well had his life been spared."

Hunter's voice seemed suddenly raw with emotion. Andrea thought she heard it crack, and the compassion in it panicked her. "Save in defense of my country and the Union I would never have had to take up arms."

"Speaking of arms," Hunter said, his voice calm and cool again, "it's high time you surrendered yours."

Andrea's arm trembled from the strain of the weight of the gun, yet her mind battled with her stubborn pride. J.J. had given her this gun. She could not just toss it away. Then again it was of no use to her right now, not with the trouble she was having controlling the beast beneath her.

"If you surrender, you'll be treated kindly as a prisoner of war despite the blood you've cost me," he said, riding toward her, his voice louder than it needed to be since she was so close.

"And if I do not?" Andrea was proud that her voice did not shake like the rest of her. She already knew his edict—surrender or die—and neither alternative appealed to her at the moment.

"There'll be no quarter," was the unemotional, merciless reply.

From the tone of his voice and the challenge in his eyes, Andrea felt he would much prefer she put up a fight, that he would take great pleasure in extracting the worth of his dead lieutenant in her blood.

The sound of pounding hoofbeats suddenly echoed from behind her, removing all thoughts and hopes of escape. The men at the barn had probably grown suspicious about the lending out of Hunter's mount.

"For your own safety, I must ask you again to drop your weapon," Hunter said, his voice sounding almost jovial now. "The fellows coming behind you get quite offended when the enemy is pointing a gun in my direction."

Andrea wondered if his words were an attempt at humor. She yielded to the inevitable and allowed the gun to drop to the ground with a thud.

"I'm glad to see you are a reasonable young man." Hunter sat his horse with easy arrogance, watching her try to regain control of Stump. "That horse is accustomed to being ridden with a strong bit and a heavy hand—not a rope. I'm surprised you made it this far."

"He should be hooked to a blasted plow," Andrea said miserably. Hunter sat only a few paces away now. He would soon be close enough to grab the horse's halter, and her fate would be sealed. "What do you use him for anyway? Pulling artillery?"

"No." Hunter displayed a lazy, confident smile, apparently finding her comment amusing. "He's certainly not a blooded horse, or the easiest to ride, but he'll jump a house if asked."

The hoofbeats behind Andrea grew steadily louder as Hunter drew steadily closer. "That's how he got his name. He'd actually rather jump a stump than go around it."

Andrea supposed Hunter made the remark thinking she had surrendered or had no means of escape. But in a flash she assessed the wall and appraised the possibilities. Nerved with the courage that God gives the desperate, she buried her spurs deep into the most sensitive part of her unruly mount's flanks, causing him to bolt forward in confusion and irritable protest. The resulting collision between the two horses made Hunter briefly lose his balance and his aim.

Before he had time to recover, Andrea turned the horse at a right angle toward the wall, clutched handfuls of mane in tight fists, and closed her eyes. Airborne for what seemed like minutes, she landed so hard on the other side that her teeth rattled in her jaw and she had to gasp for the breath knocked from her lungs. But through it all she clung to the beast with leg and hand, somewhat stunned at the horse's ability, and completely astonished she was still alive.

From behind her, Andrea heard the sound of Hunter emptying his revolver into the wall. But the action did him no good—and her no harm.

"You've made your choice," he yelled loud enough for her to hear. "There'll be no quarter next time!"

"There'll be no next time," Andrea said to herself as she rode away in an uncontrolled gallop, recalling the words Daedalus said to his son Icarus on their escape from the labyrinth.

"Escape may be checked by water or land, but the air and the sky are free-ee!"

ℋ ℋ ℋ

Neither J.J. nor Daniel was at Colonel Dayton's headquarters when Andrea wearily reined Stump past the pickets. She endured an interrogation by Dayton, but welcomed the unexpected—and temporary—reprieve from the other two colonels.

And then she slept, slept so deeply she didn't hear the commotion caused by Daniel's arrival when he received word of her return. But when her eyes finally fluttered open, she saw him pacing.

He stopped and knelt beside her. "Holy Jupiter, Andrea. You gave me a scare."

"Really?" Andrea forced a smile as she sat up stiffly. "I just needed some sleep. A little food now and I'll be fine."

"You'll be *fine?*" His voice grew distinctly more hostile. "You were more dead than alive a few hours ago."

Andrea barely heard him. Despite the fact that both hands were wrapped in gauze for the rope burns caused by her makeshift reins, she fell upon a table of leftover food like a ravenous wolf.

"Andrea." Daniel stopped and swallowed hard. "Andrea, I'm afraid I must agree with Colonel Jordan. This is getting far too dangerous. You—"

"For me? And it's not too dangerous for you?"

"That's different. I know this means much to you, but—"

"Have I not succeeded so far?"

"Of course you have."

"But you can replace me without a second thought?"

"Of course I can't." He began to pace, then stopped and faced her. "If they catch you, they'll show no mercy."

Andrea shrugged, but said nothing. Something in Daniel's eyes told her he did not expect an answer anyway.

"I admire your courage, but darn your judgment, Andrea." His voice grew stern again. "You came within an inch of your life yesterday!"

"No, not an inch," Andrea replied, her face serious. "More like four feet."

62

She burst out laughing at the thought of jumping the wall and slapped the table repeatedly with the palm of her bandaged hand.

"You have an answer for everything, don't you?" Daniel threw up his hands. "How dare you ride into an enemy camp, Stuart's no less, with no orders to do so!"

You gave me permission to reconnoiter," Andrea said, defending herself.

"I did not give you permission to fall in with the ranks!"

"You did not explicitly tell me not to," she replied, deeming her argument was no weaker than his.

"Why do you have no fear of death?" He stopped in front of her and leaned down with his palms on the table, his face even with hers. "Perhaps I should rephrase. Why are you so foolish with your life?"

"Why do you believe I'm foolish with my life?" She batted her eyelashes. "Why do you and Colonel Jordan always think capture and death are not far away?"

"Perhaps it's because you go more than halfway to meet them," he thundered. "Life is sufficiently short without shaking the sand that measures it!"

Andrea stood and tried to sound serious. "Colonel Delaney, I promise you I won't die until my times comes."

"I don't find you the least bit amusing," Daniel answered dejectedly, turning his back.

"I'm sorry," Andrea said, walking around to face him. "I know you're in earnest, but I—" When he looked down at her with his brilliant blue eyes, Andrea lost her train of thought.

"You've nothing to gain by giving your life." He gazed into her eyes almost wistfully. "Andrea, I couldn't bear it if you—"

She grabbed his hands with her bandaged ones. "Nothing will happen to me. I promise."

"You can't promise that," he said sullenly.

"Nor can you."

"You worry about *me*?" He put his hands on her shoulders and searched her eyes as she searched his.

"Of course I do, Daniel! I—"

A knock on the door interrupted them, quickly followed by Daniel's adjutant walking in without waiting for an invitation. His eyes shifted from one to the other they each took a hurried step back. "S-sorry, sir, an urgent dispatch for you."

Andrea felt the heat rising in her cheeks as the adjutant shot one more questioning glance in her direction before turning toward the door. "I'll wait for your orders outside."

Chapter 13

"Wilt thou set eyes upon that which is not?"
— Proverbs, 23:5

C aptain Hunter pulled on a clean shirt and sighed with exasperation. "A ball for bloody sakes," he said out loud.
Inwardly, he cursed the events that had brought him to Richmond. "You need to relax, Captain Hunter," General Stuart told him, "and
spend an evening off horseback." Then with a twinkle in his eyes and a knowing nudge Stuart had said, "Reap the rewards from a social engagement rather
than a military one for a change."

Stuart's remarks would have been well received by any of Hunter's men,
but to Hunter, they were aggravating. He rarely allowed himself time to rest, let
alone actually relax.

That is why Stuart had made it an official mission. "It's business, Captain. I
need your eyes. We have reason to believe that spies have infiltrated the city."

A sense of duty overtook Hunter's reluctance at attending, but he still envisioned the evening with disdain. Spending time with the social elite of Richmond, who knew little of the war and even less about fighting it, seemed a
miserable and constrained affair at best.

But by the time his carriage rolled to a stop in front of the estate, Hunter
had talked himself into making the best of it. After making his entrance, he
slowly surveyed the crowd. From across the room he saw a familiar face frantically waving at him in a striking, and quite revealing, red gown. Nodding his
acknowledgment to his old friend Victoria Hamilton, Hunter began to relax.
Perhaps this will not be such a bad evening after all.

Turning to accept a drink from a servant, he caught a glimpse of another
striking face he thought he recognized reflected in one of the tall mirrors in
the ballroom. But when he turned to locate the original visage, it was not to be
found.

ℋ ℋ ℋ

Andrea fiddled with the ornate brocading on the side of her gown, then
forced her hands to her side. She knew how perilous this night could be, yet the
amount of information she could glean made it well worth the risk.

She mused about how quickly things had moved since her ill-received trip
into Stuart's camp. Daniel and J.J. had each chastised her, then closeted themselves away in one of their secret meetings for hours. The next day she had

ridden with Daniel to Fredericksburg, where he had explained how she would get into Richmond and what was expected of her. She had been rehearsing ever since with her new "aunt," who escorted her here tonight.

It seemed unreal to Andrea that just over a week ago she had been dressed as a young boy and riding Justus through the gauntlet at Thoroughfare Gap. The only reminder of that life now was a still-sore ankle. Tonight, dressed in a pale green gown draped in layers of shimmering silk, she felt like a princess. And when she stood in the entrance to the ballroom, the thought of war seemed like a far-off dream.

A touch on her arm by her aunt brought Andrea from her reverie. This was not a dream—she had a duty to perform. Smiling brilliantly during introductions to a few of Richmond's most distinguished residents, she found herself abandoned while her aunt sought refreshments. Passing a large mirror, Andrea paused and stared at the unfamiliar image reflected back at her, then jumped slightly when a man behind her placed a hand on her shoulder.

"Pardon me, miss," came a low, polite voice. "Might I offer you some refreshment?" A young officer handed her a glass without waiting for a reply. Andrea smiled, and the butterflies in her stomach disappeared in an instant as she began to play her role with ease.

When the musicians took a break, Andrea took a deep breath of satisfaction. The South Carolina accent she usually tried so hard to disguise had come back to her with little effort. The slow, measured, ladylike walk she had been forced to practice endlessly as a child almost felt natural. This was so much easier than riding through muck and mud. Why had Daniel and J.J. been so reluctant to allow her come?

But her feeling of contentment became one of terror at the sight of a tall, dark-haired man surveying the crowd. Almost spilling her drink, she ducked behind an officer who appeared pleased to find himself the sudden focus of her attention. Peeking out discreetly from behind him, she watched Captain Hunter stride boldly in her direction. She stood in awe and dread as he moved through the crowd, the onlookers parting before him with obvious reverence and admiration.

Much to Andrea's relief the music started again, and she became caught in the flow moving to the dance floor. Losing sight of her nemesis, she continued to look over her shoulder, even as someone grabbed her hand and led her onto the dance floor. She scanned the room behind her one last time, and exhaled deeply when the dark-haired officer did not reappear. She was safe.

"Are you looking for someone?" Her partner pulled her to face him.

Andrea's heart stopped beating. She forced herself to look from the impeccably polished knee boots, past the gray trousers and snug gray coat and finally up to the steel-gray eyes. Her heart came to new life now, fluttering in her throat as if seeking the nearest way out.

"Uh-h, no. Well, yes." Andrea stumbled over the words, shocked by his sudden appearance and shaken by the light touch of his iron hand. "Just trying to locate my . . . uh, aunt. And my dance card." She looked down at the piece of paper, pretending to seek the name written there.

"Ah, yes, your Aunt Adkins," Hunter drawled the name. "As for your dance card, I see no one here to contest my claim."

The sound of his voice sent a shiver down Andrea's spine, and the feel of his hand encircling her waist almost caused her to pant. Never had she felt such enormous physical strength. And when she rested her hand upon his arm, she stared at it, trying to convince herself she was not grasping a piece of steel.

Andrea raised her head slowly to meet Hunter's gaze. She remembered well his penetrating eyes, and tonight, this close, their depth and intensity disturbed her even more. They were of a shade so piercing, she became convinced of the truth of Union gossip—that a single intimidating look from Hunter in the heat of battle could persuade his six-shooter to yield a seventh shot.

"I don't believe I've had the honor," Andrea said, surprising herself at how confident she sounded. "I am—" She faltered. His stare overwhelmed her. She could not remember the name she had repeated at least a hundred times this night.

"Miss Maryann Marlow if my information is correct," Hunter finished for her in a rich, deep voice. His tone was laced with confident sophistication, most unlike a guerilla leader of his reputation, throwing Andrea even more off guard. "The honor is all mine, Miss Marlow. Captain Alexander Hunter, at your service."

Andrea tried to look surprised and recover her composure. "Truly? *The* Captain Hunter?"

"I see my reputation precedes me," he said coolly.

"'Surely everyone in this room knows your reputation and the gallant exploits of your command." She managed to stifle the shiver that swept through her, but just saying the words was enough to make her skin crawl with revulsion. She swallowed hard and took a deep breath, half of her afraid to look at him again, the other half knowing she had to.

"You are acquainted with my aunt?" she finally asked with the best smile she could muster.

"No, I've never had the pleasure."

"But you knew her name."

"Miss, every man in this room with eyes in his head knows that you are Miss Maryann Marlow, lately of Maryland, and that you are in Richmond visiting your Aunt Abigail Adkins."

"Indeed? I had no idea I was so popular." Andrea tried hard to relax.

"Indeed," was his simple response as he led her expertly around the dance floor. His eyes, though focused over her head, revealed that his mind was alert and observant. He was aware of her every move.

Andrea's heart began racing again like an out of control racehorse. *If he discovers my identity, will he kill me on the spot?* Her gaze wandered down to his holster where he carried but one revolver tonight. *Or will he wait until sunrise and hang me?*

Clearing her throat, Andrea tried to sound more composed than she felt. "So, Captain, what brings you here? I was under the impression that a dance in which gunfire furnishes the music is more to your liking than a ball."

"Were I a gentleman, I'd say I'm present to see all of the patriotic Virginians here assembled." He looked disdainfully at the women along the edges of the room chattering like magpies.

Andrea smiled. "And since we can presume you are no gentleman—"

"Ah, you do know my reputation." Hunter's gaze remained moodily upon the crowd. "I suppose you could say I'm here scouting for enemy forces."

"Here?" The words creaked out like a seldom-used door. "Tonight?"

"Spies." He looked straight into her eyes. "There are those among us who are not as they appear."

Andrea inhaled sharply. She assumed she had awakened no memory of their earlier encounters, but now she was not so sure. "I-I-I cannot imagine such a thing." Deigning to look at his face again, and trying to keep her eyes from landing on the bulging biceps that lay beneath her hand, she tried instead to focus on imaginary objects in the air. But she could feel the heat of his eyes burning into her, could sense he was staring. *Would the music never end?* It seemed they had been dancing forever. The brightly colored ball gowns and glowing candles reflected in the mirrors around her began to make her dizzy.

Stop it, Andrea. You cannot fail. Not now.

Bit by bit she managed to push his fearsome reputation and ominous threats from her mind. Truthfully, he was not nearly the roguish-looking man she remembered. Shaved clean of the stubble that had shrouded his face when last they met, he appeared like a Virginian aristocrat. Indeed, Andrea decided she could picture him as easily sitting on a throne as sitting on a horse, so courteous and polite did he seem tonight.

"So what brings you to Virginia, Miss Marlow?"

The way he looked directly into Andrea's eyes gave her the uncomfortable feeling he was attempting to read her thoughts before she had the opportunity to lie about them.

"My aunt invited me to stay with her. As I'm sure you are aware, Maryland is quite, um, undecided about the war."

"And you?" Hunter quickly asked.

Andrea blinked, not knowing his meaning.

"And you are decided about the war?"

"Oh, yes, quite," she said, biting the inside of her cheek so hard it bled. "I am loyal."

Hunter did not appear to notice she did not say to whom her loyalty referred. "You and your aunt are close?"

"Yes, of course." Her heart banged again as she tried to decide if she'd heard a trace of suspicion in his voice.

"So your visit will be a lengthy one?"

"So long as it is pleasant and agreeable, I believe I will stay." His inquiries began to agitate Andrea. If he knew who she was, or suspected it, why did he not just say so? Her heart pulsed with new resolve to shield herself from his barrage of questions.

"Well, tell me," he continued in a voice pregnant with arrogance, "in a state with such mixed loyalties as Maryland, how is it that you decided to cast your allegiance with the imperial South?"

Andrea's heart pounded, but no longer with fear. Imperial South indeed! She suddenly felt the urge to tell him and all the regal Rebels within earshot and a long ways beyond what she thought of the imperial South.

But remembering her promise to J.J., she suffered in silence, hoping her face was not red from the suppression of intense emotion. She answered his question with a question and did not lie. "Why, Captain, how can you ask such a thing? I would not be in Richmond but for the Confederacy."

"By necessity or choice?"

The feeling of loathing and aversion at having to tolerate his infuriating Southern pride became so strong that Andrea could no longer conceal it.

"Sir, is this an interrogation or a dance?" She cocked her head to one side and looked into his eyes defiantly. "Because had I been aware that your intent was a military grilling rather than the privilege of a waltz, I most certainly would have declined the *honor*."

Andrea watched the corner of Hunter's mouth turn up unexpectedly as he threw back his head and laughed. The effect knocked her off guard. She had never seen such an engaging smile radiate from a man before and never dreamed it possible from this one. The lifting of his lips revealed straight, white teeth, and exposed two small dimples that completely changed the look of his usually stern visage. And those eyes—those cool, stern eyes, now literally twinkled with amusement.

"Miss, I apologize. You were, however, forewarned that I am no gentleman."

Hunter's voice was warmer now, his face much less severe. But the smile quickly disappeared as if he was not accustomed to wearing it.

"I was beginning to wonder about your motives for dancing with me,"

Andrea said boldly. "To my knowledge, I've asked you to divulge no military secrets. Yet you seem to think me a spy."

"On the contrary. It's my understanding that you are new to Richmond, and I wanted to make you feel welcome."

Andrea gave him a coquettish smile. "And you conceive it your duty, Captain, to make the young ladies of Richmond feel welcome?"

"In some cases, yes. In this particular case, not my duty, my privilege."

Andrea felt the color rise in her cheeks. She could feel her resolve almost melt away at the sound of his rich, persuasive voice. She forced herself to remember who he was.

"I so seldom attend events of this nature, I merely wanted to dance with the belle of the ball," he continued. "Be assured, you have nothing to fear from me."

Andrea laughed inwardly at his last statement, but responded to the former one. "Me? The belle of the ball? You know what they say about flatterers, do you not?"

"No. What would that be?"

"Flatterers look like friends, as wolves like dogs."

Hunter's face broke once again into a smile. Well, not quite a smile. Only one side of his mouth took part this time in a half-cocked grin that was somehow even more captivating. "Perhaps in Maryland," he finally answered. "But Virginian women love to be flattered."

"Is that why they all know you so well?" Andrea nodded toward the women staring with open admiration at their dashing hero. "It would appear my notoriety among the men is matched only by yours among the ladies in the room tonight."

Hunter shook his head and locked his eyes on hers. For a moment she wondered why she had thought them so frightening before. They were nothing but sparkling and brilliant and full of expression now.

"The ladies here, I can assure you, are familiar only with my reputation on the battlefield."

✠ ✠ ✠

Hunter felt strangely content matching wits with his new dance partner, as opposed to the endless banter with which he had been deluged the rest of the evening. Most of the women in the room seemed utterly devoid of intelligent thought, yet amused themselves by buzzing into his business and annoying him like so many bothersome bees. To converse with a woman whose intellectual capabilities were equal to the task was enjoyable. But something about this young stranger troubled him.

For one, her eyes revealed a strong suggestion of cleverness, mixed now

69

and again with something that definitely resembled contempt. He studied the vibrant, green orbs once more and tried to decipher what lay in their depths. Although they appeared calm and serious in their expression at the moment, something within them gave him the impression they could erupt into flames if driven to anger or excitement. He sensed, even if he could not see, a soul with deep feeling. He wondered what lay hidden beneath the mask.

"Do not accept as fact what in fact is not," his grandfather had told him once in reference to horseflesh. But even with the warning, Hunter did not envision that the gown that swished so alluringly against his legs concealed muscles that were nearly as strong as his own. That they could, in spite of fatigue and fear, carry their owner into streams, and even bareback over stone walls, if circumstances required.

"Are you certain we've never met before? You seem strangely familiar to me."

His partner laughed a bit nervously. "I'm certain, sir, any encounter with you would be inexorably branded in my mind."

Hunter pondered her response, wondering if she had really answered his query.

"Likely, you will wish to forget me," she said then as if to prevent him from mulling over the statement. "You would perhaps find that I am vain and overbearing."

"I can say that of most women." He hadn't meant to say the words, but it was too late now to stop them.

"And I can say that of most of the officers in this room," his partner quipped. She quickly flashed him a smile, as if she too regretted the rashness of her words. "Though, I dare say, you boast less than others of equal military rank."

Hunter laughed softly. "Pray don't compare me to them. One only need boast when his record does not speak for itself."

"Then pray don't compare me to most women. I believe you will find the resemblance equally unreliable."

"Fair enough, Miss Marlow." Hunter fell silent then, but his mind remained busy. He was both bewildered by his partner's boldness and fascinated by her charm. He found it refreshing to speak to one who was well mannered, yet not reverent or fawning like the others in attendance. This young lady did not seem the least bit in awe of his power or reputation. Rather, she seemed content on disproving he was worthy of possessing either one.

If she was hiding something, she was doing a good job. He had never met anyone whose eyes could be so expressive one moment, expressionless the next.

"So what did you do before the war, Captain Hunter?" she suddenly asked, as if feeling the weight of his stare upon her. "Before you became a soldier?"

"My men and I are not soldiers. We are citizens of Virginia defending our native soil."

He watched her cheeks turn crimson and her eyes a deeper green before he answered her question. "I am a horse breeder by trade."

"Truly?" The frustration in her eyes turned to intense interest. "And what bloodlines have you?"

"You really want to know?"

"Why would I not?" She appeared sincerely confused.

"Most women are not interested in such things." He felt his partner stiffen in his arms, and her brows drew together. Gone instantly was the demure lady-like demeanor and the lovely green eyes that had seemed to dance.

"Again you presume to know me so well as to assume I am like most women."

Yes, the innocent, young girl had disappeared. The chin and firmly pursed lips now clearly bespoke the strength of a lion. Eyes that had sparked now flamed, lit from a spirited fire within.

"Pardon my presumption," Hunter responded as he watched her reaction curiously. "My stock is in a state of decline with the war, but Lyonhart is my main sire."

That cannot be so," she replied, almost stopping in the middle of the dance floor. "Why, everyone knows Lyonhart stands at Hawthorne."

"Your information is correct."

She responded with a disbelieving stare. "You? Hawthorne?"

"Alexander Hawthorne Hunter at your service. I shall assume you've heard of my estate."

Hunter had no way of knowing how many hours his partner had spent in the loft above her father's stable in South Carolina, listening to men below discuss horses and that far-away breeding farm Hawthorne where so many of the bloodlines originated.

"And Fearnaught—"

"Ah-h, you do know bloodlines. Fearnaught, our original sire, lived to quite an old age."

Hunter could tell his partner listened intelligently, a trait he found rather unusual for a woman. "Now how would a young lady from Maryland be so knowledgeable about Virginia horseflesh?" Hunter watched a curtain descend upon his partner's eyes, blanking out any clues hidden there.

"Everyone knows of the famous sire of Eclipse," she said, referring to the legendary racehorse. "I just heard it somewhere." The smile planted on her face faded as she stared wistfully into space.

As if on cue, the music ended. "Welcome to Virginia, Miss Marlow." Hunter disengaged himself from her grasp and gave a low bow with cavalier grace. "I hope your time with us is pleasant and agreeable for a long time to come."

ℋ ℋ ℋ

A dull throbbing in her ankle as she stood dumbfounded on the dance floor brought Andrea back to her senses. Declining a number of requests for her dance card, she made her way to the door, trying not to limp as the pain grew more intense. She needed a break, some fresh air, and a chance to rest her ankle. And she needed a moment to think. Had she unwittingly said too much? Something that would incriminate her? Everything about the last few minutes seemed a blur.

Andrea fought the urge to run toward the door as the heat of the room grew oppressive. Sidestepping groups of women who stopped to talk in front of her, she became increasingly frantic. Memories of a dark, hot enclosure started to surface, causing her heart to beat in a frenzied panic. She began nudging people out of the way—some none too politely. She had to get a breath of fresh air, get outside, feel the night on her skin.

Finally squeezing through the door, she rushed to the railing of the veranda, leaned over, and gulped in the cool air. But even the veranda was crowded. Despite the pain in her ankle, she walked through the garden until the voices from the party finally hushed to a whisper. Half sitting in the notch of a huge oak tree, Andrea closed her eyes, leaned her head back, and let out a long sigh.

"I see I'm not the only one who feels like a caged animal in there." His voice came smooth and deep from out of the darkness. Andrea stood quickly, losing her balance when her ankle gave way. Two strong arms caught her, and once again Andrea found herself staring into the eyes of Captain Hunter.

"Are you all right?" He sounded surprisingly sincere.

"Yes. No. I mean ... I'm afraid I sprained my ankle during a ... ah ... riding accident." Andrea sighed in exasperation. "And dancing has made it worse."

"I confess I noticed you limping and wanted to make sure my dancing was not the cause."

"Not at all." Andrea began to regain her composure. "If you fight as well as you dance then the Yankees have much to fear."

"So you ride?" Hunter ignored her last statement.

Andrea's heart floundered in her chest again like a fish flopping out of water. Now she knew she had said too much. "N-n-not very well ... obviously."

Hunter grinned slightly at the comment. "Well, you must be quite an actress." He continued holding onto her waist, forcing Andrea to remain holding onto his thick forearms. The man was as solid as the oak tree behind her.

"Actress?" She tried to sound unconcerned, but it came out more like a fearful question.

"Yes, to be able to dance so effortlessly all evening with an injured ankle." He stared at her thoughtfully another moment. "You know, you have the most unfathomable eyes. They seem only to show what you want to be seen."

"Is that not the way for every woman?"

Hunter did not return her smile this time. "I can tell what most women want at a glance."

"And you find that most women want something?"

Hunter did not answer with anything other than his eyes, which appeared eerily blue-gray in the moonlight and seemed to betray a suggestion of disdain toward the subject.

"Then again, sir, I hope I stand apart."

Silence stretched between them, yet neither turned away until another couple came walking toward them. "My aunt will be worried."

Hunter looked at her intently again, tipped his hat, and nodded. "Yes, and I'm afraid I've made myself late for a train."

"You are leaving Richmond?" Andrea feared her voice sounded too relieved. "I mean ... I do hope you have a safe trip, Captain."

"And I do hope your ankle feels better, Miss Marlow."

Andrea gave him a quick nod, then picked up her skirts and turned toward the house. She controlled the urge to run, despite feeling the stabbing effect of his penetrating gaze until she was well beyond his view. It was then that Andrea compared her evening with riding a hundred grueling miles under punishing temperatures and wind-driven rain without benefit of sustenance or water or rest.

And she wondered why she had ever thought this night was going to be easy.

Chapter 14

"From the first moment I beheld thy face,
I felt a tenderness in my soul towards thee."
— John Endicott

Fredericksburg
November, 1862

Andrea sat with gloved hands clenched together in her lap, trying to maintain her balance in a carriage that careened violently over a rutted road. She blamed her trembling hands and banging heart on exhaustion and nerves, not on the fact that in a few minutes she would be standing in front of Colonel Daniel Delaney for the first time in several months, and not on the fact that he had no idea she was coming.

She took a deep breath to calm herself when the carriage began to slow. The wearying ride across an endless succession of ruts and potholes rattled her nerves, causing her to question the decision to embark on this journey. She possessed no pass to cross into Union territory. And though the soldiers at the last outpost had been kind enough, the officer of the guard sent along an escort to ensure that Colonel Delaney could vouch for her character. Andrea hoped he would not be too disturbed by her sudden appearance to do so.

The sound of shouts and the clatter and clank of horses and artillery warned Andrea that she neared her destination. The road became even more crowded with soldiers, horses, and caissons, forcing the carriage to slow still further. Loud voices and music joined the sounds, and a large mansion came into view. Andrea stared at the magnificent home, lit from top to bottom, inside and out, with every conceivable size and shape of lantern.

"This is the Lacy house, miss." A soldier held out his hand and helped her out of the carriage. "Who did you say would wish to see you?"

Andrea gazed at a two-story porch that overflowed with officers and soldiers. Suppressing the urge to run, she cleared her throat. "Colonel Daniel Delaney."

As the soldiers escorted her toward the house, Andrea gazed around. There were soldiers everywhere. Some talked and laughed in small groups, while others appeared to be departing or returning from a nearby field of campfires.

"Might you know a Colonel Delaney?" One of her guards questioned a group of soldiers holding a discussion under a walnut tree. An officer nodded toward the river, "There he comes now."

Andrea pulled her full-length cloak more tightly around her against the chill as she watched Daniel stride purposefully in her direction with true martial poise. His gaze was locked on the ground, but he nodded his head occasionally, apparently in serious conversation with the officer beside him.

Andrea turned away, the sight of his tall, manly form causing a strange sensation of fear and excitement to engulf her. She had no idea what she planned to say. *What if he does not wish to see me?* She heard muffled voices and knew the guard had approached him. Although actual words were lost in the wind, she could tell from Daniel's tone he was irritated by the interruption. Her face grew warm. Her hands trembled.

"Miss?" His voice from behind her made her jump. Andrea took a deep breath and turned.

"I'm Colonel Delaney. You asked to see me?" Daniel looked curiously from her, to her escorts, and then back again, waiting for someone to speak.

Andrea could not bring herself to look into his eyes. Instead, she stared at his broad shoulders and powerful build, and then his boots. "I am ... Maryann Marlow." She mumbled the name she had used to get across the lines, then glanced at Daniel to see his reaction. There was not a hint of recognition on his face.

"What can I do for you, Miss Marlow?" he asked somewhat impatiently. "We are extremely busy here as you might imagine—"

Daniel stopped in mid-sentence when Andrea raised her gaze again and his blue eyes locked directly onto her green ones. Without moving his head, his gaze perused her body, moving from her face, slowly down the length of her gown, inch-by-inch to her toes, and then just as slowly back up.

"Sir, we need to know if you are acquainted with this woman," one of the escorting soldiers asked. "She didn't have a pass to come through the lines and was traveling from the direction of Richmond. She says you will vouch for her."

Daniel did not remove his gaze. "Yes, I can vouch for her character. Thank you for escorting her here safely. You are dismissed."

Daniel continued to stare, though whether the look was an approving one, Andrea could not tell. What she *could* tell was that his eyes were not the blue, laughing ones she remembered. They looked strained and tired.

"What are you doing here?" He pulled her into the shadow of a tree.

"That is not *exactly* the greeting I had hoped for." She laughed to hide her nervousness.

"That does not *exactly* answer my question."

Andrea looked down at the ground, upset at his cold tone. "I have information to report, Colonel Delaney."

"I believe we have an established method of communicating that does not require you crossing the lines. You might recall that was part of the agreement with Colonel Jordan."

"But I wished to see you." Andrea could not bring herself to look into his eyes.

"Why?" There was not a hint of warmth in his voice.

Andrea raised her head, disappointment and regret turning to anger. "I was not aware that I needed a reason."

"Were you aware there is a war going on?"

"Yes, but I ..." Andrea looked up into the intense blue eyes gazing down at her and could not finish. "Perhaps I should leave." Without waiting for acknowledgment or consent, she whirled around and headed in the opposite direction, toward what she hoped were the stables.

"Miss Marlow!" Daniel shouted, striding after her. "Where are you going?"

"To see if the horses are still hitched."

Daniel grabbed her arm and pulled her to a stop. "And if they are not?"

"Then I will hitch them, and I will drive them back to Richmond, and I will forget I ever came here!" Andrea struggled from his grasp, picked up her skirts, and ran toward the barn.

"Wait! Please, Andrea!" The desperation in Daniel's voice made her stop, though she did not turn around. "Please ... wait."

Andrea heard him exhale behind her.

"I'm sorry. Can we begin again?" Daniel put his hand on her shoulder, his voice low and gentle, the way she remembered it. "Miss Marlow, it is indeed a pleasure to see you again."

Andrea allowed him to turn her around, but her gaze remained averted. Daniel put his finger under her chin and lifted her head. For a moment he did not speak, just stared solemnly and earnestly into her eyes. "I'm sorry, Andrea," he finally said. "Please forgive me."

"It's my fault, Colonel Delaney. I should not have come."

"My friends call me Daniel." He stared at her, unblinking.

"I apologize." Andrea could not meet his gaze. "I was not sure I had the honor to be considered among them."

Daniel remained silent for a moment and then pulled her into his arms. "Andrea, there's going to be a battle here. A big battle. And I never expected ... I never dreamed that you—"

She waited for him to finish, but he did not. He just increased the tightness of his embrace so that she could feel his heart pounding against her cheek.

"Oh, pray forgive me!" he finally whispered. "You must realize ... I never saw you like this."

Andrea pulled back. "I know you have duties. If you wish, I can wait here for you."

"Nonsense," he said, bowing gallantly. "I am devotedly at your service. You must be frozen. Come in and warm yourself by the fire."

"No." Andrea glanced toward the crowded house. "I'd rather speak to you … privately."

Daniel took a deep breath and offered her his arm. "Very well. If you're sure you're warm enough, let's walk."

Andrea linked her arm in his, and he led her silently toward the river.

"Colonel Delaney!" An aide came trotting toward them. "Colonel Delaney, I'm sorry, sir," he said, looking at Andrea appraisingly. "The general wishes to see you."

Daniel groaned. "About what?"

"Dunno. He was asking about Richmond though."

Daniel looked at Andrea. "If he wants a report on Richmond, I suppose you should be the one to give it to him." He grabbed her hand and led her toward the house.

"Daniel, no!"

He stopped and looked at her with a puzzled expression. "What are you afraid of, Andrea?

"There are things I need to tell you first."

"They'll have to wait. The general does not like delay."

Andrea did not speak as he led her through a back entrance and down a hall. But she knew he could feel her trembling when they stopped in front of a closed door. "Daniel, wait—"

"Relax, he won't bite," he whispered, knocking once and opening the door at the sound of a rough voice telling him to enter.

An officer who was seated behind a desk reading when the two stepped inside, quickly rose to his feet when he saw Andrea.

"General, it's my pleasure to introduce you to … ah … Maryann Marlow."

Andrea strode across the room with her hand extended, a shy smile masking her true emotions. "It's such a wonderful privilege and honor to meet you, General."

"Miss Marlow." The officer bowed and took her hand, looking curiously at Daniel to explain.

"I understand you are interested in news of Richmond," Daniel said, "and since she has just come from there, I took the liberty of inviting her.

"From Richmond?" the general croaked. "Today?"

"Indeed." Andrea walked over to a large map on a table, pretending that getting in and out of Richmond was no serious matter. "I'd be honored to tell you what I've discovered, sir. I'll not take too much of your time."

The general looked confused, but Andrea ignored him. "I have learned that there's an immense line of embankments and heavy artillery in a circle of about two miles from the city … from Battery No. 1 on the north side of the James to No. 17 on the south side." She cocked her head and looked up. "I'm sorry to report, I'm only aware of the specifics of No. 15. It has only one company of light artillery—eighty-five men, commanded by a Captain Hanns. The battery is here," she said, pointing on the map.

"Tell me, Miss Marlow, just how did you get through Confederate defenses to go traipsing wherever you pleased in enemy territory," the general asked, regarding her doubtfully.

"Sir, she is our replacement for Winslow in Richmond." Daniel stepped forward. "I vouch for her character and the reliability of her information."

"I never authorized a woman to go to Richmond!"

"No," Daniel answered, "but you asked me to find the most capable person I could."

Andrea stared at the map, pretending to have no interest in the conversation about her.

"That still does not explain how you know about these fortifications." The general gazed at Andrea suspiciously.

"To answer your question ... I mentioned to an officer that I wished to see the sunrise from the highest point of Richmond."

"And he complied," the general finished for her.

"Yes, he did. I have found the enemy's proclivity for gallantry makes them most accommodating in that fashion."

"Splendid." He walked over and took Andrea's hand while she looked over his shoulder at Daniel. Unlike the general, whose face beamed with approval, Daniel's expression was one of melancholy and concern.

"I must commend you on a job well done, Miss Marlow. I would never have permitted it had I been aware, but I'm glad Colonel Delaney had the sense to see the benefits of using a woman's grace and charm to our benefit." He turned to Daniel. "Well done, Colonel."

He pulled out a pocket watch and then clicked it closed. "My dear, it's almost midnight. You must be exhausted. Colonel Delaney will show you where you can get some sleep, and then we can talk in more detail tomorrow."

Daniel impatiently took Andrea's hand and started pulling her toward the door.

"I will, of course, need all this written up into a formal report," the general said.

Daniel turned around like he'd been hit. "But she's only here a short while."

"There should be plenty of time to write a report. That will be all."

Chapter 15

*"Gather ye rosebuds while ye may, Old Time is still a-flying;
And this same flower that smiles today, tomorrow will be dying."*
— *Robert Herrick*

Colonel Delaney did not speak another word until they reached the bank of the river. "You seem to have made quite an impression on the General."

Andrea shrugged and looked up at the night sky, pulling the hood of her cloak tight. "I simply told him what he wanted to hear." She laughed. "It is usually the easiest way to deal with men."

"*All* men? It seemed to come rather naturally to you."

Andrea looked over at him, surprised at the allegation and shaken at the accusing tone of his voice. "No. What do you mean?"

"You told me earlier you traveled all this way because you wished to see me. Was that because you thought it was what I wished to hear?"

Andrea blinked at the insinuation and felt hot blood coarse through her veins. "Of course not, Colonel. How could you think such a thing?"

Daniel took a deep breath of exasperation. "I told you before, my friends call me Daniel."

"I'm sorry, Daniel." Andrea put her hands to her temples. "To answer your question, I came because I missed you. And the more I thought about coming, the happier I felt. And, oh, never mind. I don't know why." She turned around and sighed with frustration.

"Then stay."

Andrea looked over her shoulder at him and frowned wistfully. "You know I can't stay. They're expecting me—"

"I mean stay. Don't go back." He turned her around. "It's too dangerous."

Andrea pushed him away. "We've been through this, have we not? No one is promised tomorrow. Not me. Not you. No one."

"But you don't have to tempt fate by constantly pushing it to the limit!"

"I face no more danger than you do, or any of our men in the field."

"But you should not be risking your life like a—" Daniel stopped.

"Like a man?" She finished for him.

"Dash it all, you are but a child." His voice sounded distressed.

"Is that what you think of me?" Andrea asked incredulously. "I came to prove to you that I am capable of doing my duty. What must I do to win your esteem?"

"Dear Andrea, you must know you already have my esteem." He pulled her closer. "You cannot blame me for worrying about you."

"I worry about you too," Andrea said. "Yet I do not ask you to stop doing what you do."

"You do think of me then?" Daniel held her at arm's length, probing her eyes for the truth.

"I told you I worry about you. You are in a far more dangerous position than I, yet you are too noble to worry about yourself ... instead, always thinking of what could happen to me."

"Andrea, it's not nobility that makes me worry about you." Daniel brought her close to him again. "From the first moment I met you I felt ... a connection ... an attraction." He laughed nervously. "And now I— And now seeing you like this I—"

Daniel stopped in mid-sentence and sighed. "You must think I'm foolish, rambling like a schoolboy."

Andrea wrapped her arms around his stalwart soldierly form, glad that her sweet Daniel had returned. "No, not a schoolboy," she said, laying her cheek on his chest. "I shall always think of you as my knight in shining armor, the gallant soldier who rescued me from Hunter on that hillside."

Daniel remained silent, but Andrea felt his body stiffen at the name. "Well, that's behind us," he finally said. "And, thankfully, you won't need rescuing from Hunter in Richmond. For that, at least, I can be grateful."

Now it was Andrea who stiffened and held her breath, hoping he would say no more ... hoping she would not be forced to lie—or worse, tell the truth.

But Daniel seemed to sense trouble in her sudden silence and pulled away to look at her. "You have not seen Hunter in Richmond."

Andrea looked down and bit her cheek, contemplating her options.

"You have not seen Hunter in Richmond," he repeated louder.

"He did not recognize me," Andrea mumbled to the ground.

He did not recognize you?" Daniel shook her. "You *talked* to him?"

"Not intentionally," Andrea defended herself. "I mean, it would have seemed strange not to converse during a waltz."

"During a *waltz*? This is folly!" He stepped away from her and began pacing. "I cannot allow you to return! Colonel Jordan would never forgive me, and I could never forgive myself. No duty of war could be so trying as knowing I sent you into danger—to death!"

"He did not recognize me." Andrea grabbed his coat sleeve to stop him and force him to listen to her. "The worst is over."

"How do you know that?" He stood so close she felt him trembling. "How would you know if he recognized you and is only waiting for you to fall into his trap? Hunter would never do anything rashly. He would wait until the time is right. Why must you trifle with him?"

"He did not recognize me. I am sure of it. And I am going back." Andrea crossed her arms and turned away from him.

"What are you running from?" Daniel asked from behind her.

"I'm not running from anything."

"You must be. Why else would you not be able to see reason? *Be* reasonable?"

Andrea stared at a thousand tiny reflections in the river but did not answer.

"Is it your past?" Daniel continued prodding her. "That of which you never speak? What is it that consumes your soul? Perhaps I can help you."

Andrea shrugged and sighed. "My past? It's another world."

"Then let it go." Daniel turned her to face him. "Whatever it is, whatever it was, let it go."

"It's—not—that—easy." Although she tried to erase the images of the slaves she had seen punished at the hands of her father, Andrea's words came out in short, choking sobs. "I allowed things . . . things to happen when I was young. And now—I must sacrifice—to make it right."

"Sacrifice your life?" He shook her as he spoke. "For something that happened when you were but a child?"

Andrea's eyes filled with tears of grief and pain, but they did not overflow. She gazed over his shoulder a moment, then took a deep, shaky breath. The effort it took to suppress her true emotions and force a faint smile was considerable. "Oh, Daniel, why must we talk of such things? My time here is too short."

"Yes, let's walk," Daniel said, taking her by the hand. "It will do us both good."

After only a short distance, Andrea paused and stared out over the vast expanse of river and the campfires reflected there. "It's beautiful. I'm so glad I came." She looked over at Daniel. "Even if you are not."

"Oh, Andrea, I'm glad you came." Daniel turned her toward him and brushed a tendril of hair from her face. "You must forgive me for being overly protective. It's a natural reaction, the way I feel . . ."

Andrea looked up at him, her eyes questioning.

"I wish I could stop the hands of the clock, right at this moment." Daniel gazed at her intently. "Though I suppose I would have as much success stopping Father Time as stopping *you*."

Andrea laid her head upon his chest. "Oh please, Daniel, don't speak about time. Nowadays there is never enough of it."

"I know," he said, running his hand down her back. "But I cannot help but wish this evening might last forever, that you would not go."

"Please don't be angry with me, Daniel." Andrea put her hands on his arms and clutched his coat with her fingers. "Truly, I cannot bear it."

"I'm not angry. I only wish you would reconsider."

"But what would I do here?" Andrea asked dejectedly, her cheek against his coat.

"You could let me protect you, care for you, the way a man cares for a woman."

Andrea looked up at him. "Why would you wish to do that for me?"

Daniel smiled. "Andrea, you are a woman, are you not? I am a man."

"I don't know. You said I was a child a few minutes ago."

Daniel frowned and stared into her eyes. The look softened when his eyes rose to the chignon on the crown of her head. Her hair, which had always been cropped short when she was in camp, had grown much longer during her months in Richmond.

"Take down your hair," he said.

Andrea blinked and tried unsuccessfully to read the expression on his face. She was only too happy to comply and free her hair from the uncomfortable style. But she demurred for a moment.

"Might that be an order from my superior? Or a request from a friend?"

Daniel lowered his eyes as if losing his courage, then raised them again and grinned. "Let's say it is both. So if you cannot obey the one, perhaps you can grant the other."

"Then it would seem I am doubly obliged to consent." Leaning back against his strong hands, she pulled the single comb from her hair and unwrapped a green ribbon. Shaking her head once, she let the river breeze pick up the soft locks and blow them gently back.

"I've dreamed of seeing you like this," Daniel whispered, running his fingers through the blonde tendrils.

"You think of me?" Andrea looked up disbelievingly, her hands holding onto the lapel of his coat. "Like this?"

Daniel smiled out of the corner of his mouth and dropped his gaze down to meet hers. "More than an honorable man would care to admit," he said hoarsely.

Andrea's cheeks grew warm at the attention, and she was suddenly breathless and warm and confused.

Daniel's gaze drifted back to her hair, and again he ran his hand through its length, staring as if unable to grasp how a recurring dream had suddenly materialized into reality. Andrea saw him swallow hard, felt his hands move from her hair, to her neck, to her face.

"Andrea," he whispered, just before his lips lowered to hers. He barely touched them at first, an action that appeared to be nothing more than a cordial impulse. But then he lingered in a long, sensual, affectionate kiss that implied much more than simple friendship.

Andrea pulled back, her eyes wide. "Dan," she said, her fingers clutching his arms. "You move too fast."

"My apologies," he whispered, his chest rising and falling heavily against hers, his arms refusing to relinquish their hold. "As you said, time is so fleeting these days. It is that which dictates the pace."

Andrea relaxed into him, sensing his urgency and feeling helpless to resist. "But I—"

"My dear Andrea. I will try to go slow," Daniel whispered, his arms wrapped around her protectively. "But you must know I ... adore you."

"I am unfamiliar with this," Andrea said softly, confused at her own emotions, hoping he would understand that men had been nothing but comrades to joke with, fellow soldiers to be ridiculed by, or officers to take orders from. Then her thoughts drifted to her father, the only other male figurehead in her life. "My father," she began, trying to explain. "My father showed me a side of men that I ... that I ..."

Daniel tightened his grip around her. "Then I would be honored to be the one to make you familiar with the other side of a man."

Andrea lifted her head, wanting to read his eyes.

"I want to protect you from everything and stand ready to take every possible burden off your shoulders. You will let me try, won't you?"

"I never had anyone wish to take care of me." She gripped his coat, her heart racing. "I don't know how."

"Do not fear," Daniel whispered, his hand moving to the small of her back. "I will teach you." He ran his other hand across her shoulder like he was calming a frightened horse.

Andrea tried to keep the distrust from showing on her face. But memories of her childhood came crashing back.

"Andrea, please know I will protect you with my life, guard you with my honor, if you will but let me." He placed her hand over his heart. "Can you not feel my desire for you?"

Andrea gazed at her hand as she felt the rapid pulse there, and then up into his eyes. "Yes, Daniel. And it frightens me."

"I was unaware you felt fear." He laughed, a gentle, rolling laugh, and pulled her to him again.

"I don't know what I feel anymore," Andrea said, her voice cracking with despair.

"I know you would not have traveled all this way, risked so much, if you did not care for me," he said. "If you cannot trust me, trust your own heart, Andrea. Don't fight it. I will attempt to win your heart *and* your trust."

Andrea leaned into him. "I can promise nothing. But I will try."

"Your being here is like a dream come true," he said, stroking her hair. "It will sustain me for what is to come."

Andrea pushed herself back at his words. "Promise me you won't take any risks, Daniel! This battle. You must not—"

He put his finger to her lips to stop her. "We will take Fredericksburg, and then we will go to Richmond. And I will personally carry you away from there, and all this madness will end."

Andrea put her head against his chest again. "My knight," she said smiling. "I will wait for you there." She sighed deeply then, thinking of the distance between them. "We will be but fifty miles apart. Yet, it will seem we are separated by eternity."

"Here." Daniel pulled a ring from his finger. "Take this. My grandfather gave it to me when I was a boy. It means much to me. And it would mean much more if you wore it."

"I cannot accept such a gift," Andrea said softly, staring at the ring. "It belongs in your family."

"I trust that you will justly value it on that account," he said, his eyes sparkling. "And perhaps, some day, we can arrange to have it stay there. Please." He opened her hand. "It would give me much pleasure to know you had something of mine to look at each day, something that is only shared between you and I, so that you understand there is no one else for me."

He slid the ring onto her finger. "But, I don't know what I'm promising with this." Andrea's voice shook. "I don't know if I can—"

"All you are promising is that you will think of me when you look at it."

"That I can do." Andrea smiled. "And I will value it dearly."

"It's a part of me." Daniel's voice was low, his eyes soft and solemn.

"Then I shall feel like you are with me always," Andrea said. "I will never remove it, no matter what. It is a part of me now."

"This is better than running, is it not?" he whispered in her ear.

Andrea sighed. "You will be patient with me, Dan? You won't rush me?"

"My darling, Andrea," he said, squeezing her tightly. "I will do anything for you. I will submit to any conditions you desire, for as long as you will allow me to."

Andrea exhaled and laid her head against his heart. The wool of his coat rubbed harshly against her face, yet she felt so comfortable there within his embrace. In the circle of his arms, she was the most fulfilled and satisfied she had ever been in her life.

For a moment, she thought how easy it would be to stay, to try to become the woman he wished her to be, to forget the past. And then she pulled away, panicked at the idea that she would renounce all, simply for this feeling of utter contentment.

"We have to write that report," she said, a hint of desperation in her voice.

Daniel stared at her a moment, bitter disappointment evident in his eyes. "Of course," he said unable to keep the distress from his voice, though he made an obvious effort to sound agreeable. "As you wish, Miss Marlow, follow me."

Chapter 17

"War requires sacrifice and men are ready to pay it in their blood."
— Colonel Thomas S. Garnett to his wife, Emma

Fredericksburg, Virginia
December 15, 1862

Andrea stared straight ahead as the carriage wheels rattled beneath her, clutching the message that had arrived hours earlier.

"Brother wounded," was all it said. It did not say "come," yet she knew what it meant. Brother was the code name for Daniel. And they would not have taken the trouble to send the message if it was not serious.

As she nervously played with the ring on her gloved finger, Andrea thought back to her last meeting with Daniel only a few weeks ago. The visit had been so hurried, she'd never had the chance to question him about the large 'H' engraved in the ring's center, or the intricate lettering of the phrase: *Honor Above All Things.*

She longed to ask him about his grandfather, about his family, and his life. She knew so little about Colonel Daniel Delaney, and he so little of her. She yearned to learn about his past—and, perhaps, in time, share a little of hers.

Shifting her gaze to the window, Andrea shivered at the sights. All along the road walked bandaged and bloodied men with the litter of war strewn beyond them. According to soldiers they had passed, a hospital just ahead held the worst of the injured. Andrea found herself holding her breath, willing the horses to go faster and praying she would find Daniel safe.

After what seemed like hours, the carriage rolled to a stop. Andrea stepped down before the driver had time to assist, and lifted her gaze to the building in front of her.

"This is the hospital, miss. Will there be anything else?"

Andrea heard the words but could not answer. She stared at the house, unblinking and unmoving, placing her hand on the carriage wheel to steady

85

herself as the past collided with the present.

The brightly lit mansion where she had spent a few hours of serenity with Daniel stood before her now ruined and ravaged by war. Even the lawn, once neat and well groomed, appeared as a vast swampland of muck. She turned her head away, toward the river, but the wreckage was not reserved to the house alone. Scattered everywhere, seemingly unaware of the chaos and mayhem around them, laid men indistinguishable from the dead.

Andrea choked back the bile rising in her throat and slogged through the mud to the house. Rushing up the steps, she stopped in horror at the doorway. The walls and floor of the home were spattered with blood, and the injured and dying lay sprawled in every available space, many of them shivering convulsively with the pain of their wounds. Andrea could hear surgeons in the back of the house shouting above the din of delirious cries that made her bones ache with revulsion.

Lifting her skirts, she stepped through the foyer, frantically studying the faces of the men at her feet. None appeared to be Daniel, though many were so covered in blood and mire that it was almost impossible to tell. Turning into a room off the hallway, a whimper of anguish escaped her. Lying on a door placed upon four bricks, she recognized the uniform of an officer.

Andrea dropped to her knees beside him and took his hand in hers. "Daniel, are you awake?" She wiped the sweat from his brow with her glove. Daniel opened his eyes, stared at her face for a moment, then re-closed them. Andrea feared he did not recognize her.

"Am I ... in heaven?" he asked weakly.

Andrea thought she saw a hint of a smile on his lips, but dismissed it as her imagination. "No, you're not in heaven." She glanced up at the corner of hell she sat in, then bent down close to his face and stroked his forehead.

"You're not ... an angel?" This time Andrea knew he was trying to smile.

"Not according to the Rebels." Andrea took both his hands in hers and squeezed them gently.

Daniel remained quiet for a breathlessly long time, but Andrea knew he was only mustering the strength to speak.

"You have ... come ... to me," he murmured.

"Dan, of course I came." Andrea's heart picked up its pace at how pale and despondent he looked. "I came as soon as I received word! I'll stay and nurse you until you are completely healed."

His eyes fluttered open, but only for a moment. "I believe ... too late ... for that."

Andrea's gaze shifted down to the blanket lying across him, to the large red splotch near his stomach. She bravely looked back up to his eyes.

"Don't be silly," she said, stroking his forehead. "I will nurse you until you are completely healed. You will see."

"Surgeon ... said ... nothing he ... can do."

Andrea looked at his strained face and blinked at his words, refusing to believe they were true. Yet she felt her blood begin to throb with a faster cadence through her veins as the reality of what he said sank in.

"No, Daniel, don't say that. He doesn't know. Like I said, I will stay!"

"We made ... good team," he said, interrupting her. "I hoped someday ..."

"We *make* a good team." Andrea cut in, her voice now pleading. "Surely your hopes are no different than mine."

Daniel opened his eyes and gazed into hers as if trying to read the sincerity of her words. "No one . . . promised tomorrow." His speech was now slurred and barely audible over shouts outside of a soldier coming in under a flag of truce.

"Right this way." Andrea heard an officer bark the command outside the window.

"I wanted to ... protect you," Daniel whispered.

"I will let you protect me!" Andrea felt a tightening in her stomach as panic began to grow. "I will stay. I will do whatever you ask, Dan. Just please, don't leave!"

"Must ... stop ... Andrea." He spoke with his eyes closed, yet there was urgency in his voice. "Please! Say you will ... for me."

Andrea leaned down close to make sure she had heard him. "Dan, I will do whatever you wish," she said, her heart breaking at the sight of him. "But please don't ask that of me now. Not like this."

A shadow fell over them as someone entered the room and blocked the only light coming in. Glancing briefly over her shoulder at the intrusion, Andrea turned her head back for a second look. Captain Alexander Hunter stood in the doorway, a slouch hat pulled down low over his face, the uniform of a Confederate private stretched across his large frame.

Andrea's mind was too confused to wonder why he was here, her heart too numb to care. She watched a similar look of surprise flash across his eyes when he recognized her, but it was quickly replaced by concern for the man lying before her.

"How is he?" He kneeled on the other side of Daniel.

Daniel opened his eyes. "Alex?"

"Yes, Dan, I'm here." Hunter bent down close.

"You shouldn't ... have come." Daniel coughed and winced. "Too ... dangerous."

Andrea could not help but agree. She surmised Hunter had not used his real name to cross the lines, for the Federals would never consent to letting him back out if he had—not even under a flag of truce.

Hunter grasped Daniel's shoulder firmly. "You're going to be all right, Danny boy," he said in a voice that urged the man to live. "Just hold on." Then Hunter raised his head and looked around. "Where's the blasted surgeon?"

Andrea looked incredulously at Hunter. She had never dreamed it possible to see so much compassion and concern shine in those cold, gray eyes.

"Don't think …you can fix it … this time …big brother." Daniel's breathing grew even shallower. Andrea blinked and gazed up at Hunter, but he was looking down at the hand Daniel was trying to raise. Hunter grasped it, and Daniel smiled weakly.

"You're … the best … Alex," he whispered. "I wish that we …"

"I understand, Dan." Hunter's voice trembled. "Don't try to talk. Just rest."

Andrea took a deep breath during the ensuing silence, willing herself not to look up at Hunter, and yet half afraid to glance down at Daniel. After what seemed like an eternity, Daniel opened his lids again, his eyes bright and glazed with pain. "You will … let no harm … befall her."

It was not a question, nor a statement, but was spoken clearly in the tone of an appeal.

Hunter's gaze lifted and met Andrea's, then lowered again. "You have my word."

The promise had no effect on Daniel, save make him more restless. He struggled to raise his head. "But there are things … things you know not of." He sounded frenzied as he looked deep into Hunter's eyes.

Andrea pushed Daniel back down. "Daniel, please rest." She felt Hunter's gaze burning into her.

"No matter the circumstances, Dan," Hunter said reassuringly "You have my word."

Daniel closed his eyes and relaxed then as if a great weight had been lifted. When Andrea stroked a lock of hair from his forehead, his eyes fluttered open at the contact. He gazed glassy-eyed at her as if he wanted to speak again. Andrea leaned down close, her face just inches from his. "It was an honor … to have known you," he murmured, his breathing growing raspy.

Andrea kissed his cheek. "The honor, Daniel," she said softly in his ear, "is all mine."

He must have heard the words, because he opened his eyes and took another deep, raspy breath. "Andrea, remember me …"

Andrea barely heard his whispered, feeble words. She leaned even closer, waiting breathlessly for him to finish, but not another word was spoken. The gallant soldier closed his eyes and was still.

Desperate to believe he was just gathering strength, Andrea continued to hold her breath and listen for the sound of his voice. Hunter reached over and touched her arm. "He's gone."

Andrea stared at Hunter intently for a long moment as if the language he spoke was foreign to her. Then to prove him wrong, she reached down and picked up Daniel's hand to give it a gentle squeeze. It felt cold, not at all like Daniel.

Dropping it in revulsion, Andrea heard the limb hit the floor with a thud. She sat back on her heels and looked at Daniel's face. His eyes, half-open now, stared vacantly at the ceiling.

Blinking repeatedly, Andrea looked accusingly at Hunter, as if he should do something. "But—"

Hunter stood and offered his hand to help her up. "There's nothing more we can do."

Andrea continued to shake her head, wringing her hands and rocking back and forth. *Dear Lord, they killed him!* She raised her eyes and glared at Hunter, who now conversed in low tones with an orderly. Already they wanted to move Daniel. They had a body, a living one, to put in his place.

"I'll take him back to my family home for burial."

The orderly nodded. "Very well. I'll get some men to help."

Andrea struggled to stand, grabbing Hunter's arm as she stumbled to her feet. "Wait! No!"

Hunter looked down at her hand like he was unaccustomed to people touching him without permission. "I beg your pardon?"

"In the *ground?*" Andrea's gaze darted from the man on the floor to the man standing over him. "You're going to put Dan ... *in the ground?*"

Hunter looked her squarely in the eye and responded in an unemotional voice. "I don't know how they do it where you come from, Miss Marlow, but that's generally how they bury people in Virginia."

Andrea felt a wave of nausea overcome her. Suddenly the stench of the room, the sounds of dying men, the blood soaking into the bottom of her dress in this ghastly house of suffering was more than she could take. She picked up her skirts and ran out the back door, past the very tree where she had stood with Daniel a few weeks earlier—the same tree whose bare limbs now stood guard over a haphazard heap of mutilated arms and legs.

Hand over her mouth Andrea ran, the cold air stinging her face, until at the river's edge, she could hold it no longer. The sights and sounds and smells rendered her convulsively ill. Clinging to the side of a tree for support she choked and retched as the river lapped playfully at the banks below. For so long, death had passed her by. Now it was real. Andrea could hear the clods of dirt falling on Daniel as clearly as if they were falling on her, smothering her, choking her. Her heart shuddered; her chest ached. She was sweating and freezing; she shook, yet was numb. Daniel. Oh, Daniel. So many things she had meant to tell him. *Dear Lord, I never even told him my full name!*

Andrea started to pace. It was a dream. It must be a dream. She would wake up soon. *Dear God in heaven, don't let it be real!*

But when Andrea glanced to her left, the reality was all too real. Fresh mounds of earth told of the dead that already slept below. The vaguely penetrating odor of blood and death grew inescapable and overpowering. Andrea grabbed her chest, pulling and tugging at her cloak to give her heart more room to tremble. Hearing the sound of wood sliding on wood, she turned to see men loading a pine box in a wagon behind her. She flinched when an icy drop of sleet fell from the sky, stinging her cheek and confirming it was not just a dream.

"The favorites of the gods die early," her Mammy had always told her, "and then the angels cry." Andrea raised her face toward heaven and let the angels' frozen tears fall unhindered upon her face. When she opened her eyes, she saw Union soldiers mounting to accompany the wagon back through the lines, and Hunter striding toward her. She turned back to the river.

"Are you all right, Miss Marlow?" His voice came from just behind her shoulder.

She nodded, but continued to gaze out over the water.

"They will allow you safely back through the lines to Richmond?"

Andrea nodded again.

"Very well." He turned to leave.

"Captain."

"Yes?" Hunter came back to her and she turned around.

"That is a good man you'll be b-b-burying." Andrea stumbled over the word, as if by saying it she admitted he was gone.

Hunter took a deep breath as he gazed over her head. "I know that."

Andrea stepped forward when she heard the pain in his voice. She did not see him as an enemy at this moment, but Daniel's brother, his own flesh and blood. Tentatively reaching out for him, she felt his arms wrap hesitatingly around her, a concession that he needed her comfort as much as she needed his.

"The price is too high," Andrea whispered, clinging to the gray wool of his coat.

"Too high, indeed."

And so they stood there holding onto each other as the sky spit snow—he fiercely devoted to the Confederacy; she, fervently dedicated to the Union … yet joined, at this moment, in solemn unity for a man they both had loved.

Chapter 18

"Stand by your principles, stand by your guns, and victory,
complete and permanent shall be yours."
– Abraham Lincoln

Richmond, Virginia
May, 1863

Even though angry clouds gathered overhead, Andrea knew the storm would not amount to much. She hurried along the sidewalk with her head down, contemplating how soon—and how—she would depart from Richmond. Daniel's death had settled over her like a dark cloud of despair these past five months. She no longer had the heart to continue her work in the Confederacy, or the will to keep up her charade as a loyal Southerner. A s each day faded into the next, she grew more and more determined to leave.

A loud scream and the sound of thundering horses broke through her thoughts. "Runaways!" She heard the word just as a two-horse team and wagon barreled into view.

Andrea watched a soldier run alongside the wagon, jump into the seat, and haul on the reins, but the horses continued running, too frightened to stop. The street ended a mere half a block away, and an open market with dozens of unsuspecting shoppers lay directly in the horses' path.

Without hesitation, Andrea stepped onto the road. "Whoa there, boys," she said, stretching her arms in front of her. Although the horses surged toward her, Andrea stood motionless, giving no ground. "Easy. Easy."

As the team drew nearer, they continued throwing their heads and grinding the bit in their teeth, fighting the person hauling on the reins. Andrea sidestepped out of their way when it became apparent they were not going to stop. But when they got directly beside her, she grabbed the bridle of the nearest horse.

"Whoa, son!" She yanked hard with both hands, throwing all her weight into the move as the leather burned her hands. The horses jerked to a nervous stop and stood shaking and foaming in the street.

"Easy now, boys." Andrea talked in a soothing tone while patting the frothing horse on the neck. The team continued trembling and snorting, and Andrea knew any sudden movement could cause them to erupt again.

"Nice catch, Miss Marlow."

Andrea whipped her head around as Captain Hunter jumped lightly from the seat.

"Captain Hunter." She clenched the horse's bridle. "I didn't know you were in Richmond."

"And I didn't know you were such a foolish young lady," he said rather harshly as he grabbed the bridle from her hand. Andrea noted that his formerly bronzed face appeared pale.

"Someone could have been hurt." She looked at the street beginning to fill again, then at her tender, dirt-stained hands.

"Yes, and that someone could have been *you!*"

"I thought—"

"No, I don't believe you *thought* at all. No one who had any thoughts in their head would have stood directly in front of more than two tons of horseflesh!"

Andrea did not have time to argue as a young man came running up the street.

"Thank you, sir." Breathing heavily, he took the reins from Hunter. "Blasted kids lit a firecracker right under their feet."

Andrea backed up to the sidewalk. She was about to bid Hunter goodbye, when he spoke.

"I just engaged a hack. Will you permit me the favor of escorting you home *safely?*"

Andrea thought his voice conveyed true concern, but with Hunter she could not be sure. She wanted desperately to refuse, but knew it was obvious to him by now that she was on foot and had no escort. She did not want to raise suspicions by declining the offer. "That would be lovely." She took a deep breath, knowing her tone failed to communicate the words.

"It's right this way."

Andrea tried hard to keep up with his long strides, but Hunter seemed to take no notice. "Are you in Richmond for business or pleasure?" she asked, gasping for breath as he helped her into the seat of the rented carriage.

Hunter did not answer until he had climbed up beside her. Then he glanced down at her as if the word *pleasure* was foreign to his ears. "Business." His tone conveyed she would hear no more about the purpose or significance of his presence in Richmond. "And what about you?" He slapped the horse with the reins.

Andrea looked up at him confused.

"Business or pleasure? This is not a part of Richmond where I would expect to see you."

"I-I was just visiting a friend." Andrea realized Hunter could have been watching her. For all she knew, he had been following her. She remembered Daniel's words about his brother. He would wait until the time is right ...

"Without an escort? Have you no regard for your reputation?"

Andrea tried to make her voice sound cordial, but the disdain dripped from her tongue. "Do you regard all women with suspicion, Captain? Or just me?"

"Why must you think I regard you with suspicion, Miss Marlow?" He gave a laugh that sounded forced. "Could it be because you seem to have fallen from the sky into Richmond with no one to vouch for your reputation other than your aunt, whose background is not above suspicion itself? Or because I find you walking through Richmond in a suspicious area of town without an escort? Or because—" Hunter paused and looked down at her hand. "Because you wear the ring of a dead Federal officer. Shall I go on?"

Andrea looked up at his face in surprise and then down at her hand. Mechanically her gaze shifted to Hunter's right hand, where she saw a ring almost identical to the one she wore. Now she knew the reason for his sudden callousness. What she didn't know was how she would weave her way out of this web of deceit.

"Daniel gave me this, uh, right before he died." She took a deep breath while twisting the ring. "He … that is, we—"

"I find it a bit odd that a loyal citizen of the South would continue to honor the memory of a Union officer." Hunter's hands clenched the reins more tightly. "Perhaps you view it as a trophy? My brother was a good man, despite the color of the uniform he wore. He did not deserve to be used in a game of deceit."

Andrea took a sharp breath, realizing that Hunter believed she had used Daniel to gather information for the Confederacy. She wasn't sure how to respond. Though relieved to hear that Hunter believed she was a loyal Southerner, she did not wish him to think she dishonored Daniel. "It's just that … well … Daniel was a friend before he was an enemy."

"He would not have given that ring to another without much consideration." Hunter took a deep breath. "Or without being misled."

"Pray do not smell a crime where there isn't one, Captain Hunter. Daniel was not the type of man to be misled."

"You seem overly defensive, Miss Marlow. Have I unknowingly offended you?"

"Not unknowingly, I'm sure."

Hunter ignored the stab. "So how is it that you knew Daniel? You never had the chance to tell me."

Although his voice sounded gentler now, Andrea knew it was a ploy—that things were not adding up in his mind. "Well, how did you happen to be brothers? You never had the chance to tell me."

Hunter glanced down at her with a look of annoyance. "Do you always answer a question with a question?"

"Does it seem like I do?" Andrea grinned at her joke, though it was obvious Hunter did not share in the amusement.

"My father, Joseph Hunter, died when I was young. My mother remarried James Delaney and I got a baby brother, Daniel. Satisfied?"

"You were close?" Andrea heard the unmistakable sadness in his voice.

"My mother and James were about as fond of children as they were of learning how to be horse breeders. They left Hawthorne to be closer to his family in New York when I was ten, leaving us with our grandfather."

So that's why Daniel fought for the Union, Andrea thought. His father's family was from the North.

"Anyway, my grandfather knew I would eventually take over Hawthorne, and raised us until he died. I was eighteen, then. Daniel was twelve."

"So *you* raised Daniel."

He shrugged. "I did what I could."

Andrea stared at the ring on her finger. "He never told me you were brothers, but I could tell he respected you greatly … admired you."

"The feeling was mutual." Glancing sideways at her, he must have seen her staring at his ring. "It says: "*Dare All for Sacred Honor.*""

"My grandfather had them each made." He cleared his throat in such a way that made Andrea instinctively brace herself. "I've often wondered what Daniel meant when he insisted there were things I did not know."

His voice sounded casual, yet Andrea's heart pounded in her ears. Hunter had obviously replayed the scene in Fredericksburg over in his mind and was not satisfied with the end result. "Who … who can know? He was in a great deal of pain. Perhaps he did not know what he was saying."

"Yes, indeed," Hunter said, as he turned his head and stared at her. "Who can know?"

Andrea looked away and did not speak. She could not. The man beside her was back to that hostile, aloof composure that concealed his every thought. A more overbearing and intimidating man she had never encountered.

"You still haven't told me how you met him."

Andrea tried to hold her hands steady. She vaguely remembered Daniel telling her he had spent some time in Richmond. "I met Daniel here … in Richmond a few years ago," she said. "I went to school here. And then when I decided to come South, I—"

"Used him," Hunter answered disdainfully.

Andrea's breath caught in her throat, and both of her hands turned to fists. She did not speak for fear of saying something she would regret. It seemed to her the horse moved in slow motion, else the street grew longer, or time stood still. Out of boredom from the lack of conversation, her gaze drifted over to Hunter's strong hands as they expertly held the reins, then to his well-muscled forearms disappearing into coat sleeves. She shuddered at the power they conveyed and looked away.

94

"Are you chilled, Miss Marlow?"

Expecting to see a look of mockery when she glanced up at his face, Andrea was surprised to find that ridicule was apparently not his intent. He appeared honestly concerned, his gray eyes soft and sympathetic.

"No, I'm ... I'm fine." Andrea stuttered the words, wondering why his considerate side caused her heart to beat more tumultuously than his callous one had.

The two rode in silence for what seemed like hours to Andrea, though it was but the distance of two blocks.

"This is it, is it not?" Hunter pointed with his eyes and turned toward the side of the street.

Andrea nodded but did not bother to respond nor ask how he knew. Instead, she practically leaped from her seat before he even pulled the horse to a halt.

"Perhaps we can have a more lengthy discussion in the future, Miss Marlow." He leaned over and placed his hand on her arm before she could fully make her escape. "I'm in town a few days."

"The ride was quite lovely." Andrea averted her eyes, not wanting him to see the fear she knew must be reflected there. "I thank you for the escort."

"Are you trying to change the subject, Miss Marlow?"

"Does it seem like I am?" His reaction was as she predicted. He scowled and shook his head, then flicked the reins on the horse's back and drove away.

Andrea's smile faded as she turned toward the house. She had to leave Richmond!

And soon!

Chapter 19

"Oh, what a tangled web we weave, when first we practice to deceive."
– Sir Walter Scott

Captain Hunter cursed without looking up from the map he studied when Private Malone knocked and stuck his head in the door. "Sorry, sir, but you said you wanted to see anyone the pickets stopped from now on."

"What do you have?" Hunter snapped from behind his desk.

"Just a young boy traveling alone. Says he's lost, what with the weather. We can send him on his way if you like."

Hunter felt inclined to do just that. A soupy mix of fog had moved in, making it impossible to see three feet in any direction. An interrogation would likely not be worth the interruption. "Where did he say he was heading?"

"Uh, he didn't quite say." Malone paused as if gauging Hunter's reaction. "He wants to know by what authority we halted and questioned him. Says he shouldn't need a pass nor answer to people while traveling in his own country."

"Is that so?" Hunter looked up for the first time. "Well, I would be delighted, and indeed it is my duty, to enlighten him that he is traveling in *my* country now. By all means, send him up."

By the time word passed down to the pickets, more than a few minutes had passed. Hunter resumed reading a captured dispatch, comparing its contents to former notations he had placed on a map.

Malone brought the boy in, saluted, and made a hasty retreat. Hunter did not realize another person was in the room until he looked up from his communication and saw the youth staring at a large map on the wall. When their eyes finally met, the moment of recognition was simultaneous. The boy looked instantly down, and Hunter let out an oath.

Hunter continued to stare at the figure, blinking as he tried to allow his brain to catch up to what his eyes were seeing. There could be no mistake. The youth looked identical to the one he had seen from across the stream almost a year earlier. But now he was close enough to recognize the green, almond-shaped eyes and feminine lips, the same ones he had last seen just three months ago in Richmond.

"So." He stood up and crossed his arms, glowering at her. She stood stoically still, looking him squarely in the eyes, doing a good job of not betraying the terror he sensed she felt. Hunter walked around her slowly, trying to figure out how this supposed Southern aristocrat had fooled him and so many others. "It appears I finally have the opportunity to meet the war's most famous gadfly."

"I was under the assumption that honor belonged to you."

Hunter looked at her severely for a moment, then continued, his voice losing its casual tone. "Where are you going ? What is your business here?"

"I am going—" Hunter watched her eyes flick up to his and then to the floor. He could tell she had been considering telling an outright lie and thought better of it. "I'm going to visit my cousin north of here."

"Dressed as a boy?"

She shrugged and met his stare with a corresponding look of defiance. "I've grown tired of Richmond. And I ... I have no escort."

"You have no escort, so you dressed as a boy," Hunter rubbed his chin. "I don't believe that's an option most women would choose."

"Your memory is short, Captain. I believe I told you before, I am not most women."

"As to the former, unfortunately for you, it is not," he answered. "And as for the latter, yes, I believe we are quite in agreement on that point."

Despair, disappointment, and even a little humiliation, showed clearly on her face. Hunter swept his eyes over the image of her ragged and well-worn clothes. His mind drifted back to the ball in Richmond, then to Fredericksburg and his brother's final devotional words to her.

"Would you care to extend me the courtesy of telling me your real name?"

"I have no desire to extend that courtesy, nor is it my duty or obligation to do so." She turned her back on him and began to rudely tap her toe.

"Well, I guess I can call you Maryann. You are accustomed to that name, are you not?" The room filled with silence. "Or do you prefer Miss Marlow?"

She turned back toward him. "My name is Andrew Sinclair."

Hunter noticed her voice did not betray her legs trembling beneath her, but her next statement confirmed that she felt them. "Do you mind if I sit?" She did not wait for an answer, but found the composure to lower herself into the chair in front of his desk as elegantly as a queen takes her place on the throne.

Hunter muttered under his breath, and proceeded to sit down as well. "I suppose you are proud of your deceit, Miss Marlow. You almost got away with it."

She gazed over his head into the space beyond, refusing to look into his eyes. "Like I told you, it's Sinclair, so I'm not sure I know what you mean." She sat arrow straight, her hands folded gracefully on her lap as if she were a lady of distinction attending a tea party, not a spy being questioned by a Confederate officer.

"Oh, stop this game. You know what I mean." Hunter banged his fist on the desk. When he failed to get a reaction, he took a deep breath to get his emotions back under control. "Are you a citizen or soldier spy? To whom do you report?"

She leaned forward in her chair. "I'm afraid I decline to answer, and I can't believe an officer would insult me by asking it." She stood and turned her back to him.

"You evidently don't have the good sense to realize how much trouble you are in," Hunter said as he walked around his desk to stand in front of her. "Nor how much trouble you have caused the Confederacy."

"You flatter me once again, sir," she responded. "A compliment from a foe is worth a dozen from a friend."

Hunter frowned and paced the room, his hands clenched behind his back. "Miss, you may be under the illusion that this is a game, but you are being interrogated by an officer. And if your friends have not advised you of the necessity of discretion, then perhaps, out of consideration for your youth and inexperience, I should. I would not even have requested this interview had you not given my pickets trouble with your impudence."

Hunter paused for a moment, regarding the girl's calm, proud features in silent amazement before proceeding. "You're a little young for this type of service, are you not? Since when is it the habit of the Yanks to use young ladies for special service details?"

"I'm old enough to see the state of affairs," she said defiantly. "As for the Federals, it's their duty to employ every resource for the suppression, the overthrow, and the punishment of Rebels in arms. And as for citizens of the United States, of which I am one, it is my duty to do all that I can in the achievement of those objectives."

"You must admit your actions seem somewhat contrary to good sense."

"It would appear to me that rebelling against one's country is likewise contrary to good—or at least common—sense."

"Tell me, are you always this argumentative and belligerent?"

"You may draw your own conclusions, sir."

"Indeed, I will."

His sarcastic tone apparently raised her ire. "I am only argumentative when obligation, honor and vindication of the truth necessitate."

"I see. And are your seditious acts part of these obligations and necessities?"

When she did not answer, Hunter sat down and leaned back in his chair with a sigh. "Your story about your cousin can be corroborated?" He asked the question casually as he drummed his fingers on the desk, but he watched her face closely.

She bit her cheek and continued to stare at the floor. "I had no time to send a telegram. I received word in Richmond that my horse was stolen and I'm returning to—"

Hunter stood. "Your horse? Curious. I seem to recall you telling me in Richmond that you don't ride well. Yet you own a horse, one that is apparently very near and dear to your heart. Very interesting."

"How very admirable of you to commit every word of our conversation to memory," she said weakly. "I had no idea I was such a noteworthy acquaintance."

Hunter laughed. "My dear, did I not tell you that I believed our meeting would be an unforgettable one? Surely it is not one *you* have forgotten."

She looked up at him and then away into space, in what appeared to be a custom of hers when the topic was not pleasing. "No I do not forget, but I remember with regret. As I told you in Richmond, any encounter with you is inexorably branded in my mind."

"Anyway, what might he look like?"

"Who?" she asked, bringing her attention, and her gaze, back to him.

"Your horse that was stolen!"

"That is not important."

"I believe *I* will decide what is and is not important if you don't mind!"

"Then can we not confine ourselves to the discussion at hand? Let me see, I believe you were asking me—"

"This *is* the discussion at hand," Hunter roared. "Is he a bay? A gray? Chestnut? Dun?" He stood in front of her now, but she did not answer. "Perhaps a sorrel? A roan? By your silence, I shall assume none of the above. Hmm, I can think of naught another color—save black. Might your horse be a large-boned black?"

"If *you* have stolen him, it would do you well to return him." She made no effort to control the anger in her voice now. "No one else will sit him! Least of all a man!"

"Then I'm to assume we are agreed, your horse is black," Hunter said. "And if that is the case, and if indeed he's been appropriated by my men, he is now the legal property of the Confederacy and will no doubt serve our cause splendidly."

"No Rebel will ever ride him!"

"Miss Marlow," Hunter said, losing his patience. "Are you aware of the penalties of spying in the Confederate states? And once again may I suggest the prudence in being more guarded with your speech?"

She looked straight into his eyes, unblinking, defying his attempts to shake her. "Is the interview over, Captain?" She turned, as if his silence was a signal for her to leave. "I believe you have detained me quite long enough."

"Over? Are you questioning my authority to hold you here?" Hunter stood and banged his fist on the desk. "By whose authority do you operate?"

"I believe I shall pass on the question." The girl's voice indicated that she had no more interest in the conversation than if they were discussing the weather on the third day of rain.

"What are your orders?"

"Still less can I answer that question definitely."

"Miss, you are being charged with a serious crime. Have you no defense? I don't believe you realize the character and extent of my power to deal with such conduct."

"I would trust my explanation has been sufficient. I don't know what other information I can provide you."

"You have provided me no reasonable explanation—not for your presence here in my territory nor for your impudent behavior!" Hunter shouted, losing his temper again. "I must warn you, I'm finding your manner excessively insolent."

"And insolence is a crime in the Confederacy? Or is it just an offense in your jurisdiction?"

Hunter ran his hand through his hair in agitation and stared at her, trying to understand how a mere girl could show such courage under the current circumstances. "Every word you speak illustrates more clearly to me your character," he said.

She narrowed her eyes in indignation. "I fail to see the correlation. I have a solemn duty which I will not betray."

"And I have a solemn duty to see that you pay for the crimes in which you have been engaged!"

She sighed then, like a child tiring of a game, and began removing her gloves in an exasperated sort of way. "May I remind you, sir, that you have found no treasonable correspondence on me and that I wear no insignia of the Confederacy. According to the Articles of War, I cannot be charged as a spy, at most a courier." Her eyes never wavered nor changed expression. "I presume you have some acquaintance with the existence of that code, Captain Hunter?"

She then turned her gaze to her fingernails, as if contemplating whether they needed a cleaning, indicating by her actions that she felt the subject had garnered more than enough of her time and attention.

Hunter raised his eyebrows in surprise, both at her revelation and the sudden recollection of where he'd the heard the name Sinclair before. "Your knowledge concerning the usual handling of such affairs is correct, Miss Marlow. Unfortunately, your prediction of how I shall handle yours is not equally reliable."

He watched her grow alert, like someone who senses the presence of an unseen gun.

"It is indeed unfortunate," he continued, crossing his arms in satisfaction, "but I can prove you are, or have been, within our lines for the purpose of securing information. You can indeed be arrested as a spy on my word."

She stood quietly as if weighing his words, then with her green eyes glaring, leaned forward and placed both hands on his desk. "I don't believe you. Where is your warrant for doing so?"

Hunter reached down and pulled the crumpled piece of paper from his desk drawer that had been found along the stream the night he had been rendered unconscious. "Does this look familiar?" He threw it onto the desk in front of her.

As her gaze dropped from his face to the piece of paper, Hunter thought he saw her flinch. In any event, she swallowed hard before she spoke. "It is unknown to me how attempting to save the Union from destruction is committing a grave offense."

"Then you are admitting you are a spy."

"It appears to me, I have responded neither affirmatively nor negatively to any of your statements or insinuations by expression, words, conduct, or deeds."

Hunter stared at her incredulously. "I ask you again. Do you understand how much trouble you are in?"

Her eyes did not waver. She crossed her arms and sighed deeply. "I suppose I'll have to be content knowing there are worse fates than being *suspected* of providing service in defense of country."

"If you believe that you must be unaware of the conditions in Confederate prisons." For the first time Hunter saw fear flash in her eyes, thought he even saw a shudder.

"You would send me to prison?" She looked straight up at him, as if it was the first time the thought occurred to her.

Hunter noticed she had a little more trouble keeping the fear out her voice now too. "What do you think the penalty is for the crimes you've perpetrated? A blasted picnic?

"How can I be faulted if your superiors indulged themselves with wine and then divulged all manner of things to me?"

She fluttered her eyelashes innocently, yet now it was clear to Hunter she only pretended a calmness she did not feel. Beads of sweat gathered on her forehead and a nerve twitched near her eye.

"You can be faulted for seeing that the information they so graciously bestowed upon you made it across enemy lines."

"You have no proof of such a thing. You rely on nothing but your memory to link Maryann Marlow with Andrew Sinclair, and nothing but suspicion to connect me with information crossing the lines."

"Unfortunately again you are wrong, Miss Marlow." He walked around his desk to stand in front of her. "The evidence against you is ponderous."

Hunter pulled her hand out of her pocket and held it in front of her face. "For instance, this," he said, pointing to Daniel's ring. "I believe I misinterpreted its significance and owe you an apology. You are undeniably linked to a Federal officer."

Hunter's last comment brought prolonged silence. In fact, once he released her hand, his prisoner did not move. She stared at the wall behind him so intensely she seemed unaware of his presence.

"Surely you understand that the Union that once existed may be lost forever, and the Union you seek to repair may never be restored," he said to see if she was listening.

She blinked twice in rapid succession at his words, but otherwise appeared to be deep in thought. Something about her rigid stance told of a heart beating wildly.

A completely uncharacteristic feeling of pity welled up inside Hunter, and he offered her another chance. "Do you understand what you are doing?"

"It appears my fate lies in your hands," she said softly. "Therefore I have a request."

Hunter laughed aloud as he forgot instantly his thoughts of compassion. "A request? I hardly believe you are in the position to make a request." He crossed his arms and spread his legs. "What is it you would like? Breakfast in bed? A new pair of shoes?"

"No." Her eyebrows came together in a look of unyielding resolve. "I would favor, that is to say, I would like to make it clear that I prefer losing my life to losing my liberty."

Hunter noticed the slightest falter to her voice now, as if one part of her mind was convinced of the fact and another was not quite sure. She still appeared defiant. Yet, she was unable to meet his eyes and her breathing was labored.

"You prefer death to prison," he repeated, certain she must be jesting. "You value your life so little that you will not plead for it?"

Her head went up and her eyes sparked with anger. "Beg? Beg for my life from you?" She forced a laugh. "I am quite willing to accept death. To do otherwise would be to die in another way."

"Surely you have loved ones that would wish you to reconsider."

"I have no love but that of country." She glanced down at the ring on her hand. "And I would value the honor of dying for it."

Hunter swallowed hard at the thought of his brother's sacrifice, but he suppressed any feelings of pity. "And which would you prefer? A rope or a firing squad?" He sat down on the edge of his desk, his tone indifferent, as if giving her the choice between red or white wine at dinner.

"It is not for me to decide my fate," she said solemnly. "That is for you and God."

"I know nothing of God except that He did not commit treason against the Confederacy." Hunter banged his fist on the desk again. "*You* did!"

"And since you are my legal captor, you are at liberty to shoot, hang, or quarter me," she quipped with equal verve. "Whether you like it or not, the responsibility of choice shall be bestowed on *you*."

"Do you believe me of the character that would send a woman to a hanging tree?" Hunter asked curiously.

"I can assure you I have no thoughts on which I wish to expound relative to your character." Her voice was full of disdain as her determined green eyes met his resolute gray ones. For a few long moments neither one blinked.

"Perhaps the sacrifice of your life will not be necessary." Hunter went back to his chair and sat down. "I have the authority to offer you a parole." He began digging through some papers in a drawer. "You have only to sign an oath that you will not give information, countenance, aid, or support to the enemy . . ."

Hunter saw out of the corner of his eye that she took a step back as if being hit quite squarely by a block of wood. Her heels hit the floor in quick succession, making a distinctive *kerplunk*. He had never seen a face so indignant.

"How dare you insult me!" She held her hands over her ears as if to block out the sound of his voice. "I shall die a thousand deaths before I forfeit my soul and declare allegiance to your country of traitors. God in heaven strike me down should I give my word not to do something my conscience says is right. I'll not make any such humiliating concession to you or any power on this earth!"

Hunter's lips curled into sardonic smile at her outburst. "I beg your pardon," he said, not sounding sorry at all. "I had no idea I was dealing with such a prodigy of patriotic devotion. I was simply attempting to give you an opportunity to preserve your life."

"I will choose to preserve my honor if you do not mind!" The color in her cheeks made her practically glow. "I would rather meet death at the end of a blunt bayonet doing my duty for country than be saved by abandoning it."

Hunter stood blinking in frustration, staring at her in silent wonder. Walking over to the door, he signaled with a commanding gesture for Private Malone to enter. "Hold this one separate from the others."

As they began to exit, Hunter obeyed an impulse to give her another chance. "Have you nothing else you wish to say? You must know you've placed me in a most regrettable position."

When she turned around, her expression seemed one of sympathy and concern. "If it helps, you are at liberty to disregard any promises made in the past," she said, at last referring to his vow to Daniel. "I did not request, nor do I wish to be, anyone's sacred obligation."

When the door clicked shut, Hunter sank down with a groan. What a cruel joke! The fate of his most coveted prize had been placed in his grasp, yet he could not celebrate the triumph, nor even feel the smallest sense of satisfaction.

Daniel's obscure request on his deathbed was now strikingly clear. He had known she was a spy, and had feared—and suspected—this day would come. *"You will let no harm befall her."* The words rang in Hunter's ears, followed by, *"I do not wish to be anyone's sacred obligation."*

Hunter stood and paced again. *What in the hell is this confounded war coming to?*

If she had just taken the parole, his path, and hers, would be clear. She would be unable to return as a menace to the South, and he would have a clear conscience.

But now he was forced to make a decision that would cost him dearly. Betray his men, Virginia, the Confederacy—or betray his brother.

Hunter despised her for the position she had placed him in, and was so angry he feared he could carry out her preferred sentence with his bare hands. Yet how could he punish one who had done her work, served her country, and had no fear to die?

The memory of the first time he met the infamous Sinclair emerged in his mind. If *she* was *he*, then Maryann Marlow, or whoever she was, had pulled him from the water and saved his life.

But what did that matter? This was war. Rules and chivalry no longer counted.

Did promises and honor?

Hunter put his head in his hands and groaned. Could nothing in this bloody war be clear? What had happened to the world he once lived in where things were black and white, right and wrong, good and evil? Did that world even exist any more?

Making his decision, he signed the papers and called for Private Malone.

Had he believed in God, he would have prayed he was doing the right thing.

Chapter 20

"Let this lie heavy on thy soul tomorrow."
— Hunchback Richard

December, 1863

A knock at the door interrupted Hunter as he was finishing a report to General Stuart. "Enter and make it quick."

"Just some paperwork for you to sign, sir." Malone handed over the correspondence.

Hunter scribbled his name across the pages without reading them until he reached the last one. "What's this?"

Malone leaned over the desk to look at the document. "Oh, that's your authorization to have that boy moved from Libby to Castle Thunder. It's just a formality to have your signature."

"What prisoner?" Hunter leafed through the paperwork, looking for a name.

Malone took the papers and flipped to the last page. "Andrew Sinclair," he said unconcernedly, handing them back.

"I never sent this prisoner to Libby!" Hunter continued to stare at the last page, his hand beginning to tremble slightly.

"Oh yeah, that's the order that Major Simms changed. I'll just send it down for him to sign." Malone started to take the papers from Hunter.

"What do you mean he changed the orders?" Hunter' snatched the paperwork from Malone's grasp.

"He-he came to headquarters that night after you'd ridden out. He said that since you weren't here and he outranked everyone else, he had the authority to change the orders." Malone shifted his feet under Hunter's sharp gaze. "He did outrank you," he added meekly.

"He has no authority over me! I don't care if he's a blasted general!"

"I'm sorry, sir, I—

"You mean to tell me this prisoner, this Andrew Sinclair, has been in Libby for the past …" Hunter looked at the date on the paper again. "*Four* months?"

Malone nodded.

Hunter closed his eyes, trying to imagine what she had gone through, then closed them tighter, trying not to. Four months in that hellhole surely equaled four years on earth.

He strove to push all thoughts of the prison out of his mind. The deed was done. There was no time now for either sorrow or regret. All he could do is try to mend the mistake. But Hunter heard her voice even now as if she stood right beside him. *I prefer death to prison.*

"Have Johnny get my horse," he said, keeping his voice calm. "Inform Lieutenant Carter he's in command until I return."

"Yes, well, it is Christmas," Malone offered.

Hunter gazed a moment out the window. "Then I suppose the men can have a short furlough."

"Is that an order, sir?"

Hunter picked up a pen and scribbled on a piece of paper. "It's an order. See that it's carried out to the letter, Malone."

"Yes, Captain." Malone started to back out the door.

"And Jake—"

"Sir?"

"See that no one changes it!"

✠ ✠ ✠

Captain Hunter paced in his library, waiting for the doctor to finish his examination. He had not slept in three days, nor had it entered his mind to do so. After seeing the limp, motionless mound that had been loaded onto his wagon in Richmond, he'd made the decision to drive straight through. If not for the slightest hint of green showing through the figure's half-open lids, he would not have been sure he'd been given the right prisoner.

When the doctor finally entered, Hunter handed him a brandy he had already poured. "Well?"

Doc Hobbs patted his sweaty brow with a handkerchief and nervously downed the entire contents of the glass in one swallow. Known more for his gruffness and lack of sympathy than his bedside manner, Hunter thought it unusual for him to be displaying so much duress.

"What in the hell happened to that girl?"

"That's not important now," Hunter said impatiently, taking the empty glass from his hands. "How is she?"

"How *is* she? She's got a broken femur that was never set. She's malnourished, dehydrated, and suffering from exposure, any one of which could kill her. Together . . ." He never finished the sentence.

Hunter searched Hobbs' face for any sign of hope. He had seen the unnatural bend of her leg at the prison, had been told she had "taken a fall."

"But she's got a strong will. She can fight."

"Aye." Hobbs' sat down beside the warmth of the fireplace as if suddenly chilled to the bone. "If the old scar she bears is any indication of her will to live, she'll fight."

"Scar?"

"She's been whipped." Hobbs stared vacantly into the fire as if trying to imagine the atrocity. He sighed heavily and looked at Hunter. "Someone darn near ripped her in half."

Hobbs stood and poured himself another drink. "Looks like it happened a number of years ago," he said, grimacing as the amber fluid rolled down his throat. "Healed quite nicely, I must say."

Hunter looked into Hobbs' eyes and could tell they both thought the same thing. She was still very young. She must have been but a child when it occurred. "She's made it this far. I'm certain she'll fight."

"We can hope," Hobbs replied, though his tone conveyed none. "Unfortunately, sometimes the body is weaker than the soul." The doctor turned his attention to his medical bag, and shoved a small vial into Hunter's hand. "If she wakes up, she'll need this."

"If?" Hunter stared at the bottle of laudanum.

"If," the doctor repeated. "I'll give her a fifty–fifty chance." He closed his bag with a loud snap. "And that's being optimistic."

He turned to leave with Hunter following close behind. "But what can we do for her?"

With his hand on the doorknob, Hobbs paused. "Nothing really. Just let her rest. Keep her comfortable. And wait." He squinted through tiny spectacles up at Hunter, who stood a good foot taller. "She has to heal on the inside before she can heal on the outside," he said in a grave voice. "The body and the soul are too closely bound for one to suffer without the other. And I would hesitate to guess, after seeing her injuries, which is suffering more." Tipping his hat, he opened the door. "Good day, Captain Hunter."

Hunter put one hand on his forehead and pressed his temples. He had to ride out tonight and didn't know how soon he'd be able to return. His servants would have to be relied upon to take care of his new charge.

Heading back up the stairs, he paused in the doorway and watched her breathe through half-closed lips, her chest rising and falling under the covers so slightly and so infrequently that at times he could barely distinguish if she breathed at all.

For the most part she looked as motionless as a corpse, her face pale as death. Her hair, which had been snarled in a tangle of filth and mold, had been washed and combed by the servants. The long-neglected tresses now rested in soft blonde waves on the pillow. She lay on her back, exactly as she had been placed a few hours earlier, the covers tucked neatly up to her chin.

Hunter moved closer and looked at the thin arms protruding from the rolled up sleeves of one of his cotton shirts. His focus was drawn to her right hand curled unnaturally in a fist atop the blanket, seemingly unwilling to relinquish a ring that hung loosely from its perch on her bony finger. He looked closer, though he knew it was the same ring she had worn the last time he had seen her. Daniel's ring.

He blinked in surprise at her tenacity. The doctor had been perplexed that the uninjured hand had been bound, fingertips to palm in putrid, bloodied rags. It was not hard to conjecture why. By doing so, she had saved the ring from prison thieves. But what permanent damage the bandages may have caused remained unknown.

Hunter's gaze traveled to a vicious bruise above her cheek and a cut above her eye. Even in sleep, the torture she had endured was evident upon her troubled countenance. He swallowed hard at the cruelty of war. What had compelled her to endure an incarceration so tedious and painful—and unnecessary?

But that is the way of war, he reminded himself. And this is no innocent, guiltless child, but a cunning, dangerous enemy. This is the foe he had vowed to defeat—and the stranger he had sworn to his brother he would protect.

Hunter sighed and placed his hat back on his head. How he would resolve his opposing intentions he had no idea, but there was no sense in worrying about that now—not with the slim chance that she would even survive. From the corner of his eye, Hunter caught a movement in the doorway, and saw his servant Mattie standing there with a stack of fresh linens.

"I can come back later, Massa."

"That won't be necessary. I was just leaving."

As he passed Mattie in the doorway, Hunter stopped for a moment. "I'm riding out tonight. Be sure to send Zach with a message if there's a change."

"Yes, Massa," was all Mattie said. But Hunter detected a puzzled look on her face as he turned and left the room.

Chapter 21

*"He shed soft slumbers on mine eyes, in spite of all my foes.
I woke and wondered at the grace that guarded my repose."*
– Psalms 3:5

ndrea's broken body was falling. She did not know where it fell from or where it was falling to, only that it spun and spiraled out of control in a gaping darkness full of pain. She waited to hit bottom, waited for the end to come. But the bottom never came, and the end never followed, and the pain did not recede.

But little by little the darkness fell away, until it became more like a deep, hazy fog.

Sometimes in this fog Andrea saw images of herself as a little girl lying on the banks of the Ashley River in her Mammy's lap, watching the clouds float by. Other times she saw her father's face, red with rage and contorted with hate—always with a whip in his hand. The dreams made her heart pulse, and the pulse made her body throb, and the throb left her falling back into darkness to escape the pain. But still the dreams came, confusing and bewildering her, because she could not figure out what was memory and what was fantasy, what was real and what was not.

At times, Andrea thought she heard voices. They seemed to be right beside her, yet sounded muffled, like they were talking to her under water. "I declayah, she alive on de inside, but dead on de outside," she thought she heard one say. She tried to speak, to tell them she was not dead, but her two lips had seemingly fused into one. She could not move her mouth nor find a way to make a sound escape her throat. In desperation, she tried to reach them, to tell them she was there. But the figures never heard her, so she just lay quietly for what seemed like days, but just as easily could have been hours or weeks, and waited for the haze to recede.

H H H

When Andrea awoke again, everything was still far away and hazy, yet she could sense a dim light, a warmth that drew her out of the darkness. She concentrated on moving her fingers, concentrated hard. She felt a soft blanket and realized she was no longer in the dark abyss that haunted her dreams.

The sound of breaking glass interrupted her concentration. "Izzie, what is you about?" a stern woman's voice filled the room. "You clean that up, you heah?"

"She moved her fingers," a younger voice exclaimed.

"Is you awake?" the first voice asked, sounding skeptical.

Andrea tried to open her eyes. *How could eyelids be this heavy?* She had wrestled horses with less effort than this. She paused a moment to summon her strength, and then slowly they complied, revealing two black faces, mother and daughter perhaps, bending over her. They stared at her as if she had performed a miracle or had risen from the dead. "Thirsty," was all Andrea could manage to say.

One of the women helped Andrea sit up while the other held the glass of water.

"It miracular, Izzie," she heard the older woman say before falling back against the pillow. "Go get Zach. Tell him to fetch Massa drekly. She livin' agin."

Sometime later, though she didn't know if it was the next day or the next week, Andrea awoke to the sound of someone humming beside her bed. "Where am I?" she whispered in a hoarse voice.

"Don't you go worryin' about where you is, Mistis. We gonna take good care of you."

Andrea nodded and floated back into the darkness. She wanted to ask about her leg. Was it still there? But waves of pain erased the questions from her lips. She wanted to talk, yet she wanted to sleep. Sleep, more than anything, seemed to help her escape the pain.

But sleep no longer seemed possible, and there was no such thing as a world without pain. Nerve and muscle alike racked her with agony. Even the blood in her veins seemed afire, the searing heat stabbing her with lightning bolts of torment.

Struggling to open her eyes at last, Andrea took the first look at her surroundings. Her gaze fell first on the veiled light that entered through a slot in the closed drapes of a window. She blinked at the brightness, a light so intense to her sensitive eyes that it seemed alive. She longed to stand in it, to feel it. Turning her head, she studied the rest of her surroundings. She appeared to be in a room of comfort and elegance, lying in a great poster bed of mahogany on a downy feather mattress.

Without warning, a plump, black woman burst into the room with a tray. "Natchally, I thoughts you might be awoken today. How's about condescendin' to a little brekfest?"

"Where am I?" Andrea's mouth felt strange. She wondered if she spoke loud enough for anyone to hear.

"I tol you, don worry 'bout where you is."

"Where am I?" Andrea said, louder this time. Although her voice was feeble, she was amazed she could actually speak.

"I cain't prezactly say. But you's in the home of my massa." The woman's tone was indignant.

"Who is your master?"

"Don't you worry none bout dat. Ole Him a good man. Take good care of you."

Andrea saw the tray of food just inches from her hand. Without thinking of the end result, she reached up and gave a weak pull. The servant screamed in astonished surprise when dishes tumbled and crashed to the floor.

"I demand to know where I am!" Andrea clenched her teeth against the pain that seized her body.

"And I demand that you stop this behavior this instant," came a deep voice from the doorway.

Andrea looked up and blinked, hoping a second look would change the image before her. The light coming through the door behind him almost blinded her, yet his identity was unmistakable.

"*You*," was all she could say, or at least, thought she said. Andrea looked him up and down, believing he might not be real, that she might be dreaming again. His boots and uniform were mud-spattered, as if he'd ridden a long way in a short amount of time, yet he appeared to be tall as an oak tree, his eyes sparking with the light of battle. She blinked, trying to take in every detail of this soldierly figure that radiated a presence and power that filled her with rage.

"I's sorry, Massa. I din't know you was home." The servant moved away from the wall and picked up a piece of glass.

"I just arrived," Hunter said in a low, unemotional voice. "You can clean up this mess later."

Mattie backed toward the door, keeping her eyes on Andrea. "Careful, she got de devil in her head," she whispered before exiting.

"Miss, in the future, I would appreciate it if you could try to act civilized in my home." Hunter strode into the room.

His biting words made Andrea angry, and the rush of blood the anger sent through her body brought with it so much pain that her eyelids trembled. "In your *home*?" Even to her own ears the words sounded as if they came with great effort and from a great distance. Andrea took a deep ragged breath and tried again. "Have I not endured enough of the South's hospitality?"

ℋ ℋ ℋ

Hunter raised one eyebrow, amazed at her quick tongue so early in her recovery. But when he gazed upon her pain-filled countenance, a feeling of sympathy arose in him.

"I apologize on behalf of the Confederacy for your treatment," he said in a gentle voice. "There was a ... miscommunication concerning your imprisonment."

The girl squinted at him with a look of pure revulsion. "Mis-communi-cat-ion?" She stumbled over the word, as if it were more than her muddled brain could manage. "So I am a prisoner here, now?" The look on her face, even with her weakness, was hostile. "Here for you to take out your vengeance?"

"Miss, you are not a prisoner here. You are free to leave as soon as you are able."

"I am able," she retorted, making an attempt to rise. Although she appeared to make a valiant effort, her head barely made it off the pillow.

For a moment, Hunter pitied the girl for what she had tolerated in prison and what she would endure in her recovery. Her weary and distrustful eyes stared strangely, as if unable to comprehend the events that were yet unfolding.

Deciding to let her rest, Hunter turned to leave, but stopped with his hand on the doorknob. "You need not fear your treatment here. I pledge my word."

He waited for a response, but none came. The girl had become occupied with the ring on her finger, staring at it as if it were new to her—or she just now remembered from whence it came.

"Daniel is here?" she asked, not removing her eyes from the ring.

The question caught Hunter by surprise. "Yes, he is here."

Her countenance grew peaceful. The knowledge of his brother's presence, even in death, apparently gave her some sort of comfort.

Deciding that silence was his best ally, Hunter exited the room and hoped a good night's sleep would cure his houseguest's irritable demeanor.

℈ ℈ ℈

Hunter discovered the next morning that an amiable discussion was not to be. Arriving in her chamber a few moments after his servant entered with breakfast, he heard her mumble, "I'm not hungry."

"Miss, you must be hungry." Hunter tried to pretend the events of the preceding day had never occurred. "You haven't enough flesh on your bones to provide decent forage for a buzzard."

Izzie sat the tray down and scurried from the room.

"I trust you slept well." Pretending to fix his collar in the looking glass, he studied her reflection. She appeared pale and exhausted, her eyes deeply sunken. She blinked hard as she glared in his direction, apparently trying to see through clouds of fog and pain.

"Are you comfortable?" He turned around at her quietness.

"*Now*, Captain Hunter?" she replied scornfully. "Or before you came in?"

Hunter laughed, unaffected by her demeanor. "You need not feel distressed at being here. I'll do all in my power to help you recover."

"Then you are more kind than wise."

Although stung by her sarcasm, Hunter thought it best to ignore the stab. "You have the advantage of me. You know my name, but I don't know yours." He stared at her hard. "Not your real one, anyway."

The girl turned her head away and studied the wall for a moment before answering. "Andrea." She paused, still gazing at the wall. "Evans."

Hunter pondered the chance that the name was real. Regardless, she appeared to have resigned herself to the fact she would be recovering in his house. "Well, Andrea Evans, is there anything I can do for you?"

Andrea favored him with little more than a suspicious stare. "Let me go."

"I can't do that. You're in no condition—"

Hunter watched her eyes shut violently against his words, as if hearing them spoken aloud was more pain than she could endure.

"Miss Evans, I wish to assure you that I am an honorable man, and despite the fact you are my enemy, your treatment here will be just. I can hardly be more generous."

Her head turned slowly toward him. "You did not possess the common decency to grant me my preferred punishment then, and I have little hope you have acquired that trait now."

Hunter forced a laugh and tried to control his rising temper. "My dear, there is nothing *decent* about this war, nor the crimes you perpetrated against the Confederacy."

"My crime against you was devotion to my country, her laws and her Constitution," Andrea snapped. "The worst, most despicable punishment you could conceive would be to bring me *here*. I may well die within the confines of these walls."

"I have no reason to be concerned about that possibility," Hunter responded sarcastically, "because you are obviously too stubborn to die on enemy soil."

Andrea turned her head as if warding off a blow, and stared blankly at the wall.

"I apologize for your imprisonment," he said more softly now, "but as for being caught, you have no one to blame but yourself."

For a moment Andrea did not speak. Then her gaze shifted toward the window, and her hand lifted in silent supplication. "Then confine me if you must … but I beg of you, do not make me bear this burden without seeing or feeling the sun."

Hunter stared at her sallow skin, and could not help but agree that the sun would do good for one who had risen from the dead.

He sighed and walked over to the window. Opening the curtain, he stared out at the cold, gray sky. Situated as it was on the north side of the house, the guest room never received direct sunlight, even when not veiled by snow clouds as it was today.

When he turned back to Andrea, she appeared to have drifted into a restless sleep.

Exiting the room and starting down the stairs, he called for his servant.

"Yes, Massa?" Mattie magically appeared at the top of the stairwell.

"Prepare the bedroom on the east wing," he said over his shoulder.

"You mean—"

He stopped and turned around. "Yes, Mattie. I said the *east* wing."

Mattie walked away, but Hunter heard her mumbling under her breath. "A person cain't keep up with such transforminations as is going on aroun' heah."

Chapter 22

"O, with what freshness, what solemnity and beauty is each new day born."
— Harriet Beecher Stowe

Hunter was up as the first rays of light began brightening the night sky. Passing Andrea's new quarters, he paused in the doorway when he noticed she was curled up on the windowsill. "It's magical is it not?" she said without altering the direction of her eyes.

Hunter did not answer at first. He just stared at the figure silhouetted in the window. With her hand pressed against the glass, it appeared she was trying to touch the sun as it entered the morning sky.

"It's ga-lorious no matter how many times you see it!"

She glanced around when no one answered. "Oh, it's you." She turned back to the window in grim silence.

"I'm glad to see you're feeling better."

His words were met by icy silence. She leaned her head back and closed her eyes, though he could tell the action was not from weariness. The way in which a nerve throbbed in her temple revealed that each movement, no matter how slight, caused her great pain. How she had managed to pull herself onto the wide sill he could not see. But he was glad he had taken the added precaution of moving the bed next to the window.

"Do I repulse you so?"

"No more than anyone who fights against the flag of their nation."

Hunter took the blow like a true soldier. His young houseguest had apparently awakened from her long slumber with a soul no less full of hostility than when he had seen her some months before.

He watched her gaze turn back to the landscape, and when she spoke again, it was in a low, confused tone. "The seasons seem to have changed without me."

"It's February," Hunter said, knowing she was trying to calculate the lost months. "You were in Libby through December. I petitioned for your release as soon as I heard about your imprisonment."

"*Heard* about my imprisonment? And it somehow came as a surprise to you?"

Hunter looked down at the floor, knowing his story sounded like he was shifting blame. "As I told you, there was a miscommunication."

Andrea dismissed him once more by closing her eyes, and he dismissed the thought that he would ever again see anything but a scowl upon her face. The warm, enchanting smile she had worn at the ball must have been part of the act, because he had yet to see any semblance of it here.

"It may please you to know, there's been a rather large escape from Libby."

"The tunnel?" She turned her gaze toward him. "When?"

Hunter cocked his head and stared at her intently. "Yes, they escaped through a tunnel ... just a few days ago."

"Was Colonel Streight among them?" For the first time all morning, she looked him in the eyes with something other than hatred.

"Yes. He was listed among them."

Andrea sighed, and Hunter thought he almost saw her lips turn slightly upward.

"You were aware of the plan?"

She turned her head away like a cat that pretends not to see or hear its master. Hunter interpreted the action exactly as it was meant, as one of rebuke and defiance. Although she was gaining strength, she was also growing more remote—and irritable—if that was indeed possible. The fever of her illness had passed, replaced by the fever of unrest and hostility. The former had been capable of killing her, the latter, everyone else in the household.

Hunter did not repeat the question, but stared at her countenance reflected in the warm buttery light. She appeared tired, her eyes heavy with fatigue. Yet still they glowed with the untamable spirit he knew lay hidden within. He wondered which was worse, the battered being he had brought into his home or the caged animal that now resided in the room adjoining to his.

She turned back toward the meadow that now blushed in the soft glow of morning light. "It heals my soul," she said of the sun that shimmered like gold through the window. Then she glanced over her shoulder shyly, as if embarrassed at having spoken aloud.

"I appreciate the new accommodations."

Hunter found himself speechless that she actually expressed words of appreciation. It appeared that simple sunshine and the bountiful gifts of nature could nourish her health in ways bed rest alone could not. If watching the sun come up each morning was going to help warm the cold spirit that dominated her being, Hunter was doubly glad the change in chambers had been made.

She interrupted his thoughts in a tone that once again hinted at approbation. "So this is Hawthorne."

"Yes." Hunter followed her gaze to the fields beyond. "I hope you approve."

"How could I not? It seems I closed my eyes in hell and woke up in paradise."

Fearing the consequence of changing her mood again, Hunter decided against asking her if she needed anything. He began backing out the door to allow her to revel in the dawn of a new day.

"Who in the blazes decorated this room?" Andrea's gaze darted around for the first time in full light.

Hunter looked around too, as if seeing the red rugs, lavish wall-hangings, and ornate full-length mirrors for the first time himself. In fact, he had kept the room locked and not laid his eyes upon its interior for at least three years now. "My former wife," he said without feeling. "If you need anything, do not hesitate to call for Mattie. I will not be around today to provide company."

"How very disappointing," Andrea replied, turning back to the window.

For once, Hunter could not tell if she was being sincere or sarcastic, but decided on the latter before exiting the room.

ℋ ℋ ℋ

Izzie arrived a short time later with food, and Andrea ate voraciously of everything she brought. When finished, she thought about her conversation with Hunter and tried to picture him married. Captain Hunter? A wife? It did not seem possible.

"What happened to Mrs. Hunter?" Andrea asked innocently as Izzie gathered up the dishes. For a moment, Andrea thought the servant was going to drop the tray.

"Don't ever mention Mistis 'Lizabeth again!" Izzie warned in a loud whisper, her eyes as big as the saucers she carried.

"I didn't mention her name, you did," Andrea replied. "Where'd she go? Did he kill her and bury the body in one of the fields?"

"Mistis Andrea, you stop speakin' like that!" Dishes clattered on the tray with her shaking hands. "She just gone. Dat's all. Now don't ever ask agin!"

Andrea shrugged her shoulders and looked around a second time at her new surroundings. French doors, sided by two large windows with deep sills opened onto a warm balcony that faced the rising sun. Oaks, at least a century old, stood right outside her window, though they did not block a spectacular view of the fenced pastures, fields, and valleys that rose gently to reach the hills farther east.

In the dim light of dawn, Andrea had failed to see the true majesty of the estate. It was just as she had pictured it in her dreams, if not more spectacular. Now bathed in full light, she could see stone walls running in rectangular patterns across the field, the boundaries of paddocks and pastures. A carriage turnaround sat directly in front of the house, its center filled with the promise of future blooms of every description. Farther beyond sat a large stone barn, bordered on three sides by rolling pastures, each filled with horses of every size and color. Still farther she saw the glistening sparkles of a wide stream that offered a natural barrier to anyone approaching from the east. If ever there were a more beautiful vista or more perfectly situated property for natural defense, Andrea had never beheld it.

As she sat in dreamy indulgence, Andrea noticed the temperature outside had risen with the awakening sun. The remnants of snow remaining from the previous night's storm were melting and creating a beautiful mist through which everything looked like a dream.

Andrea opened her eyes wider. A large black man appeared from out of that mist, leading the big, gray horse that Hunter often rode. "Who's that?"

Izzie leaned forward to see. "That Zach, my papa, and Dixie."

"And Mattie is your mother?"

The girl nodded proudly. "They been here since befo' Massa was bawn."

"And you like it here?" Andrea scrutinized the girl.

The slave's gaze fell at the inspection and then rose with honest resolve. "Ole Him a good man." She turned with her tray and disappeared through the door.

$\mathcal{H}$ $\mathcal{H}$ $\mathcal{H}$

Andrea's head nodded, and she soon drifted off to sleep again. Upon awakening, she saw that the room had been cleansed of all signs of the mysterious former wife during her deep slumber. The garish furniture had vanished, replaced by pieces from her previous room. Only two original items remained—a trunk and a wardrobe, both of which seemed to be overflowing with women's clothes.

"Ole Him say you can find a dressing gown in here," Izzie said.

Andrea looked down at the man's shirt she wore and, for once, agreed with Hunter. She allowed Izzie to help her change into a simple nightgown, then watched the servant disappear at the sound of an approaching storm.

Lightning soon lit the room with brilliant flashes and the wind began to beat its fist against the glass. After a struggle and much pain, Andrea opened one of the large windows. She was instantly rewarded with a cool blast as the wind and rain rushed in and surrounded her.

Fresh, clean, delicious air greeted her, smelling so good and feeling so cold that it made her chest ache. Never did she think she would feel and taste and smell clean air again!

"What are you doing?" Hunter strode to her in a single stride and reached out to close the window.

"Oh no, wait." Andrea wrapped her fingers weakly around his wrist. "Please, it's been so long ... let me feel it."

Hunter paused, but only for a moment. "You are soaked!" He slammed the window closed.

Andrea sat silently for a moment, staring straight ahead. "You take for granted the offerings of Mother Nature," she said solemnly. "Perhaps if you had to go without them you would look at the world differently."

Before he had time to answer, Mattie appeared in the doorway. "Gal, you gonna ketch you death of cold!" She rushed over to the trunk and pulled out a dry gown. "Put this on. I don't wanna hear no argumentations."

Andrea heard Hunter retire to his chamber to do the same, and determined from his heavy tread that he found her newfound strength a nuisance rather than a blessing.

Chapter 23

"In a minute there are many days."
– Shakespeare

Andrea lost count of the days she spent staring out the window, listening to rain pelting the house and watching the picturesque meadows of Hawthorne reduced to fields of muck and mud.

She wondered how Hunter and his men continued their raids, but apparently the weather did not slow them. The Captain returned only to bring in captured horses, catch up on the affairs of Hawthorne, and, every so often, sleep a few hours. After only a brief rest he would be back in the saddle and, presumably, causing chaos again.

For the most part when Hunter was home, he did not seem conscious of Andrea's presence. Or rather, he made it a point not to *be* in her presence. She rarely saw him and never spoke to him, so despite living under the same roof they remained as divided as two enemies could be.

Andrea appreciated the separation. The inevitable response of rage that crept into her body when she saw him, or even thought about him, fueled the throbbing pain she faced daily. Dark thoughts of vengeance controlled her, and became what motivated her to make it through another day.

The sound of a rider galloping hard through hock-deep slop disturbed Andrea's thoughts of retribution. Before she could ask Izzie who it was, the hoof beats charged back out the lane.

Minutes later, Mattie entered with a package in her hand. "Ole Him sended something for you."

"Really" Andrea stared at Mattie, stunned that Hunter would think of her, let alone send a courier with a package. He had not been back to Hawthorne for more than a week by her estimates, and she had begun to think he was no longer in the land of the living.

But what she held in her hand gave her second thoughts about her unchristian wishes for Hunter's demise. Newspapers, almost a week's worth, lay neatly bound with string. Most of them were out of Richmond, but one, a dated one, was from the North. How thoughtful of him to think of her—and how she hated him for it. Desperate for war news, Andrea glanced through the stack. A headline from one of them instantly caught her eye.

Appreciating the public interest in the recital of everything connected with the recent exploits of Captain Alexander Hunter's activities behind the enemy's lines, we have gathered, from reliable participants in the affair, these additional particulars, when with but fourteen of his men he captured thirty Yankees with no shots fired . . .

Andrea read the story with disgust and then wondered if Hunter had seen it. The papers did not appear to have been opened. She spent the rest of the day and most of the next catching up on the world, and forgot, for a while, about her throbbing leg and the unfortunate circumstances into which she had been thrust.

When Andrea awoke later from an afternoon nap, she listened with closed eyes to a melodic sound coming from outside. Sitting straight up in bed, she looked to the window and smiled at the joyous strains of birds welcoming the arrival of the sun. Golden rays dappled the floor, their warmth melting away the shadows of gloom that had darkened the room for so long.

"Izzie, I want to sit outside today," Andrea said, her gaze sweeping the landscape. "Oh, please! Get your father to carry me, won't you?"

The pounding of hoofbeats and the jangling of spurs and bits interrupted the discussion. Andrea pulled herself to the windowsill and watched a group of ten riders, each leading at least two extra horses, draw rein in front of one of the paddocks.

Hunter was easy to spot in the group of disheveled men. Although mud-spattered and careworn, he looked vibrantly strong and lethal. Even from the window, he appeared to her the incarnation of knighthood. But Andrea's mind was not on the muscular physique of her captor. Her pulse raced at the opportunity to be within earshot of Hunter's feared band of Rebels.

At that moment Hunter looked toward the window, his eyes meeting and penetrating hers. Andrea shivered and turned away from his piercing glare. When she looked back, he had returned his attention to the horses. Leaning his bronzed arms on the fence, he appeared to be commenting on each one turned loose in the paddock. When all had been released, Hunter removed his hat, wiped the sweat from his brow, and headed toward the barn with long, powerful strides.

His men followed, but Andrea's gaze now lingered on the martial figure in the lead. "What are they doing here?" Andrea asked, turning to Izzie.

"Dunno. His mens don't mostly come heah."

Andrea turned back to the window, but by now they had all disappeared. When she looked back for Izzie, she too had disappeared. There was nothing to do but wait for her return.

ℋ ℋ ℋ

Hunter stood unnoticed outside his houseguest's door and waited for Izzie to complete her chore. He heard the sound of the drapes being closed and then the shrill ring of Andrea's voice.

"What are you doing?"

"Him ax that you stay away from the windows."

"I beg your pardon?"

"Ole Him ax that you stay away from the windows," Izzie said again, just a little louder.

"And his Majesty the King is too cowardly to come and tell me himself?"

Hunter took a deep breath and strode into he room. "No, Miss Evans, I am not too cowardly to come and tell you myself. I was simply trying to avoid a—" He stopped and searched for the right word. "Confrontation." Looking into her angry eyes, he paused. "But I can see I was not very successful in that endeavor."

"You expected no confrontation?"

Although Hunter had found Andrea's thoughts difficult to read in Richmond, he found interpreting her mood no difficult thing now. All signs indicated a swiftly falling barometer, and the clouds upon her countenance thickened and darkened by the moment.

"You will not allow me to avail myself of the only liberty of these four walls?" Her entire body heaved with hostility against the alleged violation of her freedom. "You call me a houseguest, yet lock me away like a common prisoner? I could well die from the roar of silence in this room!"

Hunter had never met anyone quite so intolerant of confinement. "As for the courtesies I've extended you," he said in a calm voice, "your door has not been locked nor is there a guard standing outside. Both, I might add, against my better judgment."

He paused, for indeed it had crossed his mind that not confining her to this room could be unwise. But as he kept little in the house of military importance, he had decided to be lenient. Truth be told, he valued his men too much to place one of them within spitting range of this defiant, Rebel-hating houseguest.

"Oh, yes. You have shown me every courtesy, save liberty," Andrea argued.

Hunter shook his head. "Though inconvenient, I do not believe closing the curtains will cause you fatal injury. In fact, I believe I told you before, I rather think your indignation for the Rebel race will prevent you from dying in the home of one."

Andrea seemed to quake with indignation. "You are prohibiting me from looking out the window—here, where hours pass like days. This, sir, is torture in its most revolting, unrelenting and painful form. I've simply been obliged a transfer from Libby Prison to … to Camp Misery!"

Hunter tried to suppress a laugh, but nearly choked in doing so. "Camp Misery?" He glanced around her room at the accommodations. "No one could object to such agreeable terms as I have bestowed upon you. What depredations have you been made to endure, pray tell?"

"I do not have to undergo depredations to know I reside in a worse place than hell!"

"Miss Evans, I am merely *requesting* that you stay away from the windows for a few hours." Hunter knew she comprehended that his request was not a request at all, but most certainly a command that he intended to be followed. "Contrary to popular belief, Miss Evans, I am a very easy-going fellow."

Andrea met his gaze with a mixture of curiosity and disgust.

"Simply do as I say and we shall get along fine."

"Surely you are not under the illusion that my gratitude for being rescued from hell is going to outweigh my resentment and loathing for the one who placed me there."

"I have not been under that illusion since the moment you awoke, I assure you," Hunter responded. "But certainly, Miss Evans, you can understand that I'm not anxious for my men to discover there is a *Yankee* residing here."

For a moment there was no sound, save Andrea's rapid intake and exhalation of air. That she understood no other epithet conveyed a bigger insult to the Southern ear than the word Yankee was obvious. He wondered if he had gone too far in using it to describe her.

"Then hide me away behind closed curtains you must," she said, her voice trembling with offense. "For no earthly power shall keep me from denouncing the enemies of my country!"

Hunter stared at her with furrowed brow. The intrepid young lady seemed to have no fear, and as for emotions other than fury and hatred and rage, they appeared to be undiscovered or were dead or had never been born. She was, without a doubt, the most untamed creature with which he had ever had to deal. He pitied any man who would attempt the challenge of trying to domesticate her.

"Then it is evident that your imprisonment is self-imposed," he said in response to her fierce pride. "As well may be your untimely departure from your earthly bounds if you do not learn to control your temper."

"Do not dare talk to me thus." Her voice grew hushed. "I will not submit to it."

Hunter laughed at her brazenness. "Submit to what? My threat or my order? Beg pardon, I mean *request*."

"You spoke not the truth when you told me I was not a prisoner?"

"Miss Evans … I mean, Andrew Sinclair. Your sudden great respect for the truth is incredible, since you so rarely use it yourself. In fact, I don't believe I've ever had the privilege of meeting someone who was so adept at telling a lie on such short notice."

"I resent that," she said, pointing her finger at him. "I have never lied to you."

"So you are a native of Maryland and your name is Evans?"

Andrea turned her head away. "Some half-truths were necessary."

"I thought as much." Hunter started to leave, but then stopped and turned toward her. "For the record, it is my belief that a half-truth is a whole lie."

He watched Andrea's eyes turn a darker shade of green as she muttered an imprecation he could not quite hear. "If I may offer some advice," he said. "Concentrating on your recovery, instead of ways to aggravate your host, may prove to be a better investment of your time. I would encourage you to accept, with gratitude, the offerings I have bestowed upon you."

"Over my dead body."

Hunter did not respond verbally, but tried to convey by his look that her wish could be easily arranged.

"Do not jest with me," she said, reading the gaze accurately. "You have not dealt with the likes of me."

Hunter tilted his head to one side. "Yes, I believe on that point we are in complete agreement." He turned to leave. "I regret the necessity for the inconvenience, but be assured, you may enjoy your houseguest privileges the moment we depart."

"But . . . this is unjustifiable imprisonment!"

"Miss Evans, there are enough charges against you, of which I can personally substantiate, to make a rope around your neck justifiable. You will please pardon me if I decline to debate legitimate forms of punishment with you." He pulled a small watch out of his pocket, glanced at it and then back at her. "Time is valuable, and you've taken a considerable amount of it. Have a good day."

"How dare you speak to me this way," Andrea yelled when he started to depart. "You are brutal and malicious and can go to hell, Captain!"

"It's *Major* now," Hunter said over his shoulder. He stopped then and leaned back in the doorway. "And Miss Evans, can you not restrain your temper and control your language? It's most unbecoming—even for a Yankee."

Andrea responded with a whole inventory of curses—of which she possessed a goodly store—to do justice to the occasion. "I'll be damned if I can! And the hell I will! And too bloody bad if it is!"

"Glad to see you're feeling better," Hunter said under his breath as he descended the stairs two at a time.

Chapter 24

"An army of sheep led by a lion would defeat an army of lions led by a sheep."
– Arabian Proverb

Captain Carter watched Hunter sitting in the shadows with a remote look on his face, while some of the men talked and bragged in small groups around him. No one appeared mindful of the danger of the enterprise upon which they were about to embark—except perhaps Hunter himself. He stared at the distant horizon, apparently envisioning in explicit detail every facet of the conflict yet to come.

As usual, Hunter had spun a veil of secrecy around the expedition. But from the looks on the men's faces, Carter saw they were content to trust their fate to the one that led them.

"You men looking for trouble?" Hunter came out of his trance when five of the men rode close enough to cause Dixie to lunge forward with teeth bared.

"Yes, *suh*," they shouted in unison.

A devilish grin spread across Hunter's face. "Good. Let's go find you some."

Carter could not help laughing along with the men. Hunter appeared to be in a fine mood, and that usually portended plenty of action. As a result, he knew he would hear his leader's characteristic speech at least one time today. It always began with, "The enemy is in force before us, gentlemen," and ended just a few sentences later with, "Who here is with me?"

"What say you we go stir up some Yankees?" Carter noticed Hunter's voice held a ring of impatience, indicating his eagerness to start the foray ordered by General Stuart.

Although Carter did not know where they were going, he knew what they would be doing: By keeping the Yankees so busy worrying about Hunter at their backs, they would have little time to think about Stuart in their front.

The sky had turned dark and angry clouds massed when the group finally rode south. Not long after, hat brims began dripping with a wind-driven rain that soaked man and beast alike. Hunter, at first, seemed to disregard the deluge as he rode at the head of the column.

But Carter looked at the man riding beside him and winked when he saw Dixie's head sweep around to face the ranks. It was time for Hunter's customary statement about riding through a storm. No matter how often they rode in the rain or the sleet or the snow, which was often, Hunter never said, "sorry, men," or "try to stay warm, men," or "we'll find a place to get out of the weather."

It was always the same words said in the same low voice. "Keep your powder dry, men."

After two hours of steady riding, and plenty of jokes and laughter, a call went back the line for no talking. Not more than a mile farther, through a maze of pines and shrubs, Hunter directed his men into the shelter of a grove of cedars where they dismounted. Carter soon learned the reason for the need of silence. The campfires of the enemy burned so close to their right, he could hear the voices of the soldiers talking around them. To his left, farther away, came the muffled sound of a Union band playing. They were encamped midway between two enemy outposts, probably about fifteen miles from support of any kind. Here, Carter knew, they would lie, watching and waiting for the proper time and opportunity to venture forth and strike.

Carter sat down and leaned against a tree with his horse's reins wrapped around his hand. Hunter, dressed in a rain slicker, mounted and rode away, an indication that the tranquility of their current situation would not last. In another few minutes Carter was asleep, despite his soggy bed.

Sometime later, the sound of Hunter's voice woke him. "Carter, wake the men."

After all had gathered, Hunter reported what he'd found. "I discovered some good news, men," he said, in a low voice. "They have doubled their pickets."

Carter looked at the confusion on the faces of the men as they tried to figure out how that was *good* news.

"That will double the number of horses for us and they are prime," Hunter continued, ignoring their bewilderment. "I am inclined to go right in and help ourselves. Who here is with me?"

Carter stood in the shadows and smiled at the way Hunter talked to his men. He was always a man speaking to men, never bragging about his rank or power or authority. As for the unpredictable change in pickets, Hunter's reaction was completely expected. Double the pickets or no pickets at all, it was one and the same to him. He never focused on the possibility of failure, only the chance for success. If his men were in the proper mood for a fight, which was pretty much all the time, he felt justified in disregarding the inequalities of force and firepower.

"Let's go recruit some Yankee horses to the Confederate service, men," Hunter said before turning on his heel and mounting his horse.

And so with double the pickets, which Carter knew would make it hard to get *in*, and surrounded by five hundred of the enemy, which, likewise he understood would make it hard to get *out*, he and the rest of the band of rebels mounted and followed their leader.

Dressed in rain slickers and armed with courage, they rode straight into the outpost. The slumped, weary position in which they sat their horses and the casual way in which they nodded at the sentries, led the Yankee guards to believe they were a returning scouting party of their own men. Once within, they went to work with practiced haste, each knowing his duty and performing it without words and little noise. Twenty minutes later, the group rode out of the camp accompanied by another seventy-five horses without a shot being fired.

Hunter sent the horses back to Hawthorne with a small detachment of his men and headed deeper into enemy territory. Once a respectable distance from the Yankee encampment, he allowed his men to lie down and rest in the mud in another grove of cedars. Hunter nodded at Carter, indicating he wanted some company on a scout.

Carter had learned long ago that Hunter's reward for liking someone was to order the person to accompany him on a risky expedition. Carter therefore considered himself *very* well liked. Often called upon to "probe the enemy's numbers," Carter knew that in Hunter's command that meant, "ride forward and start firing, then count the number of guns firing back."

Thunder rolled in great booming waves as Carter followed Dixie's shadowy form at a full gallop through a blinding rain. He lost sight of the duo when they veered off the road and into a grove of pines, but a lightning bolt illuminated their misty figures before they disappeared.

Blinking a few times to clear his lashes of raindrops, Carter saw why they had stopped. A few hundred Yankees materialized in the mist about fifty feet away—more than likely the advance for the wagon train they sought. He watched Hunter gaze out of the darkness like a wily wolf, staring hard, unblinking, reluctant to take his eyes from the quarry he stalked. Carter knew he was busy counting their numbers, inspecting their array, and satisfying himself of their armament and readiness. If he thought the force too strong, he would move on in search of other prey.

"Let's get back," Hunter whispered. "It appears we've found some game worthy of pursuit."

ℋ ℋ ℋ

Hunter awakened Carter well before dawn and ordered him to push the men forward. The sun had just begun to spread its golden fingers upon the horizon when the group drew rein on the summit of a small hill. Carter took in at a glance what Hunter had ascertained the night before. A wagon train, heavily guarded in the front and rear, moved through the valley below them. Amazingly, it had no escort in the center. Before them sat a feast of riotous abundance.

Hunter stood on the hill enshrined by the early morning light and stared at his imprudent enemy below. "Well, go to it, Captain Carter," he said, never taking his eyes off the enemy's careless movements.

Carter followed his instructions, waiting until there was a break in the train, then stopping and directing the next wagon down a secluded bridle path that branched from the main thoroughfare. When he rode forward and pointed toward the road, the teamster just nodded, turned the wagon, and the rest of the train obediently followed.

About twenty wagons had disappeared down the path when an irate officer rode up behind Carter and shouted in a tone more forceful than polite, "What is the meaning of this? Why have you turned these wagons?"

At first, Carter ignored him and continued his business of waving the wagons on. "Orders, sir," he snarled over his shoulder.

The officer rode closer and grabbed Carter by the arm to get his attention. "Whose orders?"

Carter pulled his revolver and held it to the man's head to get *his* attention. "Hunter's, sir."

Meanwhile, on the other side of the hill, Carter heard the men laughing at the audacity of their commander and the carelessness of the enemy, as they disgorged boxes and crates of their contents and began to partake of the delicacies within.

ℋ ℋ ℋ

Hunter did not share in the festivities. Although at ease, he was not disarmed of caution. He sat on the hill watching the horizon and listening for any sign of alarm. With eyes wandering, he scanned the landscape with the avidity of a hawk. His smile of contentment turned to a frown of annoyance at the unwelcome sound of a bugle call floating to him on the breeze. He waited only an instant more. The thundering reverberations produced by the hooves of galloping hors-

126

es reached his ears at the same time a moving dot appeared on the horizon.

Hunter gave one swift whistle to warn Carter, then galloped down the hill full tilt to his men. "Put the prisoners in front," he yelled. "Keep the horses and mules together."

His men unhitched the remaining horses while Hunter rode up and down the line, urging them to hurry and ordering them to leave behind the most cumbersome of their loot.

"Sir, Gus Dorsey reporting."

Hunter reined to a stop. Gus, his foremost scout, had been ordered to watch and report on the enemy's movements. "Yes, Gus, what do you have?"

"Ran into one of Stuart's men. He was looking for you. Wanted me to give you this."

Hunter opened the dispatch and scanned it quickly.

Headqrts. Saddle
Major Hunter,
I am in receipt of your latest intelligence as well as telegraph reports from the enemy of your exploits to date. Your diversion has worked well, but Yankee patrols have been dispatched in every direction to effect your capture. If you can, cross Gooseneck Creek, burn the bridge, and head north to an abandoned house and barn. Gen. Lee wants that piece of ground held at all costs. We are en route and will provide support.
Your obedient servant,
Gen. J.E.B. Stuart

Hunter sighed deeply at the unwelcome and unexpected news, but otherwise provided no indication to those studying him whether the communication held good or bad news.

"Let's go, men." Hunter ordered the men forward, intending to move at a pace that would render pursuit difficult. But any hopes of fusing speed and distance were soon dashed. The horses slipped and slogged through the greasy Virginia mud, their progress hindered by the deplorable condition of the road.

At length the bridge came into sight, and horses, mules, and men clattered across. Hunter ordered Carter to withdraw the prisoners and the battalion to the farmhouse, then requested four volunteers to hang back and serve as rearguard—a perilous and possibly deadly obligation considering the size of the approaching enemy.

The call for such duty caused its usual uprising. Several men shouted and argued that it was their turn to serve; others dismounted and announced they were willing to settle the matter with their fists. It took Hunter several minutes to calm them down and choose who deserved the honor. With the choice made, the four men went about their job of trying to burn the structure. "May as well try to burn the creek," one of them said in frustration after fifteen minutes of trying to light the wet wood.

"All right, let's go," Hunter said. The thundering sound of a heavy body of cavalry followed his words. Hunter sent the four men to the top of a hill behind him to make a show of force, while he stopped his horse on the road and gave the approaching Yankees something to look at.

"Let your guns speak loud and clear men," Hunter yelled over his shoulder. "Tell them what you're thinking. Let's jam 'em back over the bridge."

The enemy, who had been rushing forward at a gallop, slowed at the sight of the single horseman standing in their path. Hunter watched their eyes simultaneously rise to the four men behind him. He knew the undulating road made ascertaining the strength of the potential force behind those four impossible. And he knew, as Yankees, they would be reluctant to find out.

They did not charge, but drew up in line of battle and waited for the attacking force, which came without delay. Hunter spurred Dixie toward the enemy, firing six shots and emptying five saddles. Howling at the top of their lungs, the remaining four followed his lead, charging the enemy like enraged demons and firing with the rapidity of lightning.

With four men on jaded horses, Hunter deceived the oncoming foe into thinking his entire command attacked. Unwilling to fight such a force, they fired a few ineffective shots, then turned and clattered back across the bridge to regroup, while Hunter galloped back to his men.

"Follow the road to an abandoned house. I'll meet up with you there."

The men needed no further orders. They urged their exhausted mounts on, at times pausing long enough to wheel around and pay their respects to the now-pursuing enemy. Again and again they turned and stung the Yankees with their lead, while Hunter, riding a parallel route, took occasional pot shots as well.

Even in the midst of the gunfire, Hunter heard the sound of a heavy engagement in front of him. He smiled grimly. Stuart had neither implied nor insinuated in his dispatch there would be no enemy to dispute their taking the farmhouse.

When the four men who had been with Hunter galloped up the narrow lane, the firing picked up its pace. Despite the barrage of bullets, they rode hell bent into the bloody fray, cracking away with their revolvers, showing nothing but elation at having so much action in a single day.

Hunter covered his men from a sheltered corner of the property as they rode across the open ground, then sat with head bent, attempting to reload for his own trip across the yard. Catching movement out of the corner of his eye, he looked up to see a man in blue step from behind a tree, his gun leveled and steady. Unable to move or fire, Hunter heard a shot, and blinked when the soldier's life-blood—not his own—shot like a fountain to the limbs above him. Moments later, one of Hunter's men rode by at a gallop, smiling. Hunter spurred Dixie and followed him to the barn.

"Pierce!" He dismounted and grabbed the younger man by the shoulder.

"Sir?"

"Why are you out here? I ordered your company into the house!"

"I wanted to be in the fray with you," was the simple reply.

Hunter stared at him, trying to decide whether to reprimand him for not following orders or thank him for saving his life. He decided on neither. "That will be all, Pierce."

Hunter turned and found his way to the back of the barn where he assessed the layout of the farm. The house and the barn lay at the base of a rather large and steep hill, from which he doubted the enemy could launch an attack. His men had corralled the captured horses in a large paddock beside the structures. The prisoners, about a dozen or so, were held in the barn.

The thirty-foot sprint to the house felt like a mile and a half to Hunter. He dove to the safety of the back porch and was pulled inside by a serious-faced Carter.

"What is the situation here?" Hunter strolled through the rooms, examining where Carter had placed the men.

"We cleaned out maybe a dozen or so," Carter said. "There's still a couple out there though."

"There will soon be more. How much ammunition do we have?"

"Sufficient I believe. We captured enough carbines and shotguns from the wagons to give each man two—some have three."

"My orders are to hold the house." Hunter stared vacantly through the window, refusing to look into Carter's eyes. "We should be able to resist them, provided they do not resort to artillery."

Hunter said the words as if the use of artillery meant little to him. But he knew Carter understood that when the enemy unloaded its cannons, the house and everything in it would be turned to jelly. It was simply a matter of when, a race of time, and a question of who would make it first—Stuart's cavalry or the enemy's big guns.

"Have the men barricade every door and window with furniture or whatever they can find," Hunter said. "And tell them not to fire unless they receive the order or have a good target."

Hunter went from room to room giving laconic orders, making sure no point of defense had been overlooked. He reminded everyone there would be little commanding after the firing began. As usual, it would be each man for himself. When done, Hunter joked with his men, giving the impression he thought the enemy was retreating instead of gathering and preparing to attack in overwhelming numbers.

But the shouting of officers, clanking of sabers, and whinnying of horses soon made that fact undeniable. Hunter's men watched the threatening phenomenon with grave expressions as they began to acknowledge the deadly significance of the numbers and weaponry assembling outside.

"Damnation. I wish we had some artillery to bear on them," Carter said.

"Since we cannot take them by force, we shall have to take them by strategy," Hunter said.

"And we can do it," Carter said, "God willing."

Hunter paused and looked over his shoulder. "You can wish for God to be on your side, but *I* will rely upon Stuart."

Gus, who had been walking by after distributing ammunition, asked innocently, "Sir, what are we going to do?"

"Do? Why, we're going to shoot them."

"But, Major, there are hundreds of them, maybe thousands. That's impossible."

Hunter smiled like he had just been told the enemy had turned and run. "Then we shall do the impossible."

As night slowly closed in around the command, sporadic gunfire continued. The Yankees seemed intent on keeping those in the barn and upstairs windows on their toes, though the wasteful use of ammunition did little to alarm Hunter's men.

When the night abruptly turned quiet, Hunter stepped to the window and watched a white flag move across the yard. Expecting something of the sort, he removed the coat that showed his rank and went outside to meet the two officers who bore the flag. "Gentlemen," he greeted them. "Excuse the informality. We were not expecting callers tonight."

"Are you Hunter?"

"I am an officer with the authority to accept your communication."

One of the men, a colonel, stepped forward. "I am Colonel Joshua Walters. You must know, sir," he said, looking Hunter's muddy uniform up and down, "that you are, for the most part, surrounded."

Hunter looked over the man's shoulder with a stare of colossal calm, but decided the statement required no response since the situation was obvious.

"You don't have a chance of surviving," the second spoke up. "We have an entire division within bugle call."

The arrogant attitude of the Yankees disturbed Hunter, but he did not allow it to show. "I am not unaware of that fact nor uncomfortable with my ability to deal with it," he replied, leaning one shoulder against the front porch post and shoving the other hand into a pocket. "So to be fair, I must ask that you please make your men aware they will have their work cut out for them."

The two officers took a step back and began whispering together in council. The plump officer stepped forward again. "How do you intend to defend this house against a brigade?"

Hunter blinked and bristled at the audacity, but then, again, calmed himself. "That is for you to find out when you come and attempt to take it."

The man muttered oaths, indignant at the bold effrontery as Colonel Walters stepped forward again. "Daylight will show you the hopelessness of your situation," he said in an insistent voice. "We are trying to diffuse a volatile situation without needless bloodshed."

"Thank you, gentlemen, for your concern." Hunter pushed himself off the post. "But I believe I shall bring an end to this conversation. We are Virginians, and we intend to stand and fight. We hope to see another sunrise, yet we are willing to perish nobly here."

"That is pure foolishness. How many men have you in there?" The stout major stamped his foot as if demanding an answer from a subordinate in his own army or snapping a command at a disobedient dog.

"Sufficient for the purpose, I believe," Hunter answered with a calmness that emphasized his determination. "You must know, gentlemen, I would not attempt such a defense without a number I believed adequate to settle the matter conclusively in our favor. I believe it is you who have drawn a tough assignment."

"Sir, you do not understand," Colonel Walters said. "We are here to demand your immediate surrender."

Hunter's smile faded. He cocked his head to the side and blinked in rapid succession to ward off the sound of a word he refused to acknowledge existed. "I regret greatly to disappoint you," he said, his voice hostile and threatening now. "But as I can still draw breath, I shall decline your generous offer. We will sell our lives dearly. And I fear many of yours will be part of the cost."

"But, sir," Walters continued, his voice quaking, "If you surrender you can trust in the mercy of the government."

Hunter looked each man full in the eye. "As I said, the men in this house are prepared to die here, not show their backs to the enemy. And if you gentlemen are not out of range within three minutes, we shall be obliged to open fire. Good evening."

Without waiting for a reply, Hunter stepped inside and closed the door, giving vent to a loud expletive that startled his men. Then he turned to Carter and tried to cover the emotional display. "How many men do we have?"

"Twenty-four. But four are in the barn guarding the prisoners and two are out watching the horses and the hill behind."

Hunter nodded and drew a deep breath. "Parole the prisoners and hope for the best with the horses. We're going to need every man in here."

He didn't bother to say it, but it seemed doubtful any of them would get

131

out alive to need a horse.

"It can be held, sir, under favorable conditions," Carter said. "And the good Lord might be able to provide us with that."

"If it is your custom to make requests to a higher authority," Hunter responded, "tell Him we need only two things: enough ammunition and adequate time."

Hunter knew his successes over the past two days had dealt the enemy a severe blow. This was the Yankees' chance once and for all to establish their supremacy in Virginia. Getting his entire command out under cover of darkness while the Yankees sat planning their attack would be no hard matter. But Stuart had ordered they remain until he arrived. It was an order that could not be questioned.

Hunter went through the house and assigned two men to stand guard for two hours while the others slept. Within five minutes of the order to rest, a line of corpses would not have been more motionless than the bodies strewn helter-skelter throughout that house.

"You better get some sleep too, sir," Carter told Hunter. "You'll be no good to us otherwise."

Hunter felt drugged by weariness, but his strength of will and resolve were more potent. He looked at the tired men who seemed oblivious to what the morning would bring, and listened to the ominous noises of the enemy making preparations for slaughter.

Sliding down the wall and putting his head on his knees, Hunter dozed fitfully for a few moments. Rising to gaze through the darkness, he remained vigilant for any movement or sound, half-fearing to see the view the gray light of dawn would bring—for he knew full well it would contain far too much blue for his liking.

❦ ❦ ❦

The rising sun had not even begun to affect the darkness when Hunter told Carter to awaken the men. Gathering them in one room, he spoke in a tone of mingled gloom and tenderness. "Men, we have been asked by General Stuart to defend this house," he said, swallowing hard, "and this we must do, at any price."

None made a comment. Rather, they stared back at him with supreme confidence, ignoring the growing evidence that the forthcoming match would not be an equal one.

"I knew well when I chose to fight for Virginia, the difficulties and dangers I would face. I yet resolved to live or die in the cause of my country, the honor which I owe to her." Hunter's gaze roamed from man to man in the room, and when he spoke, it was with the cool, quiet dignity that signifies command. "Men, we must hold this house, or sacrifice all in the attempt. This is Virginia soil, men. And we are Virginians. Shall we not defend it? Who is with me?"

"Son of thunder!" shouted a man who leaned near a window. "Here they come!"

The final preparations for defense were established in a moment, and then they waited impatiently for the carnage to commence. Despite being aware that extensive bloodshed was unavoidable and inevitable, Hunter's men did not show it. Rather, they smiled and winked at one another from their posts. This was the material he used to wring triumph from defeat. This was the material of victors.

Hunter paced behind the men making his final and fatal plans while the enemy gathered with a collection of men and guns it seemed no mortal power could withstand. "Men," he yelled, "hold your fire until you hear the word."

Desultory gunfire erupted from outside, but it evoked no reply from within. Hunter's ranks remained silent, waiting for a shot that would make firing worthwhile. Hunter held his breath. The living wave of blue came closer, halted and poured a volley into the house. Moisture ran down his temples and into his eyes, making it even harder to see. When they were almost to the porch he yelled, "Fire!"

His men obeyed, their guns crackling in a single deadly chorus. Flames shot from the front of the house as his men gave the enemy an unpleasant reminder of the accuracy of Hunter's guns.

The noise was loud, but Hunter's voice rose above the clamor, fierce and commanding, encouraging his men to hold their ground. The desperate assault met a determined repulse, but only for a moment. As quickly as it began, it ended. All became silent except for the chaotic sound of the Yankees' retreat.

Hunter, who kneeled at the front window, saw that perhaps a half-dozen Yankees had made it onto the porch, and there they remained, bloodied and unmoving.

Stumbling to his feet, Hunter moved from room to room through the smoke and haze, inquiring about casualties. It appeared that three men had been wounded by splintering wood and one was shot in the arm. None of the injuries seemed serious. He sat down to reload his own weapons and smiled. They had held their positions as he knew they would. No one would fight harder or be more ready to sacrifice all for their beliefs than this group. Hunter's heart swelled with pride that he had the honor to lead them.

Sounds outside announced the enemy rallying for another charge. Inside, with weapons reloaded and wounds bound, all was quiet and somber and still. The smoke had cleared somewhat by the time the Yankees lined up to attack, this time from both the sides and front. Hunter's men, determined to perform their duty, rearranged themselves and waited.

When the Union troops moved close enough, Hunter again gave the command. The house erupted, throwing flames and lead into the very faces of the men who attacked. Yet on and on the masses surged toward them, and on and on his men worked like fiends, instinctively loading and firing, loading and firing, through the smoke and suffocating air. Mad with battle fever, they began to fight more with the courage of desperation and frantic survival than battlefield valor.

The roar of the guns became deafening and the concussion of the weaponry jarred the eardrums until nothing was distinguishable. Hunter could see nothing through the smoke and breathe nothing but its caustic vapor. His clothes clung to him, soaked with sweat. His throat was parched; his face blackened by powder.

Time stood still. The Yankees remained defiant in their determination to overpower those inside, and those inside remained determined to repel them. Nothing existed but bullets and smoke and noise as the men fought amidst flying lead and splintering walls. Both sides remained unwavering, neither side willing to be the first to quit.

In what seemed like hours, Hunter's men were forced to go from carbines and shotguns to revolvers. Hunter heard a loud bang and watched the front door come crashing in. Flames from a dozen revolvers erupted around his face, and when the smoke cleared, three dead Yankees lay just inside the threshold.

Yet, again, as suddenly as it began, all grew still.

Hunter took a few moments to regain his senses. He lay on his back on the floor with two empty, smoking revolvers, his chest heaving with exertion. When he looked up, he hardly recognized his men, so blackened with powder were their faces. "Prop that door back up," he ordered, jumping to his feet and gasping for a breath of air in the choking smoke that filled the house The men hurried to obey, pushing the door up and propping it in place.

Hunter went from room to room, assessing the damage. Two of his men lay dead, and seven were wounded, three seriously. He called the rest together, knowing it would be impossible to contend any longer with the vastly superior and fresh force of the enemy.

Looking at his men's expectant faces, Hunter's gaze fell. "It is unlikely we can survive another assault, and I believe we must discard the thought of receiving reinforcements." He took a deep breath and stared vacantly over their heads.

Without warning, a loud roar from the back of the house almost knocked him off his feet, and caused what plaster remained on the walls and ceiling to come crashing down. The men covered their ears from the deafening thunder.

Artillery!

Hunter brushed the white dust from his eyes and ran to the front of the house to gaze at the chaos. The cannon fire had come from the hill behind the house. It continued firing into the mass of blue in front of them.

"It's Stuart!" one of his men yelled. "They're here!"

"Yes, I believe the general has taught us a lesson in the value of minutes," Hunter said with a slight grin.

"How in the hell did he lug those guns up there?" Carter smiled, his teeth showing brilliantly against his blackened face.

"Don't know," Hunter said. "But I'm damn glad he did."

Hunter had little time to meet with his comrade Stuart, who, even with the use of artillery, found it hot work dispersing the enemy. Instead he turned over the captured horses and mules that Stuart desired, then set out to deliver the remainder to an outpost about fifteen miles away.

Well after midnight, Hunter ordered his band of weary horsemen to halt their mounts in the shadow of some trees to wait for the intense moonlight to dim behind a cloud. This cautiousness, though necessary, cost them precious time. Hunter ignored the men's impatience and grumbling. He and Carter gazed at the moon and consulted, until at last he gave the order to mount.

Moving forward again Hunter picked up the pace, knowing both man and beast were bone weary. But while still some distance from their headquarters and with perhaps only another half-hour of darkness remaining, he hit an unexpected enemy picket post. The single sentry ambled out of the woods, scratching himself and yawning.

"Where ya headin', boys? Need the countersign."

Hunter was so tired he merely laughed, and so did his men. Almost home after three days of constant riding and fighting, a single sentry was not going to stop them now.

The picket, obviously not seeing the humor, brought his gun up to a more intimidating position and asked again. "I said I need the countersign."

"Do you know who I am?" Hunter leaned forward, crossing his arms over the pommel of his saddle.

The picket apparently took him for the leader of an uppity cavalry unit out on a lark, because he spoke with unbridled audacity. "I don't care if you writ the dad-blame Ten Commandments. You ain't getting through this post till I hear the countersign."

Hunter leaned down to talk to the man confidentially, but his voice was clearly heard by all. "I didn't write them," he said, placing his hand on the sentry's shoulder, "but I've broken quite a few in the last couple of days." He paused, while his men chuckled in their saddles. "As for the countersign," Hunter cocked his gun in the man's ear. "I am confident this will suffice."

And suffice it did. Hunter, desperate to get back into friendly territory and exhausted beyond even his own endurance, decided to parole the sentry on the spot instead of taking him prisoner. Now only ten miles from home, he rode forward without hesitation, assuming nothing could stop them now.

Riding about thirty yards in advance, as was his custom to protect his men from ambush, Hunter glanced up at an eminence ahead and noticed the rising sun glance off a metallic object. Drawing his revolver, he turned in his saddle to warn his men. Suddenly, from behind some trees, a dozen or more enemy sharpshooters appeared, their guns concentrated on him alone.

Hunter did not have time to react. A tumultuous noise arose, followed by a loud whack, and a jolt that nearly threw him from the saddle. His upper body exploded in pain, and the agony and fire that surged through his veins left him dizzy. His vision blurred, though he tried to give orders through the haze and the fog.

Two men rode to his side to help him, while others dismounted and started up the hill, blazing away with their guns. He saw little else. Faces blurred. Sound became muffled. He tried to gain control of his balance, to restrain the nausea rising in his throat. But he could see nothing save an undulating swirl of motion, and then not even that, as an ominous, dark cloud descended and carried him away.

Chapter 25

"He's mad that trusts in the tameness of a wolf."
– King Lear, *Shakespeare*

Andrea's arms trembled, but her determination to make it around the room one more time superseded the pain. Leaning on the crutches Hunter had sent from the field, she suppressed the urge to curse him. How arrogant of him to give her a gesture of kindness after his cruel treatment. How she resented his gentlemanly generosity.

Concentrating on how to place the contraptions, Andrea looked toward the window at the sound of approaching horses, and watched a group of men dismount in unison near the house. In silence they gathered around a single rider who remained in his saddle, though barely.

Andrea realized it was Hunter at the same moment Izzie screamed from the porch below her. "He hurt! Ole Him hurt!"

"It's not serious," Andrea thought she heard Hunter say. But his voice sounded weak, and his shirt was covered in blood, and he was only standing now with the aid of two of his men.

"I's can't stands blood," Izzie screamed, putting her hand over her eyes.

Her animosity toward the injured man for a moment forgotten, Andrea made it to the stairs in just a few strides on her crutches. "Bring him up here," she yelled when the men entered the door below.

"Izzie," she commanded, seeing she would have to take charge. "Tell Mattie to boil some water and bring up clean linens. And you, get some whiskey."

Opening the door to Hunter's chamber, Andrea paused at the threshold, looking for the first time upon the large, sun-swept—and masculine—room. Her sense of intrusion lasted only a moment. Heavy footsteps sounded on the stairs and the figures of three men appeared in the doorway. Their faces and clothes, masked with smoke and mud, made them unrecognizable—more like some frightening creatures from the depths of a swamp than anything of flesh and blood.

After they laid Hunter down on the bed and removed his boots, Andrea noticed he did not move. "He's lost a lot of blood," one young man said, his brow creased with concern. "Doc's in Richmond."

"We'll do what we can for him." Andrea ripped away what remained of his tattered shirt, the condition of which showed he had passed through a dreadful battle or bad weather, or both. The seeping condition of the bandage placed on his shoulder in the field gave proof that he had been bleeding copiously for quite some time.

"That will be all," she said, looking up at the men gathered solemnly around the bed. She pretended not to notice their looks of surprise or their nods and winks as they exited the room. When she heard the door close, Andrea paused and swallowed hard at the appearance and physique of the man lying before her. Covered in mud, his face blackened from powder, he still radiated exceptional power and strength.

By the time Mattie arrived with the water and linens, Andrea had discovered that a clipping from his coat and shirt remained within a ragged hole near his shoulder. The lead had torn a rather large hole upon its exit, but the bullet did not appear to have hit any bones.

"I'm just going to clean this up a little." Andrea did not know if he was conscious. He had not moved.

"Keep the hot water coming," she said over her shoulder to Mattie. "He's a mess."

Wiping the sweat from his brow with a cloth, Andrea frowned at the situation. *I never could turn away from an injured animal,* she thought to herself.

H H H

Hunter heard a voice and felt fingers probing his shoulder. Although his arm throbbed with pain, the touch felt tender and soothing upon his bare flesh. He tried to force the cobwebs from his brain, to clear his blurred vision and mind.

Opening his eyes and blinking at the pain, he stared at the face leaning over him. He thought he recognized the countenance—but no, that could not be. He saw no sign of the hatred and anger that blazed so fervently when last they'd quarreled, nor any sign of the customary sullen frown.

He closed his eyes and tried to think. *Tired. So tired.*

After being hit, he had fallen. Perhaps he had hit his head and was hallucinating now. Or perhaps he was just so exhausted he was having a strange dream. Strange indeed, because the woman he had left in the next room would be more inclined to strangle him than bend over him in aid.

Hunter blinked at the intensity of light flooding through the window while gazing upon the worried face. He became more certain he was dreaming, but decided to talk to the apparition. "What do you think, Doc?" He hoped he had actually spoken the words aloud, because it was only with supreme effort that he retained consciousness.

The figure did not respond right away, seeming intent on cleaning the wound. Or maybe, Hunter thought, she really is just a figment of my exhausted imagination.

"It appears a bullet has pierced your celestial armor, Major," she answered at last. "Unfortunately, it does not appear to be fatal."

She did not lift her eyes at first, but when she did bring them up to meet his, they brimmed with amusement. Hunter thought he had never seen anything so beautiful, so exquisite, as those two dazzling green eyes filled with laughter. He contrasted the image to the raving, maddened woman he left, but could find no comparison. Where did this person come from or where had the other gone? He hoped they had switched places for good.

"I'm not the first to baptize the soil of the Old Dominion with my patriotic blood," Hunter said weakly. His words made her frown, and her eyes reflected a look so somber and wise it made his bones ache.

"Nor will you be the last, I fear." She bent back over to examine his wound. Her breath was now so near, Hunter could feel it on his skin; her hair so close, he could smell its sweet fragrance. Her touch was divine. He felt strangely out of breath.

Hunter raised his gaze to her, but she seemed not to notice. Lost in silent observation, she bit the inside of her cheek as she concentrated on her work. When a tendril of hair fell and brushed his neck, a shock surged through his body that made him shudder.

"I'm sorry. Did I hurt you?" She looked up anxiously, her eyes filled with unconcealed alarm.

"No. Go on." Hunter transferred his gaze to the ceiling and bit the inside of his cheek as well, forcing himself to concentrate on something else. Although worn with fatigue, he could no longer think of sleep.

"I appreciate the confidence, Major. I am an honorable woman, and despite the fact you are my enemy, your treatment will be just." She sounded innocent enough as she repeated the exact words he had said to her, but Hunter saw a smile twitch along the corners of her mouth. Then, like a mass of storm clouds parting to expose the rays of the sun, she revealed a smile.

Hunter was thankful he was lying down. A face that had heretofore only frowned, glared, and grimaced at him now glowed with a teasing grin. He gazed upon lips that were not merely turned upward but that lit her countenance with a lovely sparkle of enchantment. He thought the smile the sweetest that had ever illuminated a mortal face. The throbbing in his shoulder mysteriously disappeared.

"Then I shall attempt to put on as brave a front as my houseguest and endure the fate that has befallen me." Feeling slightly out of control, Hunter took a shaky breath and wondered if she had dosed him with laudanum when he was unaware. She suddenly possessed some power that made him feel light-headed and dizzy. He glanced again into her eyes and felt a dull ache in his chest begin to spread throughout his body. He forced himself to look at the ceiling again and concentrated on breathing. Inhale. Exhale. Inhale. Exhale.

He tried not to think about the soft hands gently probing his arm, tried not to think about how they would feel— His breath became ragged. His nerves throbbed and jumped involuntarily.

"I'm sorry. I know I'm hurting you. I'm almost done."

Her voice jolted him back. He attempted to ignore the roaring in his ears and the wound that had started to ache in the back of his teeth. "Tell me, Miss Evans," he said, trying to regain the self-control he prided himself on. "Are you trying to get on my good side?"

Andrea gave him a puzzled look. "That is quite impossible, Major, as I was not even aware you possessed one. But I thank you for letting me in on your well-kept secret." She smiled, her eyes twinkling mischievously, and then went back to work, her jaw set firmly as she attacked her task with renewed fervor.

Hunter smiled too, a cockeyed schoolboy grin, which he quickly suppressed. "Perhaps it's like yours, merely hidden most of the time," he said huskily.

"Perhaps," she responded. But Hunter could tell she was more engrossed in her grim work than the conversation. Maybe she was letting him know she had no intention of discussing *her* good side, which she evidently preferred to keep to herself.

Andrea sat back and surveyed her work, then her gaze drifted up to meet his. "You have a funny look on your face, Major."

"I do?" He choked the words.

"Probably just the pain from your injury." She smiled, and, in a motherly way, put her hand on his forehead to see if he had a fever. Stroking the hair from his brow, she looked with a mixture of sympathy and concern at the spot where his head had made violent contact with the ground.

Something about that look reached down to soul and made him struggle to catch his breath. He closed his eyes, lest she read any secrets there.

"Bullets have a way of humbling one, I suppose," she said as if to herself.

"It's not the first time I've been humbled." Hunter meant to say it was not the first time he'd taken a bullet, but he was so tired and confused, he could not think straight. So tired. Yet his heart banged against his rib cage like it wanted out.

Andrea did not respond to that. She lifted his arm and began wrapping his wound with the bandages.

Hunter forced his eyes open again. "You seem experienced in the art of healing, Miss Evans," he said weakly. "Have you done this before?"

"Oh, yes. I used to help Mammy with the sla—"

She looked straight into his eyes, her brows drawn together, her face just inches from his. Apparently realizing it was too late to stop, she finished matter-of-factly, "... with the slaves." Turning back to the basin, she busied herself wringing out the washcloth.

"But," Hunter said, genuinely confused, "I never assumed you were Southern by birth."

"It should not be hard to believe that I was born and lived among the misguided," Andrea snapped. "When one is reared in the presence of some six hundred slaves, a proclivity against, and an intolerance for, the institution and those who condone it can hardly be considered unjustifiable."

She turned back to the bowl of water, but the tone, the words, the savagery, were more like that to which he was accustomed. Even her eyes had taken on that all-too-familiar look that meant the mule was back.

"I didn't mean . . ." Hunter stuttered. *Please don't go*, he thought.

"My heritage is Southern. My devotion is, and shall always be, Union."

Thus ended the conversation. And thus ended the appearance of the gentler side of his houseguest. Hunter closed his eyes again. Six hundred slaves? She must have been born into one of the wealthiest families in the South, entitled to all the luxuries and comforts that such breeding grants. She had never boasted of wealth or influence, yet apparently possessed both. What in the hell was she doing *here*?

"Cans I help, Miz Andrea?" Mattie came back into the room with another bowl of water.

"No, I've just got to clean up the rest of him."

Andrea leaned toward him with the wet cloth, but Hunter grabbed her wrist before she had a chance to touch him. "Mattie, can do it," he said, not wanting to risk his reaction to her hands. "You've done enough."

Andrea looked surprised, but shrugged her shoulders and dried her hands.

"Get some rest when Mattie's done," she ordered before leaving the room on her crutches. She need not have given the command. His exhausted condition had already brought merciful oblivion.

ℋ ℋ ℋ

Hunter heard a light knock on the door the next morning, just before Andrea blew into the room like a fast-moving tornado. He watched in amazement as she flew across the room in long—albeit ungraceful—strides on her crutches.

"What do you think you are doing?" She grabbed the boot he had been trying to put on with one hand.

"I need to get back to my men."

"You'll provide no more target practice until a doctor looks at your arm." She dropped the boot on the floor. "I've already sent Gus with a message informing Captain Carter you're in bed for repairs."

Hunter looked at her, trying to figure out how she knew the names of his men, then fully realized what she had just said. "You can't send messages through my men *about me* without my knowledge or consent!"

"I can't? Or I shouldn't?" Andrea asked innocently. "Because I did, and it is done."

She waved her hand in the air and laughed as if her philosophy of seeking forgiveness rather than permission was a sound one. "Come now, Major, you are no more fit to face the enemy than you are to fly to the moon. Gus was waiting for a message to convey, and Captain Carter is perfectly capable of overseeing things for a few days. What would you have done differently?"

"That is not the point," Hunter growled, before mumbling something uncomplimentary under his breath. He reached down to pick up his boot.

Andrea slid the tip of her crutch forward and pinned the leather shaft firmly to the floor. Hunter looked up at her and then over to the chest where his guns lay, as if they would somehow be of use.

"Did you sleep well?" Andrea's voice softened just the slightest bit.

"Yes," Hunter lied. Between the pain and the dreams of her, he doubted he slept at all. He had even been awake the times she had slipped into his room to check on him. Or had he dreamed that she had knelt over him, beautiful and smiling throughout the night, touching his brow to check for signs of fever? And was he dreaming still? Had something vague and enthralling absorbed into him so that even now it pulsed through his veins?

"Well, you don't look like it to me." Andrea cocked her head and scrutinized him. "How do you *feel?*"

"Like a piece of Yankee lead ripped through my shoulder." Hunter stared

141

intently at his boot as he spoke, as if by doing so it would dislodge itself from under her crutch.

"Well, I see it did nothing to improve your mood or disposition."

He looked up sharply. "If that was its intention, Miss Evans, then I assure you it missed its mark."

Andrea laughed, humor mingled with concern lurking in her eyes. "Oh yes, Major, I *know* it missed its mark."

He watched her scan the distance from his shoulder to his heart.

"But not by much," she said, lifting her mischievous eyes to meet his.

Hunter snorted in contempt. "Then I'm sorry to have disappointed you."

"Do not raise your hackles, Major," Andrea said, placing her hand on his arm. "I did not mean to imply that I would relish the thought of a direct hit."

Their eyes met again, and for just the slightest moment, Hunter thought he saw compassion rekindled there. But he did not have time to analyze the glance.

"It will not hurt you to lie low until a doctor looks at your arm," Andrea said, turning away for a moment. "I know your blood is the highest pledge you can give to show your devotion to the Cause, but surely you're not required to give *all* of it."

"Doc is in Richmond getting supplies, and it may be days until he returns," Hunter said, as if that explained everything.

"Splendid!" Andrea turned back with a smile. "Then you will have a few days of rest. Highly deserved by the looks of you." She seemed to take great delight in the fact that their roles were now reversed. "It's easy enough to preach patience. Now you will have to learn to practice it."

"I see it's a trait that you've acquired." Hunter glanced at her before collapsing back on the bed, holding his pounding head.

"Well I hardly believe a few days rest will cause you fatal injury," she retorted, mimicking again the words that had been spoken to her. "You are a mere mortal, Commander, much as you may hate to admit it. Hence, your flesh will heal at the same rate as the rest of the human race."

Hunter put his hand to his head and squeezed his temples hard, then took a deep breath. Too exhausted and physically drained to argue, he decided to give in. Closing his eyes again, he made one last attempt to bring back the image that lingered in his memory. Had he really caught a glimpse of a woman that could be as compassionate as she was bold, and gentle as she was stubborn? Or did such a being exist only in his mind? Had she been real or an angel of the dreamy subconscious?

As if to answer his question, Andrea bent down and picked up his boots. When she reached the door, she smiled deviously, her green eyes sparkling with a light that appeared to be of frank good humor as she held them up for him to see. "I regret the necessity."

"Where are you going with those?" Hunter attempted to stand up and groaned at the ensuing pain.

"I'm making sure that my orders are executed, Major."

"Come back here this instant," he yelled, holding his head and sitting back down, hard. "I do not take orders from you!"

"Nor I from you," Andrea said over her shoulder before the door slammed closed.

Chapter 26

"Hard lot of mine! My days are cast
Among the sons of strife,
Whose never-ceasing quarrels waste
My golden years of life."
— Psalms 120:2

Andrea did one trip around her room with only one crutch and smiled. Although she gasped for breath and leaned heavily on the support, she had made progress. Her gaze turned toward the chamber door, and her thoughts turned to the one task that remained untried—the stairs.

Determined to achieve her goal, Andrea began her descent, but she soon discovered it was too soon to have made the attempt. When only halfway down, she began to grow dizzy with pain and her legs to tremble with the effort. She stopped and leaned on the banister, staring back at the eight steps she had already traversed. She knew she would never be able to induce her aching limbs to climb back up. She had no choice but to continue.

Turning back to the task at hand, Andrea swept her gaze over the room before her. Like the upstairs, the first floor appeared beautifully decorated, yet pleasantly unostentatious. A huge open foyer and elegant sitting room appeared neat and orderly, with beautiful dark-hued floors covered with elaborate and stylish rugs.

Hearing the sedate ticking of a large timepiece somewhere in the hall, Andrea renewed her journey with gritted teeth. She remained focused on a large oaken door to her right—the gateway to freedom. Although she knew it would not be today or even this week, some day soon this would be her way out. At the moment, she wished only to touch the large brass latch to accomplish what she had set out to do.

To her surprise, a loud, impatient knock echoed from the other side just as she reached her destination. Instinctively she pulled open the massive door and beheld a stern-looking man with disapproving eyes, blinking in obvious confusion at the sight of her.

"Good afternoon," he said. "Would the Major be about by chance?"

Before she could answer, Hunter strode across the foyer with his good arm extended, the other still bound in the sling she had made. "Doc. Come in. You don't know how glad I am to see you."

"I leave for a few days and you go get shot I hear," the doctor said, shaking hands with Hunter. "Thought I should stop in and check on you and the *patient*." The doctor cleared his throat at Hunter's silence. "That is, if she's still with us."

"Oh, she's still with us," Hunter said. "You just saw her."

Hobbs turned a slightly red color and looked back toward Andrea. His eyes went from her face to the crutch she leaned upon, then back to her face. "Impossible," he muttered under his breath.

Andrea, meanwhile, looked from the man, who was a stranger to her, to Hunter, and back again, waiting for someone to speak.

"My dear, I apologize." Hobbs finally said, "but I'm the surgeon for Hunter's command, the doctor that treated you, and I had no idea you would make such a … ah, swift recovery."

"It has not seemed swift to me in the least." Andrea closed the door and turned toward him.

"Well … while I'm here, do you mind if I take a look at your leg?" The doctor sounded anxious.

"Not at all," Hunter answered for her, patting Hobbs on the back as they turned. "This way."

Andrea glared at Hunter for answering on her behalf, but since he did not seem to take notice, she followed his sweeping gesture toward an open doorway at the back of the house.

The two men were so engaged in talking behind her that they almost ran into Andrea when she stopped abruptly in the doorway, awed by the magnificence of the room she entered. Twelve-foot windows adorned each side of a French door that opened onto a portico. To her left and right stood ceiling-to-floor bookshelves filled to the brim with handsome leather-bound volumes. A massive stone fireplace that looked like it would consume wood by the cord graced the remaining wall, with Hunter's desk close to its yawning mouth. No room Andrea had ever seen compared in grandeur. Yet it was not pretentious in the least. It was a room filled with warmth and inviting, manly charm.

"Come in. Come in." Hunter gave Andrea a nudge. "Have a seat."

Hunter sat at his desk, and Andrea sat with her back to him in a plush chair he pointed out. The doctor pulled a stool up in front of her, and picked up her leg, resting her foot on his lap. Andrea grabbed the side of the chair at the throbbing pain the movement caused.

"How much laudanum are you on a day?" the doctor inquired

Andrea blinked and looked somewhat surprised. "I take no laudanum."

The doctor looked up to see if she was joking, and then over her head to Hunter. "My lady, you must be in excruciating pain."

Andrea heard Hunter's pen stop moving behind her and imagined him leaning forward to better hear the conversation. She loosened her grip on the arms of the chair and tried to conjure a smile. "It's tolerable."

"How does it look, Doc?" Hunter's voice now came from directly over her shoulder.

Hobbs looked from Andrea to Hunter and back, as if he did not know what to say. "I'd like to prescribe some laudanum." He kept his eyes averted while he lowered Andrea's leg to the floor.

"You may prescribe all you like, but it shan't be used by me," Andrea said in a low, distinct voice. "I have recovered from worse."

"Miss Evans, the doctor knows what is best," Hunter said. "I think perhaps you should obey—"

"I think perhaps *I* know what is best for me," Andrea said, her voice trembling with emotion. "And I believe, sir, that you are exceeding your authority by giving me orders."

Hunter sighed. "It's not an order, Miss Evans. It is merely for your own good."

Hobbs, who had been standing by speechless, interrupted. "Miss, your leg is not fit to be walking on. It's broken and out of line."

Andrea turned her head and her inscrutable gaze to him. "I had my suspicions about the first, and never entertained a doubt about the second. Thank you for your expert opinion, Doctor."

Hobbs blinked in astonishment at her words and looked with dismay toward Hunter for support.

A knock on the door interrupted the tirade, and Gus Dorsey burst in.

"'Scuse me, sirs, ah … miss." He nodded and smiled at Andrea like she was an old friend, then turned toward Hunter and handed him a dispatch. "Sir, the men are meeting at Locust Hollow. Something's cooking near headquarters. They're moving the horses from the Talberts' now."

Hunter put up his hand to stop his scout and gave a worried glance toward his houseguest. Andrea stared at the wall as if she was not listening, but he knew she had not missed a word.

"Give me a minute, Gus," he said, running his gaze over the dispatch. "Have Zach saddle Dixie and I'll meet you out front."

"Please," Andrea said, rising with an alacrity that surprised even her, considering the depth of her pain. "Do not end your interview on my account."

Leaning heavily on the crutch, she headed toward the door, followed by Gus, who took the time to exchange a few words before rushing to follow orders.

ℋ ℋ ℋ

The two remaining men were silent until the sound of the crutch faded.

"What do you think, Doc?" Hunter handed the doctor his customary glass of brandy.

Continuing to stare at the open door, Hobbs took a moment to answer. "I think that is one remarkable woman," he said before downing the contents and plopping the glass on the desk.

"Do you believe she is in much pain?" Hunter thought back to her kind treatment of him and worried that the return of her hostility might be a manifestation of her injury.

The doctor did not pause. "Excruciating. Beyond the capability of mortal endurance I would think."

Hunter frowned. She had never complained of pain, though he had often witnessed her sitting with closed eyes and gritted teeth, as if concentrating on some unknown purpose.

The doctor cleared his throat. "I ... never expected her to be walking on that leg."

Hunter looked at him with probing eyes. "What are you trying to say?"

"It needs to be reset."

Hunter blinked with surprise. "Reset? Now?"

Hobbs walked over to the decanter and poured himself another drink, which again he downed in one gulp. He nodded. "She was too weak, too fragile. I did not want to attempt it before."

"Damnation, man!" Hunter ran his hand through his hair. "She'll never stand for it."

"She is a bit of a lioness, isn't she? I'm afraid it will require further bed rest."

Hunter groaned in response, knowing she would never consent to such a thing without a fight.

"How long will she be down?"

"She should not rise for four to six weeks."

"Four to six?" Hunter sounded incredulous.

"I fear her recovery will be slow and her impatience will be great," Hobbs said. "I don't envy you the trouble it will cause."

Hunter, incapable of speaking, groaned as he paced the floor. Hobbs had only just met her, yet already recognized Andrea's intolerance for idleness and repose.

"I am not a doctor," Hunter said, "but I believe in some cases, and with some individuals, rest can be more hurtful than action."

Hobbs grunted. "I am inclined to agree. However, it cannot be helped in this case. It must be done today." He gazed at Hunter over his spectacles. "Now."

Hunter looked up at the urgency in the doctor's voice and watched him pull a vial from his bag.

"Do not fear. She won't know what hit her."

❦ ❦ ❦

Andrea wanted to go back to her room, but standing at the bottom of the stairs, she knew better than to make the attempt. After exchanging pleasantries with Gus, she made her way to a comfortable chair in the front foyer. Perhaps after a little rest she would be able to find the strength to make the journey. For now, she needed to sit. Glancing around to make sure she was alone, Andrea did not bother to lower herself into the chair like a lady. She collapsed.

Not long after, Mattie emerged. "You want something to drink, missy?"

Andrea started to decline, but one look at the sparkling glass of lemonade and she could not refuse. Drinking none too sparingly, Andrea could almost feel the cool liquid enter her veins, easing beat by beat the throbbing in her leg.

But just as abruptly, she began to feel warm and shaky. Closing one eye, she stared at the glass, and watched it grow distinctly out of focus. Why did she suddenly feel so horribly dizzy? So amazingly tired? Andrea fought to keep her lids open, to keep her head from falling to her chest.

She looked up to see Hunter standing over her, talking in slow motion, not making sense. Mattie and the doctor appeared too, all floating in some sort of cloudy substance.

Something's wrong, Andrea thought with strange detachment. She stared at her fingers and thought how peculiar they looked, seeming to wrap around the glass like a vine.

She looked up again at Hunter, alarmed now, and tried desperately to read his lips. But the more she concentrated, the more his image began to distort and fade away like smoke carried away on a breeze. A great gushing roar vibrated in her ears, and the room began to careen. Andrea wrapped her free hand around the arm of the chair in a panic, just as the floor in front of her opened its mouth.

She felt the glass in her hand slipping from her grasp. Did someone catch it?

She never heard it shatter. She never heard another sound before the room swallowed her whole.

Chapter 27

"To restrain her is to restrain the wind."
— Proverbs 27:16

Hunter mounted the staircase to his chamber for a welcome rest after two hellish days in the saddle. His head throbbed violently, and his injured shoulder ached with a pain so intense it nearly robbed him of his breath. He hoped his houseguest was not in similar agony.

The sound of footsteps hurrying down the stairs made him pause in mid-stride. His gaze came to rest on Mattie, and then on the tray she carried—still laden with food.

"The lioness is not hungry?"

"She won't eat nor drink," Mattie wailed. "Say she gonna leave Camp Miz'ry one way or anutter. Tol' me if I enter her room again, she gonna—" Mattie, whose stern disposition was usually feared by all who met her, sniffled like a child and did not finish.

Hunter growled, grabbed the tray from her hands, and sprinted up the steps two at a time. Having departed before the doctor's procedure, he had hoped her anger would be gone upon his return. Yet it appeared the hopeless discord in the house had not abated, or even lessened, in his absence.

"Careful, Massa," Mattie yelled when Hunter reached the landing. "She so mad, if you put water on huh, she'll sizz."

Hunter frowned at that announcement, but did not pause. "Miss Evans," he said, striding through the door without knocking. "You are vexing my patience sorely. Must you constantly dig everyone with your spurs?"

Hunter could see with one sweeping glance he was in for another unpleasant brawl, and that going head-to-head with the girl's irascible spirit was going to be even more demanding than the skirmish he had just fought with her Northern compatriots.

"I will not eat your poison again." Andrea turned her head and talked to the wall. "I shall become food for worms before I am twice deceived by your tricks."

Hunter sat the tray down roughly on the table beside her bed and turned her face to look at him. "Look you here. Were I the evil Rebel you portray me as, Miss Evans, I would have ringed your neck with my bare hands long ago!"

"My injuries are considerable, sir, but I am not deaf!" Andrea shouted as though she were.

"I'm sorry." Hunter lowered his voice a little. "But I am weary of enduring, and having my household endure, your volatile and vicious disposition. You are free to denounce me and my allegiance in any terms you wish, but I forbid you to take out your wrath upon my servants."

"How dare you insult me after what you did," Andrea spat. "Pray excuse me if I refrain from expressing gratitude that the ailment has worsened with the treatment."

Hunter could see she was hurting. Her fingers lay buried to the knuckle in her thigh as if to cut off a throbbing nerve, and her other foot was in constant motion, as if the movement helped keep the raging pain at bay. Even with her lids closed, he could see her eyes quivering beneath the thin skin. "I'm sorry if it pains you," he said in a softer voice.

"*Pains* me?" Andrea opened her eyes wide.

"Hurts you," Hunter said, trying to explain.

"I'm not altogether unfamiliar with the word! Yes, it pains me! Had you the decency to seek my opinion on the matter beforehand, I would have informed you that having my leg broken once by vicious Rebels was quite enough for a lifetime!"

"Miss, what I did was for your own good," Hunter said. "It appears imperative that I use my good judgment since you seem to have none of your own."

Andrea did not respond, other than to stare again at the wall. But the look she allowed to flash across her face before she turned away made words quite unnecessary. In fact, Hunter decided there was nothing quite so eloquently unnerving as Andrea Evans' eyes when she was angry—save perhaps a masked battery of cannon discovered at close range.

Hunter paced back and forth beside her bed in frustration. I thought perhaps your injuries were to blame for your surly temper, but I'm beginning to believe it's merely a part of your Yankee character."

"Do not waste your time fretting about my character. I assure you any disagreeableness is only brought out in the presence of traitors to our flag."

Hunter stopped and whirled around to face the bed. "Young lady, I did not come in here expecting to be eaten up with fondness, but neither did I intend to have my loyalty assaulted and my country insulted. If you would spend as much time trying to recover as you do feeling sorry for yourself, you would likely be up and running by now."

Andrea drew a deep breath like she had been slapped. "Tell me, sir," she said, narrowing her eyes to mere slits, "are you as adept at reading your own shortcomings as you are mine?"

Hunter lowered himself into a chair beside the bed and tried to cool his temper. His houseguest was, he decided, a natural born devil, possessing a temper as volatile and unpredictable as if spurred by some demon from the very depths of hell—and by the look on her face, she was consigning him to that very place at that very moment.

"It's imperative that you eat if you wish to gain your strength." Hunter stood and paced again. "It is for your own well-being."

Andrea snorted and hurled words back in open defiance. "Are you speaking to dispel your own worries or are you under the illusion you are relieving me of mine?"

"Do you never throw down your weapon? Let down your guard?"

"In the home of the enemy?" Andrea snorted with profound indignation. "What do you expect?"

"Come now." Hunter stopped and faced her. "We've lived together far too long to be considered enemies. Surely you can agree to a flag of truce."

"You forget, sir, it is misfortune, certainly not desire, that places me here."

"I assure you I do not forget. Likewise, it was necessity, not desire, which compelled me to bring you here."

"Then let us be clear. I am determined to endure my prison term. Pray do not think that I am going to enjoy it."

"Come now, Miss Evans, is it so bad?"

"Major," Andrea replied, "if I make up my mind to go to hell, allow me to cut my own throat so that I may go direct, instead of lingering in this miserable manifestation of a wholehearted hell on earth called the Confederacy."

Hunter had hoped he could silence the batteries, that they could call a truce. He frowned at the prospect. Trying to reach a compromise with her would be like trying to stop a typhoon with his bare hands.

"Miss Evans, you are simply going to have to accept the fact that you are here under my care. And you could, despite our differences, extend me some gratitude, allowing you to stay here as I do while I am out defending my native soil."

"Defending your native soil?" Andrea gave an enraged laugh. "Is that what you call the midnight mischief created by your mob of marauding miscreants?" Andrea squinted at Hunter with one eye in such a way, he was beginning to learn, meant things sat ill with her.

"May I inform you, Miss Evans, that I practice a completely legitimate method of warfare. In fact, my men live by the Golden Rule at all times: Do unto others as they would do unto you—but do it first."

"Your nomadic tribe of trigger-happy horse thieves knows nothing but pilfering and pillaging and plunder," Andrea said with a toss of her head. "The only thing your bloodthirsty gang of guerillas would not steal from Union troops is their valiant dead!"

"I can hardly be blamed if the fear of a hundred of my men in the Yankee's rear is equal to the fire power of ten thousand in their front."

"Union troops cannot be blamed for fearing the ferocity of those who know no laws! You are nothing but an engineer of evil!"

"Engineer of evil? You wound me," he said, placing his hand on his heart. "I had no idea my reputation was so misconstrued in the North, no doubt by those who have been painfully, and, dare I say, frequently, defeated by my *avengers* of evil."

Andrea stared at him for a few long moments, her cheeks turning an unusual shade of red at his quick-witted comeback. Hunter noticed her foot had begun to move even faster beneath the covers, a sure sign she was not at peace.

"Can we call a truce in the war of words?" Hunter pleaded. "I have undertaken to provide you a comfortable place to recover. I am not obliged to listen to your constant volley of insults. I regret that we had to resort to the measures we did to reset your leg, but it was for your own well-being."

Andrea's mouth dropped open in a most unladylike fashion, then snapped shut like a nutcracker.

"Surely my hospitality deserves some degree of respect," Hunter said.

"You fight against the flag of your nation." Andrea's tone indicated that such an action demanded no respect.

Hunter blinked at her impudence. "I fight *for* my state. In case you did not know, Virginia followed her Southern sisters in secession after an invasion by your government."

This made Andrea's jaw drop again. "You have the audacity to place the blame on the North for this cruel and needless rebellion? You fault the Union, when it was the South that commenced hostilities with her traitorous uprising?"

"We have the right—and the duty—to guard our homeland from incursion, our property from desecration, and our institutions from destruction." Hunter grew decidedly uneasy at the direction of the conversation. He could not recall ever having a discussion about the war with a woman. Still, she had started it. And though he had learned that few could trade insults with her and come out ahead, he was determined to give it a soldier's try.

"You invaded our country and kill us for defending it."

Andrea groaned as if he had assaulted her. "The North's so-called invasion is due to armed aggression by a traitorous regime of Southern fanatics. Our government is obligated to defend and maintain itself against acts of rebellion."

"Miss Evans, the compact of the constitution was broken by the North when they invaded the South, making Virginia no longer bound by it. Therefore our actions are not an act of treason or rebellion, as charged."

"You are deceived. Disunion by armed force is treason," Andrea responded. "And a government using force in compelling obedience to its own authority is not war or *invasion.*."

"It is my, and Virginia's ardent belief, that the Union was a partnership voluntarily entered into by the states to secure liberty and self-government," Hunter argued. "The right to withdrawal was never surrendered, and the power to coerce a state to remain was never delegated—nor does it exist."

Andrea half-choked, half-laughed. "I believe it is safe to assert that no government ever had a provision in its law for its own termination!"

Hunter stared at her for a moment, weighing the benefit of continuing the argument. Even if he was right, he did not seem destined to win. Her opinions were fervent and fanatical, and she felt no reserve about expressing them.

"I believe you are failing to see the line of distinction between the Constitution, which it is the duty of citizens to obey, and the unconstitutional edicts of a military despotism we are, in fact, obligated to resist. The sufferings we now endure are heavy and severe, but they are nothing compared to the evils we would suffer if forced to live under the rule of a tyrant."

Hunter took her sudden silence as an acceptance of his logic. "We severed our relationship with the Union peacefully through ordinances of secession, with no contemplation of war."

"The ordinance of secession is but a cloak behind which you try to conceal rebellion and treason," she said, refusing to relinquish the field.

"It is our belief that coercion is more to be despised than secession. We did not agree to the severance of ties without just appreciation of the significance of the deed, I assure you."

"Yes, and now you show the solemn convictions of your deed through boundless expenditures of blood," Andrea said, staring at the ceiling again. "You have successfully opened a vein that is bleeding a nation to death."

Hunter let out his breath in exasperation. "Every drop of blood shed is a price freely paid by a soldier for his inherited beliefs and cherished convictions in the Constitution." He made no pretense at calmness now. "It was the only option left open to us."

"You are deceived if you believe that. The Union torn asunder is not a remedy for any evil in government—real or imagined."

"My dear, we, as Virginians, will not have terms dictated to us by tyrants. Surely you do not believe the Old Dominion is made of a race of cowards who will easily surrender the most sacred rights of self government."

Andrea pretended to reflect a moment upon his question and then gave him a wintry smile. "As to the qualities of the race that is spawned upon the soil of Virginia—I prefer not to comment."

The words were spoken with such an air of disdain that Hunter clenched his fists. The sneer had awakened his combativeness, and her insolence and dogged invincibility of opinion destroyed his capability for restraint. He had no intention of being driven back from ground he had already captured.

"Allow me to enlighten you," he said. "No it *is* not, and no we *will* not—especially not to those who have chosen to override the Constitution and demand terms revolting to our sense of justice! Perhaps you do not understand the culture of Virginia. We are a separate society. We honor valor and we value honor."

"Then it is a pity honor did not keep you out of the Confederate army," she quipped.

Hunter blinked in surprise at her audacity and spoke in a strained, emotional voice. "I will grant you full liberty of your personal opinions, but that does not give you the license to thrust them upon me, nor am I obligated to listen."

"Then why did you introduce the subject?" Andrea inquired, her eyes full of innocence.

"Miss Evans, I have tried to excuse and overlook your irritable temper, but these intellectual gladiatorial encounters, truly, are pushing my patience to the limit. I understand your burning impatience to take yourself from my humble abode, but I hope, most fervently, that we can have some semblance of peace until that day comes."

"You are at liberty to hope, I suppose," Andrea replied indifferently, "since it is the concept upon which the entire Confederacy rests."

"If there is any cause imperiled it would have to be the Union's. Why else would they ultimately, and by no means infrequently, retreat with more haste than dignity?"

"You dare come in here to torment and enrage me," Andrea yelled. "To discredit the character of our brave men—men who peril their lives to defend, restore and perpetuate a constitutional government that you are laboring to destroy!"

"I believe I came in here to see that you get some nourishment, and how I strayed from that endeavor I don't well see. However, I am beginning to see, more clearly every minute, the rationale and the necessity of the methods of discipline at Libby Prison."

Andrea's eyes opened wide, seeming to double in size. She made a deep guttural noise and possessed a wild, animal-like look that gave him the inclination to put his hand on her shoulder to quiet her. "Miss Evans, please do calm down," he said with a touch of contrition in his voice. "I regret the remark."

His words appeared to provide little comfort. When Andrea turned her full gaze upon him, Hunter actually took a step back, as if to evade a punch. Her eyes, he believed, spoke better battle English than even her mouth could convey. He held up his hands. "I apologize. Truly I do. In fact, I feel I must make amends. Pray stay where you are."

Hunter flashed a smile, realizing Andrea had no choice in the matter, and then retreated from the room. When he returned a few minutes later, her head was again turned to the wall.

"As you seem to manifest a great impatience with confinement, and as I am sure you are aware that crutches are rather cumbersome, I ... retrieved this from the attic."

Andrea turned her head and Hunter watched her eyes light up when she saw the cane he held out to her. "It was my grandmother's. Made for her by my grandfather."

Hunter stood by the bed, awaiting her pleasure, secretly hoping she would not decide to use the instrument as a weapon. Andrea's eyes scrutinized the elaborate walking stick. A horse's head and flying mane made up the handle, ornately carved in smooth and polished cherry, beautifully elaborate in its detail.

"It is magnificent."

Hunter worked hard to suppress a smile. *Ah, perhaps I will be able to tame the lion after all.*

But her eyes turned distrustful again, and then grew vacant, an apparent habit of hers when she feared her feelings were becoming visible. "You think to bribe me now?"

"I told you before, I won't try to hold you against your will."

Andrea half-laughed, half-choked her reply. "I fancy not! As well ask the sun not to rise!"

"This may ease your transition." Hunter's voice grew businesslike. "Though I hope you won't rush your recovery by putting it to use before the recommended time of recuperation."

Andrea did not answer.

"You have no reason to distrust me."

"Trust *you*? Why, I'd as soon trust a dog with my dinner. But pray don't take it personally, Major. Trust is not in my nature. I do not trust anyone."

"Really? No one? Not even your family?"

"I have no family."

"They're all dead?" Hunter continued to probe.

"My mother is dead. My so-called father would be if I had any say in the matter."

Stunned, Hunter looked at her, thinking he misunderstood. "You wish your father dead?"

"I believe I could survive anything if only I knew I could live long enough to see *that* act of God."

She said the words matter-of-factly, but the conviction in her voice and the cold fury in her eyes sent a shiver down Hunter's spine. He scarcely had time to recover before she changed the subject. "I'll eat," she said, as if it were a part of some ultimate plan. "And I don't need your blasted help."

Andrea took the proffered cane and laid it beside her on the bed, placing a protective hand on it in case he should change his mind.

Hunter looked at her questioningly, suspecting some devious scheme. He had not expected the coon to come down from the tree quite so easily. "Very well. But there is one more thing."

Andrea stared at him with a mixture of curiosity and distrust.

"I must urge you not to be reckless with your strength and health. The doctor says you must not put weight on that leg for"—Hunter paused and swallowed hard—"for four weeks at the very least, six being desirable."

"Surely you jest," Andrea said, unblinking.

"No. I do not. You will do irreparable damage if you walk before it is mended."

Andrea closed her eyes and turned her head away from him, her chest heaving. "You ask too much of me."

"It is for your own good," Hunter offered.

"It is for the good of your Command that you can lay me up for four more weeks! You are trying to prolong my agony by hindering my recovery!"

"You cannot believe that is why the procedure was done," Hunter said, annoyed at the outburst. "Surely you must know, putting up with your obdurate personality for four more weeks shall not be an agreeable proposition for anyone in this household."

"I cannot make too emphatic a statement that it is my desire and purpose to leave here as soon as possible," Andrea said, as if reminding him of something he could easily forget.

"And I assure you I am doing, and will do, everything in my power for the accomplishment of that purpose."

"Good then we agree on something." Andrea crossed her arms.

"Yes, we agree. Now can I trust you to eat, Miss Evans?"

"If I can trust you to leave," she said with a hint of sarcasm in her tone. "Like the Confederacy, I wish to be left alone."

Chapter 28

"Sounds and sweet airs that give delight and hurt not."
— The Tempest, Shakespeare

A soft breeze carried the aroma of budding growth to Hunter as he made his way into the house. In the weeks following his latest encounter with Andrea, he had been in the saddle almost continuously. Now he was home at last for some much-needed rest. He paused at the stairs with one boot on the bottom step, then turned and proceeded toward the back veranda. He needed to soak up the peace and quiet of Hawthorne and clear the battle scenes from his mind before retiring.

"Mistis Andrea, you need a wrap?" he heard Izzie ask. "It getting chilly out heah."

"That would be nice, Izzie, thank you," came the reply.

When the coat settled on her shoulders, Andrea laughed. "Thank you, Izzie. That was fast."

"You're welcome," Hunter said, taking a seat on the step beside her.

Andrea glanced around in surprise before focusing her attention back on the descending darkness. "I was not aware you were back."

"Just got in. Came out to listen to the silence." He pulled out his pipe and struck a match on the stone step. As he touched the flaming head to the tobacco, his mind wandered to their last meeting—though the same did not seem true of her. She appeared more intent on ignoring his presence than thinking about the last time she was in it. "I see you've been making much progress," he said to break the tension. "Hard to believe it's been four weeks since the … procedure."

Andrea cocked her head, apparently trying to decide if he was asking a question or merely delivering an assessment. She must have decided on the latter, because she did not respond.

"I think perhaps you are pushing yourself too hard," Hunter prodded. "I believe Doc had hoped you would not put weight on your leg for six weeks."

"Did you not say you came out to listen to the silence? If so, you may find that the quieter you become the more you will hear."

Hunter shrugged and leaned back, placing his elbows on the step behind him. He had the feeling that his houseguest's spirit of intolerance, if anything, had grown since last they had met.

But then she surprised him.

"Hawthorne is a perfect paradise," she said staring out over the fields.

Hunter sat up and gazed at the serious look on her face. "And you are disappointed it is owned by a Rebel?"

"No." She almost cracked a smile. "I can't allow that to detract from its splendor."

"Well, I'm glad the fact that we're in Virginia does not reduce its value in your eyes and estimation."

"It's quite magical, actually." Andrea averted her gaze to her hands.

Hunter decided to push his advantage. "And yet you wonder why I fight for it?"

She looked back over at him, her brow furrowed, pondering his simple question.

"The decision we faced was with or against blood and kin, for or against the Old Mother," he said, leaning forward, eager to get her to understand. "Fighting against Virginia would be like fighting against a piece of myself. I love this soil, perhaps more than I love my own soul."

Andrea nodded, the fight and challenge in her eyes replaced by a heartfelt look of understanding. "I suppose it is natural to choose to fight for the soil from which you came."

Her words and tone caused Hunter to pause. He followed her gaze from the giant shadows of horses in the fields to the wisps of white scudding across the sky.

"Look, the clouds are racing the moon." Andrea pointed heavenward, her countenance suddenly radiant and childlike.

Hunter glanced up just as a shooting star streaked across the velvety cloak of night. Andrea leaned into him and grabbed his leg excitedly. "Quick! Make a wish!"

She closed her eyes, while Hunter stared at her hand as if it were a branding iron searing his flesh. Indeed when she withdrew it, he flinched, imagining he felt a scorching handprint there. Clearing his throat, he returned his gaze to the sky. "So what did you wish for?"

"The first thing that came to my mind, of course. Peace." Andrea looked up at him. "You could not have guessed?"

"No. I would have thought your first wish would be to leave here."

She simply shrugged. "You are mistaken."

Nothing disturbed the peaceful silence for a few more moments, until Andrea pulled the coat draped across her shoulders closer around her. Looking down, she shrieked, then stood in one swift movement. "How dare you!"

"What's wrong?" Hunter asked, surprised by her sudden change in attitude.

"What's wrong?" Andrea cried, her lightning temper apparently ignited. "You, sir, may pledge your allegiance to the Confederate States of America, but I do not!" She took the military coat off her shoulders and threw it at him. "Nor will I. Pray do not dress me in Confederate gray while I'm being held here against my will!"

The warm and innocent eyes suddenly blazed, the peaceful serenity of the evening shattered. "Miss Evans, I assure you, I meant nothing by it."

"You call yourself a gentleman." She flung the words over her shoulder in disgust, leaning heavily on the cane. "Circumstances may require that I live under the folds of your godforsaken flag, but I shall never owe my allegiance to it!"

"Miss Evans." Hunter stood and followed her. "My only intention was to keep you from catching a chill, I swear to you. You may be sure of my pardon if you've taken offense."

"You mock me," she spat, turning back to shake her cane at him in an act of utter contempt. "If you think I will ever betray the Union, you are mistaken.

"I believe you've made that point before." Hunter shook his head. How could he have known that draping his own coat across her shoulders would bring out this demon of rebelliousness? He listened to Andrea let out another string of curses that was neither polite nor especially easy on the ears. The words she used were of the type that should never have been *heard* by a lady, let alone cross the lips of one.

He stood dazed, shaking his head in amazement, while Andrea continued her tirade. She uttered maledictions all the way into the house, making it abundantly clear he had committed a sin that should not, and could not, be pardoned in this world or the next. Nothing he or his ancestors had ever done since their arrival in America was left untouched, nor did she fail to suggest where he and every human being in the Confederacy might go if the decision were up to her.

She was, without a doubt, the most perplexing, unpredictable, infuriating woman Hunter had ever met. Never had he seen a creature whose emotions went to such extremes, a wide-eyed, innocent child one moment, a willful, wild demon the next. There was no way of knowing which would appear or when, and he was tired of trying to figure it out.

If she is determined to remain enemies, I will have to respect her wishes. He glanced over his shoulder at the sound of a door slamming in the house. *On second thought, I have no choice in the matter.*

Chapter 29

"You prepare a table for me in the presence of mine enemies."
— Psalm 23

Andrea paced back and forth on the front porch five days later, her cane clanking against the planks with each step. She paused when she noticed Hunter walking up from the barn, sweaty and dusty from helping the servants unload a wagon.

"Miss Evans," he said, pushing his hat back from his forehead and resting his arms on the porch railing. "Something wrong?"

"Yes, something is wrong! Andrea nodded toward the pasture. "I sent word down to you a half hour ago about removing that roan from the field. He's been causing a commotion all morning."

Hunter turned his head in the direction of a horse viciously nipping at another, and then rested his gaze back on Andrea. "Yes, I heard," he said dryly, "but I had other duties to attend."

Andrea snorted with indignation. "Then I'll remove him myself!" She drew up her skirt up with one hand and started limping down the steps.

Hunter grabbed her by the arm. "Miss Evans, there's no need to alarm yourself. Zach will be moving him to another pasture in a few minutes."

"In a few minutes?" Andrea yelled. "That horse needs to be moved now!"

"Major Hunter?"

Hunter and Andrea whirled around simultaneously. Andrea could not believe she had missed the advance of three horsemen, for the corpulent rider who addressed Hunter wore a lavish saber that clanged on the hardware of his saddle each time his horse moved.

"Yes, I am Major Hunter."

Andrea eyed the man in the saddle with suppressed amusement. He was a veritable mountain of flesh, his vast proportions quivering with each movement of his mount. She saw no evidence that the flamboyantly dressed soldier had ever seen combat, for the simple reason that the target he made was unmissable.

Amid even more clanking and banging, the man dismounted hastily, and none too gracefully, and presented his papers to Hunter. "My letter of introduction from General Stuart, suh," he said, bowing as if to a king.

Andrea stood just behind Hunter's right elbow and, with a slight twist of her head, was able to read part of the contents. " . . . Colonel Wellington, my wife's cousin, is en route to Richmond on my behalf. As one of my cherished friends Major Hunter, I ask you to please do everything in your power to make him feel the importance he has not, nor will ever, achieve, during his short respite with you."

Andrea watched Hunter's face and saw the muscles in his cheek twitch, though whether from mirth or anger she could not discern. Taking a deep breath as if stepping into a torture chamber, Hunter extended his hand. "Colonel Wellington, I presume?"

"Yes, suh." Wellington saluted Hunter, then grasped his hand in a cordial, though loose, grip. Andrea saw in a glance that Hunter's handshake was not nearly so lax, because Colonel Wellington grimaced, indicating his fingers were being mashed to a pulp.

When Hunter released his hold, the stranger turned his attention to Andrea, and all memory of the pain he had just endured seemed to vanish. He stood gawking in unmasked wonder, rudely eyeing her while licking his lips as if she were a leg of mutton hot from the oven.

"This is Miss Evans, my houseguest," Hunter said, noticing the man's gaze.

"A pleasure, madam." Wellington removed his hat and bowed so low Andrea feared he might fall.

Andrea nodded but did not come out from behind Hunter. She had not failed to notice the way the man stared at her, and almost grabbed Hunter's well-muscled arm for protection from his gaze.

One of the men behind Wellington cleared his throat, and other introductions were made. Corporal Bailey, a strapping, barrel-chested young man, grinned profusely at Andrea, while the other man, Private Tate, stared at the ground.

"Beautiful home you have here, Major," Wellington said, walking a short distance, his saber jangling at his side. "Mind if we get a short rest before dinner?"

Andrea looked up at Hunter for his reaction, and smiled when he successfully suppressed the agitation she knew he felt. She knew now his friendship with General Stuart was a strong one, because it would take a great camaraderie to keep Hunter from throwing a man like this out on his ear.

"Indeed," Hunter answered. "I will have a servant show you to your rooms."

Hunter turned and headed into the house, expecting the entourage to follow, but Wellington held back. "We will, of course, have the pleasure of your company at dinner, Miss Evans," he said, reaching out to touch her arm.

Andrea took an evasive step backward as if about to be kicked by a horse and successfully avoided contact. Hunter turned around and glared at her with a look that indicated he thought the entire situation entirely her fault. Then his gaze lowered to her bare toes clearly visible beneath the hem of her gown and his look turned to disgust.

Wellington cleared his throat and spoke in a loud voice. "I would not think of dining without your presence, Miss Evans."

Andrea's eyes fell at the look Hunter fired at her. "Of course," Hunter answered, though his tone no longer conveyed warmth or welcome. "She'll be there."

♂ ♂ ♂

Andrea assumed Hunter had shown his guests to their rooms and that all were napping before the dinner hour. She further assumed that Izzie and Mattie were busy in the kitchen preparing a feast for the visitors, because no one was anywhere to be found. Desperate for a drink of water, she decided to risk a quick trip down the stairs. Plopping herself on the polished rail, and using her cane for balance, she rode it to the bottom.

"Miss Evans!"

Hunter's voice brought an instant reversal to the smiling position of her lips. It was the voice, Andrea surmised, he used on the field to order his troops to battle. "Sir?"

"That railing is for your hand, not your seat."

"Yes, sir, but I—"

"I am trying to run a civilized household here. What have I told you about wearing shoes?"

Andrea was just about to ask him if he'd been born with his boots on, when he spoke again.

"Don't come down here again without shoes on," he ordered before turning away.

"Yes, *suh*!" Andrea held herself up to full attention and saluted him, mimicking his order with exaggerated gesticulations.

Hunter turned. "I saw that."

Andrea looked at the mirror hanging behind him and limped up the stairs, forgetting her thirst in her hurry to escape. Sitting in her room, fuming over his discourteous behavior, Andrea heard a curt knock on the door, followed by his entrance.

"Dinner is at seven."

"You seem to insinuate that I am the cause of this mess," she said angrily, "but I find the aspects of dining at your table about as enjoyable as being kicked by a horse."

"You've made yourself known to the Colonel, and he expects to see you. I only ask that you have regard for certain topics that must be . . . embargoed."

Andrea stared out the window, waiting for him to finish.

"I know you may feel uncomfortable . . ."

Andrea looked back in surprise, thinking for a moment Hunter was going to express sympathy for forcing her to share a meal with a bunch of Rebels.

161

"… having to act like a civilized young lady for an evening."

Andrea turned around. "You believe me incapable of the feat?"

Hunter remained quiet for a moment. "How shall you play a role for which you've had so little practice?"

Andrea's cheeks blossomed. "I shall not essay to enlighten you on the subject now, but I assure you, Major Hunter, I can behave like a lady."

He snorted. "Really? Sometimes, my dear, I believe you possess a disposition that is no less ferocious than that of a chained bulldog protecting a meaty bone."

"That is not the impression I wish to convey," Andrea said, forcing a smile. "I shall make every effort to change it."

Hunter fell silent for a moment, apparently contemplating what she meant and what she might do. "Nevertheless, I find it necessary to advise you, for your own sake, to be civil this evening."

"Civil?"

"*Civ-il-ized*," he said, pronouncing each syllable.

"I am familiar with the word," Andrea snapped with righteous indignation. "I do not know why you think you must school me in its meaning."

Hunter took a step into the room and closed the door behind him. "Surely you understand the fine line I am treading with you in my home. Or must I explain the complexities of sheltering a Yankee spy?

"You underestimate me, Major," Andrea said, regaining her composure. "I promise you that those men will believe me every bit as cultured as one of your Virginia damsels."

"Does that mean you'll suppress your usual temperament and try to gain some measure of control over your unguarded tongue?"

"That means I'll advance no opinion unless I feel it is required or requested."

Hunter sighed and placed his fingers on his temples, as he so often did in her presence. "If you've been dining on gunpowder again, Miss Evans, I sincerely hope you'll keep the ammunition of your thoughts to yourself, and that you'll refrain from discharging words of war at my table. Do I make myself clear?"

Andrea brushed a piece of lint from her skirt. "Are you saying you wish me to remain voiceless in the presence of my enemies?"

Hunter laughed. "Since when have you been voiceless under such conditions? Or under any conditions for that matter?"

"You are being unnecessarily vicious."

He held up his hand to stop her from speaking. "I am here to tell you that your obstinate behavior will in no way be tolerated tonight."

Andrea planted her cane in front of her and stood her ground. "And so you simply expect me to submit to your demands?"

Hunter put his hat back on. "I've said all I came to say. I'll appreciate your forbearance on all issues relating to the war. Pray do not take it lightly." He spoke with the authority of one who is not to be ignored or refused. When he turned to leave, Andrea turned her back on him. But a moment after the door closed, she heard it reopen. "Miss Evans, this is somewhat of a formal affair. You will kindly wear shoes?"

Andrea whipped her head around and glared, but the door had already closed. She stuck her tongue out in his direction anyway before throwing herself face down onto the bed. As far as she was concerned, he had thrown down a challenge. She was not one to refuse it.

❦ ❦ ❦

"Your guest will not be joining us?" Wellington picked up a glass of wine and drank thirstily before turning his attention to his host.

Hunter glanced at the clock and almost hoped she would not. It took no power of prophecy to know she would either come to the table miserable and moping like a sulking child, or temperamental and explosive as a wounded lion.

But before Hunter could answer, the sound of a cane tapping down the hall fell upon his ears. Its leisurely pace confused him. Usually when Andrea approached, the movements were fast and furious, and doors blew open when she entered a room like a storm moving through.

Hunter waited breathlessly and expectantly for the gale to come rushing in, both fearing and anticipating her reaction when she found there were not four, but seven Rebels to contend with. But to his surprise the door opened slowly, allowing the light from the hall to enter first, then surround, the vision of beauty that lingered there. The tempest he had expected was nowhere to be seen or heard. The only sound was the soft, pleasant rustle of feminine attire as it gracefully sashayed into the room.

"Gentlemen," Andrea said, her eyes roaming the room.

If she noticed—or cared—that the table was filled to capacity with her enemy, she did not show it. On the contrary, she smiled demurely at those gathered as if honored and humbled to be in their presence. It appeared that somehow, somewhere in his home, a bewitching transformation had taken place. The beast of a few hours earlier had been exchanged for one of alluring majesty. The creature that had the delicacy and sensitivity of an angry bull had apparently departed. In its place was one whose deportment was ladylike, whose appearance was refined.

Smiling entrancingly, Andrea looked every man in the eye, save Hunter, who she notably failed to pay the courtesy of a glance. "Ah'm so very sorry for keeping y'all waitin'. Ah hope you gentlemen will forgive me."

She did not look sorry at all to Hunter. Rather, she seemed to be enjoying the spotlight. She acted with such sophistication, Hunter almost forgot this was the same barefooted she-devil that caused him so much distress; the same Union-loving patriot that, if she had a gun in her hand, would have every man in this room begging for his life.

Hunter's eyes swept over the yellow silk of her gown, which in the flames of the flickering candlelight appeared more like shimmering gold. The flowing of a great concourse of ruffles made her radiate with something akin to the warm rays of the sun. She stood by her chair with all the presence of grace and royalty, her head held high as if there should be a crown upon it. Hunter could see no flaw in her poise. A stranger, seeing her for the first time, would swear she had the blue blood of a Virginian ancestry running through her veins.

"It was well worth the wait," Wellington said, taking her extended hand from across the table and kissing it.

Hunter did not fail to notice that Andrea seemed well practiced in having her hand kissed by someone she would rather shoot than touch. "You are too kind, suh," she replied, batting her lashes. "It's such an honah for you to permit me to dine with you."

"Ah, but my dear, it's your presence that makes the food taste better and the company so much more enjoyable," Wellington said, still holding her hand.

Andrea smiled with her fingers locked in his mushy grasp. "Oh la, suh. Now you are paying me a compliment and ah was only stating the truth."

Hunter stood dumbfounded during the exchange. Even her accent was deceptive, sounding musical in manner, soft and alluring in tone. Just like she had warned him, every motion radiated the attitude and presence of the well-bred Southern lady. Clearing his throat, he found his voice. "Gentlemen, may I have the pleasure of introducing Miss Evans. Miss Andrea Evans."

Andrea curtsied at the sound of her name and hid the wince of pain the movement caused from all but Hunter. "It's such a pleasure to meet such honorable membahs of the Confederate ahmy. Please do be seated, gentlemen."

Hunter pulled out her chair, and took advantage of the moment to lean forward and whisper in her ear a line from Hamlet. "The devil hath the power to assume a pleasing shape."

Andrea turned her head away with offended majesty, her countenance revealing a moment of surprise, and then a hint of anger, before returning to stone-faced indifference as she lowered herself into her chair like a queen.

"Miss Evans, I don't believe you've been *formally* introduced to my second—in—command, Captain Carter."

Andrea glanced at Hunter at his choice of words, then nodded demurely toward Carter. The officer did not bother to smile, but took the time to nod in her direction. Hunter could tell by Carter's expression that he'd already made his assessment of the young beauty—that anyone who mistook those brilliant green eyes and seductive smile for anything but a sharp mind and quick wit was making a big mistake.

"And one of my scouts, Gus Dorsey."

Andrea smiled at the handsome young scout, and the wink he gave her in return did not go unnoticed by Hunter. He wondered how well the two had become acquainted during his convalescence, and then wondered why he cared.

"And my aide, Johnny," he continued. "And I believe you've met Corporal Kroger and Private Tate."

Hunter felt like he was watching an actress on the stage as Andrea smiled and nodded at each introduction. She exuded nothing but wisdom, grace, and charm tonight, yet this was the same woman who possessed the added skill of being able to rattle epitaphs with the ease and fluency of Vesuvius casting lava.

"How long might we have the privilege of your company Colonel?"

"Only one night, I'm afraid." Wellington leaned forward across the table. "I'm on very important business for General Stuart. I thought it advantageous to make Major Hunter's acquaintance in the event we find ourselves working together in the future."

Hunter saw Andrea's lips twitch with amusement, but she successfully suppressed any outright laughter.

"So you and Major Hunter are old friends?" Wellington asked. "I've not heard General Stuart speak of you."

"I do not enjoy the honah or distinction. We met—"

"She's here to recover from an injury," Hunter interrupted. "A fall from a horse."

"Well, might you be related to an Olivia Evans of Virginia?" Wellington continued. "She married a fellow, a horse breeder I believe, from South Carolina."

Hunter watched the smile vanish from Andrea's flushed face as a haunted, hunted look replaced it. "No, suh, I don't believe ah've heard the name." Her voice did not waver, but she swallowed hard and stared intently at her plate.

"I see. Well, she's dead now, but she had a daughter about your age."

"Is that so?" Hunter leaned forward.

"Yes," Wellington continued between mouthfuls of food. "However, she ran away at a young age. There was some sort of trouble over escaped slaves, if my memory serves."

Andrea had no response, but picked up her glass and appeared to be forcing herself to drink slowly.

"Yes, though from what I understand, the slaves were very much abused by Olivia's husband." Wellington barely paused before launching into a new conversation. "So you are recovering from an accident on a horse?"

Hunter saw Andrea sigh, relieved at the change of course. "Silly of me, is it not?"

"Ain't nothing to riding but keeping a horse between yourself and the ground," Carter mumbled under his breath.

"Ah'm still a little fearful of the beasts, ah'm afraid," Andrea said, shivering in such a believable way, Hunter was almost convinced she was telling the truth.

The table fell silent for a moment, but then the chatter began anew. Hunter saw Andrea pretending to listen with only remote interest as Gus and Carter discussed a recent foray into enemy territory. Her manner conveyed she did not understand the military topics discussed and that she had no interest in learning more about them. Yet he knew she could probably repeat the conversation verbatim if she was ever compelled to do so.

"How was that now?" Wellington asked. "You caught seventy prisoners without firing a shot?"

Hunter demanded with his eyes that Gus desist in the telling of the story. Unfortunately for him, Gus was not looking his way.

"Well, it was pourin' down rain and dark as could be. Major Hunter went galloping into a Union outpost, yellin' at the top of his lungs for the men to mount up and follow him—he'd found Hunter's hideout in the pines." Gus paused for a moment to take a bite of food. "Course, he didn't lie. We *were* in the pines." He looked over at Andrea and winked. "Waitin' with open arms ya might say."

Wellington looked from Hunter to Gus and back again in utter amazement, then put his head back and laughed, his jowls flapping together like two large pancakes.

The rest of the room also exploded in laughter, all except Andrea, who stared into space, her gaze fixed and intent like she was replaying the scene in her head. Hunter almost interpreted it as a deferential gaze, one that appreciated the daring and boldness the feat required, even when attributed to one of her most loathed enemies.

"I only wish I'd have the same opportunity," Wellington said, rising unsteadily to his feet with wine glass in hand. "I'd like to propose a toast to Majah Hunter and all he's done for the Confederate cause. Here's to honah."

Andrea's hesitation at being forced to link her host's name with the word did not go unnoticed. "Do you have something against honah, my dear?" Wellington asked.

"Not at all, suh," she said with a forced smile. "I believe there is nothing worse than dishonah. However, I would prefer a toast to—" She looked at Hunter defiantly. "Freedom."

The table grew silent until Hunter cleared his throat. "She means, I believe, freedom of the Southern states from the oppressive powers of the North. If I may—" Hunter stood and gazed at Andrea, whose brows had narrowed, as they always did when forced to listen to views that were at variance with her own. "Here's to the Confederacy. May she always maintain her honor, her rights, and most of all, her *freedom*."

Hunter made an extra effort to wink and toast his proud houseguest, who sat with a straight back, looking acutely annoyed but nonetheless regal. He smiled, for he could tell she was cursing violently enough to educate all the sailors at sea—even if, for once, the words were not spoken aloud. She had apparently taken his warning before dinner to heart, a surprising turn of events considering she generally did not listen to him, let alone obey.

Chapter 30

"What a plague to thee is this mistrust!"
— Polyeucte by Pierre Corneille

Andrea entered the gray shadows of the kitchen, feeling her way through the darkness with the tip of her cane. This was her favorite time of day, the quiet, peaceful moments before dawn when all the world lay wrapped in peaceful slumber. Humming softly to herself, she began to rekindle the large fire for coffee, anxious to surprise Izzie and Mattie whom she knew would be along soon.

"Ah-ha, I see I've caught the fox in the henhouse."

Andrea jumped at the sound of the voice behind her and whirled around to face it.

"Sorry, did I startle you?" Hunter's tone made it obvious he was not sorry in the least.

"Major, you're ... back." Andrea tried to keep her voice from shaking. She felt uncomfortable beside his looming form, her mind flashing back to their last unpleasant encounter. The urge to run seized her, but when she looked into his laughing, gray eyes, she had a strange desire to stay.

"Just got here," he said holding up a large sack. "Mattie said we are getting low on coffee, and now I understand why."

Hunter's voice was rich and deep, making it difficult for Andrea to keep her hands, and her voice, from trembling. Usually he treated her with cold politeness when he noticed her, ignoring her altogether when opportunity allowed. His behavior today was unexpected and confusing.

"I admit I have an affection for coffee," Andrea said, trying to avoid his eyes.

"And you have no problem drinking *this* coffee?" He held up the sack marked U.S. PROPERTY.

Andrea realized it was captured coffee, spoils of war—plunder taken by his men on a raid. "I do not believe my comrades will suffer if I drink a few cups of their coffee."

Hunter grinned. "Good. Then I shall keep the Union provisions coming."

Andrea frowned at the way he twisted everything to suit him. "Major," she said, trying to squeeze past him on the way out the door, "you'll no doubt do as you please. But don't place blame on me for your thievery and propensity for plunder."

Although she attempted to make a hasty retreat, Hunter took a step backward, barring her path. "Thievery? My dear, this is war, and I'm regrettably forced to share the same quartermaster and supplies as the U.S. army."

"Well, I hope you used your manners and asked for it nicely." Andrea tried to breathe normally, though his closeness made that well nigh impossible.

"Armed men do not ask permission. But if you must know, it was furnished *gratis*."

"I see," Andrea quipped, deciding to play along. "And did you compel the quartermaster to offer it *gratis* while you were stealing horses with the U.S. brand?"

Hunter cocked his head to one side. "Yes. But those horses all had riders. And those riders all had guns. This, my dear, is legally acquired spoils of war, by right of discovery, capture, and possession." He paused for a moment and smiled. "And by the fact that when the Yanks saw my men, they did not care to fight for it."

Andrea was at a loss for something to say—a strange state of affairs that did not go unnoticed by Hunter. He laughed loudly, a deep, rolling laugh that almost made her smile. Instead, she shook her head in exasperation, sidestepped him, and headed toward his library. She wanted to get a book to read before he settled in there.

In a hurry, Andrea did not bother to light a candle, relying instead on the few rays of early morning light shining through the windows. Giving a hurried glance and little thought to the layout of the room, she failed to notice a chair out of place until it was too late. Trying to steady herself, her cane slipped on the floor. She tumbled onto the desk, knocking papers, documents, and books to the floor.

"Miss Evans, what are you doing?" The room filled with light when Hunter entered carrying a lamp.

Andrea regained her balance and bent down to pick up the articles she'd disturbed. "Major, I'm sorry. I-I couldn't see in the dark—"

"That's what the lamps are for," he said, not unkindly, bending to help pick up some of the scattered items.

Andrea barely heard him. She stood scanning a piece of paper she had picked up, which read in part:

I forward Andrew Sinclair, a young man arrested on suspicion of having communicated with the enemy. I have agreed that he shall be placed over the lines by the first flag of truce, which is in accordance with his wishes. No specific charges or information has been lodged against him.

Capt. Alexander H. Hunter

"I-I-I thought—" She looked back to the date at the top of the order. Her brow wrinkled in perplexity.

"Miss Evans, that is none of your business." Hunter ripped the paper from her hands, a deep breath escaping him when he saw what she had discovered. "I told you before," he said, continuing to tidy his desk. "I had nothing to do with your imprisonment. This order was changed without my knowledge."

Andrea stared at the paper, and then up at Hunter, blinking in bewilderment. She reached out and grasped the back of the chair for balance. "I didn't believe you."

"Yes, you've made that abundantly clear," Hunter replied, his eyes masked with apparent indifference. "Now if you are looking for a book, please select one and retire. I have work to do."

Andrea stared at the floor now, going over the events in her head. "But it's not ... I didn't have to sign ..."

"Miss Evans, I only brought up the issue of taking the oath the night of your capture to watch your reaction. And it was all that I thought it would be."

Andrea looked up at him, through him, her brow drawn in confusion.

"I understood that sending you to prison would do more harm than good, as your tendency to provoke would only cause immeasurable suffering to you and those around you," Hunter said. "It appears I was correct since you apparently decided, either through lack of judgment or lack of control, not to restrain your tongue, predictably at your own peril."

Andrea looked down at her feet. The room grew hush and Hunter turned back to his desk.

"You are wrong about that, Major," she replied at length. "My mistreatment occurred when I refused to talk, not because I did."

Hunter straightened back up. "Colonel Streight? The escape?" His voice grew serious, the lightness of his mood gone.

"The warden wished me to share what I knew of the plan." Andrea took a deep breath and looked away. "I declined."

"I see," Hunter said. "And you were aware of the consequences?"

Andrea chewed her cheek, but did not answer. She had a question of her own. "You had the authority to gain my release once you discovered my imprisonment?"

Hunter rested his hand on one of his pistols. "I carry the authority to do as I please."

Andrea's gaze moved from his face, down to the gun, and then to the window, trying to picture her liberation, to picture him in that hellhole demanding her release.

"You may recall, I gave my word to my brother to let no harm befall you. It's a promise I feel bound to abide and intend to keep." He looked her dead in the eye. "No matter how difficult you make it."

"But I told you that night ... I told you to forget the promise." Her voice was little more than a whisper.

"Miss Evans, I did not agree to do one thing while Daniel lived and expect to do another when he died."

Andrea looked down and played with the ring on her finger. "I fear I'm more trouble to you than I—"

"I don't want to hear about or discuss this topic ever again. Is that clear?"

Andrea looked up into his eyes and nodded. "Yes, sir. It's very clear."

And though she never again mentioned the topic, neither did she ever forget it.

Chapter 31

"Courage and comfort, all shall yet go well."
— King John, Shakespeare

Hunter entered his library a week later, his gaze focused on a newspaper in his hand. At the sound of a loud clap of thunder, he glanced toward the window and observed a silent figure standing with her face pressed close to the glass watching the storm rage without.

Walking quietly behind her, Hunter observed the trees outside bending and swaying as the storm hit with all its fury. "Amazing, the power of the wind."

Andrea jumped. "Oh. I beg your pardon. I didn't know you were here. I-I just came to get a book."

Along with surprise, Hunter thought he noted a hint of welcome in her eyes, making him glad he had interrupted her musings. "I can come back later," she said.

170

A face that usually displayed open hostility, today, appeared soft and reti-
cent. Hunter hoped it was a sign that her irritable behavior was a result of the
pain she had endured, not her true character. "No need." Hunter nodded his
head toward the bookshelf. "Help yourself."

"It's very kind of you to allow me this indulgence."

Hunter smiled to himself. The servants must have forewarned her that
this room was his refuge. He generally tolerated no interruptions when present within its walls. Remaining silent, he studied the changes in his houseguest
and tried to guess their cause. She appeared to be in tolerably good spirits
today—more shy and reserved than angry and rebellious. And she spoke with
an air of well-bred elegance, making it difficult to conceive this was the same
person equally capable of spewing insults when riled.

Andrea ran her hand along the volumes as she read the titles. She had color
in her cheeks again, Hunter noted, and a little more meat on her bones. Tall
for a girl of her age, yet not overly so, she had the type of figure that gave the
appearance of delicacy. And though dressed in a plain cotton gown of a rather
drab hue, she looked somehow elegant and stylish.

Hunter turned to walk back to his desk, but failed to conceal a heavy limp.

"You are injured?" Andrea turned around at the sound of his unsteady
tread.

Hunter eased himself down onto his desk. "I ... had a horse fall on my
leg," he said, making it clear it was nothing he cared to discuss. "Just a little
sore."

Andrea swallowed hard, obviously understanding he had a horse shot out
from under him. "Dixie?" Her voice was barely above a whisper.

"No," Hunter cocked his head, surprised she knew the names of his
mounts. "Fleet."

Andrea nodded in recognition. "Nice horse."

"Yes, he was."

Andrea gazed into his eyes for just a moment with a look of sympathetic
understanding. Then she turned back to the bookshelf.

"You're finding our Southern hospitality a little more agreeable now, I
hope," Hunter said, making an effort to change the subject.

"I've been quite comfortable, thank you."

"And *your* leg?" Hunter cocked his head as he gazed at her.

"It's getting stronger each day."

The smile on Andrea's face appeared to be forced, and the way she leaned
on the cane, he saw she placed very little weight on the limb. She was gaining
steadily, but by no means rapidly.

"Well, I hope you're making yourself at home. Don't be bashful about asking for anything."

"You think me timid, sir?"

Hunter's lips turned upward. "Miss Evans, I believe you to be about as timid as a cornered grizzly bear protecting a week-old cub."

She smiled but did not respond.

Hunter rustled some papers around on his desk and then cleared his throat. "Well, I hope you don't find it overly difficult ... adjusting to our Southern traditions and culture here—"

Andrea gazed at him curiously. "I am familiar with the customs of Southern aristocracy, I assure you."

"Oh yes, I remember." Hunter paused while pretending the papers he held contained something of interest. "You mentioned once you were born in ... South Carolina, I believe it was?"

He pretended to be unsure, though the fact stuck in his mind as soundly as a boot lodges in Virginia mud during the month of March. Andrea remained silent, and he looked up to make sure she had heard.

"Your memory serves you correctly," she said in an unemotional voice.

"And ... six hundred slaves, I believe you mentioned." He put the papers down and walked toward her with one hand on his chin. "Must have been quite an estate. Certainly Hawthorne pales in comparison to that which you are accustomed."

Andrea sighed, her breath sounding like it was being forced out by a great weight placed upon her shoulders. "Indeed, Hawthorne has none of the characteristics to which I am accustomed, Major Hunter," she said, solemnly, looking into his eyes. "I hope you take great satisfaction in that fact."

She returned her attention to the bookshelf, and Hunter could see the conversation had come to an end. He walked up behind her and attempted another change of subject. "By the way ... I may have forgotten to mention, I've received word about your friend, Colonel Jordan."

Andrea jolted and faced him. In her eyes he saw deep concern bordering on panic. He recalled the day she had approached him with the newspaper article listing Colonel Jonathan Jordan as severely wounded. She had literally trembled with alarm, causing him to wonder what type of relationship she had with the officer.

"He's expected to make a complete recovery and has been promoted to brigadier."

Andrea took a step forward and put her hand on his arm. "Oh thank you, Major! Catherine must be so relieved. I was so worried for her."

"Catherine?"

"Yes." Andrea took a step back, her cheeks turning red at her emotional display. "His wife. My cousin, Catherine."

"Ah, *that* Catherine. Then I'm happy for her too."

Andrea turned back to the row of books. "I see you enjoy Shakespeare," she said, fingering through the volumes. "What might be your favorite?"

When Hunter did not answer at first, she looked around to question his silence.

"I fear you won't believe me. Or you will think me a hopeless romantic," he said.

Andrea's eyes carried a hint of amusement when she met his gaze. "If you're thinking to tell me, *Romeo and Juliet* ... No, I wouldn't believe that."

"And why not? You do not believe me capable of admiring selfless devotion?"

"I would have to admit it seems out of character." Andrea looked him up and down boldly. "From what I know of your reputation."

"Come now. You wouldn't judge someone based on their reputation."

Andrea shrugged and turned back to the bookshelf.

"I wouldn't judge you on yours."

"I have no reputation to speak of," she said, whirling around to face him.

Hunter laughed at her reaction. "Now that depends. Perhaps Miss Evans does not. But Sinclair does, I assure you."

"Oh?" Andrea looked surprised and uncomfortable.

"Well, perhaps not by name. But my captain often referred to you as the little kid with the big backbone."

Andrea half-smiled at his words as if recalling a distant memory, but the smile was pensive and heart wrenching to him, so infinitely touching and reflective did it appear. She returned her gaze to the books. "How well might you know it?"

"Know what?"

"*Romeo and Juliet.* You said it was your favorite."

"Test me," he said.

"*My only love sprung from my only hate,*" she began.

Hunter smiled and picked up the passage instantly. "*Too early seen unknown and known too late ...*"

"*Prodigious birth of love it is to me . . .*" she continued.

"*That I must love a loathed enemy,*" he finished the verse.

"So you enjoy Shakespeare as well," Hunter said after a moment of silence. "You appear to be well educated, Miss Evans. Were you tutored at home or abroad?"

Andrea shrugged and dodged the question. "I enjoy reading."

"Come now, Miss Evans. You must admit your level of female cultivation is entirely unusual."

"Anything beyond the knowledge of the proper performance of domestic duties is unusual within the Southern household, is it not?"

Hunter tried to recover his blunder. "Be that as it may, a solid education should be considered among one's most valuable possessions. And you seem to possess an abundance of it."

Andrea looked back at him now with furrowed brow. "I am of the belief that loyalty and personal honor should be more highly revered."

"Indeed," Hunter said, crossing his arms. "Few virtues are more courted. I suppose that goes without saying."

"Yes, of course, it goes without saying." Andrea gazed thoughtfully at the Confederate banner in the corner of the room. "It is honor for which you fight, is it not?"

"Yes, the honor of Virginia. The honor of the Confederacy."

Andrea gazed up at him. "The honor of your own principles and convictions."

"Yes, it's as priceless a commodity as the blood spilled to defend it."

Andrea had a distant look in her eye when she spoke again, and her tone seemed somewhat colder. "Then if you can accept the premise that a woman can possess principles and convictions, surely you can understand that my honor is more precious to me than my education."

Hunter was about to ask why every conversation seemed to place them on opposite shores, when a knock at the door interrupted his thoughts.

"Rain's stopped, Massa," Mattie announced. "And the wagon's ready."

Hunter turned at Andrea. "I'm going to check some fence in the upper fields. Care to join me?"

Andrea's eyes opened wide, and he thought for a moment she might jump up and down with excitement. Instead, she fell back on the education granted her and responded quite calmly.

"If you please, a little ride outdoors would not be unwelcome."

Chapter 32

"There would I find my settled rest, while others go and come;
No more a stranger or a guest, but like a child … home."
– Psalms 23:6

Andrea sat wide-eyed as the wagon rolled down the lane. Turning around in her seat, she took in the view of the palatial estate for the first time from a distance and gazed upon an enchanted world of beauty and charm.

The mansion itself rested on a crown of rising ground wreathed by elaborate gardens and trees. Along the back, hedges of boxwood bushes fell in a series of terraces toward a large lake that swarmed with geese and swans.

To the north, a grove of mighty oaks bordered the home, their huge spreading branches shadowing a vast, velvet lawn that seemed never ending. Andrea's gaze drifted toward the barn, and then to the rolling land beyond, where horses stood knee-deep in clover.

Even the birds seemed eager to join in on the festive occasion, providing a riotous concert along the wagon's path. Andrea looked from right to left, taking in the sight of magnificent dogwoods already robed in white and wildflowers saluting spring in rich profusion all around her. Along the fringes of the drive, and especially along the stream they approached, more colorful blooms flourished. Andrea clenched her hands together in restrained delight when the wagon rolled across the stone, triple-arched bridge. She glanced behind her once more at the imposing vista behind her. Never had she seen such a mingling of beauty and elegance.

"We might have to move some horses up there," Hunter said, pointing to the next ridge and interrupting her thoughts. "I want to make sure the fence is in good shape."

The wagon suddenly veered off the road, and Andrea held onto the seat with all her strength to avoid grabbing the driver. Hunter did not seem to notice her struggle. His gaze was intent on the fence now as they trotted beneath a tracery of bud-laden oak boughs. It did not take long for him to find something amiss, and he pulled the wagon to a halt.

Andrea watched him drag a large tree limb off the fence and begin to restack the rocks. "I wish I could be of some help."

"That's quite all right," he said turning around, breathing heavily. "Just enjoy the view."

Andrea lowered her eyes, feeling her cheeks grow warm at the view before her now. The cotton shirt Hunter wore stuck to his form, revealing the power of his broad shoulders and the strength of every swelling muscle. Glistening with sweat, his bulging forearms looked like they could bend steel. Both frightened and fascinated, Andrea quickly turned away to the safer vista in the opposite direction. The effect of the breeze as it danced with the sunlight through the leaves above soon captured her attention.

"That should do it." Hunter wiped his hands on his trousers and jumped into the wagon. "There's a creek up a little ways. I think I'd better wash off."

Andrea nodded, keeping her eyes averted. She dared not look at him. It confused her that a mere glance from those gray eyes suddenly caused her heart to pound and her cheeks to blush.

But Andrea forgot her apprehension when the wagon broke out of the forest that sheltered them. Not even the surroundings through which they had just passed could compete with the majestic splendor spread before her. A sparkling creek, the same, she surmised, that separated Hawthorne from the rest of the world, trickled through a meadow where nature had spread a blanket of floral glory. Here and there, large oak and birch trees seemed to stand guard to any unnatural intrusion, and above it all, the sun poured out bountiful rays that turned everything they touched to golden splendor. The scene surely rivaled Eden in its indescribable beauty.

"Are you going to get down?" Hunter sounded impatient, but the pleased smile he wore showed his satisfaction with her reaction.

Andrea smiled and stood, but continued to cast her gaze across the teeming hills in utter amazement. Sighing, Hunter reached up and grabbed her around the waist, lifting her out of the conveyance.

"This is part of Hawthorne?" she asked, clasping his arm for support.

He nodded. "One of my favorite places."

Andrea sat on a large rock, touching and smelling the flowers that surrounded her while Hunter washed his face and splashed water over his head. When he finished, he flung himself lazily upon the bank. "The water's cold and clean if you want some."

Andrea removed her uncomfortable shoes and stockings and hopped over to the side of the stream. "Ah, this is truly heaven." She lifted her skirts to her knees as she stood near the bank, letting the mud rise between her toes.

"Indeed," Hunter answered, looking up from her ankles to meet her gaze. "Actually it is the next best thing—it's Virginia."

Andrea grinned at his intended jibe and hopped over to the crevice of a fallen tree. Sitting down and leaning back, she stared at the sky, watching a hawk circle above them.

"Daniel and I used to come here to fish, and always ended up doing just what you're doing."

Andrea raised her eyes and studied him, trying to form the image of a daydreaming youth staring at the sky. She discarded the attempt almost immediately, but wondered how there could be a man with such dual and different natures—leading his men against inconceivable odds one day, discussing his childhood or quoting Shakespeare the next. What kind of person, she asked herself, could be occupied in the deliberate destruction of one's country, while lounging before her like a courteous and considerate gentleman?

"You ready to go?" Hunter stood abruptly and spit out the blade of grass he'd been chewing. "There's one more stop I want to make before we head back. It's getting late."

Andrea found herself talking quite freely once the wagon began rolling, as she tried to identify the different varieties of birds and butterflies that flitted across their path. But when they crested another hill, she grew instantly silent.

Directly in front of them hung the sun in an outrageous flaming sky of violent red and orange. This was apparently what Hunter had been in a hurry to show her—and his timing was perfect.

"It appears close enough to touch," Andrea whispered.

When the horses stopped, she departed the wagon, and limped to the very crown of the hill. Leaning on her cane, she stared mesmerized at the fiery eye in the sky.

"We better get a move on," Hunter said after a few minutes of awed silence. "It'll be dark soon."

Andrea discovered that Hunter was right about the darkness. Within minutes the view changed from sun and sky to moon and stars. Fireflies danced in the meadows on each side, adding to the light display.

"Are we close to *home?*" she asked when the shades of night drew completely around them.

Hunter tightened his grip on the reins as if surprised to hear the word on her lips. Before she could analyze his response, the horses picked up their pace and she had her answer. Hunter steered the careening wagon to the back of the house, and pulled the horses to a sudden and abrupt halt, causing Andrea to grab his arm to keep from being thrown.

She looked up, bubbling over with amusement that he'd allowed the horses to dash at such a pace. But her smile froze when she met the look in the steel-gray eyes staring down at her.

"Truce?" Hunter's voice was barely audible, though his face was only inches from hers.

A long, breathless moment with no words ensued.

"Massa?"

They both jumped.

"Sorry, Massa," Zach said, "but Miz Victoria is waitin' for you in de house."

Hunter cursed under his breath and hopped out of the wagon like it was on fire. "How long has she been here?" His voice was full of impatience as he took the steps three at a time without a backward glance at Andrea.

ℋ ℋ ℋ

Hunter was not in a hurry to see Victoria, but he knew better than to keep her waiting. He followed the heavy scent of perfume to the parlor in the front of the house, where he found her powdering her face.

"Oh, Alex!" She rushed over to him. "I'm so glad you're here at last. Your insolent servants wouldn't tell me where you were or when you'd return." Victoria sniffled and laid her head on his chest. "You just wouldn't believe what this awful war is doing to Richmond. I thought perhaps Cassie and I could stay with you for a while, until things settle down there." She looked up with a flutter of eyelashes.

Hunter glanced over at the young maid standing apprehensively in the corner. "Of course, Victoria," he heard himself saying, though every nerve in his body told him it was a mistake. "I'll have the guest room made up for you."

When he glanced up through the open door, he saw Andrea in the hall making slow, painful progress toward the stairs. Her hair ran riot from the swift pace they'd taken, but when he cleared his throat to make introductions, she turned with the mien and beauty of a queen.

"Miss Hamilton, I would like you to meet my . . . other houseguest, Andrea Evans. She's staying here while she ... recuperates from an injury. Miss Evans, Miss Hamilton."

Silence hung in the elegant home, interrupted only by a palpable sensation of instant dislike on both sides of the parties being introduced. Victoria boldly examined Andrea from head to toe with a slow, unbelieving swoop of the eyes. "How very lovely to meet you," she said, making it clear by her tone that it was not. Then she grabbed Hunter's arm. "I'm sure Alex has told you all about us." She looked at him with a knowing and intimate smile, then shifted her gaze to Andrea.

Andrea looked blankly at Hunter. "I fear he has not had the time. But if you'll pardon me, I'll retire and allow you to get ... reacquainted." Nodding toward each but looking at neither, she turned and began her slow and tedious ascent up the stairs.

Victoria fell back in Alex's arms again. "Oh, it's so-o-o good to see you're all right. I was afraid you'd be out fighting. We have so much catching up to do."

"Actually, Victoria, I'm afraid you've come at a bad time. I'll be leaving in the morning."

"Oh, no, Alex. You simply can't leave me here alone with that ... that stranger," she whined. "Please stay."

Victoria cried and held onto him as if he intended to depart for many years and to a distant country, but Alex eased her away. "I'm sorry the war doesn't run according to your schedule, Victoria."

"But is this an important mission? Can't it be put off for one day?"

Hunter looked at her coldly. "They're all important, Victoria. And no I cannot."

"Oh, have you no other thought but the service of your country?" she moaned, with her face in her hands. Looking out between two fingers and apparently seeing her pouting had no effect on him, Victoria raised her head and smiled.

"Well, we have tonight. We can do some catching up tonight." She wore an open invitation on her face as she took one of his hands in both of hers and pressed it against her cheek.

Chapter 33

"When woman once to evil turns,
All hell within her bosom burns."
— English poet

A bright sun spurted its rays through a thin shaft of clouds as Hunter cantered across the bridge to Hawthorne. The warmth of the beams felt good on his back, like tender hands after a hard day's work. Considering the violent storms he'd ridden through over the past week, the sun felt even more welcoming.

But Hunter's thoughts were not on the sunbeams. He mused over the morning he'd left Hawthorne and reflected on the two houseguests he'd left behind.

"Welcome home, Massa." Zach grabbed Hunter's bridle rein and waited for him to dismount.

"Thanks, Zach," he said wearily, dismounting and untying a saddlebag. "It's good to be back."

Hunter didn't hear the front door open, but he couldn't miss the unearthly squeal that followed. "Oh, Alex, you're ho-o-me!" He barely had time to brace himself for the assault that followed. Victoria ran down the steps , none too ladylike, and threw herself into his arms. "Oh, I missed you so!"

"A man could get used to such a greeting, I suppose," Hunter said, his tone sounding more annoyed than pleased.

"Oh, darling," Victoria whimpered, "it has been perfectly dreadful here without you. Why don't you go change into some fresh clothes and then we can dine together, and then—"

Hunter pried her arms away from his neck and turned back to his saddle. "I'm afraid that is impossible, Victoria." He turned his attention back to Zach. "See that he's rubbed down and fed well. He covered a lot of ground this week."

Yes, suh. But, uh Massa … I has something to tell you."

Hunter held up his hand. "Not now, Zach. I'll come down to the barn later. I'm sure it can wait."

"Yes, suh," the slave answered dejectedly, leading the horse away. But he continued looking over his shoulder, indicating that perhaps it could not.

"Victoria," Hunter said, springing lightly up the steps. "Will you kindly find Mattie and tell her to draw a bath?"

"Well, I can try, I suppose," Victoria said from behind him, obviously perturbed at being put off so abruptly. "Likely she is still waiting on your *other* houseguest hand and foot. Why, that girl stays abed all day. One would think she invented sleep by the way she loves to practice it."

Hunter half-laughed at the absurdity of the statement, but then stopped just outside the door and looked at her closely. "Miss Evans? In bed at this hour? Surely you jest."

"Laugh all you like," Victoria snapped. "She closets herself away like a queen. And your servants seem to feel it necessary to treat her as such."

Hunter just shook his head as he made his way toward his library. He knew Victoria well enough to know that Andrea was likely trying to stay out of her way. But then again, that Miss Evans would attempt to avoid a fight did seem a little peculiar.

"You condescendin' to take a bath, Massa?" Mattie asked from behind him.

"Yes," he said wearily, putting his saddlebag on his desk. "Right away."

He looked to the open door when he heard Victoria's squealing voice upstairs. "Mattie! Mattie! Show yourself this instant!"

"Why she yelling that?" Mattie asked irritably. "She gonna wake up—" She stopped herself and looked at Hunter. "The dead."

Hunter sat down at his desk and put his head in his hands when Mattie departed. Hawthorne was once a place where he retired to escape the turmoil of war. Now he was not sure which was more chaotic—his home or the battlefield. To help answer the query, the door flew open and a flurry of skirts bustled in. "I found your insolent servant and she's heating your water," Victoria reported.

ℋ ℋ ℋ

After a bath and a few hours uninterrupted sleep—his first of both in days—Hunter crept back down the stairs toward his library, hoping to avoid Victoria. He therefore spoke in hushed tones to Mattie when he encountered her on the staircase carrying an armful of wood. "You're building a fire on a beautiful evening like this?"

"Miz Andrea has a chill," Mattie said hesitantly, "from dat lazy ole wind the storm brought."

"*Lazy* wind?" Hunter stopped and looked at her.

"Yezzah," she said, continuing up the stairs as if she did not have time to stop. "Miz Andrea say it too lazy to go around, so it go drekly through."

Hunter watched the woman disappear and shook his head. His own household was becoming more remote and mysterious to him by the minute. Where was Miss Evans anyway?

The remorse at having left so suddenly had weighed constantly on his mind during his absence. He hoped to have a word with her in private before he departed again. Did she regret his leaving? Or did anger and resentment keep her locked in her room? He sighed heavily. He did not have the time or the inclination to ponder the inner workings of a woman's mind—especially one as erratic and unpredictable as Andrea Evans'.

Hunter continued to his library to clear away some mounting paperwork. He was astonished when he heard the clock in the hall strike midnight some fleeting hours later—and even more surprised when the chimes were followed by a hesitant knock on the door. "Yes, enter," he said somewhat sternly due to the lateness of the hour.

"Massa?"

Hunter glanced up to see who it was, and then looked back at his work. "Yes, Izzie, what is it?" He could tell she was nervous. Yet she always appeared like that to him.

"Massa, I, umm ... prominist I wudn't tell." Izzie's voice faded as she played with the folds of her dress.

Hunter looked up again and his heart unexpectedly quickened. "Tell me what?"

She cleared her throat. "U-m-m ... Well ya-see ... it be that ... I mean ... Miz Andrea—"

"What about Miz Andrea?" Hunter stood and came around the desk to stand in front of her, apparently intimidating her even more.

Izzie cleared her throat again. "I can't prezactly say ... since I prominist I's wudn't tell."

No longer waiting for her to answer, Hunter ran up the stairs and pushed

181

open Andrea's chamber door, startling Mattie who leaned over the bed, and Zach, who stood at the footboard with his hat in his hand.

As for the form on the bed, she gave no response to his sudden entrance. Beads of perspiration on her forehead showed she had a fever, and the raspy sound of her breathing indicated she had been ill for quite some time.

"What have you done?" Hunter placed the back of his hand against her clammy, hot cheek. Her damp hair lay plastered to her skull.

Izzie stood at the door wringing her hands. "She tol' us not to tell anyone. She say she all right."

"How long has she been like this?" Hunter looked up at the servants who all stared at the floor. "Did everybody in this household know of this but me?"

"She tol' us not to tell," Izzie said again under her breath.

Hunter turned his attention back to the bed. "Miss Evans, can you hear me?"

Andrea's eyes were open, but they were glassy and staring. Her face showed deep lines of exhaustion as she gazed fixedly up at him. "The foal," she said weakly, trying to sit up. "Is ... all right?"

"The foal?" Hunter looked up with questioning eyes to Zach.

"I try to tell you," Zach said. "Dat mare Lightning done go into labor during that storm the utter night. You know how she hate storms. And the baby be breach. And Miz Andrea, she come down to help, and it was pawhing down rain. I din't mean for it to happen, Massa."

Hunter let out his breath in helpless exasperation. Lightning was one of his best mares. He knew if Andrea had set her mind on saving the foal, no one alive could stop her.

"I understand, Zach. Go fetch Doc at the Talberts." Hunter looked at Andrea and then back at the servant worriedly. "And tell him to hurry."

Leaning over the bed again, Hunter put his hand on her burning forehead while she mumbled in her sleep. A racking cough, sounding like it might split her open, interrupted her meanderings. She faded into semi-consciousness then, though her lips still moved as if in conversation.

Hunter turned and left the room. He didn't like the way his legs felt weak, or the force with which his heart banged in his chest ... or his thoughts. She'd already survived one brush with death—but this time she knew what she was coming back to. And it did not take a prophet to predict that she may not think it worth the effort.

Chapter 34

"Blessed is the silent horse who bonds himself
to us in silence and does our will so freely."
— Anonymous

Hunter paced in his library, once again awaiting the doctor's report. "Pneumonia?" he asked when the door opened. "In the name of all that is holy, how could you allow her to go out in the middle of a storm?" Hobbs sat down and dabbed his brow with a handkerchief. "For heaven's sake, Major, in her weakened condition."

"I wasn't here. She was trying to save a foal of mine. Actually, she *did* save a foal of—" Hunter followed the doctor to the door. "But what do you think about her chances?"

"I'm not sure." Hobbs shook his head. "She surprised us all before. But I'm afraid she needs something I can't give her this time."

"What's that?"

"The will to live," he said bluntly, before heading out the door.

Hunter closed his eyes. So Hobbs sensed it too, that vague, indescribable feeling that she no longer had the will to fight. Closing the door, Hunter returned once again to her chamber.

"Tell Papa . . . all my fault," she mumbled while holding onto Mattie's arm. When the servant did not answer, Andrea opened her eyes. Spotting Hunter, she stared at him in a feverish daze. "Papa!" She reached out and grabbed his shirtsleeve. "It's my fault ... please ... don't hurt them!"

"It's all right." Hunter's words seemed to relax her. She released her grip and closed her eyes, but her stillness did not last long. In a moment, she appeared wide awake. She continued to talk and ramble incoherently, her gaze sometimes vacant, at other times roaming frantically around the room as if seeking someone she wanted to find, or searching for someone before they found her.

When Mattie returned with fresh, cold water to sponge Andrea's forehead, Hunter retired to the balcony hoping to clear his mind of the images.

"What are you doing?" Andrea's voice broke the silence. It sounded cold and threatening.

Hunter turned to see her holding firmly onto Mattie's wrist. The servant stood frozen, her eyes big and white with terror at the vengeful look on Andrea's face. Hunter hurried to the bed and pried her fingers from Mattie's wrist. "She's trying to help."

Andrea looked up at him, her eyes slanted and disbelieving. "Papa sent you."

"No. You're safe here."

"You speak not the truth," she said, turning her head away. "I am safe no-where."

How many times had this same haunted, troubled look appeared in the depths of Andrea's eyes? Now he knew some of the history it masked. Hunter nodded at Mattie to resume her place by the bed and turned to go. He feared leaving her now, but he could not stay. He would be departing again within the hour.

When he stopped one last time to check her condition, she had apparently awakened from her dream. But she stared vacantly at the ceiling as if surrendering to the illness or contemplating the alternative.

ℋ ℋ ℋ

Constantly on the move for six days, Hunter had received no word about Andrea's condition. Fearing what he would find when he finally returned to Hawthorne, he was relieved to see her sitting up in bed, propped against a pillow. Izzie sat by her side, attempting to place a spoonful of broth in her mouth.

"You gotta eat." Izzie sat back in the chair, exasperated. "Mama said mebe you'd eat for me. Jus a little?"

"Not hungry," Andrea answered weakly, as if uttering those two words was more than she could physically endure.

"If you'll excuse us a moment, Izzie." Hunter walked to the bedside, removing his hat.

The door closed behind Izzie, but the room remained silent for a few long minutes. Andrea's head remained turned toward the wall, though her stolid eyes were open and staring.

"Glad to see you're feeling better. I guess Zach told you that filly is a real handful." Hunter took a deep breath when he received no response. Accustomed to her sharp tongue and keen wit, her silence disconcerted him. The image of her glowing, vivacious face on the day of their wagon ride arose unbidden in his mind.

Hunter sat down beside the bed, and picked up the bowl of broth. "You must eat, you know. You don't want to die on enemy soil do you?"

"It matters not to me where I die," Andrea said, staring at the ceiling.

The severe indifference of her expression caused Hunter's heart to pick up its pace. "Don't talk like that," he said, slamming the bowl down and standing.

"I'm not afraid of dying." Andrea's gaze shifted to him with a look so cold and detached that it sent a shiver down his spine.

"Then it must be living you fear."

Andrea looked away quickly. "I do not fear it," she said emphatically, as if

184

she'd given it much thought. "Nor do I care to endure it."

"Come now. You've had a setback." Hunter sat down beside her again. "Nothing that can't be overcome."

"All is lost." She blinked rapidly, as if that admission of defeat was difficult for her.

Hunter knew she alluded to the strength in her legs. Once again she would have to start over, one step at a time, to rebuild the muscles. The task did seem daunting, even to him. Her physical endurance and vigor before her stay in prison must have been incredible. To jump a four-foot stonewall bareback would have taken nothing less than legs of steel.

"I've been here four months and still cannot walk." Her voice was weak, but Hunter detected a small spark of anger in her eyes now. "I may well spend the rest of the war in this house."

"Come now. Would that be so bad?"

Andrea turned her head and focused on Hunter with such a contemptuous look that he worked hard to suppress a grin. He saw within her eyes an agitated flicker that mimicked a candle just catching flame.

"Get out."

Hunter smiled and picked up the bowl. "Not until you eat a few bites."

"You are trying to bribe me? If I eat, you will leave?"

"That's right," he said, his spoon ready, waiting for her to open her mouth.

"And if I do not?"

Hunter sat back in the chair and threw his long legs in front of him, getting comfortable in anticipation of a long wait. "You will learn the power of my patience—one of the few traits I possess that is superior to yours."

"What devil art thou, that dost torment me thus?" Andrea said in a tone of morose rebellion, her defiant eyes still shadowed with gloom.

Hunter ignored the look and instead laughed at her Shakespearian quote. "Come now, Miss Evans. I'm not trying to torment you. I'm trying to help you."

Andrea opened her mouth, and he quickly filled it with a spoonful of the broth. "I can feed myself," she said, her eyelids obviously getting heavy.

"One more," Hunter said. "Then I'll let you rest. I'm leaving again in the morning, and I want to see make sure you've eaten."

Andrea complied, but Hunter knew it was only because she was too weary to argue. She swallowed, and, half to his disappointment and half to his relief, fell asleep.

H H H

With a sense of impatience, Hunter finally returned to Hawthorne after three days. He probed Mattie with an inquisitive eye when she met him at the door.

"She gettin' her sass back," Mattie said, before he had time to ask a question. "That tongue got more sauce than a beehive got honey."

The sound of shouting from the direction of Andrea's bedchamber interrupted the conversation. Charging up the stairs, he noticed from a glance over his shoulder that Mattie hurried away in the opposite direction.

He entered the room to find Andrea waving her cane in the air like a mighty sword. "Pray don't feign more courage than you possess, Miss Hamilton. If you take another step, your shoulders will be lonesome for your head!"

When Victoria saw Hunter standing in the doorway she ran into his arms, sobbing. "Alex, she's trying to kill me. I only came to see how she was feeling."

"Miss Evans, cease this instant! What is the meaning of this?"

Andrea collapsed back against the pillows and closed her eyes in apparent acknowledgment that she had been baited and bested by Victoria. During her silence, Hunter ushered Victoria from the room and then conversed in a low voice on the other side of the door. When he re-entered, he stared at Andrea before speaking. "Do you mind explaining what was going on here?" Her pale and wane appearance worried him, yet the familiar go-to-hell look she shot in his direction encouraged him that health was returning.

"Ask your friend, the high priestess of pomposity," Andrea said with a flip of her head toward the wall.

Ah, her vocabulary is back too. Another good sign.

"I'm asking *you*." Hunter tried to suppress a grin. "But I'm profoundly pleased to see your pleasant disposition has returned."

Andrea glared at him, then closed her eyes. "Why should I bother explaining anything to *you*, the one who sent your misery-making mistress of malice to torment me while I lie helpless?"

"You? Helpless?" Hunter laughed. "Hell will undoubtedly freeze to the core before that day comes." He walked over to the bed. "I'm not a doctor, Miss Evans. But were I to guess, I'd say your only ailment now is a rampant infection of self-pity."

Andrea snorted, looking at him with unfriendly eyes. "Say what you will, Major. It is of no consequence to me."

Hunter's gaze fell upon the crutches leaning idly by the door. He had hoped by now the fever of unrest would have overtaken her illness and she would be attempting to climb the walls. Instead, she appeared to have recovered in health, but not in spirit.

"Are your spurs so cold you can no longer dig me with them?" Hunter tried to make a joke. "I fear I've missed our little sparring matches."

His attempt to provoke a response failed, but the sound of a carriage caused her to turn toward the balcony door. "That would be Victoria leaving for a few days to visit friends. Perhaps in her absence you'd like to come down and sit on the front porch."

Acting on instinct, he did not give her time to refuse. He scooped her up in his arms, carried her down the stairs to the porch, and deposited her in a chair splashed with sunlight. "I thought you might like to see Storm Dancer, the filly you saved."

He nodded toward the paddock where the foal grazed contentedly by its mother. Folding his body into the chair next to hers, he looked over at Andrea. "Comfortable?"

She did not speak, but the smile she flashed him had the same effect as an enthusiastic hug of gratitude.

At the sound of banging and shouts coming from the direction of the barn, both Hunter and Andrea looked up. Hunter stood and walked to the edge of the porch as one of the servants ran up.

"Dat black hoss, Massa. He kickin' down the stall."

"Did Zach try turning him out with the other horses?"

"Yes, Massa. He done attacked the other hosses."

"Excuse me a moment," Hunter said to Andrea, before he hopped off the porch and strode toward the barn. "Move those two horses," he yelled to one of the servants. "I'll turn him out up here where he has no one to pick on."

As Hunter led the horse out of the barn toward the paddock by the house, it reared and whinnied at every step, straining his strength and temper. The animal looked emaciated and was so covered with dust and dirt that it appeared more brown than black. Its mane was one large knot of hair, its face scarred and bleeding.

After being dragged a few steps by the rearing horse, Hunter saw for the first time amid the flurry of hooves that Andrea leaned heavily on the porch rail, and was trying to make it down the steps. "Miss Evans, what are you doing?"

"Justus?" Her voice sounded weak and shaky.

The horse snorted and reared high in the air, lashing out with its front legs and pulling the rope out of Hunter's hand. Trotting a few steps toward Andrea, it stopped, put its head down, and snorted again, like a bull getting ready to charge. Andrea took another step down, still holding onto the railing, her legs visibly shaking.

"Miss Evans, don't," Hunter warned in a low voice, afraid the stallion was going to charge her. He saw Zach and another servant coming up to encircle the animal, but he feared they would only add to its terror.

Andrea put out her hand. "Here, boy." The horse took another step toward her, breathing heavily, its eyes wild with terror.

Hunter held his breath, afraid of what might happen next. The horse was only steps from her now. It looked unsure of itself, like it may bolt or charge.

"Miss Evans, get back!" Clearly it was hard for her to remain upright. Even though she still leaned on the railing, her entire body quivered from the effort.

The horse took another cautious step and Hunter froze when Andrea let go of the railing and fell into its shoulder, burying her head in his neck. "Justus. Oh, Justus." The horse raised and lowered its head, nickering all the while as if holding a private conversation with his mistress.

Hunter let out his breath, both from relief and exasperation. Perspiration dampened his forehead, and his heart pounded as if he'd been in hand-to-hand combat. "This beast yours?"

Andrea nodded with her head still buried against the horse. "Thank you."

Hunter realized she was under the impression he'd deliberately brought the horse to her. Seeing her standing once again, he took no pains to remove the notion.

"Ever think of teaching him some manners?" Hunter reached for the rope.

"He doesn't like men," Andrea responded in his defense.

"I can't imagine where he inherited *that* trait," Hunter said dryly, giving the animal a tentative pat on the shoulder. The beast had settled down now, seemed almost docile.

"I'm going to turn him out right here." Hunter nodded toward the paddock. "You'll be able to keep your eye on him."

Andrea nodded, but could not let go of her pet's neck. Hunter put one arm around her waist and gently sat her on the porch step. "Rest here a minute. I'll be right back."

The horse took another step forward and nuzzled Andrea, then he obediently followed Hunter to the paddock.

"Where? How?" Andrea asked when he returned.

"We'll talk later." Hunter scooped her up again. "You need some rest first."

Andrea was asleep in his arms before he even reached her bedchamber.

As far as Hunter was concerned, the horse was precisely what she needed to revive her shattered spirit. Although he could take no credit for his arrival, he was thankful for whatever circumstances had occurred to place her beloved mount at Hawthorne. It was the closest thing to Divine intervention he'd ever had occasion to witness.

Chapter 35

*"In great contests, each party claims to act in accordance with
the will of God. Both may be, and one must be, wrong.
God cannot be for and against the same thing at the same time."*
— Abraham Lincoln

Dark clouds, their bellies swollen with rain, had devoured the last remnants of a beautiful sunset when Major Hunter galloped up the drive to Hawthorne.

"Look like you outrunned the storm, Massa." Zach took the reins and led the prancing horse toward the barn.

By the time Hunter dashed up the steps, the first great drops began to fall, followed closely by a deafening assault as the full tempest hit. Rain lashed the windows, and the wind caused bushes and tree limbs to writhe and shake. He entered the house, grateful to have missed a soaking, and headed toward his library. Hearing the rapid footfalls of Victoria, he pressed himself against the wall in the shadowy hallway and held his breath.

"Mattie! Mattie! You impertinent slave," Victoria muttered, then louder, "Hello? Anyone? Is Alex home? Did I hear his horse coming up the lane?"

Not stopping to light a lamp, Hunter continued through the darkened corridors and escaped out the back. Just as he stepped out on the porch, a brilliant flash of lightning created a silhouette of a lone figure already there. Andrea glanced at him and nodded when he took a seat in the darkness beside her, but seemed too lost in her own thoughts to pay much attention to his presence.

Hunter sat back in his chair with a sigh and lit his pipe, delighted to have found a place of refuge to escape Victoria and her wagging tongue. The storm convulsed in the sky with brilliant displays of lightning, causing Hunter to assume that Victoria had retreated to the safety of her chamber.

The one beside him, on the other hand, appeared to take immense pleasure in the celestial display. With each dazzling bolt that lit the darkness, her smiled broadened.

Glad for the opportunity to sit and relax after two days almost constantly in the saddle, Hunter sank deeper into his chair. When the wind diminished its ferocity and the thunder retreated, he finally spoke. "Quite a hellish brew that was. Looks to be another one coming."

Andrea's gaze remained locked on the sky. "Yes. Let's hope so."

Hunter looked over at her in surprise just as the sky burst with a brilliant flash that lit her face in perfect relief against the darkness. She stared straight ahead with a serene look upon her countenance, and he found her peaceful appearance in the midst of a raging storm perfectly beguiling.

Relighting his pipe, he stretched out his legs. "Did you see the gray Johnny brought in?" Hunter was well aware she saw every horse that came and went on the estate since the arrival of Justus.

Andrea nodded, continuing to stare straight ahead. "It's sad the horses must give so much. Suffer so."

Hunter leaned forward with his elbows on his knees and peered at her through the darkness. "Everyone and everything has suffered during this war. Nothing has escaped it. Including you."

Andrea tilted her head to the side, and even in the dim light he knew she stared at him intently with those big green eyes. "You are wrong, Major. Perhaps pain is inevitable." She took a deep breath. "But I believe now that suffering is optional."

Hunter studied her profile, amazed at the resolve and strength of one so young. "Your wisdom is beyond your years."

"Again you are wrong," Andrea replied. "Were I wise, Major, I would not be *here*."

A flash of lightning lit her features for an instant, and Hunter could see that the good-natured Andrea had mysteriously returned. She smiled at him then as if together they shared a secret joke.

Hunter smiled too while drawing contentedly on his pipe, and made the decision to take advantage of her light mood. "I want you to know you can stay here as long as necessary. I know it's difficult with our ... differences. But you're most welcome."

"And you won't try to convert me to the Southern Cause while I'm here?"

Hunter answered without thinking. "I'd as soon ride a stubborn Yankee mule into battle."

"Are you comparing my temperament to that of a mule, Major?"

Hunter's smile faded, and he remained silent as he tried to think of a response that would not rouse her volatile temper. Prone as she was to spontaneous fits of anger, he wanted to choose his words carefully.

"I believe I was thinking of willful—not stubborn." He suppressed a grimace, waiting for the remorseless wrath to come.

"How very diplomatic of you," she said just as the moon made a brief appearance, sending shafts of light over the garden.

Hunter stared at her spellbound, unable to suppress the sense of accomplishment he felt—like he had finally ridden a horse that heretofore had tried to buck him off.

Nothing remained of the storm now except a few clouds sailing across the moon, but thunder growled in the distance, indicating another tempest approached. Hunter wished to take full advantage of the short respite. "Too bad your loyalties are misplaced," he said, taking a short toke on his pipe. "But I respect them."

From the corner of his eye he saw Andrea's head turn toward him and could feel the green eyes flashing like the lightning that still flickered in the darkness. Perhaps he had gone too far now.

"Had you witnessed the brutal atrocities I have, you'd not say my loyalties are misplaced."

"Had you been reared in Virginia, you'd agree that they are."

Andrea amazed him again by expressing neither anger nor resentment at his reply, but sat back as if to analyze it. Finally, she leaned forward. "Virginia means much to you."

Hunter eyed her intently and saw she was prepared to weigh and compare what he told her, and then draw her own conclusions. "It is the land of my birth. Every obligation binds me to my state and my home."

"Then you are fighting for what you may never keep."

"No," he responded in a determined voice. "We are defending what we will never part with."

Andrea remained quiet as dark clouds swallowed the moon again. Hunter's gaze drifted toward the west, where the wild skirmish line of another storm approached. Large drops of rain, already falling, foretold another downpour was imminent.

"I hope Zach took Lightning and that filly into the barn," he said. "It's too bad that mare is so afraid of storms."

"He did. I made Izzie help him."

"Izzie helped him?"

"Yes, it takes two. I've never seen a more headstrong, stubborn, obstinate foal in my life." Andrea closed her eyes and rested her head back against the chair.

"Perhaps you've spent too much time with her."

Hunter's heart twitched at the sound that followed, for it was the richest, most mirthful laugh he had ever heard. Unlike the flirtatious, restrained giggles that emanated from the throats of most women, this was a deep, gurgling, infectious laugh one hears only between friends.

"Yes, I'm afraid you've uncovered my plot." She gazed over at him, her eyes sparking with amusement. "I've been planning to turn your stock, one by one, into headstrong Yankee mules."

"I do not doubt your success with such an enterprise." Hunter kicked his legs out in front of him again. "But I'm afraid you won't have any luck with your scheme on Dixie. She has the soul of a true Virginian."

"Oh, I see." Andrea nodded. "So she is *already* headstrong and obstinate."

Hunter raised his eyebrows. "That is what you think of Virginians?"

"I've known only one. I suppose it would be unfair to judge an entire breed of humanity on but a single man." She looked over at him and smiled shyly.

Hunter shook his head and leaned toward her. "But you did know another."

"Yes." A shadow crossed her face and she sighed deeply at the thought of Daniel. "I did know another. But it seems like forever ago and barely at all."

The sound of rustling skirts brought a hasty end to their discussion.

"Alex, there you are. Whatever are you doing out in this beastly weather?"

"Alex," Victoria said again. "I've been searching all over for you! Why don't you come—"

The sudden change in the atmosphere when she saw Andrea was unmistakable. The temperature dropped so swiftly Hunter half-expected to see his breath. Yet at the same time, the air crackled around the three as if heat lightning sent spasms of jolting energy through the surroundings.

Andrea stood. "Good night, Major." She nodded in his direction but deigned to meet his eyes. "I hope you enjoy the next storm."

Hunter wondered if she meant the one in the sky or the one that sat down with a great heave in the chair beside him. In any event, he knew that Victoria would make amends for the peaceful minutes of silence and good conversation he had just shared.

"Oh, I'm so glad you're home," Victoria began before Andrea had even made her way through the door. "Why I hardly know how to occupy myself. Did you know I just received a letter today from Peg, and she said that Dottie Lane and Ben Collins are—"

At once, the contrast forcibly struck Hunter. *They are so different*, he thought, looking wearily at the flashing sky. *As different as the lightning bug from lightning.*

Chapter 36

"Ah! Soldiers to your honored rest,
Your truth and valor bearing,
The bravest are the tenderest,
The loving are the daring."
— Bayard Taylor's "Song of the Camp"

Hunter stopped at a fallen tree and gazed out over the lake. Every color of the sunset's spectacular display were reflected in the water before him, the deep hues even more brilliant than those in the sky above.

Instead of noticing the flaming exhibit of glass and fire, he sighed deeply, placing one foot on the fallen timber and crossing his arms over his bent knee. Two swans lifted off the glassy surface, their reflections rippling across the water in a blurred, mystical effect as their mirrored wings and feathers merged with the vibrant colored sky.

"Major?"

The soft voice startled him. Hunter turned to find Andrea standing behind him with an envelope in her hand. He reflexively looked back toward the house at the distance she had walked to bring it to him. "A dispatch for you, sir. You appeared to be waiting for something important. A courier just brought it."

Hunter nodded, wondering how she had grown to know him so well. "You needn't have walked all this way," he said a little more coldly than he intended as he took the missive from her outstretched hand.

Andrea did not seem to mind. She stood staring over his shoulder at the molten light of the setting sun casting soft hues of bronze and pewter over the water. "It was worth it." She took a deep breath and gazed at the dark outline of the mountains in the distance. Clouds that had been puffy and white earlier, now shone pink and violet as if lit from within. But their bellies were slowly turning dark and gray as the last bit of light trickled out of the western sky.

Hunter watched Andrea's gaze drift over to a small rise that overlooked the pond, and then to the single tree that stood like a stoic guard. She turned back as if she'd forgotten his presence for a moment. "Daniel is ... there?" she asked, motioning with her eyes.

Hunter nodded, his thoughts moving to the lone tree and the single headstone beneath it.

"I believe he'd be pleased." Andrea's gaze moved to the family burial grounds that lay some distance from where Daniel was interred. The spot where he rested was a lovely one with a bird's-eye view of the estate.

"You cared for him." Hunter's voice was low and husky.

Andrea blinked repeatedly as if recalling the day Daniel's life trickled out before her very eyes. "I was not acquainted with him for very long," she said at length, "but a greater loss I have never known."

They both fell silent for a moment, and then Andrea spoke. "I trust it's not bad news." She nodded toward the unopened letter.

Hunter turned the dispatch over and then back again. "I believe it may be."

"Would you like me to open it?"

Hunter did not answer at first, then hesitantly handed her the envelope.

The diminishing light made it difficult to read, forcing Andrea to turn the page toward the setting sun. Hunter watched her eyes sweep over the missive and knew the report was unpleasant.

"It's news of Stuart?" His voice cracked with anguish.

"Yes, I'm sorry." She took a deep, shaky breath as if feeling the weight of the news herself. "I'm afraid his wound was mortal. He died yesterday in Richmond."

She reached out and put her hand on Hunter's arm. "There is honor in dying for one's convictions, yet it seems an inconceivable loss. I'm sorry."

Hunter did not say anything. And now, neither did Andrea. Yet somehow, just as when Daniel had died, they found themselves in the embrace of each other's arms, enclosed in a cloak of shadowy comfort.

Andrea finally broke the spell. "I'm sure he is at peace," she whispered to console him. "He fulfilled his duty to God and country."

Her words did little to ease Hunter's deep sense of loss. He stiffened and drew away. "My dear, you are mistaken. *God* is nowhere to be found in this war."

Without another word, he stalked away into the darkness.

Chapter 37

"Good night, good night! Parting is such sweet sorrow,
that I shall say good night till it be morrow."
— Romeo and Juliet, Shakespeare

Major Hunter pushed his weary mount forward through the darkness, as eager as he'd ever been to see Hawthorne come into view after two weeks on the move.

"Come on, Dixie," he said, leaning down and patting his horse's neck. "We're heading toward a good night's rest."

The animal, seeming to understand his words, picked up her pace when they were a mile away and soon cantered across the bridge to Hawthorne. At first glance the house appeared silent and dark, matching Hunter's mood. But when he stopped in the front, he noticed a candle burned in a room on the second floor. Although well past midnight, that lone beam shining out of the darkness appeared like a warm, welcoming light.

Turning his mount loose in the nearest paddock, Hunter glanced again at the window and saw the silhouette of Andrea sitting in the amber light with a book. The sight drew a smile to his lips. This was not the first time that solitary flame had greeted him after a long night's ride.

Finding his way through the dark house to the stairs, Hunter slowly ascended, his legs and body so weary he found himself holding onto the banister for support. He could hardly wait to take off his boots and fall into bed. Yet as he passed her room, with its door slightly ajar, he found himself knocking once and pushing it open. "Permission to enter Camp Defiance."

Andrea stared at him with a look of half welcome and half rebelliousness, which prodded him to continue his jesting. "Waiting up for me again, Miss Evans?" He tipped his hat back as he spoke.

"You are doomed for disappointment, Major." She lowered her eyes to her book. "I am reading."

Hunter laughed and strode into the room. "I'm beginning to think you believe it your responsibility to stand picket duty while I'm away. But if you can leave your post, you really ought to take a look outside." Hunter nodded toward the window.

"Oh my!" Andrea stood and stared at the full moon shining in through the door. "But it was cloudy earlier."

Hunter stepped forward and offered his arm to help her out to the balcony.

"I always loved and dreaded a night such as this." Andrea leaned forward over the railing as she stared up at the sky. "So beautiful and yet so dangerous."

195

The night breeze cast its magic, catching her robe and twirling it out behind her. She turned and looked at Hunter, causing him to quickly avert his gaze. In fact, he had been thinking the exact same thing—but not about the moon.

"What a ga-lorious evening!" Andrea turned back to the fields and gazed at the horses silhouetted in the moonlight. The stone walls resembled dark rivers flowing through the fields, twisting and turning over the hills until they disappeared into the deep shadows. Fireflies flitted across the pastures like sparkles on an endless sea, their flashing golden globes illuminating even the shadows where moonlight failed to hit.

"I would hardly call it evening. Do you never sleep?" Hunter pulled a chair from the shadows and helped her sit, then pulled a second one to the railing. "You're not afraid of the dark, are you?"

"I do not fear the darkness or the night," she said, her voice suddenly somber and serious. "Just the dreams."

Before he could think of something to say, she nodded toward the field where his horse now lay in a patch of lush grass. "Looks like you've exhausted your mount."

"Covered a lot of ground in the past few days." Hunter stretched out his long legs and propped his booted feet on the railing.

Andrea gazed back at him, cocking her head to one side. "Yes, you look a bit tired yourself."

"Let's just say it's good to be home." He took off his hat and rubbed his temples.

"You take great risks being out on a night like this." Andrea's voice held a hint of concern. "It would appear you possess an unseemly appetite for battle if you dare to ride in the deathly light of a full moon."

Tipping his chair back on two legs, Hunter laughed softly. "It's my duty to have an appetite for battle. As for the moon, I generally trust the clouds to be on my side—as they were tonight."

"You rely much on luck and chance, Commander." Andrea draped the edge of her gown over her bare feet and propped them up on the banister beside his. "Surely it's not your bravery and devotion alone that the salvation of the Confederate army depends."

Hunter shrugged. "I don't go into battle with the slightest desire to come out alive unless I've won. My life is a small price to pay for Virginia."

"Do not speak like that," Andrea scolded.

Hunter sat his chair back down on all four legs and met Andrea's gaze with a curious grin. "Ah, my dear, could it be you were worried about me?"

Now it was Andrea's turn to laugh. "Major, your arrogance is as astounding as your apparent good fortune at commanding the clouds. If you weren't to return, it would be no concern of mine."

Hunter leaned over and put his hand on the arm of her chair, willing to forget his rank and status as an enemy officer tonight since she was so willing to ignore it. "Come now, Miss Evans. You wouldn't miss me just a little?"

Andrea looked into his eyes, a hint of humor illuminating her face. "I suppose I *would* miss your overbearing attitude, your stubborn pride, your inflexible—"

"Aha, despite our differing philosophies on war, it appears we have more in common than I thought."

His quick response apparently caught Andrea by surprise. She looked up at him with a straight face, but a smile tugged at her mouth. Hunter felt his heart thump in his chest as a feeling of serenity began to overcome him. Whether it was the moon or her mood, he did not know, but he suddenly had a desire for the night he had longed to end, to go on forever.

The moon's rays became partially shielded by a thin veil of clouds, then emerged again in even more brilliance. The leaves above them stirred in response, seeming to writhe with a sense of exhilaration at the emergence of the night star in its radiant splendor.

"The odds are great against you." Andrea's voice sounded serious again.

"I find that patriotism and determination generally make up for lack of numbers." Hunter gazed out over the fields. "Just because the enemy is better armed doesn't mean our resolve is any less. In fact," he said, pausing to pull out his pipe, "I dare say the North may have overestimated its strength and underestimated our power."

Andrea crossed her arms and sank down deeper in her chair. "It seems a pity to engage in a war in which a soldier's safest armor is his determination to fight."

Hunter lit the tobacco and leaned back in his chair. "Not just determination. We have cause and will."

"And we, strength and means." Andrea leaned her chair back on two legs. "I suppose your resolve is commendable, if not your prudence. You dare to continue your campaign where your enemy is all around you."

Hunter put his head back and laughed. "My dear, it is my duty to be in closer contact with Washington than Richmond. I dare say I was within hailing distance of your Capitol this morning."

"We are close to the Union lines now?" Her voice was full of surprise.

"We're less than fifty miles from Washington. Much of the time we are within Yankee, I mean Union, lines."

Andrea nodded with a faraway look in her eye. Whether she was surprised at her proximity to Union encampments or not, he could not tell.

Hunter leaned back and watched a smoke ring lift and hang in the air. When he glanced sideways, he found her staring at him. "Is something wrong?"

"Just trying to figure you out," Andrea said contemplatively.

"And are you having any success?"

"May I talk without restraint?"

Hunter laughed loudly and majestically. "Miss Evans, you have shown me no hint toward possessing such a thing."

Andrea joined in with a laugh that sounded in perfect harmony with the music of the night.

"Well first tell me, Miss Evans, do you find the Northern gossip a faithful portrait of the powers I'm alleged to possess? What did you think of me as a foe?" Hunter leaned back contentedly in his chair, waiting for her reply as if he regarded her as an old acquaintance whose opinion he valued.

"I understood you to be a dangerous opponent, due in part to the close bond you hold with your men."

"And would you not charge that as a fault to my character? Does it not seem unwise to become close to men you may potentially have to hurl at the enemy and to their deaths?"

"I avow I never regarded it quite like that." Andrea drew her brows together. "I thought of it more like a mother ferociously protecting her young."

Hunter put his head back and laughed heartily "My men would take great humor in the analogy. I must remember to tell them." He grew serious again. "What else?"

Andrea spoke quietly, and Hunter knew it was from the heart. "There was no one I respected more, nor wished to confront less."

He smiled. "Ah. I shall take that as a compliment."

"Richly deserved, no doubt. But only because of your seeming unquenchable thirst for blood."

Hunter looked over at her, surprised. "I am not bloodthirsty, I assure you. We are at war, Miss Evans. Therefore, any Yankee soldier who places a foot on our soil justly forfeits his life." He stopped for a moment to re-light his pipe before continuing. "As Virginians, we would rather give up our lives than our honor or liberty."

"You speak like you believe bravery is exclusively restricted to the men of the Old Dominion. Do you think because I am a woman my loyalty to the Union is less than yours for Virginia? That honor means less to me?"

"No." Hunter stood and stretched, then sat on the railing where his feet had been. "But most women choose to show their loyalties in a less ... perilous way."

Andrea raised her gaze to meet his. "Protecting the integrity of the Union is incentive enough for peril. As for hiding behind my skirts, trust that I will never do."

He smiled broadly. "I could certainly never accuse you of that. Your convictions are commendable, if not your loyalties." Hunter watched her stare musingly into the sky, seemingly trying to figure out how to end the conflict herself. "It's too beautiful a night to be talking about war," he said to get her attention.

Andrea looked over at him and smiled. "On that point, I can agree." Her eyes drifted back to the moon.

"Yet still you are thinking of it. I can tell by your expression."

Andrea shrugged. "What else is there to talk about?"

Hunter stared up at the heavens and then lowered his gaze to her. "How about you?"

"Me?"

"Yes. You puzzle me. You are a complete contradiction."

"The contradiction is only seeming. My convictions are firm."

"The latter is accepted, the former is not." He laughed. "Let me assure you, young lady, you are a paradox in every sense of the word."

Andrea laughed half-heartedly at his words, as if to end his scrutiny, but he noticed the smile never quite reached her eyes. They held in their depths, as they always did, a solemn sadness that seemed reluctant to depart.

He leaned closer. "Which tell the truth? Your lips or your eyes?"

Andrea turned her head away. "I don't know what you mean."

"Your lips are smiling, but your eyes are not." He chewed on the end of his pipe for a moment. "And I'm trying to decide who might be the real Andrea Evans."

"Do not waste your time," she snapped, her gaze intent on the field below.

"Why not? She may be someone I wish to know."

"I can assure you *that* is not the case. I'm not of the type that makes good company. You of all people should know that by now, Major."

Hunter continued looking at her, trying to read down to the depths of her soul. "I do not presume to know you well, Miss Evans. But I believe ..." He paused, unsure he should continue. "I believe that perhaps pain and despair have been a substantial part of your life, and to fight the world seems more practical to you now than to tolerate or endure."

He watched an unmistakable grief steal into her eyes. "There you have it, Major, my life in a sentence. Well done."

Hunter's heart thudded at the look. He leaned forward to touch her shoulder. "I didn't wish to upset you, Miss Evans. Pray forgive me if I did."

Andrea continued staring skyward. "There is nothing in the truth to forgive."

Hunter let his hand drop. "I apologize for speaking so frankly. You possess a pain in your eyes that has nothing to do with your injuries. I believe it is this pain that has thrust you into the war."

"Suffice to say, I do what I do willingly. The reward is equal to the sacrifice."

"It seems an unreasonable sacrifice to me."

"Is it so unreasonable to believe in a cause, defend it, attempt to protect it, endeavor to preserve it, and—if necessary—die for it?"

"As I said before, those are hardly choices required of a woman, nor sacrifices for which many yearn to make."

"I'm not the first to submit to the mysterious law of pain and sacrifice for deliverance from evil. Pray don't give me the honor."

"But I know you've undergone great hardships," Hunter said, knowing it was too late to stop now. "Great risks that were perhaps unnecessary."

Andrea stared over his shoulder with a faraway look as she absently rubbed her leg. "Be content to know I am justified in my actions."

"Frankly, I can see no justification for fighting against your birth land."

Hunter said the words without thinking, and wished he could take them back.

Andrea cocked her head to one side. "Agreed. I was born in the United States."

Hunter frowned, hesitating to oppose her will. "You were born in the South."

"I don't believe that geographic birthplace is reason to defend organized barbarism." Andrea's voice sounded a little unsteady now. "Until the South rebelled we were all one and the same, as we will be again. Our duty is to Union and flag, preserve the one and uphold the other."

"But surely you can agree that the right to use military force for the purpose of coercing a state to remain in the Union against its will finds no warrant in the Constitution."

"What I can agree on is that it would be wiser for the South to endure, rather than commit a worse crime than it resists."

"Why should we endure?" Hunter inhaled deeply from his pipe, somewhat enjoying the way she dug in and defended her beliefs. "Secession involved no war. We withdrew from a voluntary union of states in the same dignified and peaceable manner in which we entered it. We deplore secession, but coercion is a far greater crime."

"Yes, and you defend your decision with armed resistance against your own government, creating an enemy of your own countrymen."

"Tell me, what else have the Yankees infused into your poisoned mind?" Hunter cocked his head. "The enemy I fight is a vandal who preys upon helpless civilians. Our goal is no less than expulsion of the invaders from Virginia soil."

"Place not the blame on the Union, sir," Andrea fired back. "The war is the fault of aggressive traitors. We seek only peace."

"Yes, and you are determined to have that peace, even if you must fight and kill every remaining Southern man for it. I've told you before, I can find no power in the Constitution that allows the abolishment of our domestic programs without the consent of the individual state."

"The Constitution also does not give you the right to secede."

"Nor does it take it away."

"But you fired the first shot!"

Hunter laughed. "That's like saying I fired the first shot at an intruder who broke into my home."

"Those who deny freedom to others deserve it not for themselves," Andrea said. "Such is the price of sin."

Hunter did not respond and his face lost all signs of playfulness. All was quiet, save the gentle rustling of the wind in the newborn leaves of the trees. Then he spoke softly, but not gently. "We will not allow the destiny of our state to be placed in the hands of an irresponsible Republic who knows nothing of our Southern culture."

"Southern culture? By that I suppose you mean the continuation of a system that promotes free labor."

A heavy silence ensued, as thick and perceptible as the scent of honeysuckle in the air. Never before had their bantering touched on the sensitive matter of slavery. But the ugly topic hung between them now like an indefinable barrier.

"The South did not make war in defense of slavery." Hunter's voice grew strained. "Less than one man in a thousand in the army has any property interest in slavery. And the fact is, when the Constitution was created, slavery existed in every state."

"It's a cursed evil no matter how long it has existed or where it began."

"We have a right to defend our way of life—"

Andrea's voice grew softer. "I know you are convinced of the righteousness of your Cause, Major, but I believe your convictions are misguided. Can you not see the soil of Virginia is soaking in the blood of your misplaced patriotic devotion?"

Hunter leaned back and crossed his arms, pondering the fact that he admired her spirit despite the fact that she remained determined to be his enemy. He sighed with exasperation. "Someday, Miss Evans, I hope I can get you to see my point of view."

"Major, I already *see* your point of view. I simply don't *agree* with it."

Hunter shook his head in feigned dismay. He knew she could not be induced to yield a point when she thought she was right … and she pretty much always thought she was right. "Miss Evans, in the end we believe in the same things, preservation of constitutional liberties and the right of self-government. I desire peace as much as you do. But we won't purchase it at the price of the honor and the interests of Virginia."

They were both quiet: she staring at the sky, he gazing at her. "I suppose we've solved one thing tonight. "We both follow the dictates of our conscience."

Andrea looked up at him sharply, as if she understood where he was taking the conversation. "As for the dictates of my conscience, do not fear, I have my reasons."

"Your father?" Hunter saw her wince before her gaze locked in on his.

Eyes that were sometimes the color of emeralds turned dark as a thunder-head. "What know you of my father?"

"You ... spoke of him in your fever."

Andrea blinked repeatedly, then looked away. "It is ancient history."

"But the scars cannot be so easily forgotten." Her eyes darted up to meet his again. "Doc told me," he explained.

Andrea stood and turned away, leaning heavily on the chair, obviously shaken at the thought that he was peeling away the layers of her past. Hunter could see her chest heaving as she appeared to reflect on the pain and horror of her childhood. It was hard for him to imagine a child living through the trials and anguish she must have endured; harder still to conceive the strength and resilience that grew from it.

"You needn't talk about it. I don't wish to revive unwelcome memories."

Andrea took a deep breath and gazed up at the stars. "It was a long time ago." She shrugged as if it meant nothing to her now. "I placed myself between my father's whip and a slave thinking it would stop him." Her voice trembled at the memory. "But clearly, it did not."

Hunter closed his eyes, imagining the scene. "The sacrifice was worth the cost I hope."

"It did no good." Andrea turned back to him. "He sold the slave, a boy of eight, the next day. And his mother . . ." She swallowed hard as if the words would choke her. "His mother hung herself that night."

She said it matter-of-factly, but the pain in her voice was unmistakable. When Hunter looked into her dry, staring eyes, he saw more sadness than a thousand tears could hold. He understood now why hostility and vengeance were a part of her soul, recognized that her impervious nature was a veil to cover the inner turmoil. All this, because she carried on her narrow shoulders the burden of two lives for which she could in no way be responsible.

Gone was the rebellious, defiant spirit to which he was so accustomed. Before him stood an innocent, fragile child, whose only companions had been anguish and torment.

Hunter watched her head rise another notch, as if rejecting the memories that consumed her. For a brief moment, he had glimpsed the pain behind the mask, but the curtain descended again as she stared out at the night. At least he had learned another slice of truth from her past. She had apparently inherited her beautiful eyes from her mother; the grief and anger in them from her father.

"I'm sorry," she said, taking a deep breath and looking down. "No one knows about that. I don't know why I told you."

"Those people ... like your father," Hunter said, his brow creased at her distress, "they are not the ones fighting this war."

"But they are the ones it's being fought *for*!" Her cheeks turned red with passion.

Hunter sighed, knowing it would be useless to argue. His words of conciliation were not going to change her emotional animosity toward the South. He stood beside her in silence, his shadow touching hers as the moon continued its dazzling slide across the horizon.

"Hawthorne looks beautiful in the moonlight," Andrea said at length. "Did you command the heavens to produce such a display tonight, Major?"

Hunter looked skyward at the moon behind her head, and shrugged. "I'm home now. My control over the celestial bodies was completed hours ago."

"I think I shall always remember this night when I see a full moon." Closing her eyes, she opened her hand to the night air and brought it toward her, closing it as her fingers touched her heart.

"What are you doing?"

She looked up at his gaze of confusion. "Saving the moment." She closed her eyes again and smiled. "I close my eyes, feel the breeze on my face." She paused and inhaled deeply. "I smell that honeysuckle right below us, envision the horses grazing in a pasture flooded by moonlight ... Then I catch it all in my hand and save it forever in my heart." She brought her closed hand once again to her heart.

The sound of thundering hooves interrupted the conversation. A group of horses came into view, galloping in the path of a moonbeam before disappearing over a hill. Hunter watched Andrea stare out into the darkness, her face taking on a wistful, radiant look at the scene before her.

"You are so blessed to have a home in paradise," she whispered.

"It gives me great pleasure to know you enjoy Hawthorne. Where do you call home?"

Andrea looked genuinely surprised at the question and fell silent for a moment. "I ... well ...before the war, I lived with my cousin Catherine."

"Well, what about after the war? You have to have someplace to call home. Certainly you've thought about marriage, a home of your own."

Andrea laughed that soft, infectious laugh he loved to hear. "I have no intention of bowing to a man's authority, Major. Why should I expect one to bow to mine?"

"You may have a point there." He winked to show her he was joking.

"And what of you?" She gazed skyward again. "You will marry again? Or have you given up on love?"

He gazed at her, contemplating the question. "I've not thought about it in quite those terms. Let's just say I've given up on the thought of perpetual and everlasting companionship."

She smiled at his attempt to evade the question. "I suppose I'm lucky to have never known companionship. I don't know what it is, so I cannot miss it."

Hunter frowned at her rationale. "You're much too young to think of going through life alone."

"I'm nineteen. Almost anyway. Old enough to know that trusting a man enough to marry him would require more courage than is within me.

Hunter blinked. "*Almost?* You told me a year ago you were nineteen!"

"I did not wish you to think me a child," she said, shrugging.

He stared at her as he thought back. Then she was only seventeen while eluding him. Just a youth … yet possessing the cunning, courage and commitment of someone much advanced in age. Woman or child? She could scarcely be considered one or the other, yet possessed distinctive elements of both.

He reflected on her earlier statement. "It does not require courage to love someone and marry."

"I didn't say I could not love a man, nor do I doubt the divinity of the institution. I said I could not *trust* one. I told you before, Major, it is not in my nature." Her gaze turned skyward. "Trust is an ability that I have lost or has died or was left out of me at birth."

"You can't go through life without trusting."

"Trusting. Needing. They are one and the same. I prefer to rely on myself, depend on no one, and expect nothing in return."

The pain in her voice startled him. "You can't allow your past to dictate your future."

"You speak from sympathy?" Andrea looked as if she yearned for him to impart some magical insight upon her.

"I believe I speak from experience."

He watched her gaze slowly drift away to somewhere over his shoulder, then her eyes grew wide with amazement.

"Major," she said, pointing behind him, "I fear the sun is rising."

As if on cue, a cock crowed. Hunter turned so see the first pearly glimmers of light slicing through the darkness. In the far, far distance, the jagged shapes of trees emerged against the slightest patch of pink.

They had talked all night.

"I apologize for keeping you up." Andrea's eyes remained focused on the sunrise. "It wasn't my intention, truly. The hours fled so swiftly …" She drew her attention away from the spectacle for a moment to meet his gaze. "But I thank you for the discussion. It was quite … fascinating."

Hunter knew she meant the remark sincerely and smiled, then wondered why her words had elicited such a response. He generally found conversations with women nothing less than tedious, yet he had just conversed the night away with one. He sighed at his own confusion.

When he looked back around, the sky had taken on the impression of an artist's masterpiece, with swirls of deep pink and lavender floating in stratified layers of lacy wonder. He felt he was witnessing a miracle, and knew he had never seen the dawning of a new day arrive with such splendor.

But as magical as the vista in front of him appeared, the beauty that stood beside him was also not without effect. She stood so near he felt her dressing gown touch his leg, and he tensed at the contact.

"I believe I shall never see its equal." Andrea's voice was soft as they stood in the lingering glow of dawn, sharing the spectacle before them.

Hunter studied her, thinking he should perhaps admit aloud that the glorious beauty of the sun in the painted heavens was nothing compared to the one who stood beside him watching its appearance.

"I'm sure you wish to get some sleep, Commander." Andrea casually reached for the support of his arm. When she looked up, her eyes met his and lingered for the breadth of a heartbeat—long enough for Hunter to get the impression he had just witnessed a miracle that had nothing to do with the dawning of a new day.

He smiled again, dazed, remembering his weariness of a few hours ago that had vanished at the sight of her. Dismissing his confused thoughts, he helped her back into her room.

"Good night, Miss Evans," he said, bowing.

"You mean, good morning, Major." She smiled broadly.

He smiled too, but the smile quickly faded. "I stand corrected. Good morning, Miss Evans."

After closing the French doors behind him, Hunter could not resist one more contemplative glance to the East. Something had awakened in him with the dawning of this new day. Something vague—yet something so distinct, he knew he would never look at sunrises or full moons the same again.

Chapter 38

"Even God cannot change the past."
— Aristotle

Andrea lifted her eyes from a book to gaze at the rays of soft sunlight drenching the lawn in a rich golden blanket. She heard the front door close, then the familiar sound of Hunter's spurs clanking across the porch. Seemingly unaware of her presence, he leaned one shoulder against the ionic column and gazed meditatively over the gorgeous panorama of the valley he owned.

Andrea could not draw her eyes away from the indomitable figure. With one hand wrapped around a cup of coffee, the other stuffed indifferently in his pocket, his image suggested little of the intrepid character she knew so well. Dressed casually, without his Confederate coat, he seemed tranquil and relaxed. Yet his large muscular frame, with his strong, tan forearms and powerfully built legs, showed evidence of his ability to put up a fight.

She lowered her eyes to her book, then lifted them once again. He was striking, she mused, irresistibly masculine and, she had to admit, very appealing. Tall, broad-shouldered, and vigorous, he was the incarnation of force and strength. A fearless soldier, he was likewise respected by others as a gracious and gallant gentleman, creating a puzzling veil of mystery that made him all the more mysterious.

Andrea cocked her head and scrutinized him. Most officers dressed flamboyantly. Hunter, on the other hand, always wore a uniform that displayed nothing but hard usage. She could not help yielding him the tribute of admiration, for he was almost impossible to dislike.

Almost.

Andrea looked away as her thoughts began to disturb her, and a sigh involuntarily escaped her lips.

"Oh, there you are." Hunter turned around.

He moved toward her with a brilliant smile, revealing a hidden handsomeness all the more captivating. Placing his cup down on the table opposite her, he took a seat. Andrea detected an uncharacteristic twinkle in his eye and tried to decipher its cause.

$\mathcal{H}$ $\mathcal{H}$ $\mathcal{H}$

"I forgot to mention that I had a chat with some fellows from South Carolina last week," Hunter said as if simply making conversation.

Andrea lifted her gaze and then lowered it again, but otherwise did not respond.

"Yes, the Charleston area to be exact." He leaned back, relaxing in his chair.

Hunter noticed that his houseguest stared at the book in her hands, but her eyes did not move, a hint to him that her thoughts were not on the words. "Maybe you know the area? Something-Crossroads, I think they said."

Andrea closed her book and looked up at him with questioning eyes.

"Anyway, they can't recall any Evans from the area," he continued, "but they do know about this chap Charles *Monroe*"—Hunter emphasized the last name—"who, oddly enough, was married to an Evans—of Virginia."

Andrea swallowed hard, but for the most part, her impassive face revealed nothing. "Anyway, this Charles Monroe owns half of South Carolina." He swept his arms to show the magnitude. "A place called MontRose."

Hunter knew with certainty he had struck a chord now. Despite her best efforts to maintain an appearance of indifference, his young houseguest appeared troubled.

"I'd be somewhat surprised if you hadn't heard of it with your knowledge of horseflesh. It's quite a reputable breeding establishment. In fact," he laughed, "can you believe Fleetson's dam was bred at MontRose? You remember Fleet, don't you?"

Andrea stared straight ahead, but the color blossoming in her cheeks revealed that she recalled, not only Fleet, but most likely his dam Lady Fleet, one of the plantation's most blooded broodmares. "Yes," he continued, not giving her time to answer, "my grandfather dealt with Charles Monroe quite extensively apparently."

"This is really a very nice story, Major." Andrea stood. "But I fear I do not see what it has to do with me."

"Oh, wait." Hunter took her by the hand. "I haven't gotten to the best part. I do insist." He plopped her down in the chair next to him and stared at her musingly as he took a leisurely sip of coffee. "Anyway, according to these men, this Charles had a daughter, an only child, an heiress to all his wealth and power." Again, he spread his hands to show the magnitude.

"How nice." Andrea sounded bored, but she stared mournfully out over the pastures while her fingers fumbled nervously with the pages of her book.

"But instead of being content with all that fortune, do you know what she did?"

"I have a feeling you're going to tell me."

"She ran away," he said bluntly. "At a very young age, I'm told."

Andrea stood to leave again. "Heavens, I was so hoping your story would have a happy ending. Now I really must go talk to Izzie."

Hunter took her arm and guided her back to her seat with compelling force. Leaning forward with brows drawn together, he whispered, "That's not the worst of it."

"You don't say?" Andrea settled in the chair as if annoyed, but her quick glance toward heaven did not escape Hunter's searching eyes.

"Oh, yes, I *do* say. She disappeared the same day that all the outbuildings and warehouses on the estate burned to the ground. Of course, everyone believes she set the fires. Cost her father a fortune."

Andrea put her hand to her mouth as if dismayed. "Why the little demon. How dare she?"

"My thoughts exactly." Hunter nodded in agreement. "They told me other stories that I scarcely know if I should believe."

"Truly? I hope you don't care to share them."

He chuckled. "Oh, yes, there is one I must tell you."

He leaned back to get comfortable and gazed at Andrea. Her eyes were upon him, but their shaded depths revealed nothing except a sort of melancholy detachment.

"It seems this Mr. Monroe was losing slaves, almost regularly, for a year or so before the daughter left. It was suspected at the time, and later confirmed, that the child was giving them clothes, food, what have you, and sending them on their way."

"That's not much of a story," Andrea said, looking him in the eye. "That sounds like the mindless tongue-wagging of neighbors and the abstract speculation of gossips."

"Well, it gets even better. It was discovered that in order to throw off the hounds, this young lass tied a bundle of the escaped slaves' clothing behind her horse, and dragged it all around the countryside—in the opposite direction, of course." Hunter slapped the table to get Andrea's attention. "Can you imagine? The hounds running around with a scent for hours in one direction, while those slaves were escaping with impunity in the other? Quite a bit of ingenuity that!"

Hunter's smile faded at the anguished look on Andrea's face. "No doubt it was not accomplished without serious risk," he said gently.

Andrea swallowed hard. "I'm sure the child was aware of the risk and willing to face the consequences." She stood and smoothed the front of her gown. "And now if you're done telling your wonderful tale, Major, I'd really like to go lie down."

Hunter stood too, as all gentlemen do, and waited until she was almost to the door. "By all means, Miss *Monroe*. Get your rest."

She paused a moment and glared at him, then swung the door open with violent force before slamming it shut with a thunderous bang.

Hunter sat down, took a sip of coffee, and grinned. "Well, well. Andrea Marie Monroe. The creature has a name."

Chapter 39

"There is no animal more invincible than a woman,
nor fire either, nor any wildcat so ruthless."
– Lysistrata

Andrea had successfully avoided Victoria for some weeks now, but she knew it was only a matter of time until the two collided once again. When a shadow crossed her path at the foot of the stairway one warm afternoon, Andrea knew the moment of calamity had arrived.

"My darling," Victoria said with icy sweetness, "you really should do something about your hair. Do you not know it's unfashionable to wear it down?"

Andrea took a deep breath to calm herself and smiled politely. "I have attempted to mind my own business, Miss Hamilton. I hoped you would do the same."

Victoria ignored the comment and looked Andrea up and down with amused contempt. "I do declarah, no hoops, no shoes half the time, your hair all ... blowsy. I don't understand why Alex—"

"Miss Hamilton," Andrea interrupted, her temper wearing thin, "pray do not waste your breath barking at me. I have no fear of dogs. Even *distempered* ones."

"How dare you insult me, you little Maryland magpie," Victoria spat. "You have no idea how to speak to a lady, let alone *be* one!"

With self-control she did not know she possessed, Andrea ignored the comment and tried to continue on her way.

"I believe you are of the mongrel breed," Victoria said, grabbing Andrea's arm.

"And I believe you are the misbegotten spawn of hell!" Andrea shot back in angry retort, pushing Victoria away.

"Stop this instant!" Hunter strode across the floor to the rescue of Victoria, who gasped and flattened herself against him, sobbing convulsively in his arms as if she'd been struck.

"Did you hear what she said to me?" she wailed.

Hunter gave Andrea a stern look. "Don't you think you owe Victoria an apology?"

Andrea let out a small gasp of her own. She looked at Hunter, first with surprise that he should suggest such a thing, then with dismay that he *could* suggest such a thing, and then with anger that he *would* suggest such a thing. "Most assuredly not!"

"Make her apologize." Victoria sobbed, endeavoring to call up some tears. "She has the manners of a ... b-b-billy goat."

"No, *you* make me apologize!" Andrea lunged at Victoria before Hunter had a chance to react.

"Stop this minute!" Hunter tried to keep the two women separated.

Even after being held at arm's length by Hunter, Andrea made one last, strenuous attempt to reach Victoria's throat, intent on manually removing the woman's noisy windpipe.

"A truce to this!" Hunter tried again to gain control.

"She's mad! She's bloody mad! Keep her away from me," Victoria screamed before swooning against his broad shoulders.

"I give you fair warning, Victoria, do not provoke me again." Andrea shook her finger at her antagonist who now lay moaning in Hunter's arms as he carried her up the stairs.

"Enough," Hunter said over his shoulder. "I expect my command for a truce to be obeyed by God!"

"Perhaps *God* shall obey your cursed truce, but *I* shall not," Andrea hurled back.

Hunter stopped dead in his tracks. Even Victoria ceased her sniveling for a moment to glare through imagined tears and hear what was going to happen next.

"I will settle with *you* properly later." Hunter swiveled on the stairs and gave her a stern look.

Victoria grinned over Hunter's shoulder with a look of sweet victory once he continued up the stairs. Andrea smiled back, pointed her cane like a shotgun, and mouthed the word *pow* while pulling an imaginary trigger.

Victoria let out a blood-curdling shriek that caused Hunter to stop and turn around again. But by the time he did, Andrea was leaning nonchalantly on her supposed instrument of carnage and smiling innocently.

❋ ❋ ❋

Hunter's declaration of "settling" with her later gave Andrea an uneasy feeling about when and in what manner that threat would be carried out. She attempted therefore to avoid him, but he discovered her in the far reaches of the garden sitting on a crude bench under the bowers of an overgrown grape vine. He appeared without warning, his hands resting on top of the natural doorway, his body leaning forward as he talked.

"You wouldn't be trying to avoid me, would you?" He greeted her somewhat cheerfully.

"Why would I do that?" Andrea averted her eyes from the muscles his stance produced.

"Well, I've come here to ask"—Hunter cleared his throat—"*demand* the truce that was earlier mentioned."

Andrea's eyes glazed over. "A truce?"

"Yes. And the truce will begin tonight when the three of us dine together." Hunter removed his hands from above him and turned to leave.

"I find the thought slightly less pleasant than being buried alive," Andrea said just loud enough for Hunter to hear. Then louder, "Sir, permit me to thank you for your most courteous invitation, but I fear I have no appetite and therefore must regrettably decline the *honor*."

Hunter returned in an instant as if fully expecting her predetermined refusal. His look was now that of a warrior preparing for battle.

"Dinner is at seven. I insist you attend, hungry or not." He looked her in the eye and repeated his mandate. "Think of it as a *privilege*, and see that you are there."

Andrea coughed as if his words actually choked her. "I regret I must plead ignorance of the privilege of the invitation," she said coldly, abandoning her feigned indifference to the idea. "It is my understanding that your houseguest is prouder than Lucifer of her family name, but frankly, I see no reason for the tribute."

"Be that as it may, it would be most advantageous to your personal well-being if you were to heed my wishes voluntarily."

Andrea blinked in surprise. "Would this be an order, Major?" She tried to keep her voice from shaking with agitation. "For if it is, I must earnestly beg you to reconsider."

"I do not order it, Miss Monroe. But I advise it. Strongly."

"Pray don't call me Miss Monroe!"

Hunter gazed at her, somewhat bemused. "That is your name is it not?"

"My name is Evans. I shall answer to no other!"

"As you wish," he said curtly. "May I remind you that dinner is at seven?"

Andrea cleared her throat. "I ... believe I declined the invitation."

"I don't recall offering you that option Miss Evans," Hunter said, his voice growing strained. "The invitation is for an appearance at a dinner table, not an appointment with a hangman's noose."

Hunter's tone made it clear he believed the latter a more appropriate response to her behavior, and Andrea did nothing to hide from her expression that it was one she found exceedingly more desirable to endure.

"Heed my words, for they are not spoken in jest."

Andrea bit the side of her cheek, contemplating his ultimatum and the possible penalties. She decided she would rather cast her lot with the fate of his punishment than spend another minute of her life in the presence of Victoria Hamilton.

"Then, Major, may I at least go on the record stating that if I had the choice of dining with your houseguest or riding a hundred yards through a hell storm of Confederate lead, I would, without hesitation, choose the latter?"

Hunter blinked at her impudence and stared at her so intensely Andrea felt she was being burned alive by his eyes—yet this did not stop her. "Make that on a *balky* horse. A balky, *three-legged* horse. A *blind*, balky, three-legged horse."

"I am sorry I'm not in the position to offer you that opportunity at this time," Hunter said interrupting her tirade in a perfectly calm voice. "But perhaps in the near future that arrangement can be made."

Andrea felt a stinging sense of defeat at his latest comeback. He was learning to spar with her a little too well.

"Ah-h, Miss Evans."

"Yes, Major?" she snapped.

"Let's try not to have a battle of wits like this tonight."

"You mean with Victoria?"

"Yes, I mean with Victoria."

"Trust, sir, that won't happen," she said in a reassuring voice.

"Good." Once again Hunter turned to leave.

"I would never pick a battle of wits with an unarmed person!" Andrea yelled after him.

She watched him stop for a moment, but he did not return. He shook his head and mumbled something unintelligible under his breath, then strode back to the house, his gait—and his tightly clenched fists—portraying an emotion he seemed unable to suppress.

Chapter 40

"Vengeance is mine, I will repay sayeth the Lord."
– Romans 12:19

Hunter paced the dining room awaiting the arrival of his two houseguests. He tried to think optimistically, that anything other than a dismal failure would be a splendid success. And success would mean peace. And peace would mean his household would no longer be the scene of constant skirmishes and conflicts that he inevitably had to quell. Yet his heart pounded as if preparing to face a foe of unknown strength.

Victoria arrived first, walking into the room with the arrogance and sophistication of an empress among her subjects. Hunter escorted her to the table, and then turned to see Andrea standing warily at the doorway, her gaze sweeping the room as if calculating the terrain of an unfamiliar battlefield.

"Miss Evans, Miss Hamilton," he said while the two women eyed each other from across the table. "I'm hoping we can enjoy a meal together and would be much obliged if you'd each cease and desist your ... warfare."

Hunter's eyes fell on Andrea at the end of his sentence, who made no effort to conceal her disdain. Still, as his gaze swept over her, he could not help but admire what he saw. Clothed in a rose-dotted muslin, severe in its simplicity, she looked unpretentious and charming. Victoria, on the other hand, was dressed in a shade of shimmering silk that would be hard to describe and even harder to admire. The differences in them were even more apparent tonight. One had elegant Virginian breeding and upbringing. The other, he mused, possessed the look, bearing, and character of such.

"I'll have no more of the disruptions such as I witnessed today. Do I make myself clear?"

"Oh, but, Alex, that wasn't my fault." Victoria put her hand on Hunter's arm and blinked flirtatiously. "You heard what she said to me."

Hunter glanced at Andrea and determined that the version of events running through her mind was on a collision course with Victoria's. The room turned from chilly to stifling hot with the intensity of contrasting views. "I did not place the blame on anyone," he quickly noted. "I only demand it not happen again."

Andrea sat down stiffly with the air of one being forced to watch a beheading, refusing to give him the benefit of even a simple nod. She made it clear she had gone so far as to submit to his demand, but it was obvious she had no intention of feigning fondness for the woman on the other side of the table.

ℋ ℋ ℋ

Andrea took a deep breath while Hunter helped a rabidly mirthful Victoria into her chair. She stared at the food Mattie and Izzie served like it was steaming carrion, and prepared to face an evening that promised to be anything but enjoyable.

As a defense to the babbling Victoria, Andrea focused her attention on the view out the window, letting her mind wander to happier times. She had no idea how much time had passed when a loud voice interrupted her thoughts.

"Can you attempt to come back from your remote regions of thought and join us?"

Andrea turned her gaze to Hunter, then to Victoria and back again with a feigned look of confusion. "I'm sorry, sir, are you speaking to me or Miss Hamilton?"

Hunter's hand tightened into a fist around a knife. "Is our conversation boring you, Miss Evans?"

It was evident to Andrea that Hunter was somewhat perturbed. Since she did not wish to appear rude by answering in the affirmative, or lie by answering in the negative, she did not respond at all.

"Our conversation," Hunter repeated in a louder voice, "do you not find it interesting? Or are you just disinclined to talk in *our* presence?"

Andrea took his comment to mean she should feel disinclined to *be* in their presence and was instantly offended. "No, indeed, it's quite"—she sighed like she was trying to suppress a yawn—"captivating."

Hunter leaned toward her and whispered in a lethal, threatening voice. "Miss Evans, if you are trying to conceal your displeasure, may I have the honor of informing you that you are failing miserably?"

Andrea had no time to answer before Victoria interrupted in a shrill, excited voice. "Where did you get that? How came you to have it? And why?"

Surprised, both Andrea and Hunter followed her gaze to the ring on Andrea's finger. Victoria shifted her attention to the similar ring on Hunter's hand, then fastened her eyes upon Andrea accusingly, drumming her fingers on the table impatiently, waiting for a reply.

Andrea cleared her throat. "Daniel Delaney. Daniel . . . was a friend of mine."

"But he was a Yankee!"

Andrea's gaze went to Hunter's and Hunter's went to hers. Victoria's flicked from face to face.

Hunter recovered first and turned his attention to Victoria. "Daniel and Miss Evans were friends before the war, Victoria. Such a twist of fate cannot be helped."

"But that ring is priceless," she gasped, as if that justified the immediate retrieval of the heirloom from Andrea's finger.

"Nonetheless, it was given to Miss Evans. And agree with them or not, Daniel's wishes need to be respected." He looked at Andrea severely, letting her know by his tone that his words applied to her current presence in his home as well. Victoria became absorbed in another glass of wine, taking her mind off the ring, but her attention soon returned to Andrea. "Since it is Alex's wish that we get to know each other, perhaps you could enlighten me about your past. You hail from Maryland, do you not?" She spat the name of the state like it was some sort of incurable disease. "Why, I'm only surprised you don't drink whiskey and chew tobacco."

Andrea responded coolly. "But I do drink whiskey, Victoria, preferably right out of the bottle. You should try it in preference to the wine that you drink by the—"

"Miss Evans!" Hunter's voice boomed.

"Pray don't tell me you believe that because I don't know how to run barefoot and drink whiskey out of a bottle," Victoria said, shivering and rolling her eyes, "that I am somehow deficient."

"It is not for *me* to determine in what you are lacking." Andrea rested her gaze on Hunter as if that job belonged solely to him.

Victoria looked at Alex with a mortified expression, then put her hand to her head. "Alex, I have *tried* to overlook her homespun ways and uncouth manner, but really, must we attempt to have a reasonable conversation with her? I do not believe she is capable."

"And you are?" Andrea raised her eyebrows.

"La, my dear. I have been tutored in the delicate nature of being a lady, a concept obviously not familiar to you." She paused and then added with her nose in the air, "Of course, it's not your fault that you lack the breeding and cultivation of a Virginian."

Andrea looked at Hunter, expecting him to put an end to the dispute, but with all his warrior's blood, he appeared bewildered at the catfight occurring before him and seemed equally unsure of just what should be done to stop it.

Instead of getting angry, Andrea felt a sense of calm indignation. "You are right, Victoria," she said in a conciliatory voice. "I admit, I don't have your delicate nature or cultured breeding." She paused and stared down at her hands folded on her lap. "I know that inherent within you are a distinction and superiority, which I, and others like me, can only aspire to."

Andrea thought she saw Hunter roll his eyes toward heaven—something uncharacteristic for him—but she did not stop . "Perhaps, if you'd be so kind, Victoria, you could answer a question about the refined Virginian culture that I … that I know so little about."

"Miss Evans—"

"Oh, stop, darling," Victoria hushed Hunter. "The poor girl wants some advice." She lowered her eyelashes, obviously flattered by the request.

"Isn't it true," Andrea said, leaning toward Victoria to ensure she caught every word, "that women of your refined, Virginian lineage are—"

"Yes, dear?" Victoria leaned forward as well, intent on hearing the question.

"… are usually married by the time they reach *your* age?"

Victoria's mouth gaped open, but otherwise she did not respond. Andrea decided to strike while the iron was hot. "I was always taught that a woman's virtue is presumed until the contrary is proved, but, frankly, the appearance you present is rather, well …" Andrea paused and waved her hand in the air. "La, never mind, I believe I've gone and answered my own question."

She barely had time to finish and lean back contentedly in her chair before the room erupted into a scene of pandemonium. Victoria looked at Alex in horror and then shrieked so loudly the chandelier overhead rattled and jingled like a wind chime. Andrea thought for a delightful moment she was going to faint dead away—as a true, quality-bred lady probably should. Instead, she got a little of the uncivilized hellcat about her and reached for the vase of flowers on the table. Andrea ducked when the heirloom sailed in her direction and crashed into splinters when it hit the fireplace mantel behind her.

Hunter, on the other hand, stood in a rush, apparently afraid he was going to have to catch a swooning Victoria. The movement sent his chair skidding across the hardwood floor where it crashed with the sound of a massive explosion against a small serving table, sending both pieces of furniture plunging to the floor.

Meanwhile Izzie, who was a little skittish anyway, saw the coming tempest, and in attempting to make her escape before the full storm hit, ran headlong into Mattie, who was coming through the same door in a hurry to see what the commotion was about. Dishes and food went flying, some of it landing in Victoria's hair, thereby causing her to scream all the more hysterically.

A darker shadow of tumult could hardly have fallen on the domestic tranquility of Hawthorne had the enemy opened fire with a full battalion of artillery. Andrea sat gazing straight ahead, her hands folded on her lap, her eyes unblinking. She tried to suppress any indication that she had been the cause of this macabre disturbance, but failed to control a twitch at the corner of her mouth when she thought about the simplicity of it all. *Oh, the power of words.*

But her triumph was shortly erased. As Hunter helped a bawling Victoria from the room—so pale, so pathetic, so hysterical—Andrea let out a sigh of relief. The displeasing evening had at last come to an end. She waited until Hunter and Victoria were at the threshold before she stood to take her leave.

"Don't move!" Hunter's voice from the doorway sounded so authoritative, so very convincing, Andrea deemed it advisable to comply with his command.

And so she sat and listened to his retreating voice trying to calm the insensible and inconsolable Victoria. From what Andrea gathered from the vociferous howlings emanating from above, the gallant Hunter was having little luck soothing his fair maiden's nerves.

Andrea tried to initiate a conversation with Izzie and Mattie as they cleaned up the mess on the floor, but to her great surprise, they avoided her side of the room as if she had just been stricken with some fearfully contagious disease. Occasionally they threw anxious glances in her direction as if to see what other calamity she was going to impart on their beloved master, but mostly their looks consisted of angry glares and apprehensive scowls.

So Andrea sat pouting, her elbows on the table in a most unladylike fashion, waiting for her host to return. Her mind began to wander and her lips to twitch into another smile, and she feared she would not sleep a week for the satisfaction of the whole blessed affair.

Those thoughts were forgotten when it suddenly grew quiet upstairs. Andrea stirred uneasily in her chair, finding the silence more disturbing than the noise. When she heard the unmistakable fall of Hunter's heavy boots coming down the stairs, she decided there was something infinitely worse than the silence. Izzie and Mattie apparently had the same evaluation and made a mad rush for the kitchen door.

Andrea held her breath as Hunter paused at the door behind her, presumably taking in the scene of destruction. She felt his eyes penetrating the back of her head and wondered if the intensity of that glare would blind her if she turned around. She did not have the nerve to find out.

"Miss Evans," he said, striding across the room in his usual dashing style. Andrea noticed he had removed his coat in his absence, and was now rolling up his sleeves and shaking his head, the way men often do when they are anticipating a long, drawn out battle.

"Yes, Major?" She gazed up at him innocently with her chin planted on her hands.

"Tell me, is this your idea of a truce?" Hunter's eyes flashed with a look that could halt a lightning bolt in mid-strike.

"She fired the first shot." Andrea focused her attention on a painting over his shoulder.

"*She* fired the first shot?" Hunter hit the table with his fist so hard it made Andrea jump and caused the chandelier to jingle again. "Had you a gun in your hand in place of your wicked tongue, I've no doubt not a soul in this room would have been left standing!"

The thought of such a scene tickled Andrea so that she snorted trying to suppress a laugh. She covered her mouth with her hand to hide her amusement from his gaze.

"This is a monstrous affront to my hospitality!"

"Hospitality? I thought I made it clear I would prefer crawling into bed with a nest of rattlesnakes than accept the invitation."

Andrea again tried to conceal a grin with her hand, but the attempt did nothing to screen her mirthful eyes.

"You think this is great fun, don't you?" Hunter waved his hand at the mess. "Is there no deviltry to which you will not stoop? Are you driven by some mad inner force to do whatever you should not?"

Andrea looked around the room and surveyed the devastation. "One would not think such carnage could be created without gunpowder, would one?"

"And yet you are no doubt proud to have created such havoc armed only with your wit and tongue!"

"I am not proud. I simply attacked at the weakest point, which is to say her mind ... a strategy with which you are not altogether unfamiliar, I am sure."

Hunter scowled at her attempt to be clever. "I'm sorry to diminish the honor of your triumph, but this is an outrage! We had a truce. How dare you disobey!"

"That is not true." Andrea's smile vanished in an instant. "You *demanded* a truce. I would never submit to a truce with a conniving, manipulating *she-Rebel*. Did I not warn you that this was the inevitable outcome of your ill-conceived scheme?"

"Warned me? I do not believe I was forewarned of a major engagement in my dining room!"

Andrea sighed and gazed around the room. "I was not desirous of bringing on a general engagement, but please, sir, the battle was inevitable. Alone as I am on enemy soil, I am obliged to defend myself, am I not?"

Hunter seemed for a moment almost devoid of speech. "Defend yourself? Can you not curb your propensity for warfare for one evening?"

"I believe I showed great powers of restraint," Andrea said with a toss of her head. "And as for warfare, surely you cannot believe I'd attend here tonight, outnumbered two to one, without anticipating and preparing for premeditated malice from the enemy."

"This was no occasion for hostilities," Hunter said in a voice that trembled with anger. "You could not have done more bodily damage had you beaten her with a horsewhip."

"You are much deluded if you believe *that* to be true." Andrea failed to suppress a grin. "Yet I would be willing to test your theory."

"Don't trifle with me, Miss Evans. Since you have been here this home has been the scene of perpetual turbulence, a cauldron ever ready to boil over."

Andrea smiled gleefully and then pretended to cough when he fixed his eyes upon her.

Hunter gazed at her sternly. "Will you not try to get along?"

"Frankly, sir, I'd be more inclined to watch her Rebel carcass being picked clean by the birds of hell."

"Good God, Andrea!" Hunter pounded his fist on the table again to gain her attention.

Andrea looked up at him curiously when her first name and the Almighty's rolled off his lips like they were both old acquaintances whom he had addressed as such a thousand times. Yet she could not recall him ever calling her anything but Miss Evans, and was fairly sure discussions with his Maker were even more infrequent.

"You are greatly mistaken, my dear, if you feel my leniency with you will last forever." Hunter started to walk toward her side of the table, causing Andrea to retreat to the other.

"I believe leniency has been reserved for Victoria and well it should be. One shouldn't be too hard on someone who wouldn't know a rock from a ramrod. Surely, even *you* must find her obtuseness tiresome."

"On the contrary. Sometimes I believe she has infinitely more wisdom than you."

Hunter's words had the effect of a match to gunpowder. "Retrieve that," Andrea screamed, seizing a knife on the table and slamming it down so that it stuck upright on the table. "That is an unpardonable insult!"

"She is not to blame for your constant discontentment, nor is she in any-way responsible for the circumstances that brought you here," he said calmly. "That is the fault of no one but yourself." He paused but only for a moment. "I must ask that you apologize. She has requested such."

Andrea had, at that moment, been taking a drink of water. Only with the greatest effort did she manage to swallow, rather than discharge the fluid in her throat. She whirled around and glanced at the table, obviously looking for something to throw. But what was not already lying smashed on the floor had been cleared, save the knife, which Hunter snatched and placed out of reach.

"Hang me if I will! Andrea paced erratically for a moment, then took a deep breath for control. "Major, I would tell you what else I think of your suggestion, but fortunately for you, I'm a Christian lady."

Hunter laughed. "I do not know from what great nation of Christendom you hail, but you've never concerned yourself with holding your tongue in check before on that basis. In fact I dare say I've heard you say some things that would blister the lips of a sailor on shore leave."

Andrea glowered at his half-cocked grin. "The fact remains, sir, that this entire evening can be attributed to a woeful lack of judgment on *your* part. I can only hope you do not allow it to happen again."

"You share no blame for this?" Hunter threw his hands in the air. "Your arguments are neither convincing nor persuasive, or, frankly, even logical! You cannot expect me to regard you as a rational creature."

Andrea studied her fingernails to show she had no interest in continuing the conversation. "She has but to stay out of my way and no further trans-gressions shall occur. Perhaps you can persuade or compel or convince her to comply."

"Tell me this. Are you even now? Has the appropriate justice been meted out?"

"Sir, why must you place the blame on *me*? Why do you not place the blame where it belongs—on her distemper and wickedness?"

"I *do* place the blame where it belongs—on *your* defiance and rebellious-ness!"

"I take issue with that. Rebelliousness is an admirable trait when associated with the men of your Command, yet an offensive one when linked with my ... free will."

"Free will? Is that what you call your intolerable, insolent behavior?"

Andrea closed her eyes until there was barely a slice of green to be seen. "I cannot help but find it quite fascinating, sir, that you are determined to defend and support such a supremely selfish, notoriously insincere and disgracefully vain woman, who would sell her sense of honor, which I fear is not of much value, for influence and power." Andrea raised her eyebrows to their highest elevation. "One can only speculate as to your motivation."

Now it was Hunter's turn to lose his temper. "You may speculate all you want, young lady," he said, shaking his finger at her, "and I'll determine it my justifiable duty to put you in your place."

Andrea's eyes narrowed. "*She* is the one who needs put in her place. Did you not notice that she attempted to insult me tonight?"

"You are too obstinate to be insulted," he said, throwing his hands in the air. "Your behavior today is most certainly only going to fuel her fires!"

"If I were you, I'd counsel her to the contrary. Nothing in her life could become her like leaving it."

Hunter leaned forward with his hands on the table. "Is that a threat?"

"Take it as you may," she responded coolly. "And pass it on."

"Do you believe that comment will go unavenged?"

Andrea recognized the limit of his patience and felt the color drain from her face. But much to her surprise, the cause of the evening's disturbance became the source for her escape. Victoria's shrill voice pulsated through the room, causing Hunter to cast an eye to the room above them at the sound of his name.

His gaze fell again upon Andrea, and it was one that caused her insides to writhe. "This conversation has come to an end." He strode to the door, then turned and looked her dead in the eye. "But that does not mean I'm through with you."

Chapter 41

"Wisely and slow; they stumble who run fast."
— Romeo and Juliet, Shakespeare

Andrea eased herself into the chair with her book just as a loud knock sounded at the door. She cringed, knowing Hunter had returned, and that they had not yet finished their last conversation. "Yes?" She attempted to keep her voice from shaking.

Hunter walked in buttoning up the coat of a dress uniform she had never seen. He wore a look of deep concern that surprised her. "I'm having some guests this afternoon." He gazed at her with his head cocked to one side, apparently testing her reaction to his words. "It's a business meeting. And it is imperative that everything goes smoothly."

"And you'd like me to stay out of the way?"

Hunter, who had been staring over her shoulder, brought his eyes back to hers in obvious surprise. "Yes. I'd prefer that you stay out of sight."

"Well, I'm just about to start this book, so you've nothing to fear from me."

Hunter studied her another moment, nodded his head, and disappeared out the door.

When Andrea heard the clatter of hooves in the turnaround a short while later, she could not resist the urge to look out the balcony door. The sight that greeted her caused the book to fall forgotten from her hand. She watched in awe as a four–horse team of perfectly matched dappled grays drew toward the house. Hurrying to the balcony, she leaned over the railing to get a better look at the steeds and the elegant conveyance that approached the front door directly beneath her.

"What you doin', Miz Andrea?" Izzie stood behind her.

"Oh, Izzie. Look at that coach-and-four. I simply must see those horses!"

Andrea leaned farther over the railing, but the team was now hidden from view. She straightened and turned to Izzie. "And you're going to help me."

"Why you want to see some ol' horse? They's horses all over dis place."

Andrea ignored her, and limped out of the room to stand at the top of the stairs. She heard greetings being made and saw two well-dressed men—or the bottom halves of them anyway—following Hunter into his library. Finally, the door closed.

Andrea motioned excitedly for Izzie. "Come on," she said, taking her by the arm and thrusting her down the stairs. "Go down and make sure no one is about. I'll run straight through the foyer and go out the kitchen side."

"I dunno," Izzie protested. "Ole Him 'bout as happy today as a buzz saw today. And I don't wanna go messin' with no buzz saw."

"Go on, hurry." Andrea pushed her again. "I don't know how much time I have."

Izzie crept down the stairs and looked cautiously both ways, then motioned Andrea to proceed. Just as she reached the bottom step, the door to Hunter's study opened. Knowing she would never make it back up the steps in time, Andrea decided to make a run for it. She limped after Izzie, who had already skedaddled across the foyer and disappeared.

Andrea took only a few running steps before colliding with a man hurrying out of the library. The resulting collision was swiftly followed by the appearance of Hunter, whose fury was evident, though he somehow managed to control his tone.

"I see you've made the acquaintance of my houseguest," Hunter said to the man who stared down at Andrea while holding her securely in his arms.

"Your houseguest?" The man's gaze swept over her.

"Yes." Hunter strode across the foyer and picked up Andrea's cane, which had clattered to the floor. "John Paul Clarke, may I present Miss Andrea Evans." He thrust the cane at her so she could step away.

John Paul Clarke reluctantly released her and made a sweeping bow. "I apologize for my haste and clumsiness, Miss Evans. I had no idea Mr. Hunter had a houseguest. It is indeed a pleasure to make your acquaintance."

That the man failed to use Hunter's military title when he referred to him did not escape Andrea's notice. Nor did his mocking tone of voice elude her. She studied his face, which was strikingly handsome, yet the soft feel of his arms when he grasped her detracted from the image.

"John Paul was on his way to get some papers from his carriage." Hunter's tone made it clear to Andrea that he wanted her to depart the room.

"I'm sorry. I was actually … I mean … it appears you have a very nice team," she said to John Paul.

"They are a sight, are they not?" John Paul strutted over to the window and looked outside as if to remind himself just how perfect the four horses really were. "Well, come then," he said, holding out his arm. "You simply must accompany me to get a better look."

Andrea glanced at Hunter and saw him scowl as she linked her arm in the stranger's. When Victoria cleared her throat from the stairway to catch everyone's attention, Andrea was almost certain she heard Hunter groan.

"Land's sakes, Alex. How many more beautiful women are you hiding at Hawthorne?" John Paul asked, as Victoria descended the stairway.

"Oh, John Paul, stop." Victoria elbowed Andrea out of the way, then giggled and kissed him on each cheek. "What are you doing here?" Then she turned to Hunter. "Why did you not tell me John Paul and his father were coming?"

"We're here on business," John Paul said, nodding toward the other man who stood in the doorway of the library. "Horse business."

"Oh, please, no." Victoria waved her hand in the air. "That's all you two ever talk about!"

"Well Alex is determined to get his hands on that stallion of mine."

Andrea felt a prickle go up her neck and a knot form in her stomach. Were they discussing Zeus, the gray stallion Hunter had once mentioned he wished to buy? Her heart lurched at the remembrance of how his eyes had lit up at the mere mention of the horse. Had she ruined Hunter's chance of acquiring the stud he had been trying to purchase for years?

Victoria held her hands over her ears and spoke in an overly loud voice. "I don't want to hear another word about horses, especially not while we're eating. You did invite them to dinner did you not?" She threw a probing glance at Hunter.

"You're, ah, welcome to—"

"We accept!" John Paul took Andrea's arm again as if he had accomplished a great victory. "Come now, Miss Evans. Let's have a look at that wonderful team of mine."

❀ ❀ ❀

Hunter had wearied of watching John Paul lean close to Andrea during the entire meal, and decided to put an end to the private conversation. "It's been a long afternoon, gentlemen. Miss Evans, would you like to retire?" He rose from the table and offered his arm, giving her little chance to refuse.

Andrea gazed up at him with a forced smile. "I suppose it has been a long day." She stood and turned to John Paul. "So very nice to meet you," she said, offering him her hand. She nodded in the direction of John Paul's father, "Mr. Clark, a pleasure," then reluctantly accepted Hunter's arm.

As soon as the dining room door closed, Hunter whispered in her ear, "Bravo my dear. Another marvelous performance."

Andrea cocked her head innocently to one side. "Performance?"

"I dare say anyone who did not know you could not help but be impressed." He felt anger swell within him when he thought of the looks John Paul had thrown her—and the ones she had skillfully returned.

"Does that include you, Major? I had no idea I was that *impressive.*"

"I believe I said anyone who does not know you." He pretended to be completely unaffected by her loveliness, though it was only with great effort that he drew his eyes away from her when they reached the bottom of the stairs.

"Did I in some way displease you?"

"No, my dear. You simply play the part of a devoted Rebel so well that I'm beginning to wonder who the real Andrea Evans is. In fact, I wonder," Hunter said, leaning down so his face was just inches from hers, "if *you* even know anymore."

Andrea did not answer at first. But the redness in her cheeks and the expression on her face was sufficient to tell Hunter what she thought of him. "Perhaps I find it pleasurable and refreshing to have a discussion with *gentlemen*. Your behavior today was abhorrent. You could have at least tried to be civil to your guests."

"Believe me, Miss Evans, it is an act of civility that I allow John Paul to step foot in my house."

Hunter turned away, marking the end of the conversation. "I'll call Mattie to assist you up the stairs."

Chapter 42

"Heaven hath a hand in these events."
— Richard II, Shakespeare

Andrea stepped out of the house with a large smile on her face as she gazed upon the brilliant sunlight beaming down in golden sparkles through the trees. Halfway down the steps, she noticed a carriage tied to the post in the turnaround she did not recognize.

She almost passed it by before noticing a young female slave tied to the back. Noticeably pregnant, the woman was on her knees, resting from apparently being made to walk a great distance.

Andrea hurried to the young woman's aid, but the slave covered her head and lay in the dirt like a dog cowering from the boot of its master.

"Don't hit me, missus. Please don't hit me no more."

"I'm not going to hit you. Let me help you up."

The woman lifted her head, revealing a pair of brown, frightened, disbelieving eyes. Her look of pain and distrust revived memories of the revolting spectacles Andrea had witnessed in her childhood. The reflections lashed her into a fury for the injustices committed then and now.

Before she had time to react further, a shadow appeared from the front of the carriage. Andrea looked up to see a man of rotund stature, whose sweaty forehead and pallid skin reminded her of her father.

"I do not believe I've had the honor," he said.

Andrea refused to accept the extended hand. "Have you no sense? No decency?"

"I beg your pardon." He grabbed her arm. "Do you know who you're speaking to?"

"Remove your foul hands from me!" Andrea struggled free from his grasp. "Or I'll—"

"Miss Evans!" Hunter strode out of the house seeking the cause of the commotion.

"Please control your wife," the man said, brushing off his coat like he had touched something offensive. "I've half a mind to call off the deal."

"She's not my wife, and I wouldn't attempt to control her if she were," Hunter said with a hint of anger in his own voice now.

Andrea shot him a look of surprise. "What deal have you made?"

"Mr. Potts has offered to purchase the two blooded bays." Hunter's gaze shifted from Andrea to the slave girl behind the carriage, apparently seeing her for the first time.

"You cannot possibly sell horses to someone who treats property like this." Her hand trembled as she pointed toward the man. "*This* is what is wrong with the South!"

The slave looked up curiously.

Hunter took a step toward Andrea and spoke in a gentle voice. "It's none of our business."

"None of our business?" Andrea hit her cane on the ground and turned to face the man. "I'll not turn my back on evil! How much for her?"

"She's not for sale," Potts answered. "She's leaving with me and staying where she is."

Andrea took a step forward. "And you'll walk over my prostrate form to accomplish it!"

"I said she's not for sale. I just purchased her, and need to make sure she knows who is master before I get her home." Potts brushed some imaginary dirt from his coat sleeve.

"Who is master?" Andrea spat the words. "You're nothing but a—"

"How much?" Hunter quickly interrupted.

Potts rubbed his chin while making a grunting sound. "Well now, you can see she's with child. I'd say the two of them are worth fifteen hundred dollars."

"You told me earlier you'd bought a negress for eight hundred dollars. I'll give you eight fifty, and the deal with the horses is off."

The man scoffed at the offer. "You jest. You're going to allow this . . ." his gaze swept over Andrea, "this slave lover to—"

Hunter rushed toward Potts, grabbed him by the throat, and threw him against the coach with such force that the man's feet left the ground. "It's for men like you that men like me are forced to shed their blood in defense of this country." Hunter's face was but inches away from that of the trembling slave owner. "If you'd like to leave this estate in one piece, I'd urge you to consider my proposal."

Andrea saw the strength in Hunter's one arm, and was both petrified and enthralled. When Potts responded with a nod, Hunter released his grip, causing the man to fall against the coach gasping for breath. Andrea gave Hunter no time to change his mind. She rushed to untie the slave.

"Miss Evans." Hunter's voice was stern. "Mattie will take care of her. I'd like to speak with you." He turned and strode toward the house without a backward glance.

ℋ ℋ ℋ

Andrea stormed into the library to find Hunter at the window, standing with his back to her. She could see from his stance he was agitated.

"When I started this day," he said, turning and looking into her eyes, "I thought I had two horses sold—and at a very good price I might add."

Andrea looked away from his piercing gaze.

"Now, I find my purse empty of eight hundred and fifty dollars. I am still in possession of two horses for which I have no use. And will soon have, not one, but two more mouths to feed!"

"I'm sorry if I displeased you." Andrea sounded sincere, yet she revealed no remorse.

"This estate is not a sanctuary for your menagerie of injured horses and abused slaves. I have a responsibility to feed and clothe those already here. I have more than two hundred head of horses that need my attention—"

"I'll pay you back."

"Hold your tongue, Miss Evans." His voice grew noticeably louder. "That is not the point."

Andrea stared at the floor, while twisting the ring on her finger. She could tell Hunter had reached his limit.

"I did not mean to interfere."

"You did not mean to interfere?" Hunter bellowed. "Then what did you mean?"

"I ... I was simply doing what I feel is right in my heart—"

"Your *heart*? Well, thanks to your heart, I lost more than two thousand dollars today!"

Andrea stared out the window.

"Have you nothing to say?"

"The cost of doing what is right cannot be measured." Andrea gave Hunter a penetrating gaze. "Not in pain. Not in sacrifice. And certainly not in the loss of gold."

She turned and walked out the door, leaving Hunter to mull over the fact that he knew she was right.

Chapter 43

"A faith that shines more bright and clear,
When tempests rage without
That, when in danger knows no fear,
In darkness knows no doubt."
— Hymn from Nurse and Spy

Hunter heard a blood-curdling scream from the direction of the porch and flew through the house to discover its source. He found Andrea standing perfectly still, a look of complete panic on her face. "Miss Evans. What is wrong?"

She grasped his forearm in a powerful one-handed clutch. "Spider," she whispered, as if fearing the creature would hear her.

Hunter thought she must be joking, but not even the sight of a hangman's noose could equal the terror that radiated from her eyes as she shook her hair, then her hand, as if she had touched something vile.

"A spider, Miss Evans?"

"Yes, it dropped—" She gasped, barely able to finish the sentence. "In my h-hair."

Despite her serious face, Hunter put his head back and laughed. "You, Andrea Evans, are afraid of a little spider?"

"It wasn't *little!*"

Hunter suppressed another laugh because he felt her trembling, yet he hardly believed what he heard and saw. The daring, dauntless Andrea Evans had a weakness.

"You don't understand!" Sighing with obvious exasperation at his mirth, she checked her hair one last time and picked up her skirts to depart. But before taking a step, she stared warily at the porch floor as if to make sure the creature was not about to attack her from the ground. Then she peered up to the beams in case it, or any of its many relatives, was preparing to launch an aerial assault.

"Well, I'll be!"

Hunter turned to see a pony cart pulling into the turnaround at the porch. "No wonder I never see you any more, Alexander Hunter."

"Mrs. Fox." Hunter strode down the steps. "What a pleasant surprise."

"Pleasant indeed." The woman looked at Andrea and winked. Heaving her robust figure out of the seat, she stood and waited for Hunter to help her down.

"I'm Emma Fox," she said after she dusted off her skirt and offered her hand to Andrea. "The Widow Fox is what the boys tend to call me."

"Mrs. Emma Fox, I'd like you to meet Andrea Evans. Miss Evans, my neighbor, Mrs. Fox of Hawk Shadow Farm."

"Pleased to make your acquaintance, Mrs. Fox."

"I had no idea you had a beautiful young woman hidden away up here," Mrs. Fox said, turning her attention back to Hunter.

Victoria, who must have heard the sound of the earlier screaming, appeared in the doorway and cleared her throat. "Oh, and of course, you know Miss Hamilton," Hunter said hurriedly.

The newcomer gave Victoria a sideways glance. "Yes, I do." She offered no further comment.

"Well, what brings you to Hawthorne?" Hunter stepped forward. "Is there something I can do for you?"

"No, no. I just came to deliver a message from the Talberts."

"The Talberts? Is something wrong?"

"My gads, boy, no." Mrs. Fox laughed. "Quite the contrary. I've come to invite you to a celebration Saturday."

"A celebration? For what? I was just at the Talberts yesterday and there was no mention of such an event."

"Mrs. Talbert and I and some of the boys just decided today. It's a celebration party in honor of your recent promotion—though the ladies are more interested in celebrating the fact that Colonel Hunter survived an intended ambush last week. Either one is certainly sufficient for celebration."

Hunter scoffed. Victoria squealed. And Andrea suppressed a gasp. She did not know Hunter was now a Colonel—but Victoria's excitement apparently did not stem from news of the promotion.

"Oh darling, a party! Do you know how long it's been since I've attended a party? It's Saturday?" Victoria spoke to no one in particular. "Why that's the day after tomorrow. How will I ever find something to wear by then?" She talked excitedly and hurriedly, as if the announcement was of far greater significance than the current state of the country at large.

Mrs. Fox frowned at the outburst and turned to Andrea. "You will attend, won't you, dear?"

"Miss Evans is recovering from an injury," Hunter said before she had time to respond. "She's in no condition to attend a party."

"She looks fine to me," Mrs. Fox insisted with relentless persistence. "I'll stop by and pick her up myself. I can see you will have your hands full." She gave an unflattering glance toward Victoria and turned back to the wagon, indicating the conversation was over.

"She has nothing appropriate to wear." Hunter tried one more time to turn down the invitation, while helping her into the wagon.

"Oh, come now," Mrs. Fox said. "She's about the same size as Elizabeth. I'm sure she left a thing or two lying around here."

Andrea's eyes rose in obvious surprise at the mention of Hunter's wife, but he successfully masked any emotion.

"You'll inform the other men." Mrs. Fox's statement sounded like an order, not a question. Then she turned to Andrea at the exclusion of the other two. "He's always been such a worrier. Wait and see, everything will go without a hitch."

Yes, everything will go without a hitch as easily as a wagon goes uphill without a horse," Hunter thought.

"I'll be by about seven o'clock Saturday." Without waiting for a reply, she slapped the horse and disappeared down the drive at a brisk trot.

❦ ❦ ❦

The jostling of the carriage did nothing to ease the pain in Andrea's leg once she and Mrs. Fox were on their way. Like Hunter, she had a bad feeling about tonight. Although she would never admit it, she knew he was right in trying to convince her not to attend.

But the conversation soon took her thoughts away from her nagging instincts and anxiety. The topics they discussed were light and impersonal—until Hunter became the focus of the banter.

Mrs. Fox leaned toward Andrea. "So how is it that you came to know the king of the land?"

"The king?" Andrea laughed.

"My dear, certainly you know the authority and influence the Colonel holds in this province." She sighed deeply. "Such a warrior, yet such a gentleman. Commands the affection and respect of all who meet him."

Andrea looked at her hands. "No, I was ... not aware—"

"And handsome, of course. Certainly you are aware of *that.*" The widow turned and looked directly into her eyes.

Andrea felt herself blushing. "I suppose he is somewhat attractive."

"Somewhat attractive?" Mrs. Fox bubbled over with laughter. "The Greeks have their gods, and we Virginians have Colonel Hunter. If there is a soul who can exceed him in manliness or grace of character, I've yet to meet him. Gracious me!"

The widow shook her head and babbled on. "He'd make a wonderful husband, yet he shows no sign of desiring to settle down. Who could blame him really, his mother deserting him the way she did, and then that business with Elizabeth. Certainly every eligible woman in Virginia and beyond has made him aware she's available. And then, of course, there's Victoria."

The conversation began to make Andrea uncomfortable. She brushed some imaginary lint off her skirt and then repeated the unnecessary task.

"He's changed much since then," Mrs. Fox continued, talking in a low voice as if she feared being overheard. "Not that he was ever that sociable, but when Elizabeth was at Hawthorne there were visitors and entertaining all the time. He's a regular recluse now, and seemingly perfectly content. Yet everyone's convinced he'll eventually marry someone with a pedigree. You know, take a Virginia bride."

Mrs. Fox looked over at Andrea. "Oh, I really shouldn't be gossiping like this. Anyway, you never answered my question. It's such a rare privilege to be honored with his intimacy. How did you meet?"

Andrea took a deep breath. "We met ... well . . . quite by accident."

"Oh, the war, I suppose," Mrs. Fox finished for her.

Andrea nodded, glad she did not have to go into more detail.

"If that is the case, then I'm glad to hear some good has come out of this terrible state of affairs," Mrs. Fox said wistfully. "They say it's all right to give your only son to the Cause—"

Andrea heard the woman's voice tremble.

"But I wish I had mine back."

Andrea looked up into Mrs. Fox's eyes. "I'm sorry. You lost a son?"

"He served under Colonel . . . *Captain* Hunter, at the time." Her voice was raw with emotion. "He was a lieutenant."

Andrea's heart stopped beating. She closed her eyes, and grabbed the edge of the seat for support as a wave of dizziness swept through her as her mind drifted back to that day at Thoroughfare Gap.

"What's wrong, dear? You don't look well."

Andrea looked up at her, but did not speak.

"Matthew and Alex were inseparable friends, grew up together." She looked over at Andrea sadly. "He took it hard, the Colonel did. Felt responsible, I guess. But I never blamed him. How could I? He's always been like a second son to me."

"And the rest of the command?" Andrea's voice was just a whisper. "Did make their escape that day?"

Mrs. Fox looked at Andrea curiously. "Yes, dear. Alex would draw blood with his teeth before he would let the Yankees get too close to his men. But there were some prisoners taken that day I believe." She shook her head sadly. "I think Alex took it even harder than I. He swore to me he'd extract in Yankee blood the value of my loss."

Andrea gulped. "I'm sorry, I-I-'m not feeling very well. Can we go back?"

"My dear, we're almost there. It's all this talk about Matthew, isn't it? I'm sorry to have upset you. It's been more than a year now. I should not have brought it up."

Andrea felt nauseous. The incident at Thoroughfare Gap had been a little more than a year ago, when Hunter was still a captain. If Matthew Fox died there, it was because of her. She may have caused the death of the only son of the only friend she had in this godforsaken land! Andrea tried to breathe without gasping for air, but she felt like she was drowning as Hunter's words from that night echoed in her ears. "My loss was severe, more so in the worth than the number slain." She swallowed hard, felt the blood draining from her face, and tried to concentrate on the moonbeams adorning the meadow.

"Ah, here we are," Mrs. Fox said, turning the team into a tree-lined drive. "Feeling better?"

Andrea took a deep breath at the sight of a house gleaming from afar. She looked around then, and thought the drive looked strangely familiar. Searching her mind, she could think of no reason for such a reflection. As they ascended a long, covered ally of trees, the house appeared again, ghostly in the light mist, but luminous with twinkling lanterns. Already the sounds of music and laughter floated in the breeze, and Andrea tried desperately to turn her thoughts to other things. She was here. There was no turning back now.

As they crowned the last small rise, the house appeared in full view. Horses, dozens and dozens of them, all meticulously groomed and looking sleek and swift, stood tied indiscriminately throughout the yard, along with drays, carry-alls, traps, coaches, and carriages.

It seemed that all of Virginia had been seeking an opportunity to celebrate, and Hunter's escape from an ambush had provided it. In the fashion in which the house was lit—and from the noise emanating from its depths—this party was fit to do honor to a king.

❦ ❦ ❦

Hunter had just taken a sip of punch, which he almost discharged onto the man next to him, when Andrea came through the doorway. Dressed in the colors of dawn, candlelight flickering off her hair, she appeared as magnificent as nature itself. Although holding the hand of Mrs. Fox for support, she gave the impression she was entering on the arm of royalty.

Allowing his gaze to drift to the men who stared openly, Hunter looked back to the entranceway and felt his heart uncharacteristically pick up its pace. Andrea was smiling demurely at one of his men, Lieutenant Pierce, who bowed and kissed her hand with his usual pugnacious chivalry. Apparently Pierce had not bothered to wait for the proper introductions. He was giving her his undivided attention, examining her in such a way that made his intentions obvious.

Hunter shifted his weight uneasily, thinking what could happen should the tall, broad-shouldered lieutenant discover the true identity of the one whose hand he held so lovingly now. He knew how quickly that expression of lust would turn to loathing. Pierce was well known for his ability with women, and was equally renowned for his ability with a gun. Hotheaded and temperamental, he was a man who, when riled, relied heavily on bullets and fists. Hunter would have dismissed a lesser man in a minute, but Pierce was not unworthy to be considered among the bravest in his ranks.

Taking a sip of his drink and nodding mechanically at Victoria's incessant chattering beside him, Hunter watched Andrea turn and fix her attention musingly on the crowd. He thought he saw strong admiration and a flicker of wonder cross her face before a shadow of deep regret crept into her expression. Following her gaze to the far side of the room, Hunter blinked in surprise when he saw it was the Southern Banner that had evoked the remorseful expression. Turning back to analyze the gaze, he saw it had disappeared. The smile had returned.

A movement in a side doorway suddenly attracted Hunter's attention, and he watched Carter give him the "all's quiet" sign. Hunter nodded in acknowledgment and again his gaze drifted to Andrea. Yes, all's quiet—as is a powder magazine until a match is lit.

ℋ ℋ ℋ

When Andrea entered the room on Mrs. Fox's arm, her heart beat wildly and her stomach flipped and churned. When she glanced around the room, what she saw overwhelmed her even more. The men gathered before her were not officers wearing new costumes of gray and brass like those in Richmond. Here were soldiers wearing uniforms that showed signs of heavy wear; soldiers who looked accustomed to hard living—and harder fighting.

But Andrea found she was not frightened by what she saw. She gazed upon them with admiration for what they were—noble, brave, tenacious warriors. Their weapons and their manner attested to their familiarity with desperate combat. Yet, despite their martial appearance, they did not seem to be the ruthless horde she had imagined. Rather, all had eyes glowing fervently with patriotic devotion.

For a moment, Andrea stood and stared. These were her enemies. Yet now they had faces and names. They had families and homes, husbands and wives, and sisters and brothers. Her gaze drifted to the Confederate banner hanging on the wall. *How sad, how pitifully tragic this war has become.* All hate suddenly drained out of her, replaced by sorrow and confusion. Virginia and her inhabitants had begun to affect her heart in a strange and mysterious manner.

Mrs. Fox's hand pressed hers in comfort, but Andrea felt suddenly apprehensive when she sensed Hunter's penetrating gaze upon her. Glancing over her shoulder, she saw his gray eyes trained on her like an animal watching its prey. Even with the distance between them, the sight made her tremble.

Andrea placed a smile upon her face and pretended to take no heed. "Miss Evans?" Andrea half-jumped and turned toward the sound of the voice.

"My name is Fannie … Fannie Mae Madison. I'm very pleased to make your acquaintance."

Andrea looked into the soft, warm eyes of a woman several years her senior. She appeared more shy and reserved than many of the others in the room, her fingers nervously toying with the sleeve of her gown.

"Mrs. Fox told me about you," she said, apparently noticing Andrea's confusion.

"Not too much I hope." Andrea smiled at the woman while glancing at Mrs. Fox.

"Oh, no, don't worry. Not too much. Only that you reside temporarily at Hawthorne." Fanny cleared her throat. "I suppose … I suppose you have occasion to see a good deal of Major Carter."

Andrea followed the woman's gaze to Carter, who appeared intent in a conversation with a young recruit across the room. "Yes. Enough to know that he is quite a fearless soldier … and a gentleman."

"Yes, I think so too." Fannie's words and her longing eyes revealed her feelings clearly. Before Andrea could say anything else, Fannie pointed over her shoulder. "Oh, it looks like Laura Talbert is trying to get your attention."

Andrea turned to follow the girl who had been motioning toward her, but paused in the dimly lit hallway trying to see where she had disappeared.

"Miss Evans," Laura said, grabbing her wrist. "This way." She unlocked the only closed door, hastened Andrea through, and closed it behind them. In the pitch-black room, Andrea waited for the lamps to be lit.

"I'm sorry to accost you like this, Miss Evans, but I had no idea Colonel Hunter had a houseguest other than Victoria. Why, everyone is talking about it! You must tell me everything that goes on at Hawthorne."

"Miss Talbert," Andrea said, turning to face the girl when the room became illuminated. "I'm afraid I—" Andrea stopped and gazed around the room, then down at her hands that rested on the back of a chair. She jerked them away and took a step back as if the chair had turned and bit her.

"Miss Evans," Laura said. "Is something wrong?"

Turning slowly, as if excessive movement would make her fall, she looked over her right shoulder. Yes, there was the door to the outside where they had brought her in. The room even smelled the same, the sweet odor of pipe smoke, mixed with the scent of freshly oiled floors.

Andrea's heart stopped beating for a moment as recognition slowly sank in. This was the same room where she had been brought when captured by Hunter's men. The room where Hunter had, she thought, committed her to prison. The Talbert house was his headquarters. And he did not want her to find that out—even now.

The door opened with a loud groan. "Miss Talbert, Miss Evans, what a pleasant surprise." Hunter wore his customary expression of composed nonchalance, yet he appeared and sounded like a stranger to Andrea.

"Colonel Hunter," Laura said, looking nervous. "I just brought Miss Evans in here to talk in private and get acquainted. It is so loud out there."

"I see." He stared at Andrea with a cold smile that matched the cool glint of ice in his eyes. "Why don't you offer her a seat?" He nodded toward the very chair where Andrea had sat while being interrogated.

Andrea stared at the chair as if it were already taken. She knew Laura was waiting for her to do something or say something, but she was too dizzy with confusion. "No. No thank you. I believe I'll stand," she finally muttered.

A few of Hunter's men wandered into the room, apparently thinking there was something of importance occurring.

"I cannot imagine why you would wish to get better acquainted," Hunter said in a loud voice. "Seeing that you are a loyal Virginian, and Miss Evans is a—" He stopped himself, but the damage had been done.

Laura flinched and looked at Andrea, apparently waiting for her to speak up and defend herself. Yet Andrea said nothing, revealed nothing. In silent pride, she gazed over Hunter's shoulder, her eyes fixed on a painting on the wall.

"You are a most deceptive man, Colonel." Andrea finally spoke in a tone low enough so only he and Laura heard her words. "There was a time I had almost thought you a gentleman."

Laura attempted to lighten the air. "Come now, Miss Evans, you'll break the Colonel's heart with such talk."

"Truly? I was not aware he possessed one. Now if you will excuse me." Andrea curtsied politely and nodded toward the others in the room. "Gentlemen." Her eyes lingered slightly longer on Lieutenant Pierce than on any of the others, and his eyes consumed hers before she swished out the door.

H H H

"Pierce!"

Lieutenant Pierce, who had started to follow Andrea, stopped in his tracks and turned impatiently toward Hunter. "Sir?"

"Leave her alone."

Pierce blinked and looked back over his shoulder toward the disappearing figure, obviously not willing to relinquish her quite so quickly. "But, I ..." He turned his back on Hunter and continued to scan the crowd as if the statement was a suggestion that he could heed or disregard at will.

"That is an *order*, Lieutenant."

Pierce swung back around and stared at Hunter with a look of contempt.

"Is there something about that order you do not understand?"

One of the men walked up and patted Pierce on the shoulder. "Calm down, Pierce. This is a party. No sense getting in an uproar over a woman."

Pierce shrugged the man off, while others stepped in between the two officers. That Pierce was hotheaded enough to pick a fight with a man twice his size was common knowledge. It was hoped that he would not be foolish enough to pick one with his commanding officer.

"I believe I understand it perfectly," he said, saluting Hunter with a feigned display of respect. "And may the best man win."

The words had barely left his lips before Hunter stomped over to him, at which time those who had moved forward deemed it prudent to take a few steps back. The looks being discharged by the two men boded ill for eyes and jaws and anything else in range of the fists that were being clenched.

"I have no time to stand in contemplation of who is the better man," Hunter said from between gritted teeth, "but I do expect my order to be followed."

Pierce stared Hunter in the eyes for a moment before departing in disgust. Laura, meanwhile, gave Hunter an unkind look and followed Pierce.

Hunter stood alone, breathing heavily, as he acknowledged that he had not only failed to keep the powder keg away from the flame—he had caused the incendiary spark that ignited the explosion.

Chapter 44

"Land of the South, imperial land, how proud thy mountains rise,
How sweet thy scenes at every hand, how fair thy covering skies!
But not for those, oh, not for those, I love thy fields to roam;
Thou hast a dearer spell to me, Thou art my native home."
— Land of the South by Alex Beufort Meek

Andrea kept walking. She limped out the door, breathing in gasps at the exertion and the pain shooting through her leg.

That room! This house! She had no idea what she had been getting into. Yet Hunter had, and all along. How dare he stand there so smugly, knowing she recognized the room and the memories it wrought. Damn him! And damn his men! And damn this whole damn war!

By the time Andrea came back to her senses, she had passed the gate of the estate. She did not care. If she stopped walking, she feared she would explode. The throbbing of nerve endings in her leg felt excruciating, but she was too angry to acknowledge it.

From out of nowhere, she heard the sound of a wagon coming up behind her, and then a voice. "May I take you somewhere, Miss Evans?"

She glanced up at Major Carter and walked faster. "I do not care for a ride, thank you."

Carter urged the horses forward, then pulled them across the road in front of her. "I can be as stubborn as the next person," he said. "Git in."

Andrea stopped, but only for a moment. In her rage, she struck the side of the wagon with her cane. "Move this blasted rig out of my way!"

The officer sighed, got down from his seat, and grabbed the cane from her hand. Tossing it into the back, he held her arms by her side. "You can get in by yourself, young lady, or I can *help* you." His tone let her know it was useless to argue.

Flipping her nose in the air and struggling free from his grasp, Andrea clumsily climbed aboard. Carter took his seat, picked up the reins, and clucked to the horses.

"You're not very talkative," he said after they had ridden quite a while in silence.

"I only speak when I have something to say."

Carter looked at her sideways while popping a cigar into his mouth. "Interestin' trait for a woman."

The remark would normally have angered Andrea, but tonight her mind was a million miles away. She stared at the moon as she tried to keep her thoughts from wandering back to what had just transpired.

"It appears the lady folk wished to have some inside information on the Colonel," Carter finally said as if stating the obvious.

Andrea wondered how he knew what Laura had wanted, and then grew angry all over again. "Yes, and how ironic that I have only just come to learn that I live in the same household with a man who is worshipped in Virginia only slightly less than the Lord."

"Yup. He may not be the Almighty, but he's a darn close relative."

"Oh, please," Andrea spat. "I did not accept this ride to hear about the godlike hero of Hawthorne. And please speak no more about the honor and virtue of one who enjoys the spoils of war almost as much as the blood that flows in its procurement."

Carter pulled the horses to a sudden stop. "You are misinformed on that count, young lady. The Colonel does not, nor has he ever, shared in the partaking of the spoils of war. The men are permitted to take what they need, the rest is forwarded to the Confederate government. The Colonel has never taken so much as a spoonful of coffee without paying its full price." He turned back to the horses and snapped the reins.

Andrea blinked in the darkness. Hunter had never disputed the allegation when she had accused him of taking plunder. He allowed her to think the worst, probably with the assumption she would not believe him anyway.

"Despite your hostility toward the Colonel, I think you're probably a remarkable young lady."

Andrea laughed outright at the comment, but knew the sound carried no humor. "There are those who would take issue that I'm a lady at all." She looked gloomily at the house as they pulled up to it, her wistful gaze apparently not escaping Carter.

"I believe you're probably mistaken on that point, too," he said, helping her from the seat.

Andrea held onto his arm a moment and looked up into his face. Browned by sun and aged by weather, he possessed a countenance that obviously masked more than it expressed, yet was somehow profoundly handsome. "You are returning to the party?"

"Nope. I owe you a debt of gratitude for giving me the opportunity to escape." He laughed while turning to retrieve her cane from the back.

"But Fannie will be so disappointed," Andrea said without thinking. "I would be distressed to think that I am the cause."

Carter whirled around rather suddenly for his usual slow and deliberate demeanor. "Fannie Madison?" He lowered his voice then and tried to appear calm. "Now why would the most beautiful woman still at the party be disappointed if I don't return?"

Andrea saw in his eyes the same light she had seen in Fannie's. "I just believe she would."

"She told you that?" His dark eyes probed hers in the moonlight.

"I dare not divulge what was said in a private conversation, Major Carter," she replied coyly, "but I believe you would not be disappointed if you were to return."

Carter was silent for a moment as he studied her. "I think perhaps I will take your advice, Miss Evans. After all, the night is still young, is it not?" He leaped into his seat and whipped the horses out the lane at a speed Andrea concluded was neither safe nor necessary for a wagon not under heavy fire or in imminent danger of capture by enemy forces.

Smiling, Andrea stood at the bottom of the porch as she watched the wagon disappear. But the smile turned into a frown when the sound of hoof beats did not fade away. The noise from the departing wagon overlapped with the sound of a single horse galloping over the bridge. It did not take Andrea long to recognize the rider. She started up the steps with more haste as he reined his horse to a stop.

"Miss Evans," Hunter said, dismounting. "I'm sorry you didn't find the party to your taste."

"I pray you did not leave the affair early to offer me your sympathy." Andrea tried to sound indifferent as she continued up the steps. "The celebration, after all, is in *your* honor."

"I didn't come to offer my sympathy, Miss Evans." Hunter tied his horse to a post. "I came to apologize."

"Then I'm sorry you rode all this way for nothing." Andrea heard Hunter's spurs hit the steps as her hand reached the door latch.

"It won't be for nothing." He was suddenly so close to her that she felt the words on the back of her neck. "I intend to be heard."

Andrea turned and faced him. "Colonel Hunter, I believe your time would be much better spent at the Talberts. It appears the ladies there are more interested in what you have to say than I am."

"I disagree, Miss Evans." He trapped her between his arms as he leaned them against the door. "I think you will be very interested in hearing what I have to say."

Overwhelmed by the intensity in his eyes, Andrea could barely look at him. Yet neither could she look away, for his probing gaze held her there as securely as the confinement of his arms.

"I wish to retract my earlier statement about your loyalties," he said, his voice softer now. "And I hope you can find it in your heart to consider me, once again, a gentleman."

"Where you think my loyalties lie, Colonel Hunter, is of little concern to me." Andrea stared out over his shoulder rather than meet his gaze. "And I hardly think your behavior tonight can be considered that of a gentleman."

ℋ ℋ ℋ

Hunter closed his eyes and banged his fist on the doorway above her head. It was as he had expected, the contemptuous enemy had returned. He felt as though he had just slipped a rope over a horse's head and it was backing up, getting ready to bolt and drag him off his feet.

He attempted to slacken the rope. "I would like to apologize for any embarrassment I may have caused you this evening. I spoke rashly and impulsively, and considering your lineage, I hardly—"

"My lineage?" Andrea looked up so quickly that she hit the back of her head against the door.

Hunter hesitated, but decided she could be no more surprised to hear what he was about to say, than he'd been shocked to learn about it. "If I'm not mistaken, Miss Evans," he said, never removing his eyes from hers, "you are the daughter of Olivia Evans, whose *second* husband was Charles Monroe.

Andrea stared at him unblinking, her lips pressed tightly together, her expression changing from poised to forced composure.

"Of course, it is no secret that your mother was from Virginia, and as such, that a considerable amount of Virginia blood flows through your veins. However—"

"Good night, Colonel." Andrea reached behind her for the door.

"Wait." Hunter grasped her hand. "I'm not yet finished. It has come to my attention that your mother's first husband, Nathaniel Evans, who died just before you were born, is from a long line of distinguished Virginians."

The silence was deafening, the tension palpable. Hunter did not know if her speechlessness was caused by what she had just heard, the fact that he knew it, or that it was something she refused to admit to him after all this time. He decided on the latter.

"I-I have never made that claim," Andrea stammered.

"You need not claim it for it to be true," Hunter said calmly. "Though you pretend to detest us, you cannot deny the inheritance of an honored line of ancestors. You possess a blue-blooded pedigree with not so much as a drop of tainted blood in your veins." He chuckled. "I dare say there are few in Virginia who can boast flesh that is of better dust than yours."

"Who told you this?" she demanded.

"Miss Evans, I dare not reveal my sources."

"Then you obviously have nothing but imagination to build your case upon." Andrea stared broodingly over his shoulder. "I suppose such interest in my affairs should be complimentary, but I find it curious that you've nothing better to do with your time than attempt to trace my family tree." She brought her gaze back to his just as the faint sound of a carriage reached their ears.

"Oh, it took no time. If you insist on knowing, one of my men has a lady friend from Unison, whose brother was acquainted with Nathaniel Evans. This brother told me—just tonight—he remembered Nathaniel marrying an Olivia Spencer. He further remembered the scandal it caused when Nathaniel was killed in an accident, and Olivia, with her husband barely cold in his grave and a child well on the way, married into a wealthy family in South Carolina. And, well, the rest is easy to speculate. You were raised as the daughter of Charles Monroe, probably didn't even know yourself that you were not. But when you discovered the truth, you ran away, disassociated yourself from him and his name."

Andrea met his gaze, but only briefly, as the sound of carriage wheels grew louder.

"It is not hard to surmise that you are both Virginian by birth and Southern by instinct," Hunter continued, "and that you would rather denounce or ignore your bloodlines to allay the feeling that you have regrettably placed your loyalty on the *wrong* side of the rebellion."

Andrea's mouth opened, then snapped closed, but he gave her no time to respond.

"You are made of Virginia soil, my dear, and will be made of it forever. You can never unmix."

Andrea's eyes turned darker than he had ever seen them. "Allow me to do some speculating of my own," she spat, nodding her head toward the approaching carriage. "It would be my guess that your mistress has noticed your absence and has come to seek you out. She will, no doubt, be ecstatic to find you waiting up for her. Good night, Colonel."

Andrea reached behind her with a swift movement of one hand, opened the door, and backed in, closing it in his face. Revealing nothing.

Hunter put his head against the door in exasperation and sighed. *Who are you, Andrea Evans? And why are you determined to be my foe?*

The carriage rolled to a stop, and Victoria's high-pitched voice shouted from within, "Alex! Dar-r-ling! How sweet of you to wait up for me!"

Chapter 45

"Water and words are easy to pour and impossible to recover."
– Chinese Proverb

Andrea sat on the front steps watching a small dust cloud move and hang in the air, while a larger one followed along behind. From the size of the dust cloud, Hunter was likely among them. Andrea could not help herself. She smiled.

The Colonel, after the turbulence of the ball, made no further comment about her suspected heritage. In fact, he had been surprisingly charming and mannerly as of late. Andrea found herself trying to separate enemy from man—admiring the latter and respecting the former. Yet she still found it hard to admit they were one and the same.

Once the lone rider had approached and crossed the bridge, Andrea saw it was not Hunter. When she did identify the figure, well nigh coated with sweat and powdery dust, she greeted him cordially. "Lieutenant Pierce."

The officer's mouth twisted into a confident smile as he interpreted her look as one of obvious admiration. "Miss Evans—" He bowed after he dismounted. "It's *Captain* Pierce, now." He paused and tied his horse to the porch. "I apologize for my untidy appearance."

Andrea's gaze remained on his horse for a moment, making it clear it was the animal with which she had been enthralled, not the soldier who'd been mounted upon him.

She dragged her eyes over to Pierce. "To what do I owe the pleasure? Are you looking for the Colonel?"

"Uh, no. The Colonel is behind me about a mile with the men, bringing in some horses I captured today. I rode in advance to … get some water, if I may?" He took off his hat and swiped dirt and sweat from his brow with his dusty shirtsleeve.

"Of course." Andrea grabbed his arm and led him up the steps, even though it was obvious to her he had seen an opportunity to arrive before his commander and nearly ridden the legs off his horse to do it. "How impolite of me. Come rest in the shade on the porch."

The long-legged soldier followed her eagerly up the steps with a considerable rattle of spurs and reposed himself on the vine-mantled banister while she went inside.

When Andrea returned with a pitcher of water a few minutes later, Pierce held his hand to his eye. "Captain? Is something wrong?"

"Oh, I seem to have gotten some dust in my eye." He blinked hard. "Nothing to worry about."

Andrea poured some of the water onto a handkerchief and looked up at him. "Goodness. You're so tall. If you'll move that stool over, I'll try to clean it for you."

With one eye closed, Pierce moved a footstool over to the banister and sat back down upon the railing. Andrea stepped onto the stool between his legs and wiped away the dirt around the eye.

"This is very kind of you," he said, staring into her eyes. "I hope you'll permit me to repay the favor. I never neglect my duty to a lady."

"Don't talk," Andrea said. "I'm liable to poke you in the eye. Now lean your head back a little." Pierce obeyed, putting his hands on Andrea's waist in the process for balance. "I don't really see anything." Andrea leaned forward, her face just inches from his.

"Are you certain?" he asked huskily, looking straight into her eyes.

Andrea was concentrating so hard that she did not notice the other horses coming in until they were right in front of her. She jumped at the sound of spurs clanking angrily up the porch steps.

"Captain, may I see you a minute." Hunter stormed up the steps, eyes blazing with indignation. Not stopping to wait for an answer, he pushed his way through the front door with the strength of a hurricane wind and disappeared into the house.

Pierce stood quickly to obey and in the process kicked the stool from beneath Andrea's feet. He held her body against his before letting her slide slowly to the porch. "Thank you, miss. I feel much better."

ℋ ℋ ℋ

Hunter turned at the sound of Pierce's spurs in the doorway of the library. "The order still stands, Captain Pierce. I did not withdraw it."

"The order, sir?"

"The order to leave Miss Evans alone."

"You jest."

Hunter's jaw tightened, making it clear he was not joking. "Miss Evans is a guest in my home. I have a duty to protect her."

"Protect her from what? Anyone else courting her?"

Hunter stomped out from behind his desk to the door, slammed it shut, and turned back to Pierce. "I have never liked you, Pierce, as you well know. Yet, I have promoted you because you are deserving. For the good of the Command, I demand you stay away from her. It stems from no personal interest on my part, I assure you."

Pierce snorted. "The good of the Command? How so? If you have no desire for her, why should you have no desire for anyone else to have her?" He looked Hunter straight in the eye, taunting him. "It appears to me she is of an age capable of making her own decisions. And I dare say that age is closer to mine than yours."

"She will not become one of your conquests, Captain Pierce. Not while she's residing under my roof. Let me make that perfectly clear."

"But she will become one of yours?" Pierce took a step backward at the look in Hunter's eyes. "Colonel, it is clear to me she is a lady of integrity. Are you telling me I may not call on her?"

"Not so long as you are a member of this Command."

This silenced Pierce, but only for a moment. "May I go on the record, sir, as stating that I do not believe it is fair of you to use your military status in this regard?"

The two men stood glaring at each other, both pulled up to their full heights. "You may go on the record," Hunter replied, his voice perfectly composed, "but the order still stands."

He turned away and went back to his desk. "You are dismissed."

Pierce remained glowering at him as if contemplating some action, then saluted and turned for the door.

"Ah, Captain."

Pierce stopped with his hand on the doorknob.

"I'll need a report on your other activities today as soon as possible. I'm sure to hear from Richmond about it—and Washington—when word gets out."

Pierce did not turn around. He nodded, placed his hat on his head, and opened the door.

"And Pierce, report the reasons and results, not the details."

His response was the slamming of the door.

❧ ❧ ❧

Andrea was standing by the paddock gate when she saw Pierce come out of the house. He appeared to be somewhat angry, if the dust rising from his boots was any indication. Seeing Andrea, he nodded stiffly in her direction, mounted his horse in one fluid movement, and spurred it down the lane.

"What's wrong with him?" Johnny asked from over her shoulder.

"Don't know." Andrea watched Pierce thoughtfully. "Colonel Hunter didn't seem too happy about something."

"Yea, I got the same feeling," Johnny said. "Something happened today. Haven't figured out what."

"What do you mean?" Andrea turned to face him.

"See this?" Johnny pointed to some blood matted in the mane of one of the horses.

Andrea nodded and Johnny's voice got low. "Didn't bring any prisoners in

243

with these horses today."

Andrea swept her eyes over the animals, all of which were still wearing saddles. "Seven equipped horses and no prisoners at all?"

"No, ma'am," he said, walking into the herd to begin removing the tack.

Andrea watched him, absorbed in trying to come up with a suitable explanation for what had become of these horses' riders. She was still leaning on the fence when she caught sight of Hunter out the corner of her eye making his way to the barn. She hurried to catch up with him. "I heard you brought back no prisoners today."

Hunter stopped in his tracks and stared at her with distant, gray eyes. "That is correct." His manner, his icy stare, and his expression sent a chill up her spine.

"But those horses all had riders, did they not?" She nodded toward the paddock.

"Yes," Hunter replied coldly. "And the riders on those horses all had torches, and the torches were being used to burn innocent civilians' homes to the ground."

Andrea blinked, puzzled at first. The confusion swiftly changed to disbelief, and then horror. "They were burning homes so you took no prisoners?"

"What's wrong, Miss Evans? Are the cold realities of war suddenly too much for you?"

"You shot those men in cold blood?" Hunter's lack of emotion shook Andrea no less than the ghastly scene she envisioned.

"My men came across the atrocity. The officer in charge reacted admirably to deeds that are repugnant to humanity." He stared out over her shoulder into the distance as he spoke.

"And slaying seven men in cold blood is not repugnant to humanity?" Andrea's voice grew shrill. The anger in her tone did not convey the sadness in her heart at the thought that Hunter would allow his men to resort to such a despicable act of malice. She had grown to think of him as a man who would prevent brutality in his presence and strictly forbid it in his absence. She did not know *this* man.

"Does your code of honor come from a barbarous nation I'm not familiar with? Or has mercy and civilized behavior never been a part of your code?"

Hunter started to turn away.

"I know you have no heart, but have you no soul?"

"In case you are not aware, we're in the middle of a war," he said over his shoulder, obviously trying to put an end to the conversation.

"That does not excuse barbarism!" Andrea ran after him and grabbed his arm, too angry to be fearful of the consequences. "This act is a stain upon our nation's honor! It's revolting! It's . . . unconscionable!"

Hunter swung back around. "You dare insult my men about honor?" He pulled his arm from her grasp and looked at her with burning fury. "Surely the hell your comrades are creating in Virginia is not too hot for the demonic Yankee villains who apply the torch!"

"You cannot tell me you condone these deaths," Andrea said, her chest heaving. "You cannot make me believe that, on behalf of your men, you can overlook this carnage, this … this butchery because it was performed in the name of vengeance for a policy of devastation."

She was so angry she waved her arms in the air. "War may excuse certain actions of cruel necessity, but it can never justify this! Even *you*, Colonel Hunter, cannot claim that this is legitimate warfare!"

Hunter remained silent, brooding, as if weighing the decision to defend himself. When he spoke, his words were distinct, his voice was low and his dust-stained face was just inches from hers. "You insist on justification, Miss Evans? The reprisal was indeed revenge, taken by my officer in direct retaliation for the"—Hunter paused and drew a sharp breath—"for the cruel, deliberate, merciless hangings of seven of my men last month."

Andrea did not speak. She blinked in complete bewilderment, deeming at first that he must be lying, but seeing by the look on his face that he was not. She took a step backward. "You cannot tell me a Union officer ordered such a thing."

"Colonel Clayton Shepherd," was the blunt reply. "And today his men got their payback—and mine divine revenge."

Andrea swallowed hard. Seven had perished today, victims of a bloody code of retaliation. In her absence, this ghastly, revolting war had opened a new chapter in horror. It seemed that any and all sense of humanity had taken flight from this once-peaceful land.

"They were fairly warned," Hunter continued when she did not speak. "For every Hunter man murdered, they were informed I would take ten-fold vengeance. My men were most humane in that regard, only killing those directly involved."

Andrea closed her eyes and imagined the scene. Men inflamed with vengeance dealing out a sentence of death to those who had executed their comrades.

"So you see, Miss Evans, we have been compelled, reluctantly, to adopt a line of policy as ruthless and revolting as your Northern comrades. All the prisoners I have taken since that day have been treated with the respect due them."

"You were not there?" Andrea's voice was barely above a whisper.

"I don't know what difference that makes," Hunter said coldly over his shoulder as he started to walk away. "The outcome would have been the same."

Then he stopped and turned back. "You may know the officer who was in charge. His name is Pierce—promoted today to Captain—as you may have already been informed." Hunter continued his journey to the house, his boots and spurs raising small clouds that enveloped him in a dusty mist.

Andrea looked over her shoulder when she heard Izzie yelling from the direction of the slaves' quarters.

"Miz Andrea! Gabriella havin' her baby!"

Andrea watched Hunter turn briefly with a look of concern on his face. Then he continued to the house, his long powerful strides and straight, rigid back in no way revealing the great weight he carried upon his shoulders.

ℋ ℋ ℋ

Once mother and her new daughter were resting comfortably, Andrea walked toward the lake, guided by the magical hum of insects that convened there. Climbing down a small bank, she reposed herself on a fallen tree and tried to make sense of the day. Despite the miracle of birth, there seemed little to celebrate when she thought of Pierce's crusade of vengeance and the reason for it.

Had the world gone mad since she left? Leaning forward, she put her arms around her legs and rested her forehead on her knees. What else had happened which she knew nothing of? She listened half-heartedly to a bullfrog bellowing on the far side of the pond, and jumped at the sound of a voice behind her.

"Beautiful evening."

Andrea turned to see Hunter, illuminated by moonlight, standing on the bank behind her. She nodded in answer to his question, but did not speak.

"It's peaceful down here." Hunter hopped down the bank.

"I—" Andrea stood and looked up at him. "I'm sorry about—"

Hunter stopped her. "I don't want to talk about it anymore. How's Gabriella doing?"

"She's doing fine. A daughter. She calls her Angelina." Even as she said the words, Andrea's mind drifted away from the miracle of birth to the horrifying deaths of the month before. "You could have told me," she blurted out. "You needn't have kept such an atrocity a secret from me."

"It was not my intention to keep it a secret, Miss Evans. I simply saw no point in concerning you with it." Hunter stared vacantly out over the water.

"Concerning me with it? Seven of your men were murdered by men who claim to be soldiers!"

"Miss Evans, you have spared no effort to remind me we are your enemies," he replied. "Considering your unhappy status at Camp Misery, I deemed the news would not be of interest to you."

Andrea inhaled deeply, his statement and his rationale taking the breath from her. All of the unpleasant words she had spoken in the past rose with painful vividness before her, and a feeling of shame surged at the thought of her vengeful tongue.

"But you cannot believe I would take pleasure in the deaths of your men." Andrea gazed up at him, her hand on his arm. "That I would defend the Union's ruthlessness?"

Hunter looked out over her head into the distance and did not answer.

Andrea let her hand drop to her side. "You are wrong, Colonel Hunter." Her voice trembled as she bowed her head. "I do not, nor could I ever, support such an indefensible act. And I have never, nor will I ever, rejoice in the deaths of any of your men." She paused and looked up to meet his gaze. "And I deeply regret the loss your Command has suffered."

Andrea took another deep breath, squared her shoulders, and started back toward the house. "I do deeply regret the loss," she said again, this time to herself.

Chapter 46

"We are not enemies, but friends. We must not be enemies.
Though passion may have strained, it must not break our bonds of affection."
— Abraham Lincoln

Midnight. Hawthorne stood like an island in a thick sea of haze, the air so dark and pregnant with humidity, Andrea felt confined in a cave. Rising from her restless sleep, she lit a candle and sat on the edge of the bed opening and closing her swollen fingers. Twisting off her ring, she sat and stared at the engraving as she had done hundreds of times before. What would it be like if Daniel still lived? She closed her eyes and rubbed the ring, gasping when she felt a slight movement of its face. Holding it to the candle, she opened the small, hinged compartment and withdrew a tiny, meticulously folded piece of paper.

Tenderly opening a note crisp with age, she read:

Dear Daniel,

I am in receipt of your last, and acknowledge your decision to serve in the Federal army. Yet, I too must do my duty as I conceive it to be. Never could I have envisioned an event that would lead me to stand in opposition to my dearest kin or against my cherished flag. But it is honor that I must now defend, and it is honor for which I will move forward. That you remain safe, my dear Daniel, until such time as harmony once again prevails, is the hope of your devoted brother ... Alex

Andrea closed her eyes at the depth of emotion displayed in the words and what they must have meant to Daniel. "Oh, Alex," she said without realizing it. How often had he attempted to tell her the intensity of his feelings for Virginia? Yet he had never mentioned how terribly difficult had been his decision to fight for the Confederacy.

Now wide awake, Andrea walked onto the balcony and felt the night air settle down around her, heavy and close like a wet blanket. Leaning over the railing, she tried to catch even a hint of a breeze to cool her clammy brow. All she caught was the smell of tobacco smoke coming from behind her. When she began to turn to find its source, he spoke.

"Too hot for yah, Mish Evans?" His voice was thick and rich, and uncharacteristically, had a pronounced Virginia drawl.

"Colonel. I had ... I had n-n-o idea you were—" Andrea stuttered, suddenly aware of her deficiency of a robe.

"Jush got in."

Andrea wondered why he slurred his words, but turned back toward the banister without inquiring. "It's rather a ... warm night." She hoped that would end the conversation.

"Yesh, it is."

"Are you quite all right, Colonel?" Andrea looked back over her shoulder. A bottle clanking hard against a glass in the shadows was the only reply.

"Have a sheat and join me." He patted the chair beside him.

Andrea's face reddened. She had never seen Hunter so completely abandoned in his manners. She could make him out now. His coat lay haphazardly on a chair beside him. His shirt was unbuttoned at the collar, his sleeves rolled up.

"That would be highly inappropriate, Colonel."

Hunter put his head back and laughed. "Begging your pardon, Mish Evanssssh," he said, evidently majestically drunk. "Since when have you been worried about pro-pri ... pro-pre ..."

"Propriety," Andrea finished for him, wishing again that she had put on her wrapper. "Sir, I think that perhaps you should—"

"Come here a moment," he commanded. He stood and killed his drink in one swallow before letting the glass hit the table with an unsteady hand.

Andrea obeyed, afraid to refuse. The tone he used to give the order was not one she wished to dispute, especially in his current state.

"Do you shee this?" He swept his arm toward the fields and barns below, then took a step backward, the action knocking him off balance.

Andrea reached out for his arm to steady him and nodded, though she could see nothing in the haze and darkness.

"Thish is my life. Everything ish here."

"Yes, I understand that, Alex."

Hunter stopped his ramblings for a moment and stared down at her lips, as if hearing his name on them made him lose his train of thought. Andrea blushed, embarrassed that she had taken the liberty.

"Your beauty," he said, softly now, "would create a pulsh in a marble statue. Do you know that?"

The air was perfectly motionless. Andrea felt the heat rise in her cheeks and looked down. "You should not speak like this. You don't know what you're saying."

Hunter smiled, put his hand under her chin, and lifted her head. "It's not my wishh to make you un-com ... un-fort ..." He exhaled in exasperation. "I was merely shtating a fact."

He took another half-step forward, as if talking and keeping his balance were a bit too much to be attempted at the same time. "If I lost thish place—"

The desperation in his voice made Andrea's heart swell with sympathy. She knew in a moment the source of his fears. She had heard at the ball that Union soldiers were sweeping through the valley burning homes and barns. The idea that this home could be destroyed in the firestorm had never occurred to her as a possibility. Now, from his tone, he thought it a probability.

Andrea stared into his eyes, at a loss for something to say to console him. No words could possibly bring him comfort, for he appeared sure his fear would be justified—and soon.

"I know nothing of that," she said. "But I do know that alcohol is a destroyer of human reason. Things will look brighter in the morning."

Andrea gave him no time to reorganize his thoughts. "Let me help you to bed." She grabbed him around the waist and led him through the open door of his chamber. Hunter did not resist. He sat down hard on the mattress and watched her remove his boots.

"Get some rest." Andrea gently pushed him into a lying position. When she turned to leave, he grabbed her wrist, and pulled her back.

"Even if the war takes everything else—" He stopped and gazed earnestly into her eyes, as if she should understand his meaning.

"Even if it—" he began again, his voice so low and determined it sent a shiver down Andrea's spine. "You won't ...don't let it come between us ... any more."

Andrea tried to pull away, not sure of the emotions that raged inside her.

"Promish?" He pulled her closer and this single word was a demand.

"I promise," she whispered, taking in the sweet smell of liquor on his breath.

Hunter let go of her wrist and appeared to fall instantly asleep.

Andrea stared at his careworn countenance, surprised at herself for not running from the room. Instead, she pulled a blanket tenderly over him and watched his gentle breathing. "Sleep well, Alex." She took a deep breath at the sudden tightening in her chest as she said the words. A strange feeling overcame her then, one of compassion and belonging, and it caused the rapid flight that had, for a moment, been delayed.

⌘ ⌘ ⌘

When Andrea opened the door to her room the next morning, she practically ran into Hunter on the other side preparing to knock. "I trust I did not offend you or create a disturbance last night," he said with a grave expression. "If I did, I apologize."

His bloodshot eyes looked tired. Andrea could tell he had no memory of his actions. "You were a perfect gentleman, as always." She turned away to bring an end to the conversation.

Hunter grabbed her arm and stopped her. "Now you have me worried because I know I could never be a perfect gentleman in the company of such a charming young lady in my ... undesirable condition."

Andrea turned and feigned a look of astonishment. "You think *me* charming, Colonel? I would never have guessed such a thing."

"When I say *charming*, I mean it in only in the most exasperating sort of way."

"Sir, if that is your definition of the word, then you can believe with complete confidence that you were quite *charming* last night yourself."

Andrea turned to walk away, but not before noticing that at least half of Hunter's mouth had lifted into a lighthearted smile at her comeback.

Chapter 47

"Man is so made that whenever anything fires his soul, impossibilities vanish."
— Jean de la Fontaine

Three days later, Andrea awoke to streaks of orange blazing across the eastern sky. Dressing hurriedly, fearing she had overslept, she took a moment to stand on the balcony and admire the view. Taking a deep breath of the morning air, she almost choked when she inhaled the acrid smell of smoke rather than fresh morning air.

Running back into her chamber to check the clock on the mantle, she realized it was too early for dawn to be so far advanced. Back to the balcony she ran, and now amidst the copper-colored sky, she saw columns of black, rolling smoke in the distance. She even made out the glittering sparks and flying embers that created the ghastly glare.

The hills beyond Hawthorne looked a very mass of flame, and she realized the impact of the dreadful scene unfolding. She leaned over the railing and cupped her hands. "Zach!"

In an instant, his head appeared below her. "Take the stock to the woods," she yelled pointing to the distance. Without waiting to see if he understood her command, she darted back inside, half-running, half-hopping to Victoria's room where she pounded on the door. "Get up! Get up!"

Down the stairs she stumbled and out the door, where excitement already prevailed. Zach and others had tied horses together and were leading them by the dozen to a hideaway on the side of the hill. Andrea looked to the east and trembled at the great columns of smoke dotting the horizon. She took a few steps more and a horrible groan escaped her. Just over the hill, rising over the trees, shot another column of black smoke, swirling and dancing in evil delight. It had to be the Talbert house. "They're coming!"

Andrea had hoped the Union troops would somehow not discover Hawthorne, but it appeared the home was right in their path. She had no idea how much time they had. She only knew she could not face the look in Hunter's eyes if he returned to a smoldering ruin.

Running to the barn, barely using her cane, Andrea bridled Justus. When Zach had a string of horses together, she climbed upon him bareback and led them to the hidden paddock behind the hill. By the time she returned, he had more ready to go. "Move the worst of the wounded horses into the front stalls," she ordered. "We don't have time to move them all."

Returning again, Andrea saw only one more string of Hawthorne stock remaining to be moved. In the early morning light, a column of dust rose on

251

the road—likely a cavalry unit that had discovered the turnoff to Hawthorne only a half-mile away. Blinking against the acrid smell of smoke, Andrea spied Victoria wringing her hands on the bottom step of the porch.

"We're all going to die! They'll kill us all!"

Andrea rode Justus up to the porch, leaned forward, and grabbed the panicked woman by her collar, shaking her. "Do as I say, Victoria! Go to the barn, get an armful of hay, and put it in the library!"

Letting her go, she turned Justus away. "And leave the front door open," she yelled over her shoulder.

"The library? Are you insane?

Andrea pulled Justus to a halt and shot Victoria a look that implied she might take the time to dismount and show her just how insane she was. "Do as I say!" The tone of her voice made Victoria scamper to the barn.

Grabbing the remaining stock, Andrea returned a few moments before the troops appeared in sight at the bridge. Without stopping, she rode Justus up the steps and into the house. Dismounting in the foyer, she led him to the library where Victoria sat huddled.

"Here." Andrea handed her the reins. "Keep him quiet."

"Oh no." Victoria backed up and shook her head. "No! I'm scared to death of horses!"

"Do it, or death is exactly what you'll be facing!"

Andrea hastened back toward the door, trying to straighten her ravaged dress as she walked.

"Aren't you going to take a gun or something?" Victoria mumbled from where she now stood on a chair, holding the horse's reins at arm's length.

Andrea's gaze rose to the old muzzle loader hanging over the fireplace—the only weapon she was aware of in the house, and one she surmised had been owned by Hunter's grandfather. Though the idea of carrying a weapon appealed to her, Andrea turned back and gave Victoria a disgusted look. "I scarcely think a single gun will serve any purpose against an entire regiment of cavalry, Victoria." Andrea wished she knew what *would* work against an entire regiment of cavalry, but she was at a loss for an answer.

A frightened Izzie appeared in the doorway carrying an armful of haphazard belongings Victoria had apparently ordered her to take to safety. Among the items was a beautiful black mourning gown of silk.

"Izzie!" Andrea exclaimed, making the girl jump. "Give me that!"

"That's my gown!" At Victoria's outburst, Justus jerked his head up, causing her to scream. "Take this beast!! Izzie, I demand that you stay here and take this horrible creature! Don't leave me or I'll see you whipped!"

"Follow me, Izzie." Andrea grabbed Izzie's hand and closed the door, ignoring Victoria's sobs and screams. She then took the dress, and with Izzie's help, threw it over the front door while it was open. When they closed the door, the skirt portion appeared like a large, black fan from the outside.

When Andrea looked up, she beheld a long line of riders in blue, trotting toward her in columns of two. Above and beyond them lay a billowing un-natural blackness of smoke that had spread out and settled over the valley like a thick blanket of fog.

Andrea limped down the steps, leaning heavily on her cane to exaggerate her injury, and went out the lane to greet the visitors. When they were but fif-teen rods away, her legs began to shake. The men carried torches in their hands, sabers on their saddles, and guns around their waists. She had never felt such helpless terror before. Never. Yet never did she feel more determination or carry stronger resolve. The thought of watching Hawthorne go up in smoke overcame any hesitation within her.

"Gentlemen, what can we do for you?"

"We're under orders to set fire to every building in this vicinity. We can give you the consideration of fifteen minutes to remove some personal belongings."

Andrea's heart leaped to her throat even though she had known what was coming. He had orders to lay the region to waste, and she could tell by his tone and attitude that he fully intended to obey them to the letter.

"Fifteen minutes?" Andrea's voice was full of disbelief. "Then your men will help remove the sick from inside? I fear most of them cannot get out un-aided."

"What do you mean 'sick'?" The officer gazed over her shoulder at the house.

"Certainly you were informed there are men with smallpox here." Andrea nodded toward the front door where the black gown fluttered in the wind in silent warning.

"Smallpox?" The colonel pulled his horse backward a step, his gaze shifting from the house to the disheveled, frazzled-looking girl before him.

Andrea knew that, to a soldier's mind, the disease was more painful, more prolonged, and more agonizing than death from the enemy's guns. "Yes. I have fifteen men in there." She turned toward the house and then gazed sadly off into the distance. "Sixteen if you count the one who just passed and we've not had time to bury."

Another officer rode up beside the one to whom she spoke. "Colonel, we can't take her word for it. We need to see one of these here patients."

Andrea tried to ignore the sound of her heart pounding. "Of course, you don't have to take my word for it." She motioned to the one who had spoken. "Follow me. I'm afraid they're too sick to come out. Smallpox is a deadly dis-ease you know."

The two men looked at each other and began shaking their heads. "I ain't goin' in there."

"We're wasting time," the colonel growled. "Set fire to the barn."

Andrea turned toward the officer. "Sir, I know you have your orders, but as you can see, the only horses here are those a Union regiment dropped off a few days back. They took all our breeding stock and left only these poor miserable creatures who have served your troops so nobly."

The colonel nodded his head toward his lieutenant, who dismounted at the barn and went in. Indeed all he found were poor, jaded and wounded animals that Hunter's men had captured—and all possessed the U.S. brand.

"She's right," he said when he reappeared. "Might be better to leave the barn and come back in a few weeks for remounts."

"We've got to burn something!"

Andrea looked sadly toward the large chicken house. For some reason, the hens had refused to lay in it, or even go near it, for the past few weeks. But giving the soldiers a woeful look, she pretended it would be a great loss. "Oh, not the chicken house," she said, wringing her hands.

"I'm sorry, miss." The colonel motioned for a torch. "This is war."

As the wreathing serpents of flame curled around the rather large outbuilding, Andrea realized why the chickens had neglected to lay there. A swarm of angry yellow jackets flew out, and the Yankees went riding and cursing out of the barnyard at a much faster gait than they had arrived. The officer in charge took one last lingering look at the house and the beleaguered woman sobbing with her face in her hands, then turned his horse and left with the rest.

"I could have been burned alive," Victoria shouted the moment Andrea entered the library. "You wait until Alex hears about this!"

"Miss Hamilton, there is no reason to worry the Colonel about this."

"Don't you think he's going to notice the chicken house?" Victoria smoothed her dress while watching the servants attempt to douse the flames.

"Of course he'll notice, but that's all he has to know." Andrea began leading Justus out of the library. "They set fire to the chicken house and the yellow jackets chased them away."

After thinking it over, Victoria seemed to come to the conclusion that telling Alex she had been made to hold a horse like a common slave would not be to her advantage. "I suppose you're right. Why worry Alex with the details?"

❦ ❦ ❦

Hunter and his men rode into the stable yard of their headquarters stunned and dumbfounded. The building where they had gathered and eaten and danced the night away on so many occasions was now a flowing bed of coals. The stone chimney alone stood as a monument to the barbarous destruction the Yankees had wrought. The riders drew together in the glare on the hillside and stared at the spray of sparks and smoke that continued to rise. Every now and then, when the wind stirred, flames would flare, illuminating the sad faces that surrounded it.

Laura and her mother stood in the yard, sobbing. "Oh, Colonel," Laura said, running to Hunter. "Whatever shall we do?"

Hunter clenched his jaw, knowing the same fate had most likely befallen his own estate. "Take the ladies to Hawk Shadow if it's still standing," he said over his shoulder to his men. "It appears they've turned north. I'm going to Hawthorne."

Major Carter rode up beside him. "You want some company, Colonel?"

Hunter pulled his horse to a stop. "No," he answered after thinking for a moment. He pretended calmness, but his heart beat frantically as he searched the horizon for signs that his beloved Hawthorne still stood. If the hot breath of war had come upon his home and destroyed its sacredness, he needed to see it alone.

He urged his mare forward and headed toward his birthplace. As he crested the final hill, he saw a small column of smoke rising above the trees. But when he rode into the clearing above the house, he had to blink to make sure his eyes did not betray him. First he saw the towering chimneys—still intact—then the house, untouched. Surprise, relief and pure joy washed over him in a mixture of overwhelming emotion.

"Alex!" Victoria ran to him as he rode up the lane, her skirts flapping haphazardly.

"The Yankees were here!"

"I can see that." Hunter watched Andrea's lithe form hurry from the barn toward the house without looking in his direction. Even with her cane she walked gracefully, with long fluid strides that bespoke of someone who was going somewhere and wanted to get there as quickly as possible. He watched every motion of her slender figure and was curiously enthralled.

"They spared the house?" He brought his attention back to Victoria.

"They set fire to the henhouse and were chased away by bees."

Hunter stared at the smoking charred remains of the small building. Nothing but a blackened ruin and some ashes remained, though he could see that an effort had been made to save it from the flames. "Bees?"

"Yes, bees!" Victoria led him toward the porch. "It was perfectly dreadful, but as you can see, they spared the house."

H H H

With baby Angelina in her arms, Andrea walked into the kitchen and discovered Mattie and Izzie laughing so hard tears spilled from their eyes. "What is so amusing?"

"We was just talking about that hoss standin' in the library with Victoria." Mattie wiped her eyes, still laughing.

"That were a hoot of a thing!" Izzie, who rarely showed emotion, slapped her leg in glee.

"I do not think she admired her duty." Andrea laughed along with them.

"Naw, she were scairt to def," Izzie said. "I ain't never heard tell of the likes! A hoss and Victoria in Ole Him's big room!"

The sight of the slaves' amusement caused Andrea to giggle harder, but the servants suddenly grew quiet, their faces serious. Still laughing, Andrea glanced over her shoulder to find Colonel Hunter leaning nonchalantly against the doorframe with his arms crossed. Andrea's expression, too, instantly turned solemn.

"A horse? In my library? With Victoria?" Hunter questioned with curiosity. "I don't believe I've heard this story."

His words were met with astonished silence as the three women stood grim-faced in the middle of the room for a few long moments.

"It was a dream, of course." Andrea put the baby up on her shoulder, and tried to pretend the topic was trivial. "I told everyone about this crazy dream I had that Victoria had a horse in your library."

"Oh, I see." Hunter nodded his head.

"Silly, isn't it?" Andrea stepped around him and out the door. "But you know how dreams are."

Hunter pushed himself off the doorway. "I'm quite afraid I do not," he said under his breath.

Chapter 48

"Look to the future, there is no road back to yesterday."
— Oswald Chambers

Hunter heard Andrea stomping down the stairway, her anger evident in her noisy tread. Moments later, the door to the library flung open like it had been hit with a battering ram. The impatient fury on her face at his summons turned to confusion and then nervousness when she saw Victoria, Mattie, Izzie and Gabriella standing in front of his desk.

"Ah, Miss Evans," he said. "Come in. How nice of you to join us."

With slow, measured steps now, she joined the line of women in front of him.

Hunter sat on the edge of his desk and flung one boot casually over the other. "The reason I called you ladies together," he said, scratching his chin, "is, well, it's a funny thing. I dropped a paper under my desk." He turned around and pulled something from behind him. "And upon trying to retrieve it, I found this."

The women gasped in unison at the handful of hay he held in his hand.

"And I got to thinking about Miss Evans' dream." He stood now and walked in front of them like a drill sergeant. "And I thought to myself, how odd that hay would materialize from a mere dream."

Hunter's gaze drifted down the line of faces. All were looking at the floor, except Andrea. She nibbled on her bottom lip and had fixed her eyes upon the chandelier overhead.

"Oh, it was terrible!" Victoria ran to Hunter. "*She* made us do it!"

Everyone looked at Andrea and nodded in agreement. Hunter watched her jaw tighten, saw the color rising in her cheeks as she tried to maintain her self-control, and then, amazingly to him, she dropped her head and stared at her feet.

In former times, Hunter would have expected her to explode with harsh language, and, more likely than that, with physical violence. Instead, Andrea appeared determined to restrain herself. Hunter pondered the change in her, his lip curling up with surprised amusement.

Everyone began talking at once, trying to explain how the event had unfolded. Hunter pictured Andrea barking out orders, going about the business of defending his home with great calmness and authority. He could not help but smile. Her ingenuity was as limitless as her patriotism.

Victoria began whimpering like a child, as Hunter presumed she had done that day. "I could have been burned alive! It was the most cruel and malicious thing I have evah endured!"

"Victoria, you were probably in the safest place you could be. Miss Evans would never allow her horse to come to any harm."

"Oh, no, Alex! She threatened me!" Victoria grabbed his arm and sobbed into his chest. "She told me if I made a sound, she'd see that I perished with this house! She said my Virginia soul wouldn't save me from burning into a pile of black ashes! Oh, it was so frightening!"

Hunter looked at Andrea, who stared at the sniveling Victoria as if she now wished she had followed through with her threat. He could not help but agree. "Truly, Miss Hamilton, if your conduct was as intolerable then as I'm witnessing at present, I only wonder that you escaped cremation. And I believe you should be grateful to Miss Evans for the clemency granted you."

Victoria's head jerked up as though she had received a slap. "You will take her side?"

"I take no sides. I state the facts." Hunter looked down at the hay he still held in his hand. "And now that the mystery has been solved, you are all dismissed."

Victoria turned with a toss of her head and everyone else made moves to follow.

"Ah, except you, Miss Evans. I'd like to have a word."

Victoria looked at Andrea with a smirk on her face, apparently thinking Hunter's remarks were only an effort to obscure the punishment that was about to be unleashed on the girl for her cruelty.

When the door closed, Hunter stared at Andrea as she shifted her weight under his gaze. "You wished to ask me something, sir?"

"I guess I'm wondering … that is, I'm a bit surprised that you would choose to defend my home, rather than leave with … your comrades."

Andrea cocked her head, appearing genuinely surprised by the question. "I defended Hawthorne, its future and its legacy. It never occurred to me that those men with torches in their hands were my comrades."

"But they were Union troops, were they not?"

Andrea chewed on the side of her cheek. "I suppose they were wearing blue." She seemed to contemplate the question again, and then spoke with quiet dignity. "I believe my conviction for right and wrong takes precedence over those for North and South." She crossed her arms, apparently satisfied at having come up with a better answer. "I believe we're both in agreement that the torch is not a legitimate implement of war. And I don't believe setting fire to Hawthorne is a fate on which the Union cause depends."

Hunter shook his head. She was indeed a law unto herself. Made up the rules as she went and lived by them.

"On the contrary," she continued, trying to defend herself. "To allow Hawthorne to burn would only incite more wrath among the citizens of Virginia, thereby creating more suffering and privation for the Federal troops."

"I see. So, by defending this estate, you were actually doing the Union a favor?"

"Yes, of course. You must admit, you'd be unrelenting in your revenge had Hawthorne been destroyed."

Hunter shook his head and stared intently at the woman before him. Hiding in this slender, feminine form was someone with the wit and the will, the charm and the courage to take on anything in her path—one man or an entire army—it mattered not to her. She knew when to stand up and fight, and she knew when to use cunning and persistence to accomplish her goal.

"But certainly it occurred to you that these were allies."

"My sole concern was to prevent the firing of Hawthorne. I … really had no other thought."

"So you decided it better to have your hopes turned to ashes than this home?" Hunter was amazed that she would risk the one thing she valued most—her freedom.

Andrea looked up at him sharply, the color mounting in her cheeks. "One can hardly be compared to the other. My high regard for Hawthorne suggested an alliance."

"And a sacrifice?"

Andrea said nothing more, and he assumed she did not intend to. She considered herself his enemy, yet had not hesitated to defend the home he loved. Her will alone had once again proved stronger than any shield of armor.

"You were aware, I suppose, that your chance of success was hardly favorable. May I ask what you would have done if your first plan had failed?"

Andrea surprised him by laughing, as if he had intended his statement as a joke. "Sir, I had no *plan*. I mean I did not take the time to ask myself, 'Can this thing be done?' I merely asked myself, 'Is this worth doing?'"

Hunter was unable to speak for a moment. With or without a plan, it had been a feat of unprecedented daring, one that required wisdom as well as nerve. It had always been within her character to act, rather than meditate on possibilities and outcomes. Still, her courage awed him. She had within her a faith that made indisputable opportunities out of absolute impossibilities.

Hunter cleared his throat, yet his voice was still hoarse when he spoke. "I wish for you to accept the assurance of my gratitude."

Andrea blushed and looked down. "I believe it is your servants that deserve praise. They did much to protect your stock and property."

Hunter knew of no other woman who would, or could, have confronted such peril. And yet, she acted as if she had done nothing out of the ordinary to save his grandfather's dream—and his future—from destruction.

"May I speak without restraint?" Hunter's voice was barely above a whisper as he suddenly reached for her hand.

Andrea answered with a nod and stared with furrowed brow at her hand resting in his.

"I know, that is, I-I accept, that considering our circumstances, you may never consider me a friend. But your respect, Miss Evans, I desire deeply."

Andrea's face was calm and thoughtful as she looked up at him. "That desire has already been secured, Colonel. Whatever our association is or comes to be, you can be assured of my high regard."

The reverent and respectful look reflected in the depths of her brilliant eyes caused his blood to pulse more uncontrollably than from any open invitation he had ever received from a woman. "I hope, as I have never hoped, that I do nothing to forfeit that sentiment."

Andrea stood with her hand still in his, gazing straight ahead. "It is a Virginian trait, I believe, to follow the dictates of conscience regardless of consequence. And I am honored that as a Virginian ... that I had the opportunity to defend Virginia soil."

Hunter blinked at her acknowledgment of her birthright and the emotion expressed. "May I have the honor of saying," he whispered, "that Virginia has been made more worthy by your belonging to her."

The room grew quiet. The sound of a clock ticking in the hallway through the closed door sounded like thunder. Something passed between them, something vague and indistinguishable, yet tangible and real.

Hunter took a deep breath. Andrea lifted her eyes in expectation and met his.

"Andrea ..." He said her name with a tinge of tentative uncertainty in his strong voice. "I think that ... I mean, there is something that I—"

ℋ ℋ ℋ

Carter burst into Hunter's library with a swift knock. Seeing Hunter was not alone, he hurriedly removed his hat from his head and then the cigar from his mouth.

"Miss," he said, giving a quick nod to Andrea. "'Scuse me, Colonel. Didn't mean to barge in. Just got a dispatch from Gus."

"Major Carter." Andrea smiled and greeted him like an old friend. "How nice to see you again."

He smiled politely and then looked at Hunter. "Glad to see Hawthorne made it through. From what I seen, looks to be the only place spared."

Carter watched Andrea glance up at Hunter, who still gazed intently down at her. To Carter, they looked like two children who had been discovered sharing a secret. Both wore expressions of deep affection that exposed their emotions more plainly than spoken words could reveal, yet neither seemed to be aware of the display.

"I'll leave you two alone," Andrea finally said. Her attention returned to Hunter and lingered there before she started toward the door.

It appeared to Carter there was almost physical contact in the shared looks between the two. He was accustomed to seeing sparks fly when they were in the same room, but tonight the sparks were different—more like a smoldering fire about to burst into flame.

Carter waited for Hunter's attention once Andrea left the room, but his commander continued to stare into the hallway, following her every movement. It was surprising to watch the renowned officer so engrossed, with such longing in his eyes, as he listened until her footsteps could no longer be heard.

For quite some time Carter had known that Hunter admired Andrea with almost reverential affection and that she returned the sentiment in no small way. But from what he knew of the Colonel and had learned of the girl, he doubted either of them had yet come to the same conclusion. In fact, they appeared more inclined to behave like two mules at the same hitch, each pulling in opposite directions and getting nowhere.

"That's a noble woman there," Carter said to break the silence. "She has few equals."

Hunter looked up as if noticing Carter for the first time and stared through him. "She has *none.*"

Chapter 49

"O, beauty, till now I never knew thee!"
— Midnight Summer's Dream, Shakespeare

Scouting with a half dozen of his men in enemy territory, Colonel Hunter pulled his horse to a stop without signaling, resulting in a collision behind him as the group bunched up. A number of horses kicked and snorted at the contact as the men tried to rein them in.

"Colonel, you see something?" Carter whispered, knowing Hunter's intuitiveness at finding the enemy.

Hunter stared off into the distance while the entire squad followed his gaze.

"No. Just admiring the sunrise," he answered with a vacant, but pleasant, look upon his face.

Carter studied him to see if he was serious, then followed his gaze toward the east. "It does that every morning, sir." Carter rolled his eyes and glanced over at Gus Dorsey who had ridden up beside him.

The men had all noticed a change in their commander. The differences in his character, though minor, were profound to those who knew him well. When lounging around the men he appeared a bit more relaxed, smiled a little more. Often they would see him staring in deep reverie at the moon, perfectly unconscious of his surroundings, as if picturing or remembering images that no one else could see. One of the men even swore he had heard Hunter whistling when returning from a scouting expedition, though that was not widely accepted as fact.

ℋ ℋ ℋ

After returning to friendly territory, Hunter dismissed his men and rode all night to get back to Hawthorne. It was now dawn again, and with his home in sight, he pulled his horse to a stop to soak in the beauty before him. Down below, beneath the rising sun, he caught glimpses of the sparkling waters of the stream that cut through Hawthorne. Through the early morning mist rising from the water, he barely made out the peaks of the house, and farther beyond, the hills that stood like silent sentinels guarding the prominent estate. He sat and scanned the scene, contemplating why the sight of Hawthorne caused his heart to rush after so many hours in the saddle.

Urging his horse forward, he began his descent and the last leg of a long journey home. Why try to analyze a feeling of exhilaration? It was simply a beautiful morning. *Ga-lorious* as Andrea would say.

Hunter smiled, and then tried to discount any connection between his eagerness to return to Hawthorne with any thoughts of *her*. But slowly, just like the sun eating away at the mist, the haziness of his thoughts became clear. Hunter caught sight of Andrea almost instantly after galloping across the bridge, and his eyes remained riveted upon her until she came into sharp focus. The vague feeling he had strived to conceal on his journey home was suddenly no longer vague. The notion that his sentiment was merely a manifestation of gratitude for her defense of Hawthorne could no longer be justified.

Standing on the bottom of a paddock fence with her arms draped over the top rail, she seemed to be concentrating on a horse. When Hunter was nearly upon her, she gave only a half-hearted glance over her shoulder at the sound of his approach. When she saw it was him, she did a double-take. "Oh, howdy, Kuh-nel," she drawled jokingly as he drew rein behind her.

Her eyes seemed lit with a luminous welcome before she returned her attention to the horse. The glance created a rush of warmth in Hunter's heart and caused his blood to race. For an instant, a divine dizziness possessed him. He sat motionless, feasting his eyes, his senses, his soul on the woman before him. Although slow to admit it to himself, and hesitant to admit it to others, he now felt certain he had fallen in love with the enemy. How it had happened, when it had happened, *why* it happened, he did not know.

"Spoken like a true Virginian," he said as he dismounted.

Andrea's smile flickered again and so did his heart. "Well ah cain't help my speech, suh."

"Miss Evans, your comrades shall accuse me of trying to convert you." Hunter eased himself up to the fence beside her and stood in silence while the gold light of September bathed them both in its warmth.

"That for Victoria?" Andrea nodded toward his hand.

"Oh, ah-h-h, no ... here." He thrust the wildflower he had picked on the hill overlooking Hawthorne toward her awkwardly, then stood and stared at her in an uncomfortable sort of way, knowing he should say something else but having absolutely no idea what it was. "It reminded me of ... I mean, I thought you might like it."

Up flashed her radiant smile and dazzled him again. "For me? For me?" Andrea took the flower and stuck it in her hair, making no effort to hide her delight. The outburst reflected a girlish exuberance that defied all she had passed through.

Hunter responded by shrugging, pretending that picking flowers was nothing out of the ordinary for him. Yet it did not require much knowledge of his character to know he would have had no more thought of picking a wildflower than plucking a pinecone but a few days earlier. Clumsily and nervously trying to find something to do with his hands, Hunter took off his hat and slapped it against his leg.

"It appears you are returning from a forced march," Andrea said, watching the dust rise.

Hunter just nodded, not wishing to admit that *she* was the forcing power.

Andrea turned, and, hanging on the fence with one hand, used the other to pat his shoulder, sending another cloud of powdery dust into the air. "Turn around." She tried to remove the worst of the grime from his shoulders and back by brushing and patting with her hand. "Looks like you're carrying around half the sacred soil of Virginia."

"And you no doubt enjoy beating *that* out of me, don't you?" Hunter said good-naturedly.

That rippling laugh returned at his words. It was a laugh that was hers alone, a laugh that made the desolate silence that used to reign over Hawthorne echo with happiness. And it was a laugh that brought with it a woozy, wobbly feeling that made Hunter place his hand on the fence to steady himself.

"Trust I could never remove it all, Commander," Andrea replied, making an attempt at seriousness, "for I dare say you have it running through your veins."

Hunter looked into her smiling, glowing eyes and felt a raw ache of happiness in his heart—so acute as to be almost painful. She appeared so radiant on this beautiful, sunny day that he had to look away for fear his eyes would betray what he was thinking. *Good heavens, I am losing my mind!*

Standing quietly for a few moments as she turned back to the paddock, Hunter tried to calm his rushing pulse. Speech had become dangerous, but that did not stop him from gazing at her while her eyes were trained on the horses.

"You know," he said, studying the side of her honey-tanned face, "if you are determined to spend so much time outdoors, you really should wear a hat."

Andrea shrugged, her gaze locked on the horse. "But I don't have one."

Hunter removed his and placed it on her head. "If you're not averse to wearing this one, it's yours."

The hat sank low on her head, and she pushed it up off her brow. "I suppose I should be honored to wear the hat of the gallant Hunter."

"But you are not sure?" He smiled at her uneasiness, knowing she wrestled with the idea of wearing a Rebel hat and did not wish to offend him. "Think of it as legally captured property of war. To the victor go the spoils."

She chuckled at that. "But I fear I did not legally capture it."

"My dear, just because there was no bloodshed does not mean you did not legally capture it. It is yours. And your smile is ample reward."

Andrea looked at him quizzically as if trying to see if he intended some deeper meaning from his words. Hunter quickly leaned over the fence with his arms crossed on the top rail. "I see you have your eye on the roan."

His elbow now touched hers in relaxed abandon. Although she seemed not to notice the contact, he could barely control his thoughts. He wondered what it would feel like to stand there with his arm resting possessively over her shoulders on this brilliantly sunny day while they watched horses in the paddock side by side—as if there were no, and never had been, a war.

Hunter took a deep breath at the disheartening chance of such an event occurring, and her reaction to it, then cleared his throat. "Nice looking piece of Yankee horseflesh," he said, trying to make conversation. "Not that he's comparable in speed or endurance to a Virginia-bred."

Andrea remained silent, cocking her head and examining the horse. Then she gazed confidingly up at him, almost as if a deep and comfortable affection existed between them. "Maybe not. But I know a horse that is."

Hunter put his head back and laughed, knowing she baited him. "You think Justus is faster than Dixie? Or Dash? Funny, but usually I find a woman's vivid imagination a bit tedious."

Andrea looked curiously at him, as if surprised at the sound of the warm gentle voice. "Imagination? Tedious? And in my case?"

"I find it enchanting," he said with a relaxed, boyish grin. "And someday, Miss Evans, I'd be honored to take you up on the challenge of finding out whose horse is faster.

"I look forward to that day." Andrea grabbed his arm for support when she stepped off the bottom rail of the fence. "What shall be the stakes?" She had a laughing challenge in her eyes as she kept her arm linked in his. Hunter felt the warmth of her touch, yet her weight as she leaned on him was hardly discernible.

"Leave that to me," he said in an emotional voice. "I'll think of something."

"Oh no. I believe it is *I* who should come up with the purse for the victor. You would oblige me?" She glanced up at him with a daring, and he thought, seductive look, as she allowed her hand to slide down his arm and into the grasp of his fingers.

Hunter's heart missed a beat as he continued walking in a delicious trance. The simple, casual contact of holding her hand had every nerve and muscle in his body quivering in a way that had never occurred even with the most passionate touch of a woman prior.

"If such is your pleasure." He smiled down at her with unmasked emotion. "I only hope you will make the stakes high enough."

"Colonel, you doubt me?" She pulled him to a sudden stop, a wide grin upon her face and an audacious sparkle in her eyes.

This was the sort of thing that shook him. Hunter laughed, not so much at her words, but at the beautiful way her smile made him feel. She looked perfectly enchanting with his battle hat upon her head, a flower peeking from beneath its brim—a characteristic contradiction of refinement and roughness, grit and grace. "The pleasure will be all mine—win or lose." He gazed down at her and quickly looked away. Her captivating green eyes were never devoid of power, yet today they overwhelmed him.

"I fear you don't take me seriously." Andrea slid her hand up to cling to his arm again. "When I win, I wish it to be fairly."

"I did not mean to infer I will allow you to win, Miss Evans." Hunter stopped again and tried to calm his pulsing heart. "I only meant that, should I lose, it could not be to a more deserving victor."

They were almost to the porch now, and Hunter had the sudden urge to go back—back to the fence, start over, move in slow motion. *Don't let this moment, this morning, this feeling end.* He remained silent, but his mind raced. *Tell her. Tell her.* Then, *do not hold the reins too tightly. Relax, or she will pull and run away.* He tried again to think of the right words to explain his emotions—and to find the nerve to say them out loud.

Pausing on the middle step, he looked back over his shoulder at a disturbance some horses created in the field. Andrea continued to the top step, but turned around questioningly when he did not follow.

With their eyes almost even since he now stood two steps below her, she turned all the way around and placed her hands on his shoulders playfully. "I like this. For once, I do not have to look *up* to you, Colonel."

"I believe I prefer it when you do."

Andrea tilted her head back and laughed. Gazing straight into her enchanting eyes, he knew he would remember the expression she wore on this day, no matter what else ever came to happen in the world.

"I'm sure you do, Colonel." Andrea pushed gently on his shoulders, forcing him to take another step backward and down, his spurs clanking when they hit the slate behind him. "There," she said, her eyes shining from under the brim of his hat. "This is even better. Now *you* are looking up to *me*."

The look—and the words—made him reckless. The smile faded from his face. "My dear," he said, his strong voice low and husky, "trust, I always do that."

Andrea's brows drew together as she tried to read the look in his eyes, but he did not give her time. Bounding up the remaining stairs, he took her hand once again and turned her toward the pastures with boyish enthusiasm. "Have you ever seen anything more splendid?" In the field before them a dozen horses raced their shadows along the paddock fence.

"I believe I've told you before, Colonel, you reside in a place no less perfect than paradise."

Hunter felt a surge of warmth from the small bit of pressure she placed on his hand as she spoke. "And so Virginia is heaven in your eyes, after all?"

Andrea turned to him, her eyes swimming with mirth. "Oh, Colonel, you do have a way of putting words in my mouth. I'll give you that Hawthorne is heaven—but I must still reserve my opinion on all of Virginia."

Hunter laughed at her stubbornness, and she laughed at his laughter. They stood like two children in the sunshine, thoughts of war and enemies and fighting as far from either mind as the thought of any rapport between them had once been.

Tell her, Hunter thought again. *Tell her now.*

Why his lips remained silent he could not fathom. The sparkle of acceptance in her eyes seemed to be a signal, but secretly he feared her heart would not go so far as to accept the affections of a Rebel.

"You are smiling as if you have a secret you wish to share," Andrea said, interrupting his thoughts with imploring eyes.

Hunter could not speak. He was trying to catch the breath she took away. Biting his cheek, as he had so often seen her doing, he thought about confessing what he felt. He took a deep breath as if to try, then exhaled slowly when he could not make his tongue give utterance to the words. Of all the women he had been with in his lifetime—and there had been quite a few—not one had the power to interrupt sensible thoughts like this one. He swallowed all the things he wanted to say and said something else.

"You've been content here the last few weeks?" He lifted the hat a little to reveal her eyes.

"*Content?*" Andrea drew her brows together and cocked her head.

"I beg your pardon." Hunter leaned one shoulder against a pillar, his face turning rigid. "I realize you do not know the meaning of the word." He tried to appear calm, but inside his heart plummeted. He knew with certainty now that her impatience to leave had only been subdued, not extinguished. She still thought of Hawthorne as a prison, one she would break away from when circumstances allowed. The time would come for her to go. And that time, he feared, was not far remote.

"Oh, I understand the word, Colonel. But how could I be content when the one with whom I have enjoyed so many battles of wit is forever absent?"

Hunter sucked his breath in and strained to let it out slowly. Her words and her tone indicated an attempt to make light of the situation in a polite and courteous fashion. Yet he felt sure her eyes indicated something much more complex.

"My absence is not of my own desire," he said in a low, serious tone. "There are many times I wish for nothing more than to be home. Here."

"Then it would appear your wishes have been very much in accord with mine." Andrea looked straight up into his eyes, and then out over his shoulder as if she too had trouble putting words to her thoughts. "I once believed it an unkind fate that placed me here ... but it's a kind one that occasionally permits me the privilege of your company."

Had a hidden battery suddenly opened fire at close range, Hunter could not have been more stunned. He reached instantly for her hand and drew it instinctively to his heart.

Miss Evans ... Andrea. It is time that I tell you that I ... that I—"

The door opened and Victoria burst out, driving his speech back into the depths of his soul.

"Alex, I didn't know you were home!" She dove into him with her usual rapture, knocking Andrea out of the way. Hunter watched Andrea's eyes flicker with a hint of disappointment before they became consumed with resentment and fury. Within the blink of an eye the door into her soul—the one that had taken so fearfully long to open—slammed shut. And he had no way of knowing how long it would take to crack open again.

"Victoria. I believe you owe Miss Evans an apology."

It was too late. Andrea turned around and retreated into the house without a backward glance. One moment she was there, and the next she was gone, vanishing as swiftly and silently as a shadow when a cloud covers the sun. Her quick movement knocked the flower from her hair and it was soon trampled beneath Victoria's foot.

"Miss Evans!' His response was a resounding slamming of a door. Whatever intimacy had flowed between them was gone. Her emotions were mail-clad. She was, yet again, unreachable.

Chapter 50

"Love that well which thou must leave ere long."
— Sonnet 73, Shakespeare

Hunter sought Andrea in every room in the house once he detached himself from Victoria. She was nowhere to be found.

Buttoning his coat against a cool, westerly wind that had arisen, he headed toward the barn.

"You seen Andrea?" he asked Zach when he met him leading a horse in from the paddock.

The servant stopped. "Well, yessuh, Massa. She up and took the team."

"Took them where?" Hunter looked over Zach's shoulder, thinking she may have led the two horses down to the next field for fresh grass.

"I's not sure." The servant scratched his head. "She didn't 'zactly say."

"Where's the wagon?" Hunter looked around the barnyard, his anxiety increasing.

"Well, suh, ya see, it were hooked to the team."

Hunter growled, more a sound of pain than anger, and headed at a brisk pace into the barn. She would not be running way. She could not be. *Not now, Andrea. Please not now!*

He glanced at the darkening sky and tried to think objectively. She would not try to leave until she was completely healed. Surely she would not take a risk that would cause her to extend or prolong her stay.

Within mere minutes, Hunter had mounted and was spurring Dixie down the lane. Meanwhile the storm continued to descend, bringing with it a heavy cloak of black. A low, rolling rumble to the west gave further indication of its severity.

Hunter followed the fresh tracks easily to the place they had watched the sun setting on the hill. When he reined his horse in beside the wagon, he saw her standing near a large boulder, the wind whipping at her skirt. She stared absently at the sky as angry clouds advanced toward the sun like a hungry animal preparing to engulf its prey. Hunter tied his horse to the wagon and stepped carefully among the rocks in his path. If she knew he was there, she did not let on.

"We'd better go," Hunter said gruffly, taking her hand. "This is going to be a bad storm."

Not waiting for her to answer, he dragged Andrea over the rocks so fast her feet barely touched the ground. Within moments, the elements of nature finished lining up for battle and the major engagement commenced. By the time they boarded the wagon, lightning flashed in the sky and the heavens thundered like great volleys of musketry. Hunter gripped the reins as rain pelted them in horizontal sheets. Ducking his head against flying leaves and branches, he guided the horses as best he could, then jerked them to a stop.

"Get inside!" He pulled Andrea across the seat and lifted her down.

"Inside?" Andrea blinked her eyes against the rain.

Hunter pushed her forward and moved his hand across the solid wall in front of them. Finding the latch, he opened the door, shoved her through, and then fought against the brutal wind to secure it behind them. Once closed, they both stood breathing heavily, staring at each other in the dim light.

"You look like a half-drowned kitten." Hunter stared at the dripping hair on her shoulders.

Andrea shivered. "*Half*-drowned?"

Hunter strode over to a large stone fireplace and, after getting a small flame started, turned back to Andrea. "Keep your eye on that. I'm going to put the horses in the barn."

Andrea still stood dripping and shivering when Hunter pushed his way back into the one-room cabin. He closed and bolted the door against the wind, then proceeded back to the fire without saying a word.

"W-w-hat is this p-p-lace?"

Hunter continued to poke at the fire and then turned his head toward her. "It's mine. I built it. Kind of a getaway you might say."

He watched Andrea look around the room, her gaze taking in the bed to the right, then the stone fireplace and the large bearskin rug sprawled before it, and finally the hand-hewn table and cupboards to his left. "I n-never heard anyone s-speak of it."

"Nobody knows about it except me. And now you."

He turned back to the fire and poked at it more forcefully than before, his resentment at the intrusion showing clearly. When it began to blaze, he leaned toward the bed. "Here." He grabbed the patchwork quilt that covered it. "Take off those wet clothes."

Andrea stood motionless, not blinking, not speaking.

"Come on, Miss Evans. This is no time for modesty. You need to get out of those clothes. I'll not have you lying on your deathbed again and blaming me for prolonging your stay."

Andrea opened her mouth to argue when another chill apparently ripped through her. She shivered, then turned and offered no resistance when he un-hooked the back of her gown. Hunter quickly wrapped the blanket around her as she stepped out of the wet dress.

By the time Andrea removed her soaked undergarments and readjusted the quilt, Hunter had shed his shirt and was busy once again stirring the fire.

"Comfortable?" Hunter asked over his shoulder after she sat on the rug. Andrea nodded with chattering teeth but kept her gaze averted. "Here, get a little closer." He pulled her and the rug nearer the fire, keenly aware now of the effort she made not to look at him. Deciding to ignore it, he stood and turned toward the cupboards. "I might have something to warm you up."

After much banging and clattering, he returned to the fireplace carrying a bottle of whiskey and two tin cups. "It's not much, but it will take off the chill." He poured a small amount in a cup and handed it to her as if she were a guest at a tea party.

Andrea lifted the cup, and with shaking hands, emptied its contents. Hunter waited for her to grimace or choke. But when she did neither, he poured another.

"You come here often?" She looked up at him through wet clumps of hair.

Hunter shrugged and turned back to the fire. "I used to come up a lot before the war. When I was married."

"You needed a place to get away from your wife?"

Watching her empty the cup again, he sighed. "It's a long story."

"You didn't love her?"

He threw another piece of wood on the fire, trying to decide whether to answer or not. "It was an arrangement of sorts. A match planned by my grandfather. I was young and naive and wanted to respect his wishes."

"Even though you didn't love her?"

He glanced back at Andrea, wondering if the whiskey impelled her to ask so many questions. "I would have made it work, could have looked past all of her faults … save one." He began stabbing roughly at the fire.

"She was unfaithful." Andrea whispered the words as if it was an act impossible to comprehend.

Hunter sighed and stared into the flames. "John Paul." He tried to sound indifferent, though it hurt to think about it even now. "As it turned out, she was everything I despise in women."

Andrea remained quiet as if pondering in her mind the type of woman that would choose John Paul over Hunter. "That makes it sound like you despise all women," she finally said.

He did not answer. Instead he poked again at the wood, sending a cascade of sparks up the chimney.

"U-m-m, the fire feels good."

Appreciating her attempt to change the subject, Hunter turned around and gave her a smile. "Getting warm?"

"On the inshide and the outshide."

"Looks like you've had enough to drink."

Andrea returned his smile and stretched out on the rug, causing Hunter's heart to involuntarily thump against his chest. Reaching to the bed, he threw a pillow in her direction.

"You comfortable?" He propped himself on one elbow beside her and concentrated on the fire flickering in front of him.

"I wish I could feel like this forever." She lay on her back staring at the ceiling with the blanket wrapped tightly around her.

"Like what?"

"Warm. Safe. Secure."

Hunter laughed and rolled onto his back to stare at the ceiling as well. "You're the only woman I know that could feel safe and secure locked away in the middle of nowhere in a violent storm with the enemy."

Andrea opened her eyes and turned her head toward him. "The enemy?"

"Last time I checked there was a war going on." He lifted himself up on one arm and downed a cup of the amber liquid. "You've not been unclear about telling me that I'm the—"

Andrea put her fingers to his lips. "Not here. I don't want there to be any war tonight." Then she lay back and stared upward again.

"You can't make it go away by wishing it away." Hunter laughed. "I'm at a loss to know which is greater, your will or your imagination. You are determined not to see the world as it really is."

Andrea smiled. "You should try it, Colonel. Because imagination or no, I fear we are stuck here tonight and as good as a million miles from the savage world of war. So what is the harm in pretending it does not exist?"

He gazed at her angelic face, contemplating her rationale.

"You see? Can you believe it, Colonel?"

Hunter quickly shifted his eyes to stare indifferently at the fire. "Believe what?"

"That we can have a civil conversation with one another. Talk without one or the other giving or taking offense."

"Actually, it's long been among my wishes … but realistically not one of my expectations."

"I know." She sighed deeply. "I have incurred your displeasure countless times."

He smiled. "And I, yours."

"Perhaps less often than you think, sir."

"Well to tell you the truth, you are displeasing me right now."

Andrea turned her head toward him. "I am?"

"Yes. If you insist there is no war, then I must insist you call me by my given name. Which, in case you did not know, is not *Colonel*. Nor is it *Commander*. And it is not *sir*."

Andrea looked at him questioningly and then smiled. "Fair enough ... Alex."

Hunter swallowed hard in response to the surge of warmth his name on her lips produced. Was it the alcohol that caused this confusing sensation? Or had he seen something in her eyes before she turned away?

"And this does not frighten you?" He shifted his gaze from the fire to the serene look on her face as she lay with closed eyes. "Being alone with me?"

There was no pause before she answered. "Of course not. *I trust you.*"

Hunter watched her eyes fly open the instant the words left her mouth. She seemed as startled to have said them aloud as he was to hear them.

"You trust me?" With his face just inches from hers, he probed her green eyes for answers.

She remained silent a moment as if searching for the right words. "The only fault I can find is the color of your uniform, but you wear it with honor." She paused and swallowed hard as if admitting this fact to herself for the first time. "Despite my previous tendencies, I have no reason not to trust an honorable man."

Hunter's chest rose with a deep, shaky breath. "Your trust may be ill advised. An honorable man would not think what I am thinking."

He meant the statement to diffuse a precarious situation, but it did not work. Instead, he found it necessary to avert his gaze from Andrea, because she appeared to be wearing the expression he'd wished to see all day. Hunter tried to concentrate on the flickering flames of the fire rather than those two green eyes that suddenly held so much acceptance.

"We are from two worlds," he finally said, reminding himself of their loyalties and obligations. He swallowed hard again, took a deep breath, and closed his eyes. From the very core of his soul, he strove to resist the temptation to touch her, or even look at her again—afraid if he did, sparks would fly.

"You speak as Hunter the soldier," Andrea said, her voice strangely soft. "Not as Hunter the man." She lifted her hand to his face, touched the rough stubble with her fingertips, then moved her hand back to his hair, as if it was something she had long desired to feel.

Hunter blinked at the contact and gave an involuntary shudder. His breathing came faster now, his chest rising and falling with the effort. He grabbed her wrist to stop her. "Andrea, you don't know what you're doing."

Their eyes locked. "Teach me."

A flash of lightning lit up the room at that moment, and for an instant Hunter saw her face clearly in the brilliant light. Her eyes were no longer big and innocent. They were seductive and enchanting and intoxicating, made even more so under the influence of the fire's soft glow.

"We are at peace?" Hunter's pulse throbbed. Blood tingled in every vein.

He struggled to breathe without gasping.

Andrea did not bother to answer with words. She placed her trembling fingers upon his shoulders, touching the soft skin stretched taut across hard muscles. Hunter flinched and moaned softly, the contact almost more than he could endure. With a reverent movement of his hand, the quilt fell away, and there was suddenly flesh on flesh, pounding heart upon pounding heart. With the barrier of war lifted, the long-restrained powder keg ignited into flame.

ℋ ℋ ℋ

Hunter awoke to a sense of deep, inexplicable peace. He lay in silent contemplation, staring at the flickering glow of the dying fire, intensely aware of the beat of another heart against his own.

A smile crossed his lips when his groggy mind considered the possibility of waking to this feeling each morning, and feeling this sense of contentment each day. The more he thought about it the more he looked forward to pouring out his feelings and letting his affection be known.

Then reality set in. His heart, seemingly of its own accord, began pounding in such frantic reaction to his thoughts that he feared it would wake her. He could accept having fallen in love with the enemy—but could she? There may have been no North and South last night, but there would be now. He knew well the effects of whiskey on an empty stomach and tired mind, and he feared that without its intoxicating influence, he would once again be a foe—one that had taken advantage of her youth and innocence.

Yes, she would be angry. He was sure of it. Mother Nature may have kept the world at bay last night, but it was morning now. Andrea would never forgive him for making her feel she had to make a choice between her beloved Union and him.

What have I done?

In that moment of uncertainty, Hunter decided that rather than admit something had happened between them, it would be better to pretend nothing had happened at all. But before he slipped out from under her, he did as she had done on the balcony that warm, summer night. He closed his eyes, opened his hand and brought it back to his heart to effectively store the passion and emotions there, forming a memory that would be vivid and real to him to his last breath.

ℋ ℋ ℋ

Andrea awoke to morning light streaming in through the window and a fire that was only a bed of hot ashes. Before she had time to wonder where Hunter had gone, the door opened and he appeared, wearing his coat, but no shirt beneath it.

She looked down and realized she now wore the large garment that hung

273

to her knees, but Hunter did not appear to notice. He walked by and poured a cup of coffee with nothing but a remote, detached look in his eye—the same look that had infuriated her on so many previous occasions.

"The horses are ready," he said with callous indifference. "We'd better get a move on. They'll be worried."

Andrea was stunned, then incensed, unable to believe his conduct could be so uncaring and cold after his passionate display just a few hours previous. Then again, why should she be surprised? He was after all a man—and a Rebel at that!

Removing the shirt in one swoop, she aimed for the back of his head. "You mean *Victoria* will be worried!"

By the time Hunter unwrapped the cloth from around his neck, Andrea had pulled on her dress and was limping unceremoniously to the door, picking up her undergarments as she walked.

"Andrea, wait—" She slammed the door shut before he could finish.

Chapter 51

"Look what fools these mortals be."
— William Shakespeare

Andrea successfully avoided conversation both on the wagon ride home and the rest of the day. But her attempts to avoid her own memories that night failed miserably. Although she searched her mind, she recollected no words of devotion spoken. Hunter's actions may have implied, but never really confirmed, any newfound admiration for her.

Tossing and turning in bed, she strove to push all thoughts of the incident from her head. It had been an act of simple lust, nothing more—lust brought on by intoxication and hunger and fatigue. Why or how she could have behaved that way, she could not understand. But it was over with now, over and done. She had to forget it ever happened. As Hunter had done.

Giving up on sleep, Andrea crawled from her bed a little before dawn. Tip-toeing down the steps, she hurried out the door, and gasped at three shadowy figures standing on the porch talking in low, hushed tones.

Colonel Hunter, Major Carter, and Captain Pierce seemed to be in the middle of a very important council of war. At the sound of her approach, all three heads jerked around at once. At the sight of her, all three removed hats in unison.

"Mornin', Miss Evans." Carter was the first to find his tongue.

"Major Carter." Andrea nodded. "Captain Pierce." She looked the latter in the eye, but Pierce quickly averted his gaze. As for Colonel Hunter, she did not say his name or acknowledge his presence.

"I-I couldn't sleep. I regret the intrusion." Without pausing, she continued on her way.

In a matter of moments, Andrea inhaled the soothing scent of the barn, and the violent pounding of her heart began to ease. She followed the sound of banging buckets to find Zach preparing the horses' feed. "Good morning!"

"Morning, Miz Andrea," he replied with a large smile.

When she turned back around to visit Justus, she nearly ran into Captain Pierce.

"Colonel sent me down to get a fresh horse," he said to Zach, ignoring Andrea. "Mine seems to have picked up a stone. Be quick about it."

Zach disappeared to retrieve a horse, and Pierce turned back to begin unsaddling the mare that stood in the aisle. Andrea watched his blank mien for a few moments. "Are you trying to ignore me?"

"No." He tugged at the cinch. "Just following orders."

"Orders?"

"The Colonel seems to think it's in your best interest if I don't converse with you."

"I beg your pardon?"

"Seems to think you need protection."

"Protection?" Andrea forced a laugh. "From what?"

Pierce lifted the saddle from the mare's back and placed it on the gelding Zach brought forward. "From me, apparently." He reached under the animal for the cinch.

"You jest." Andrea removed the bridle from his lame horse with expert hands and handed it to Zach.

"No, I don't." Pierce watched with apparent interest her casual and relaxed interaction with his horse and the practiced way she handled the bridle.

"Then you must have misunderstood."

"There was no misunderstanding." He mounted and then bent down, his face almost even with Andrea's as he pretended to adjust his stirrup. "Perhaps he believes I find you intoxicating and would not be able to perform my duties as a soldier with you in my blood."

Andrea's heart thumped as his deep, passionate gaze swept over her. But the suggestion he offered stirred no pulse of desire in her, only a slow building of anger.

"In any event," Pierce cleared his throat and straightened, "I'm a soldier first and remain obedient to the Commander. I fear any further discussions on the subject will have to be with him." He tipped his hat, devoured her with his gaze in such a way that let her know he did not concur with Hunter's wishes, and urged his horse forward, leaving Andrea standing in the barn, both hands clenched into fists.

℀ ℀ ℀

Hunter heard the crowing of a lazy rooster as he started out the door. With his head bent over the task of pulling on his gloves, he did not see Andrea making her way back from the barn. He almost strode right past her on the steps, but when he looked up, he stopped.

"Andrea." The image of green eyes blazing in firelight appeared in his mind unbidden. She stared straight ahead, making it obvious the memory of what transpired in the cabin had not deserted her mind either.

"Wait!" He grabbed her arm. "Andrea, if there is something I have said or done, or failed to do or say … I mean, it was not my intention to offend you—"

Andrea interrupted him in such a calm, determined voice that it instantly struck at his heart. "*Offend* me? Sir, you forget. I have spent enough time in the exclusive company of men to understand their motives." Her voice betrayed no pain, but her eyes did, noticeably.

Hunter winced at the thought of the many indelicate conversations she must have heard among soldiers in the gleam of campfire light. For a moment he tried to divine her meaning. "My motives?"

"The conquest." Andrea assumed an air of indifference she obviously did not feel. "It's the thrill of the hunt that enthralls men such as you, is it not?"

She was apparently trying to make the matter sound trivial, but Hunter could see she was so angry—or hurt—she trembled. He reached out for her hand, but she evaded the move. "No, Andrea. I fear I've bungled badly something that … that—" He struggled for the right words. She stood on the top step, he two steps down, just where they had been two days earlier when he had stared into laughing, happy eyes. Today he could not look directly into them, so agonized and distrustful was her gaze.

"Andrea, you don't understand."

"Oh, I believe I understand perfectly." Andrea drew her arm away when he reached toward it. "I'm that willful spirit which you doubtless longed to break, and certainly not the first to become a woman at the hands of—" She took a deep, gasping breath and shook her head impatiently as if losing her train of thought. "I mean, to be *conquered* by the gallant Colonel Hunter."

Hunter noticed she no longer trembled. She visibly shook. Even her teeth chattered as though bitterly cold. The strong, unwavering Andrea stood quivering from head to toe and, for once, showed no signs of being able to rally her spirit. He imagined her heart beating like the wings of a caged bird, thrashing and bruising itself against the bars.

"Andrea, please listen to me."

"And now I have caused a rift with one of your officers." She wrung her hands, staring out over his shoulder again. "I rather thought, Colonel …" She stopped to catch her breath. It was as if she were sobbing, yet there were no tears. "I rather thought that *sharing* the spoils of war was a key component of your Command."

"Andrea, you must calm down." Hunter took both of her arms and held them by her side. "Stop talking like this. Listen to reason!"

"I would have expected as much from Captain Pierce, whose motives were clear to me from the moment I met him." She looked Hunter in the eye now, staring through him with a half-crazed expression.

"Andrea, you don't understand. Pierce is a volatile man. If he found out who you really are—"

"I'm not ashamed of my allegiance!" She struggled from his grasp again. "For if I were to be shot by him or held in his arms, I'd be grateful for the former and sickened by the latter!"

After taking a deep, shaky breath, Andrea seemed to will herself to calmness. "Perhaps you can withdraw your offensive order from Captain Pierce, sir. *He* is not the one from whom I need protection."

She tried to turn and leave, but Hunter stepped in front of her. "Andrea, you must know, it was not my intention to—"

Andrea held up her hand. "I understand, Colonel, that these matters are inconsequential, more so for a man than a woman. Such things will naturally sit more lightly on your conscience than they do on mine."

"I did not mean to imply it was inconsequential! You are misconstruing my words!" Hunter suppressed the urge to drag her into his arms, for it appeared to him she would crumble to dust and blow away if he but touched her. "Andrea, I don't have time now, but—"

He gave his horse a hurried glance. His men were already gathering. Stern duty demanded his prompt return to them.

"Yes, of course. If duty compels you to leave, then leave you must."

"Andrea, I need to talk to you."

"No. No need to talk." She stared straight ahead, her face white with restrained emotion, her whole appearance one of misery.

"I swear to you on my brother's grave I never meant to hurt you."

"Oh, yes. There is the matter of that promise." Andrea laughed without smiling. "No doubt a distasteful obligation for you. But it is ironic that a promise is the only reason I am here, is it not? A promise to allow no harm to befall me at that." Her voice turned to a mere whisper. "Tell me, Colonel, do you consider that promise kept?"

She gazed deep into his eyes, and the look on her face told him that she did not. He bowed his head at her words, could no longer bear the pain in her voice.

Her next words were barely audible, with such heartbreaking emotion were they voiced. "I asked you before to despoil me of my life ... but leave me with my honor."

Hunter looked at her hard, then wished he had not. He saw her very soul in her eyes and it wept—even if she did not. "Andrea. Please listen to reason."

"Truly, Colonel, I accept the situation. It is I who construed a mere truce into a . . . into a sacred claim."

"It was not just a truce!" Hunter grabbed her arms and held them to her side. "Andrea, what must I say to make you understand?"

"Say nothing! I want nothing to do with you!"

"If I have to lock you in your room, young lady, I will make you listen to me!"

"Do not *threaten* me." Her voice was calm, though she still stared into his eyes with an unnerving, unnatural look.

"Andrea, please. This is too complicated to discuss right now. But I—"

Hunter paused, unable to decide on a course of action. He had hoped to ask her to become his wife, to make things right with the night they had shared. But he did not dare. Not now. She would not believe his words of devotion. Her emotions ran too deep for that.

In that moment's hesitation, when he did not know what to do or say, Andrea struggled free from his grasp, and half-ran, half-stumbled to the door.

"Andrea, wait! We need to talk! Don't walk away from me! I forbid it!"

Andrea turned slightly and gave him one pitiful backward glance of hopeless pain and fury before rallying her spirit enough to speak in customary defiance of his power. "Do not *dare* give an order to me!" Her eyes blazed with that old foe, hate. "You forget! I am the *enemy*!"

Chapter 52

"It is faith that saves, distrust that most quickly destroys."
— From Jest to Earnest, E.P. Roe

Hunter paced in his library, his hands clenched, his face red with anger. After returning from the field, he'd discovered Andrea was nowhere to be found. Izzie had been forced to admit she had "gone for a carriage ride" with John Paul hours earlier.

Was this her way of exacting revenge on him? His heart lurched at the thought. She had no way of knowing he would return so soon. Even he had not known that the cry of alarm that roused him this morning was a false one.

The sound of carriage wheels interrupted his thoughts, soon followed by the soft tap of Andrea's cane coming up the porch steps.

Hunter strode from the library and waited for her by the stairs. Unconscious of observation, she brushed her disheveled hair back as she walked across the foyer, her eyes cast downward. Even in her tousled appearance she radiated a glow of beauty and natural innocence. The sight of her made his heart flutter, and the thought of her with John Paul caused his blood to surge with jealousy.

The closer she got, the more his anger swelled. "Welcome back, Miss Evans," he said. "It appears you had an errand that took you away from Hawthorne."

Andrea lifted her head, obviously surprised at his presence. Yet she stood and looked him calmly in the eye. "I pray you did not return in haste so we could resume our earlier conversation." She tried to push past him.

Hunter grabbed her by the arm and blurted out the first thing that entered his mind, fully expecting a fight. "Are you intentionally following in Elizabeth's footsteps, Miss Evans? Or does lust for my neighbor fall under the category of vengeance?"

Andrea blinked repeatedly as if his words were a hard slap to the face, but otherwise she did not move or even appear to breathe. Instead of pulling away in anger or rebellion, she looked up at him with eyes that reflected surprise, then disbelief, and then a deep hurt, as if he had indeed physically assaulted her. She opened her mouth to speak, but nothing came out.

The silence for a few long moments remained oppressive, her thoughts apparently too deep for human utterance. "Once again you dishonor me, sir," was all she said before wrenching her arm free from his grasp.

Hunter looked in wonderment at her blank, detached expression, and then into the eyes that stared up at him still. His heart welled with pity at what he saw there—for he could have sworn, before she turned away, that a tear had overflowed the rim and trickled down her cheek.

Hunter felt a crushing blow to his chest at the deep hurt reflected in those misty eyes. "Papa does not like tears," she had said during her fever. Indeed, he had never witnessed a single one—not even upon Daniel's death. The tears she had pent up in her heart for so long had finally been wrung from her soul by his own accursed words.

"Wait. Andrea, I—"

A loud knock on the door interrupted him. By the time he yelled impatiently for the courier to enter and turned back, she had disappeared up the stairs.

"It's important, sir," the courier said.

Hunter tore open the dispatch. Blast it! The Yankees were heading toward town. The chance of two false reports in one day was slim.

Hunter ran up the stairs, taking two at a time. He needed to apologize before he left. It could not wait. Knocking once on her door, he burst in and found the room empty. She must have anticipated his move and gone straight down the back staircase.

Hurrying back downstairs and outside, he made a quick sweep of the gardens and the pasture where Justus stood. She was not there.

"Saddle Dixie," he yelled to Zach, while looking down toward the pond. A sudden movement on the hill caught his eye.

There he saw her, kneeling in front of Daniel's grave, her head bowed, her shoulders drooping. She placed her hand on the tombstone, and leaned her head on her hand. The scene tore at his soul, made him regret the pain he had caused her. How could he tell her how much he respected her? Honored her? Yet it was strikingly clear that it was Daniel for whom her thoughts would ever be.

Oh, Andrea. If by forfeiting my life I could place him back in your arms, how quickly and willingly would the exchange be made!

Hunter turned away. He had a duty to perform. He did not look back. He could not.

ℋ ℋ ℋ

The sound of a horse galloping at breakneck speed broke the silence in Andrea's chamber. She sat on the bed with trembling hands and closed her eyes in anticipation of what was to come. Within moments she heard the loud clank of spurs, and then his voice outside her door.

"Andrea, we need to talk." The doorknob jiggled, and then Hunter pounded the wooden barrier with his fist. "Confound it, Andrea! I'm going to put my horse away, and when I return, this door had better be unlocked—or blast it, I'm coming through!"

His fist—or his head—hit the door in exasperation one last time before his spurs retreated down the hall. Andrea heard him pause at the stairway, as if looking back one last time, before his footsteps faded away.

Even after the passage of two days, she was too ashamed to face him. Her only choice was to leave Hawthorne. For two days she'd been convincing herself of the necessity of that action; for two days she'd put it off.

Gazing out the window, her eyes fell upon a group of superbly mounted Confederate officers riding up the drive at a brisk trot. Hunter walked toward the horsemen, a look of surprise and annoyance clearly visible upon his countenance.

After greeting Hunter with formal stiffness, the entire entourage moved toward the house. Andrea sat down on the bed, a sigh of relief escaping her lips. She would have a slightly longer reprieve than expected.

Rocking back and forth in nervous contemplation, Andrea found her thoughts interrupted by the sound of voices below. When she stood and walked toward the fireplace, the voices grew even louder. Realizing the visitors had been taken to the parlor beneath her, she knelt by the hearth.

"We need that train, the gold, and the payroll, Colonel Hunter," a loud voice said. Andrea matched it in her mind with a heavily bearded colonel she had seen outside.

"Supplies are in dire shape," another replied. "It's imperative we get that shipment."

"I'm sorry, gentlemen, but I've received word of a wagon train of medical supplies expected to go through around the same time." Hunter sounded none too polite. "Considering the scarcity of medicine and the suffering of our wounded, I find that a more reasonable prize."

The next words were unrecognizable because whoever spoke had moved away from the fireplace.

"Perhaps you do not understand, Colonel Hunter," the officer's voice grew distinct. "This directive comes from General Lee. I am merely the messenger."

"The gold is coming straight from the U.S. paymaster," another voice said. "You and your men will have easy pickings at Martin's Crossroads."

"Easy pickings? I do not believe you know the nature of the business. If the train is carrying payroll it will be heavily guarded. Already, there is not a quarter mile between pickets and a mile between camps!"

It sounded like Hunter was pacing, for his voice grew strong and then so weak Andrea barely made out his words. "The wagon train of medical supplies is coming right through Madison. The success of its capture is almost guaranteed."

"We trust you can find a way to take the train, Colonel. You always do."

"Your trust will do nothing to protect the lives of my men!" Hunter's reverberating voice caused Andrea to back out of the fireplace. "Taking that train will take all that I have and then some."

"We have orders to provide you with whatever you need."

281

Hunter's words became muffled again, but she heard the final part. ". . . the medicine is worth its weight in gold to those who are suffering."

"You have your orders, Colonel. See that they are carried out."

Andrea stood and paced too, gnawing on a fingernail. Her heart raced so violently she could hear it pulsing in her ears. "I have the date and near location of a raid—"

These thoughts, and many others, flew through her mind so fast and fleetingly she could scarcely keep up. *Oh, why? Why did I have to hear this information?*

Andrea stopped and held her head in her hands. Her conscience drew her in one direction, duty in another. How had the lines of obligation suddenly become so blurred and allegiances so distorted?

How could she do this?

How could she not?

Was it not divine providence that she overheard the conversation? Was it not divine providence she was leaving anyway? Yet Andrea yearned for a sign to guide her in determining what course to take. She no longer knew what was right or wrong; no longer knew *who* was right or wrong. Confronted with these two mighty, opposing convictions, she wondered what Hunter would do in her shoes.

Then her decision was made.

If all went as planned, he would never be the wiser. It was a calculated risk, but one she was willing to take. She must go. Succeed or fail, it was her duty to try. And succeed or fail, Hunter would never know of her involvement one way or the other.

All she needed now was one quick glance at a map, the detailed, hand-drawn one of the area she had seen him studying once with Carter. With the slamming of the door downstairs and the sound of boots on the porch, her plan was launched. Hunter would no doubt be leaving tonight. And she would be right behind him.

Running out the door and leaving it open, Andrea headed for the back stairs. She knew Hunter would not be long in coming, yet she never dreamed he would be up the main stairs and standing in her doorway before she was even halfway down the other.

"Andrea!" She heard him enter the room. She stopped, pressed herself against the wall in the narrow stairwell, and held her breath.

"Damn it!" Her door slammed shut with a resounding bang.

"Alex, you're home!" Victoria's shrill voice filled the hallway.

Andrea let go of her breath and smiled.

"Where is Andrea?"

Victoria snorted. "You think *me* in her confidence?"

"Mattie!" Hunter bellowed, his voice like thunder. The servant's footsteps sounded instantaneously. "Have Zach hang the red banner and saddle Dixie. Then report to me in my study. I have some dispatches I need you to give the courier when he arrives."

"Darling, you just got here," Victoria moaned. "You're not leaving already, are you?"

Knowing Victoria would keep him occupied for the few minutes she needed, Andrea continued down the stairs and headed toward the library. Proceeding to Hunter's desk, she pulled out the map and glanced at the landmarks she could use to guide her. Her hands shook as she hurriedly refolded the map, placing it back in the drawer.

Without warning, she heard Victoria's voice right outside the library door, then the sound of the doorknob turning. She slipped out the French door into the garden as the sound of Hunter's spurs filled the room behind her. Not until she was safe from view did she remember she had neglected to close the desk drawer.

Taking her time, Andrea walked through the garden and then around to the front of the house, pretending to be returning from the barn. As she made her way up the steps of the porch, Victoria and Alex appeared at the door.

"I don't understand why you have to leave—" Victoria stopped speaking when Hunter stopped walking. "Miss Evans."

"Colonel Hunter." Andrea nodded as if nothing out of the ordinary had transpired between them. She continued toward the door, but he caught her arm. "I'd like to have a word."

"Yes," she said, her gaze settling on Victoria, "I can see that is a high priority for you." Wrestling free from his grasp, Andrea resumed her journey into the house. She did not get far. Before making it up the stairs, he was beside her again.

"You will allow me the honor of a word?" Hunter's voice was anything but calm. He placed his hand on hers as it rested on the banister to emphasize his intent.

Andrea did not answer, but did not refuse. With regret, she thought how soon she would be leaving, never to feel that strong hand again.

"I am called to duty. I ask that you stay until I return ... until we talk."

Andrea looked up at him, wondering how he so easily read her thoughts. She turned away again and spoke to nothingness, though she suddenly found it difficult to breathe. "If you wish it of me."

"I should not be gone long." His tone was unusually low and strained. Andrea thought she heard a tremor in it. "Two days at the most."

"Two days," she repeated, feigning that every minute at Hawthorne would be agony.

"Andrea." Hunter put his hand on her shoulder and spoke in a tone that made her heart thump violently. The tremor she suspected before was clearly evident now. "I regret deeply any pain I caused you."

Andrea pretended to be unaffected by his gentle and sincere manner—or his words.

"Will that be all, sir?" She turned her head back toward him, but successfully masked all emotion.

"Yes." He sighed, his eyes revealing a hint of suffering. "That will be all."

Chapter 53

"Make yourself ready for the mischance of the hour."
— The Tempest, Shakespeare

Feeling more dismay than disappointment, Hunter loped up the drive to Hawthorne, his mind occupied with the events that had unfolded on the ill-fated train raid.

As expected, the tracks had been heavily guarded. But he had not anticipated the arrival of two additional regiments of enemy cavalry on the night of the attack, a complication that resulted in the ultimate failure of the enterprise and the complete demoralization of his men. One killed, five wounded, three captured, and no gold or bounty of any kind. The raid was a catastrophe.

But his mind was preoccupied with other thoughts as well. His heart ached at the image of Andrea ascending the stairs after their last brief conversation. She had refused to look him in the eye, had gone back to calling him "sir." No action or word of hers disclosed they had ever shared intimacy, and it pierced him to know she regretted they had.

He felt her drifting farther away every minute, sensed she was pulling the cloak of her isolation more firmly around her. The door was closing again between them, and he feared it would soon be locked and barred against further intrusion.

Hunter inhaled deeply. He intended to do everything in his power to keep that from happening. By revealing all, he planned to put an end to the blessed uncertainty between them. Dismounting at the barn, he glanced up at her window. He would confess all that he no longer had the will to restrain, and then certainly she would not leave. How they would resolve their conflicting loyalties he did not know, but it did not matter. He loved her, and she loved Hawthorne, and somehow, some way, everything else would work out.

284

His optimism brought a smile to his lips. It was so much more like her than him.

Hunter handed his mare over to Zach, then noticed Justus had worked himself into a sweat. He paused in front of his stall. "What's the matter, boy," he said, tapping the stallion tentatively on the nose. "Those old girls teasing you again?"

Staring at the horse through the bars of the stall, his slight smile faded as a deep feeling of foreboding closed in on him. The stallion did not seem agitated by the mares in the barn. Rather, he appeared somewhat subdued. Tired. And though he had obviously been groomed, the faint outline of a saddle could still be seen. Hunter recognized the horse had been ridden hard, and had not been back long.

Standing spellbound, Hunter felt his hands tighten on the bars of the stall as his mind absorbed what his soul already knew. He blinked and blinked again, like a man trying to come to terms with his own mortal wound.

Hunter closed his eyes and rested his head against his hand. No matter how he tried to alter the possibilities, the same conclusion stared him in the face. As the minutes ticked by, the pain of the revelation intensified, and the rage that blossomed from the pain grew proportionately extreme.

The drum of blood in his temples almost blinded Hunter as he stormed out of the barn toward the house. Anger, disappointment, and disgust at her duplicity swept over him and became master of him. His theory on what had transpired took possession of his thoughts and obliterated every other possibility.

This now was war. War with no quarter, no flag of truce, and no negotiations! She had laid the ground rules. Now she must live by them.

ℋ ℋ ℋ

Andrea sat with a book on her lap, but she was not reading. She was thinking about the ride from which she had returned and wrestling with what she had done. She tossed the book aside, stood and paced, then sat again and stared into space. Her mission, she believed, had been a success. Yet so deep was her guilt, she could not feel exultant. This constant blurring of lines between obligation and allegiance made her feel only remorse for her actions, edging toward frantic regret.

Putting her face in her hands a moment, Andrea shook her head. She felt compelled to explain to Hunter what she had done and why. But how could she? She was not sure she knew herself.

She sighed and leaned back in despair. Right or wrong, the deed was done. There was no way to take it back. She had done what she felt was right, with her heart as her guide.

Why then did she feel so despicable?

Andrea was so deeply absorbed in her thoughts, she never heard Hunter ride in. Only when the door slammed shut below, followed by his spurred boots clanking up the steps, did she realize he was home. The echo of his heavy tread in the hall sounded ominous, causing her to feel a foreshadowing of something dreadful to come.

When her door flew open, Andrea jumped in surprise. When she saw the look on Hunter's face, her surprise redoubled. He glared at her with a look of vengeance, his expression suggesting insensate passion and fury. Standing in the doorway, legs spread, fists clenched, he appeared desperate and violent, like a great warrior ready to do battle.

Andrea gasped, but otherwise controlled her emotions as she swept her eyes over him. Had he been standing on a battlefield, surrounded by the enemy, he could not look more warlike or less human.

The room grew gravely quiet. "Beautiful sunrise this morning, was it not, Miss Evans? Perhaps you had a chance to witness it before your return."

Andrea swallowed convulsively, yet she did not speak. Breathing seemed to be the only ability she possessed, and even that took great effort.

When she did not answer, Hunter slammed the door behind him and strode across the room like an angry bull. Grabbing her by the shoulders, he picked her up out of the chair and shook her like a rag doll.

"Does your bitterness, your hatred, your desire for revenge run so deep? Could you not allow me the opportunity to explain my actions before taking your treacherous retribution?"

Andrea tried to answer, but he shook her so violently her teeth rattled. She stared into the black anger gleaming from his eyes. Though he had always appeared to her the image of massive power, today that power was frightening.

"I do not understand," she managed to say despite the sudden thickness in her throat.

"Do not understand?" Hunter let her go, stepped back, and looked at her incredulously. "My men were ambushed on the way to a raid last night, Miss Evans, and I have a sneaking suspicion you are more knowledgeable about what transpired than I."

"Ambushed? But ... I ..." She stopped, not wishing to risk a long sentence until her voice was under control again.

"But what, Andrea? You warned them of the raid and did not expect them to go on the offensive? I believe you know battle tactics better than that!"

Andrea tried to remain calm so she could explain what she had done and why, but Hunter's anger was so intense, his look one of such pitiless contempt, she feared what he might do. She remembered what his men had said about him in battle, and now she knew what they meant. The ferocity that possessed him when in the presence of the enemy had apparently overcome him now. His actions, his face, even his voice, were no longer familiar to her. "I-I-I—"

"Are words suddenly stricken from your tongue, Miss Evans? It's so very unlike *you* to be speechless." His voice, as cold as the steel of the two guns he still wore, was more effective at stripping Andrea of courage than if he had actually struck her. She could more easily pull the trigger of a gun aimed at her own breast than face him now.

"Colonel, I—"

He turned away, the action sufficient to stop her in mid-sentence. The room filled with silence, save his rapid, ragged breath.

"Did you lose any men?" Andrea pushed the words from her throat.

Hunter made a strange, angry noise that would be hard to conceive by anyone who has never heard the growl of a wounded bear. He whirled back around to face her, disdain shining from his liquid-gray eyes. "Of course I lost men! That was your intent was it not?"

His voice had taken on the intensity of thunder. Trembling, caused by suppressed rage, shook his frame. Andrea began experiencing a strange choked feeling in which she could not talk or think, or even feel. If she had it all to do over again she would not go. To hell with sacred duty!

"Your talent for deception is remarkable," Hunter said, jarring her from her thoughts. "But how could I have envisioned what deceit Yankee ingenuity could devise when you stood before me with a palm branch in one hand and the sword of vengeance in the other?"

It was not a question that required an answer. It was instead a statement that demanded an explanation. But Andrea could not speak. Instead, she listened to his insults with her eyes closed. *I deserve this*, she thought to herself. *This is war. Yes, this is war, J.J. ... And it is no game.*

"You came here with nothing but treachery in your heart!" Hunter pointed his finger in her face like a pistol. "You would use *any* means to get what you wanted, wouldn't you?"

His words penetrated Andrea's heart. Even though his voice was no longer raised, the tone carried a cutting, painful edge. She felt her body wilting like a flower too long without water under a merciless sun.

"Have you nothing to say?" Hunter bellowed as if shouting orders in the din of battle. Andrea's lips parted, but failed again in speech. Her eyes dropped and beheld the sight of the clenched fists he held close to his side, both of them shaking.

He began pacing again, while Andrea followed his every motion with her eyes. "This was your strategy all along, I suppose. Admit it! You saw me merely as an advantage to your cause!"

Andrea lowered her head at his accusations. His words slid through her like a bayonet, painful and deadly, twisting deep in quivering flesh, impaling her like a blade of agony.

Hunter stood surveying her features. "I trusted you," he said, his voice raspy and barely above a whisper. "I trusted you, and you deceived me."

Andrea remained silent, refusing to increase his wrath by speaking, even though she felt her very life draining away.

Hunter backed away and threw his hands in the air. "Our disagreement had nothing to do with my Command. It was between us. Not my men!"

"You will not allow me the honor of an explanation?"

"*Honor?*" Hunter choked. Such was the disdain in his tone that Andrea's legs suddenly felt incapable of supporting her and she sat down numbly on the bed.

He laughed at the action. "Well, then, go ahead if you have something to say."

Andrea forced herself to meet his gaze. "It appears you have it all figured out, Colonel."

"Yes, I have it all figured out! I value knowing how to put two and two together with confidence in the result of the addition!"

Andrea had no defense against his words, nor the tone in which he spoke them. Nothing in her past had prepared her for this. She struggled to push words from her throat. "What proof do you have that I'm guilty of this offense?"

"I have all the proof I need." He whirled around to face her. "Your deceit, your cunning, and your guile are sufficient proof of your character for me."

Andrea maintained a dignified silence, enduring his probing, pitiless stare without flinching.

"Dare you deny that Justus was ridden last night and returned in the not-so-distant past?"

Andrea gave a faint reply while staring at her feet. "No, sir."

"Dare you deny you studied my map?"

Andrea looked up in surprise, and then eyed him in silent contemplation, an action Hunter apparently took as a confession. "No," she said exhaling, "but I—"

"And still you are *denying* it?"

Andrea trembled from the great battle taking place inside. "If you believe I did it, what good would it do for me to deny it?"

"Blast it, Andrea. I *trusted* you!" He stared at her intently, seemingly waiting for her to admit her betrayal, or deny her involvement, or beg for his mercy or forgiveness.

Only with the greatest effort did Andrea manage her voice. "Sir, I do not believe you know the meaning of the word."

"Do not tell me what I don't know!" He stood right in front of her, his breath coming in uneven gasps. "How could you do this to me?"

There was such torment in his words Andrea stood and gazed into his unblinking eyes. The merciless glare was gone, but the despair lingering there was so pathetic, her heart picked up its pace. She lowered her eyes to his heaving chest, contemplating the necessity of telling the truth. She swallowed hard, took a deep breath, and slowly lifted her gaze to meet his. "Alex—"

"Enough!" He held up his arms as if to shield himself from her words, his name on her lips seeming to open a new wound. He took on a look of impatient intolerance and his seething anger revived.

The solid floor began to tremble beneath Andrea now. "Colonel Hunter, I believe you will regret—"

"The only thing I *regret*, Miss Evans," he said in a cruel, malicious voice, looking at her with dreadful calm, "is a promise I made to my brother—and ever having met *you*."

Andrea stared at his lips, forcing herself to comprehend that the words she heard were the same ones he had actually spoken. Words. She had laughed at their power. Now his almost felled her. This final stab had caught her unaware and pierced all the deeper because of the willingness with which she had exposed her vulnerable heart.

She raised her eyes to meet his like a convicted criminal receiving a death sentence from a judge. "You wish me to leave?" She heard her own voice speak, rather dim and far away, while feeling herself sinking fast in an abyss of unknown depth. With his hand on the doorknob, Hunter paused. "I not only wish it, Miss Evans, I *order* it. And I recommend you proceed swiftly before I change my mind—and my capacity for leniency."

He shot her a look of disgust. "And I hope to your God you have sense enough to head North."

There was no disguising the threat inferred. He would show no mercy should they ever meet again. Andrea stood silent as the door slammed closed, uttering no words of protest. She could not find the words to speak, nor find the breath to speak them. She grabbed the bedpost for support and closed her eyes, trying to block out the sound of his boots stomping down the stairs. She jumped when his library door slammed shut with thunderous finality below.

She had been willing to leave, but not like this. How could she leave when she did not know if she could move? Andrea raised her head and cast her eyes around the room she had grown to know as home.

How ironic. I shall leave just as I arrived: suffering, miserable, and hopeless.

Chapter 54

"'Tis my reward for dearest victory won,
I did that love undo – to be myself undone!"
– Polyeucte by Pierre Corneille

Not even waiting to put her feet in the stirrups Andrea pushed Justus into a gallop and ran away from Hawthorne. She barely saw the house as it flew by, a streak of white followed by a splash of green. The bridge appeared as a blur, then all was sun and shadow.

Andrea eventually looked back, but by then Hawthorne was not to be seen. How far she had ridden or how long she had been riding she did not know. She had been unconscious of everything around her, numb. But now she realized it was useless to push Justus so hard. The memories would pursue her no matter how far she went or how fast she rode.

Bending down and patting her heaving horse, Andrea tried to console herself. She knew she was well enough to leave—had been for some weeks now. It had only been a matter of time. Yet his words continued to resound in her brain, buzzing and vibrating like angry hornets trapped within the crevices of her skull, stinging her over and over with venomous force. *"The only thing I regret ..."*

Andrea inhaled deeply to clear her mind, and gasped at a sudden stabbing pain that struck her like an explosion. Clutching her chest, she looked down expecting to see blood, but there was none. *Dear Lord, what is happening?*

Dismounting shakily, Andrea put her shoulder against a large tree trunk and sucked in deep gasping breaths. Closing her eyes in agony, she felt again the sting of Hunter's words. The pain bent her in two and dropped her to her knees.

She began to cry then, softly at first, just a low moan, like someone who is unfamiliar with the act of weeping. But the moan swelled and grew until it became a gut-wrenching wail that sounded more like a desperately wounded animal than anything of human origin. Andrea gulped for air as decades of unshed tears poured forth in a great surge of pain and loss. She cried for her country and her enemy, for Daniel and her past. And then she cried because she was crying and because she was hurt and confused and alone.

When she was done, she lay quietly, and listened to a world that was intensely, painfully still.

Opening her swollen lids, Andrea took in the scene around her. Justus stood beside her amid the funereal shadows of a setting sun. He nudged her gently with his nose and she laid her cheek against his soft muzzle. "It's just us again," she whispered.

After mounting and reluctantly heading north, Andrea halted at the sound of a low rumble of thunder in the distance. Glancing up at the clear sky, she turned back toward the sound. Slowly, almost hesitantly, a smile grew upon her face. The din was not thunder. There was no storm. It was the familiar, rolling, earth-shattering throb of cannon fire.

Justus pawed the ground, eager for her to make up her mind.

Andrea's decision came like a lightning flash. For once, it was not a decision made of vengeance, nor even from hate. Retaliation and revenge had drained from her along with hope and trust. With a look of grim determination on her face, she turned her horse's head toward the sound of war.

And went forward to face the music.

ℋ ℋ ℋ

Hunter stepped out into the bright sunlight, squinting and grabbing his head at the horrific thudding the endeavor produced. The liquor he had consumed the previous night had done little to deaden the ache in his heart, and much to cause the pain and misery he now endured.

Opening his eyes, he watched a speck in the distance turn into a rider cantering up the drive with a large gray horse in tow at his side. He blinked in disbelief when he recognized John Paul and Zeus.

"Here you go, ol' chap!" John Paul tried to bring the powerful stallion under control, though it practically wrenched him from the saddle.

Hunter remained speechless.

"Did Miss Andrea not tell you? She convinced me to sell you this beast, though I don't know quite how or why." John Paul stared at Hunter curiously. "I hope you don't mind, I took the liberty of telling her it was your birthday. Today *is* the day is it not?"

Without waiting for an answer, John Paul reached into his coat pocket with great difficulty and pulled out some papers. "Got the bill of sale right here. Quite a little negotiator she is. Wouldn't go a penny higher than what you last offered me, though I insisted his value has increased substantially since then."

Hunter continued to stand silently, blinking like an owl in sunlight. The fact it was his birthday had completely slipped his mind. What he had said to Andrea after she returned from being with John Paul had not. He remembered distinctly the moment of callousness that had started the chain of events that left his world crumbling.

John Paul's gaze flicked over Hunter's unshaven face and puffy red eyes. "It appears you started celebrating the big day a little early."

"She *bought* him?" Hunter murmured, his mind beginning to catch up to what had been said moments previous.

"Well, she signed the bill of sale on your behalf," John Paul responded. "Insisted her word and your honor were sufficient to close the deal." He paused a moment. "She's a bit of a funny female if you ask me. A little standoffish ... though she seems to have warmed up to you quite nicely, judging from the way I had to listen to her constantly singing your praises."

He looked Hunter up and down in such a way that indicated he could not fathom a woman choosing the Colonel over himself. "Here, take him, he's all yours."

Hunter descended the last two steps and grabbed the skittish horse.

"Will you announce me to Miss Evans?" John Paul dismounted and brushed the dust from his suit. "Perhaps now that she's had time to reflect, she realizes who is the better man." He grinned at Hunter's blank stare and patted him on the shoulder. "You can't blame a man for trying, Alex. As you have made no claim on her, it's my duty to make her realize she's much too charming to spend her life being unnoticed by you."

Before Hunter could answer, Victoria walked out the door. "John Paul, how nice to see you!"

"Victoria, I was just asking about you!" John Paul gave Hunter a sly smile and a wink, before greeting her with a hug and disappearing into the house.

Hunter stood in the middle of the drive, holding the horse he had only dreamed of owning, the lineage of which he knew would transform Hawthorne into the legendary breeding establishment his grandfather had envisioned. There was no elation as he gazed at the prancing animal. He saw only a world falling apart around him, and felt a crushing weight of loss and loneliness that threatened to overcome him.

Dazed, he walked to the barn and handed the horse over to Zach. Anxious to ride away from the memories, he began saddling Dixie in the paddock himself, but paused at the sound of a wagon racing down from the main house at breakneck speed.

"What have you done to Miss Andrea?"

Hunter winced at the sight of Mrs. Fox looking like a ruffled hen. "Andrea and I were to meet today. The servants told me she is no longer here. What have you done to her?"

Hunter turned to his horse and continued to tighten the girth. "As you know, Mrs. Fox, Miss Evans was here to recover from an injury. She has recovered—and she has thus departed."

"You did not make her leave." Her tone was not questioning, but the statement seemed to demand an answer nonetheless.

"It was ... a ... mutual decision." Hunter talked into his saddle, pretending to adjust his stirrups. He guessed it was mutual. She hadn't really argued. Hadn't protested.

"Where did she go?"

"I do not know her intentions. She had a habit of confiding only in herself."

The widow shook her head. "She would not just leave without saying goodbye."

"Apparently she would," Hunter answered bluntly, preparing to mount.

"I hope it wasn't because of *you*, Alexander Hunter." Emma picked up her own reins. "That girl respected you, admired you. And it wasn't for your money or your *charm*, I assure you."

Hunter spun around. "She said that?"

"She didn't need to say it. I saw it every time she looked at you. Why, she well nigh worshiped you."

"I think perhaps you saw what you wanted to see, not what was really there." Hunter mounted stiffly, though he tried to appear calm. "Miss Evans did her best to endure her time at Hawthorne, nothing more. She made it quite clear to me she would rather be anywhere but in my company."

The widow leaned forward and pointed her finger. "You may be well respected within military circles," she said, staring so deeply into Hunter's eyes that he almost flinched. "But you, sir, are a darned fool!"

Slapping the reins, she left him without a backward glance.

Chapter 55

"Look back at man's struggle for freedom,
Trace his present day strength to its source,
And you'll find that his pathway to glory
Is strewn with the bones of the horse."
– Anonymous

A cold front had moved in overnight, sending Andrea deeper under the single blanket she had managed to scavenge from the trail. The action was futile, as she knew it would be. Yet shivering kept her from sleeping and not sleeping kept her from dreaming.

Andrea stared glassy-eyed with fatigue at the darkness above her. Although the first shards of light had not yet illuminated the eastern sky, an over-anxious bird had started its morning ritual overhead. She took a deep breath and listened to the music she had been anticipating for hours. Its chorus was blissful to her ears. She had made it through another night.

Soon the sun would spread its glorious rays, and she would no longer have to fear the heart-wrenching scenes that caused her to wake during the night in a feverish sweat, those scenes from a nightmare that had made her wake every night since her departure from Hawthorne.

Although she tried to push it from her mind, the dream replayed itself, even now before her open eyes. She saw herself walking side by side with Alex through the meadow by the stream. At a steep incline that appeared out of nowhere, the landscape changed from colorful and distinct to foggy and gray. Still, as happens in dreams, Andrea saw herself smiling and pulling her way up the rocky hill, even as the ground at her feet began to crumble.

Andrea squeezed her eyes closed in an effort to stop the vision, but it continued in vivid detail. She watched herself reach up through the fog in an attempt to grab Hunter's strong hand, but what she found in her grasp was never his hand at all. It was always the cold, steel barrel of his gun, its muzzle staring her in the face.

What came next tore her heart apart in both sleep and waking hours.

"Let go, Andrea." His voice was always pitiless in its tone.

"You deceived me. Let go." He cocked the gun. "Or I will make you."

As if watching the scene from a distance, Andrea saw herself look into the barrel of the gun, then at her hand wrapped around its steel shaft, then straight up into Hunter's savage eyes.

And then she let go.

In her dream, she would fall endlessly through time and space, yet never hit bottom or die. She simply awoke, sweating and crying and gasping for breath, and praying fervently, and as never before, that today God would take mercy upon her and make it her last on earth.

Andrea shivered a final time, more from the memory of her dream than the chill, and rose when the faintest promise of a new day broke through the darkness. The frosty nights had been hard on her, the cold air finding little resistance in blasting its way through her empty heart. Having grown accustomed to a warm bed, she now found the hard ground acutely painful.

When it grew a little lighter, Andrea took an overgrown path up the side of a hill to get her bearings and the layout of the land. Dismounting and securing Justus to a tree, she crept along the ground, keeping to the shadows of a small ridge. She was not prepared for the great panorama that opened before her at its peak, and felt a surge of adrenalin pulse through her body.

Below lay the white tents of the enemy, thousands of campfires reflecting eerily off the glass-like waters of the river. Men and horses, mere shadows in the early morning light, appeared to be scurrying to and fro, preparing for a major action. A long gray blur, already in motion behind them, portended something of dreadful significance.

From her position, Andrea continued to study the scene. Why would they leave their fires burning if they were moving out? She held her breath and listened. The distinct sound of a large army on the move assaulted her ears.

The war monster is hungry, she thought to herself. But they have decided to skip breakfast.

Running, sliding and tumbling down the incline, she mounted Justus, hoping beyond hope that she may be in time to stop the feast. Even with Justus at a gallop, she fancied she heard the rumble of the great army and likened it in her mind to the growl of a mighty stomach. She knew this monster's appetite and determination, could picture it in its tens of thousands of unwavering eyes. This was a monster insensible to fear and numb to death. And it was apparently intent on destruction.

From a distant place to the south Andrea began to hear gunfire, a light spattering at first, but growing more intense as daylight began spreading. She looked back in the direction of the Confederate army. She had to hurry.

❦ ❦ ❦

"Pardon me, sirs, there's a scout outside. Sinclair, I think he said his name was, to see you."

In the midst of a conversation with another officer, General Jonathan Jordan stopped in mid sentence and stared. "Did you say *Sinclair*?"

"Send him in," General Bowden, said gruffly. "I need to hear what he has."

When Andrea entered, a breathless moment passed as her eyes met J.J.'s from beneath the broad-rimmed hat. He took a step toward her in jubilant surprise, but she remained all business. "Sir, I have the honor to report—" She spoke nonchalantly as if returning after a lapse of three days, not more than a year.

"Well, go on with it," General Bowden snapped.

"If that's you I hear skirmishing to the south, it's just a feint." Andrea nodded toward the sound of gunfire. "The main body is on the move to flank you. And they're preparing for business."

The generals looked at each other. They had been discussing the enemy's movements and this is exactly what they both suspected and feared. "Chrissakes," Bowden said. "Take this to Colonel Scott. Do you know where he is?"

Andrea looked at him blankly and he pointed at the map. "He's here!" His finger hit the table violently. "Tell him to move up to Colonel Smith's right flank, holding Lawson in reserve. Do you understand? See that it is done forthwith. And tell him I said to proceed without delay and without counting the probable cost."

"Yes, sir." Andrea turned to leave.

"Wait!" J.J. held up his hand. "He's not a regular scout, sir." He looked from Andrea to General Bowden with a look of grave concern. "And Colonel Scott

295

is directly in the enemy's first line of fire."

Andrea stopped and turned. "I understand, General Jordan, and I am willing."

Her eyes seemed morose and remote and fearless. The combination made J.J. cringe. She turned to go back outside and he followed her onto the porch. "Land's sakes, Andrea, it's good to see you! I received word you were safe with friends, but still I—"

Andrea's gaze jerked up to meet his. "Received word?"

"Yes. I was wounded," he said, regarding the look on her face intently, "and received a message while recovering. I assumed you knew." J.J. watched her gaze shift to a place over his shoulder without commenting one way or the other. "You *were* safe with friends, were you not?"

Andrea came out of her trance and glanced up at him. "There's a fine line between friends and enemies," she murmured.

"Andrea." He took a hesitant step toward her, then grabbed both her arms and shook her. "Haven't you given enough?"

She looked back at him defiantly. He had her attention now. "Hasn't everyone?"

J.J. sighed and shook his head. "Report to me upon your return," he said, knowing it was useless to argue and dangerous to delay. Nothing he could do or say would change her mind once it was set. That much, he saw, had obviously not changed.

Andrea turned to leave, an expression of grit and determination evident in her mournful eyes.

"Sinclair."

"Yes, sir?" She turned back to face him.

Grabbing her arm, J.J. swept her to him in a manly bear hug. "It's good to have you back." He felt Andrea swallow hard against him, revealing the depth of emotion she tried to suppress. "We'll talk when you return. Really talk."

Andrea nodded against him, though he sensed she wanted nothing more than to lay her head on his shoulder and cry. He let her go and walked back into the house, listening to the sound of hoofbeats fade in the distance. "Godspeed," he muttered.

$\mathcal{H}$ $\mathcal{H}$ $\mathcal{H}$

Andrea's heart throbbed in wild anticipation. Destiny had set her on a perilous journey, and she could barely control the excitement that flowed through her veins. All around her men galloped hastily to and fro, rushing to obey orders shouted at them by officers, and hurrying to make final preparations for the impending conflict.

Having found and reported to Colonel Scott, she was on her way back to headquarters by a remote path when a spattering in the trees above her made Justus shy to the right. Andrea looked up at the limbs, expecting to see a flock of birds flying away. Instead, she saw small branches and leaves plunging down, mixed with the lead that had caused their descent.

Moving her eyes to the left, she stared with unrestrained awe at the sight of men and horses, followed by flying caissons and cannons, seeming to appear out of nowhere on the brow of a hill. She felt the hair rise on the back of her neck in response to the sinister apparition of evil that seemed to materialize out of the solid green earth right before her eyes.

Spurring Justus cruelly, Andrea struck back to Scott's command to inform him of the proximity of the enemy. Already the far right was skirmishing, and she knew chances were good they would be hotly engaged all along the line in the not-too-distant future.

Calm, but breathing hard from the exertion, she was in the midst of detailing what she had seen, when suddenly utter silence prevailed. Andrea stopped talking and gazed out at the horizon. Both she and Scott tensed and held their breath as if expecting something of significance to begin. Their expectations were realized in a matter of moments. Ear-splitting detonations that defied description began, and the eruptions that followed made it appear the earth itself had begun spitting fire.

"Find Colonel Lawson," Scott screamed above the fury. "Tell him to move up and protect my right! Then go to Murphy. Tell him to send reinforcements at the earliest possible instant and by every available means!"

Andrea nodded and wheeled Justus around, knowing the order would take her through the midst of the fighting. She guided her mount through seemingly impassable obstacles to where she hoped Lawson was being held in reserve. The sound of battle, already deafening, continued to swell like a colossal gale gathering strength.

An angry crackle of carbines to her left warned her she was getting close to some action, and the ensuing cloak of smoke alerted her to its intensity. Soon, to her right, more noise erupted as Federal cannons moved into place and began to talk back. The fighting began to spread and seemed to exist everywhere. Missiles of every conceivable type and every imaginable size came hurling from out of the sky, wreaking havoc on anything and everything in their path.

Andrea thought the storm could get no worse, but when she got to the crown of a small rise, the tempest burst with all its fury. Not knowing which way to turn, she pulled Justus to a stop and found herself within a sea of smoke. Pushing him back into a gallop, she watched a wave of gray crest a hill of green to face a wall of blue. Her eyes, seeming of their own accord, lifted to the hills far beyond that flashed with small puffs of smoke. Almost instantly, entire lines of men disappeared. She found herself in a surreal storm of whirling hot lead so loud and brilliant it seemed to her the world was falling apart. Not fifty feet away a horse bounded by with only the bottom half of a man upon its back. Nearby walked a steed with its entrails dragging out behind. Slaughtered beasts and butchered men, many with their vital current pulsing out in throbbing streams, lay suffering all around.

Just moments earlier, the land before her had been the picture of peaceful Virginia farmland. Now, death bloomed like a hell-spawned crop on every foot of soil. The scene affected Justus, too. Trembling in terror beneath her, he stared crazily at the ground, sniffing the sulfur smoke and the scent of blood, reluctant to move forward, yet afraid to stand still. He stepped on something that made a squishing noise, and Andrea gagged when she looked down to see what it was. She did not look down again.

Yet what she saw when she looked up was not much better. The smoke lifted, revealing a column of Union troops directly in front of her—a living, breathing mass of men plunging toward their formidable foe. Andrea lifted her gaze toward their destination on the opposite hill, where the muzzles of a dozen cannons glowered from the heights. It took a moment for her brain to grasp the surreal scene unfolding. Her mind could barely comprehend the horror about to ensue as the cannons prepared to eat everything in her midst alive.

Even then she did not have time to feel fear or contemplate flight. She watched small puffs of smoke rise from the gaping mouths of the massive instruments of death and thought how they appeared like smoke rings from a peace pipe against the blue of the sky.

But their effect was anything but peaceful. A dreadful roar reached her ears as the earth trembled beneath her—and hell exploded in her face. The unleashed fury that fell upon her was like nothing she had ever known or could imagine. All of the thunderstorms and all the lightning she had ever seen thrown together could not compare with the storm roaring around her.

Justus, startled by the thunderous clamor, reared high in the air, throwing Andrea backward and off balance. She heard an appalling thud, a loud crack, the sound of iron consuming flesh and bone. Leaning forward, she grabbed erratically for a handful of mane to regain her balance, but there was no mane to grab. There was no horse beneath her. The strong, well-muscled animal between her legs had dissolved. Disappeared. He was gone.

She hit the ground with a thud so loud it continued to echo in her ears for some moments after. Reaching up tentatively to feel her skull, Andrea envisioned that it had splintered into any number of fragmented pieces, like the vase Victoria had thrown at her at Hawthorne. She felt a sinking sensation, dizzy and faint, a numb darkness, as she attempted to regain her senses. Remembering Justus, she struggled to her knees, choking and gasping for air, trying to clear her mind of the fog enveloping it. The roar and the thunder that, minutes earlier had seemed so loud, now sounded faint and detached, like the battle was far away, coming to her from a distance of miles or years. Yet she could feel the earth beneath her fingers trembling with the great ferocity of the fight.

Crawling through the smoke that hovered above the ground, Andrea moved in the direction she thought her horse should be standing. "Justus," she cried, half expecting him to run to her through the clamor of battle. She blinked against the red haze that filled her eyes and spit blood from her mouth as she struggled and clawed and groped through the tempest of death in desperation. "Justus!"

It seemed to Andrea that she had been dropped into the very depths of Hell. She could no longer distinguish anything in the thick, gray canopy that settled over her. Closing her eyes against the stinging sulfuric smoke, she continued edging across the ground. Her fingers finally touched something wet, something soft and warm. She stopped and lifted her head. There in the dim, shadowy haze of battle, she saw the dark mound of her horse, or the pile of quivering flesh that remained, lying in a growing pool of coagulating red.

If not for the roar of battle that already filled the air, her blood-curdling scream of pain and despair would have been enough to pierce even the most war-calloused heart. But no one heard and no one cared, so she crawled beside what was left of her beloved companion and prayed for a similar fate.

Chapter 56

"Then I with flowing tears,
Allowed my doubts to rise,
"Is there a God that sees and hears
The things below the skies?"
– Psalms 73:6

When Andrea opened her eyes again, it was to a scene of heart-wrenching destruction. Moving nothing but her eyes, she scanned the field and took in the scene of massive carnage. Mutilated and disfigured horses lay everywhere, while wisps of smoke hung motionless in the air over the field of battle.

Andrea lay still, staring at the leaden sky above. Ignoring her aching muscles, she moved her fingers and then her hands. Though her stiff, bloodstained clothes made moving difficult, she finally brought herself to a sitting position.

"Sinclair? That you?" The voice sounded incredulous.

Andrea looked up to see her old friend Jasper from J.J.'s command. Leaning upon him was a Union officer she did not know. Both faces were black from smoke.

"Boonie's down yonder." The soldier pointed down the hill as he half-helped, half-carried the man toward a row of ambulances. "I'd be much obliged if you could take him some water."

Andrea stood unsteadily, and then searched aimlessly for her friend. It never really occurred to her to look *down*, down in the dirt where so many others lay. But then, at last, by chance, she saw him.

"Boonie?" She dropped to the ground on her knees.

He looked up, pain written across his usually smiling face. "Sinclair? That … you?"

Andrea felt the crusted blood on her face when she tried to smile and realized she must be hard to recognize. She lowered her gaze to Boonie's chest, to a wound from which warm blood still flowed.

"You … go on, Sinclair," Boonie whispered, his lips barely moving. "I'll catch up." He paused and sucked in some air, kind of gurgling as he did.

"I'm not leaving, Boonie." Andrea bent down still lower beside him with a choking mixture of hope and dread.

"Where? Where … you come from?" he asked after a few moments silence.

"We'll talk later." Andrea tried to sound cheerful as she attempted to stem the bleeding. But when she put her handkerchief under his shirt, her hand fell into a horrible hole.

"Rumor had it … you was caught by … Hunter." Boonie opened his eyes and stared at her. "How'd you … get away?" The way Andrea grimaced was apparently not lost on the injured man. "Betcha found out he weren't such a bad guy." Boonie paused and sucked some more air into his lungs. "Betcha if I got to know the guy who put this hole in me, I wouldn't think he was such a bad guy neither."

"Don't talk, Boonie." Andrea blinked back tears she did not want to cry.

Boonie fell silent, but only for a moment. "We had some good times … I wish—" His voice sounded weak.

"I wish it wasn't always the best blood that gets spilled." Andrea rolled up an old coat to put under his head, while putting pressure on the gaping hole with one hand. His eyes fluttered open and met hers with a look of appreciation and understanding.

"Damn it, Boonie." Tears stung her eyes as she tried desperately to stop the flow of life that gushed from him. "Don't do this."

"Don't go gettin' soft on me now, boy." He moved his fingers in the pool of red beside him as if suddenly aware how swiftly the precious fluid was draining from him. "Don't leave me here, Sinclair."

Andrea swallowed hard. "I won't, Private Boone. I won't."

He nodded slightly in recognition that he had heard her, but did not re-open his eyes. "It's Lieutenant," he said after a few moments rest. "Lieutenant Boone."

Pride swelled in Andrea at the announcement. Yet congratulations seemed so out of place when she was attempting, unsuccessfully, to keep his lifeblood from flowing through her fingers. "Are you in pain?"

Boonie shook his head, but his teeth began chattering slightly. "Just c-c-o-l-d ..."

Andrea removed her coat and laid it across him, then knelt down close to his ear. "Boonie, I never told you how much I admire you." She felt the slightest squeeze from the hand she held, but that was all.

"I'm ... not ... afraid," he whispered, gurgling again. "Tell ... my ... moth-er." Andrea squeezed his hand firmly. "I'll tell her ..." She closed her eyes and bowed her head without finishing.

He coughed deeply and Andrea wiped the scarlet fluid from his lips with the edge of her coat. "Sinclair ... I want you ... to know." His breathing grew more sporadic and shallow.

"Don't talk, Boonie. And don't worry. Best friends know everything."

Yea," he whispered so faintly she could barely hear. "Best friends know *everything*."

He lay quiet then, his face pale. His coughing had aggravated the wound, causing the blood to flow even faster. Andrea tried in vain to catch the precious fluid, tried in vain to return it to its rightful place. She pushed it back toward the hole by the fistful, but it would not go in, would only come out, bubbling and gushing between her fingers. "Oh, Boonie!"

He looked up once more, a mute appeal filling his eyes even though he could no longer speak. That's when Andrea stopped trying to stop the blood. Instead she contented herself with stroking his hair and speaking bravely to him, easing his passing as best she could. Within minutes, she raised her head and gazed statue-like over the field of battle, knowing her friend's spirit now floated above—up there where his eyes vacantly stared.

Andrea looked back to the spot where the soil had drunk the last life drop from his bleeding breast. She stared disbelievingly at her own hands soaked in sticky humanity, then gazed up at the sun. Sinking behind crimson clouds, it appeared to be fleeing into its own sea of blood. The sight caused her to shud-der, then shake uncontrollably. A scream rose up from the deepest recesses of her heart. "W-h-h-y-y???"

She pounded the ground by Boonie's corpse in a delirious rage, though it was not because he had died. "Please," she beseeched with her cheek against the blood-soaked dirt, "take ... M-E-E!"

Andrea awoke to the drone of a low, moaning wind that sounded almost human. She turned her head side to side in an effort to stop the noise, then realized it was coming from her own throat.

"Andrea."

She heard her name faint and detached, like it was coming through fog, or water, or from a thousand miles away through the distance of time and years.

"Andrea," the voice said again.

She tried to open her eyes, but could see nothing but darkness. Then someone began to unravel a bandage she had not known was there. When it was off, she attempted to focus her eyes. She could see only that the uniform standing before her was blue, the face too blurry to identify.

"Andrea," the voice repeated. "It's J.J. How ya feelin'?"

Andrea took a deep, pain-filled breath, trying to remember where she was. She could only see out of one eye. The other was swollen shut. Her confusion must have been evident.

"You're in a field hospital. You took a fall."

Andrea closed her eye and remembered the battle, remembered galloping through the smoke, remembered— She gasped, struggling to sit up. "Justus?"

Memories rushed back. No, it could not be memories! It had to be the vision of a frightful dream, like the one about Hunter that seemed so real upon awakening. How silly to think that mere mortals could produce the scenes of horror she recalled.

J.J. gently pushed her back down.

Squinting with one eye, Andrea looked up in desperation, her hand grasping his sleeve. She pulled him down closer and tried hard to focus on his face. She could see now that it was full of concern—and it told her all she did not wish to know.

"You've been through a lot," he said, ignoring her questioning stare. "Try to get some rest."

Andrea closed her eyes, whimpering involuntarily. *If Justus is gone, then Boonie is gone—and how many others? My God, how many others?*

"Boonie?" She mouthed the word.

"I saw that his— He was sent home."

Andrea continued to cling to his hand in desperation. "How I envy him," she said after a long silence. "He would not take me."

"Don't talk that way," J.J. scolded her. "This pain will pass."

Andrea did not believe him. "Thousands are dead." She closed her eyes tightly to shut out the memory. "All for glory, I suppose."

"Listen, Andrea." J.J. sounded desperate. "Just try ... try to forget—what you saw, what you heard, what you felt. It's over. You just have to forget. We all do."

Andrea sighed again. Indeed she wanted to forget. Yet she knew her memory would never be erased as quickly and as effortlessly as had all those once-living souls on the battlefield.

She tried again to banish the image of the guns, the smoke, the cannons—the terror, the dead, the dying. Her horse had reared an instant before the fatal blast, had taken the death shot intended for her. He had been no match for that death-dealing ball of iron that consumed everything in its path. But that's what a cannon was for, was it not? To devour flesh and bone? And that's what the war was for, was it not? To destroy as many souls, as many lives, as possible?

Andrea kept her eyes closed and lay still, thinking how silly and senseless had been her arguments with Hunter. Who cared anymore who was right or wrong? This war was nothing but a killing machine now, a living, breathing killing machine devouring all in its path, wrecking everything, and destroying what everyone thought they were fighting for. Nothing and no one could stop it now, until perhaps everyone in the whole country was dead. Or like her, longed to be.

"I'm going to get you out of here," J.J. said. "In a day or two."

Andrea moaned softly at a searing, stabbing pain in her arm and wondered how long she had been here. Was it one day? A month? She wondered how he would move her. The pain was too great to open her eyes. She could not imagine the prospect of having to travel.

A tear squeezed through Andrea's swollen eyelid. Her other eye was open, but it focused on nothing. "I have lost everything, save that which I have been most willing to give," she whispered.

She felt J.J. grip her hand firmly. "God has not willed the sacrifice of your life, Andrea. And neither should you."

She responded by mumbling something she knew he could not understand, then something he could. "No, he was right all along J.J.," she said, her voice cracking with pain. "*God is nowhere to be found in this war.*"

Chapter 57

"I cannot love as I have loved,
And yet I know not why.
It is the one great woe of life,
To feel all feeling die."
– Robert Bulwer-Lytton

"What is your name and rank?" Colonel Hunter leaned slightly forward in his seat and looked the Union officer who questioned him in the eye. "Lieutenant Maxwell Harrison."

"What were you doing in the Turner house when we captured you?"

Hunter leaned back in the chair and took a deep breath of exasperation. "Sleeping. Obviously."

The two interrogation officers—one a major, the other a colonel—took a step back and began to consult with each other in hushed tones. Hunter knew the routine. He had done it himself a thousand times.

"Let's get to the point." The colonel stepped forward. "I have reason to believe you are lying."

Hunter did not flinch. Although he had been captured while catching a few hours sleep in the house of a citizen, he had been taken without his coat. The papers within its pockets and the stars denoting his rank on the collar would provide the Federals all the verification they needed. But they did not have it.

Or did they?

"Upon what grounds do you make that absurd accusation?"

"Upon the grounds that we were told, by some excellent sources, that Colonel Hunter was in the house where you were found."

"Then I'm sorry to disappoint you." Hunter's voice was utterly calm, though his heart picked up its pace just a little. "It appears you have been given some erroneous information."

"If we can't settle this one way, we can settle it another." The colonel stomped to the door and waved for an aide. "Is Sinclair still in camp?"

"He was this morning, sir."

"Go find him!"

When he shut the door, the room grew quiet. An icy sensation crept up Hunter's spine.

"Tell me, while we're waiting, Lieutenant," the colonel began, his voice dripping with disdain, "why is it, do you suppose, that you Rebels win so many victories against a superior army?"

"I assume by *superior* you are referring to numbers. In which case, we have

304

found that audacity and a righteous cause doubles ours."

The silence that followed was broken by voices outside.

Hunter squinted at the sudden burst of light when the door opened. Even though her face was not visible beneath the hat pulled characteristically low, he could see it was her. She returned the officers' salutes in a purely mechanical manner that had nothing of respect in it, and looked down, trying to remove her gloves. This appeared to be tedious work, both mentally and physically.

Hunter swallowed hard, accepting the fact that his death warrant had arrived. He lifted his eyes to meet the inquisitive stare of a general who walked in behind her. Quickly averting his gaze, Hunter chose a mark on the wall on which to concentrate.

"General Jordan. Sinclair," the colonel said, "thank you for joining us."

Hunter looked down at the floor a moment and thought of all the times he had wondered how he would feel if he ever saw her again. Would it be anger for what she had done? Remorse for what he had done? He found it was neither. It was concern, forgiveness, and now even regret for the position he placed her in—betray the Union or seal his fate.

Hunter willed Andrea to look up, to see him before being taken by surprise, but she stood with head down, still concentrating on her gloves. His gaze flitted across her faded, threadbare coat, too big for her small frame and marred with more than one bullet hole. He winced at the thought it was on her when they were collected, and it disturbed him that she had been placed in harm's way.

Andrea did finally look up, but not at him. She stood directly in front of the two officers, close enough for Hunter to reach out and touch her back.

"You wished to see me, sir?" She addressed the colonel in a dull tone that made it evident she did not carry a favorable impression of him either.

"Yes, Sinclair. I was hoping you could identify this man as Colonel Hunter."

Hunter tried to look relaxed, but every muscle, every fiber of his being was taut with the expectation of exposure.

Andrea turned slowly, painfully, and looked at him for the first time.

Hunter watched her closely, expecting to see a hint of surprise, or anger, or maybe even compassion flash across her eyes.

But he did not.

The surprise was all his when she lifted her head high enough for him to see beneath the brim of her hat. One of her eyes was barely visible, so swollen was the lid. The other one sent a chill down his spine. It stared at him cold and emotionless. No fire or ice glimmered there as he so often remembered. No joy or sorrow, no flicker of hope or spirit. He beheld no trace of the Andrea he once knew, nor any indication that any thread of that being remained within her.

The room grew quiet. Hunter removed his gaze from her, swallowed hard, and looked straight ahead. He felt the eyes of General Jordan boring into him from where he stood silently observing, and wondered if he had given himself away already. Had the pain in his soul at seeing her again—at seeing that lifeless look—been reflected in his own eyes?

"Why do you think I can identify this man as Hunter?" Andrea turned back to the officers, giving no indication of what she was thinking. She held her right arm against her body and rubbed it like it caused her great pain.

"He is the one who captured you, sent you to prison, is he not?"

The room grew deathly quiet for a long moment. Hunter held his breath. Any hope that he had for freedom, for life, was dashed. He knew she would not lie. It was not within her to be disloyal to the Union. Hunter cleared his throat. He would not make her answer the question. He would admit to his true character and save her honor. He owed her that at least.

As he opened his mouth to speak, he saw her raise one finger down low by her side, anticipating his intentions behind her back. Her sign of warning, intended and seen only by him, cautioned him to silence. He pretended to cough instead of speak.

"Indeed, I was captured by Colonel Hunter and know his image well."

Hunter's heart banged in his ears. He discerned no emotion in her voice.

"But I have the duty to inform you, the man behind me is not the one who sent me to prison."

Hunter sat looking straight ahead. If he had expected her to say something else, he did not allow it to show, though it took every ounce of his strength to hide the admiration in his eyes. Once again she had shown her resourcefulness. He should have known she would find a way to spare him—and yet, she had not lied.

"You are certain?" The colonel's disappointment was obvious.

"As I said, sir, that is not the man."

Hunter found himself holding his breath. He was close enough to touch her, to take her in his arms and protect her from everything and everyone that would ever dare harm her. The feeling to do so was so strong, despite what she had done to him at Hawthorne, that the strength it took to overcome it caused his muscles to tremble.

Hunter watched Andrea give the officer a truculent nod of her head in response to his and turn to leave. He noticed her limp was present, but less pronounced than when he had last seen her. Yet she moved stiffly, as if now her entire body pained her, not just her leg. He contrasted the Andrea who had been forever in motion with this one, who now moved as though an unseen blanket of weight hindered every move. She appeared like the walking dead, her body seeming to have aged by minutes, rather than by years.

"Will that be all?" Andrea did not wait for an answer as she proceeded to the door. Reaching for the door latch, she twice came up with nothing but thin air before General Jordan stepped forward and opened the door for her.

"Yes, that will be all," the colonel sneered, apparently enjoying the sight of the young scout struggling with double vision from only one eye.

ℋ ℋ ℋ

The misty, damp night adequately reflected Hunter's mood. Most of the other prisoners sat around a smoky campfire playing cards with the guards, but Hunter stood apart, staring into the darkness. Although successful in hiding his true identity, he knew he was still destined for a Union prison. But the thought of losing his freedom did not weigh as heavily on his mind as the image of a spiritless Andrea.

The scent of pipe smoke on the breeze reached him at about the same time as a voice from out of the darkness behind him. He recognized it as General Jordan's, but could not make out his form in the inky blackness.

"That Sinclair is really something, is he not?"

Hunter hesitated to answer, fearing a trick. "I suppose so," he said noncommittally.

"A little headstrong sometimes," the officer continued.

Hunter failed to suppress a snort of agreement but said nothing more.

He heard the general take a few puffs on the pipe and smelled the sweetness of the effect. "We've known each other a long time, Sinclair and me," he began again, seeming to choose his words carefully. "And I know that if he ever protected a Confederate officer over all that he believes in, and fights for, and protects so passionately—then he has a darn good reason."

Hunter held his breath and waited for him to speak again.

"He's a strong one, no doubt, but having his horse shot out from under him ... he hasn't really recovered."

"Justus? Is dead?" Hunter turned toward the direction of the voice in the darkness, forgetting entirely about staying noncommittal. He knew the enormity of that loss.

"Yea. She was lucky to get out alive."

Hunter winced, not even noticing the general's change of gender.

"She lost one of her best friends there too," he said sullenly. "I don't believe she's quite made it back to us yet."

Hunter closed his eyes, knowing by *us*, he meant the living. What scenes of suffering and death had she witnessed? And what he wouldn't give to have protected her from them—yet if not for him, she might have been spared the experience.

"We had a bit of an argument after the interrogation today," General Jordan said, his voice quivering ever so slightly. "Due to the state of her health, I felt compelled to inform her that her services were no longer needed

307

Hunter let out his breath.

"I should not have, I realize. But I was trying to protect her!"

Hunter slid down the tree he was leaning on to a sitting a position with his head in his hands. He knew her duty to country meant everything to her—was all she lived for.

"Too bad it's so dark, tonight. You can almost see the river from here," Jordan said softly.

Hunter blinked hard, understanding immediately his intent.

"It's a bit steep and rocky on the way down, but a couple hundred yards, there it is. Darn Rebels are right on the other side."

"Is that so?"

"Yea, they're close. I should probably have camp guards on this side, but we're shorthanded and the men are tired."

Both men were silent for what seemed an eternity. Then Jordan spoke in a voice barely above a whisper. "I fear for her safety. She's gone."

"Gone where?" Hunter knew his tone was far too full of concern to deceive the general.

"I wish I knew."

Hunter closed his eyes, and for the first time in his life, said a quick prayer. By the time he opened them, he knew the general was no longer there. He glanced over at the group playing cards and began to form a plan of escape. He did not care if it was a trick. Did not care if a firing squad of twelve or the whole bloody Union army was waiting for him at the river. General Jordan would be looking for her on this side. By Jupiter he would be looking for her on the other!

Chapter 58

"Noble is the courage that performs without hope or without reward."
— Anonymous

It was that time of year when leaves on the trees change from gold to gone, seemingly overnight, leaving no doubt in the minds of those who gaze upon them that winter will soon descend.

Three weeks had passed since Hunter's escape from the enemy camp, yet no trace of Andrea had yet been found. If General Jordan's search yielded better results, Hunter had received no word of it. It pained him to know that he probably never would.

"A courier is here with a dispatch for you, Colonel."

Hunter lifted his gaze from the plate of untouched food before him to the smiling face of his hostess.

"At the door, sir."

Excusing himself, Hunter went outside to accept the communication. Before he opened the envelope, a strange, sinking feeling overtook him, as if a part of him knew that somewhere, something had gone terribly wrong. He broke the seal and hurriedly devoured the contents.

November 15, 1864
Col. Hunter,
It is my undesirable duty to inform you that a deserter from my command has been recaptured. It appears he relayed information to the Federal forces concerning the intended raid on a train by your men in September, having heard of your intentions through careless members of my staff. It can be presumed this was the reason for the fateful events that followed.
I will supply additional information as it becomes available.
Your most obedient servant,
Colonel Wade Burton

Hunter read the dispatch again, his hands trembling as his mind absorbed the words. A deserter was responsible? Could Andrea be innocent of the charges of which he had accused her?

He dropped the note to his side and stared into the darkness. No. Justus was proof enough that she had ridden out that night. And that the horse had been ridden she had not bothered to deny. Even the servants had corroborated that she had been absent from Hawthorne. Hunter went quietly back into the house, trying to make sense of the dispatch.

"That was the same night as the train raid." Captain Pierce held a newspaper and scanned its contents. "You can be sure that it was no one from *this*

Command. We had our hands full as it was."

"Well, I was just curious," their hostess said. "The article does, after all, give you men credit."

"We get a lot of credit for things we don't do," Gus Dorsey said jokingly. "But usually it's not for *good* things."

"What have we gotten credit for now?" When the hostess handed him the paper, Hunter's gaze fell upon the article they discussed. As he began to read, a dark haze descended, enveloping him and threatening to snuff him out.

By the grace of God, a Union medical supply train bound from Washington, was confiscated by Confederate troops south of Chantilly Saturday last.

The wagons reportedly were lost when a new guide led them straight into a Confederate infantry unit. No lives were lost, but the Confederacy gained twenty prisoners, nine wagons, fifteen horses, eighteen mules, and all of the supplies therein. The guide, apparently on a swift, black horse, was the only one to escape.

Though this correspondent can find no official report filed, it is widely speculated it was a member of Hunter's command—or perhaps the gallant Hunter himself.

Hunter's hands visibly shook. He looked back to the story, then to the date on the paper, and then stared into space. His heart did not doubt the truth, even while his head balked at accepting it. Never could he have envisioned any news that would have brought more of a shock to his mind or hopeless anguish to his soul.

It couldn't be! She couldn't have! Surely, she wouldn't have!

But the pieces fit. With her knowledge and her cleverness, she could have passed herself off as a guide. It would have been difficult, but not impossible for one daring enough and reckless enough to make the attempt. Her plan must have been hurriedly conceived, yet zealously and methodically thought out. Only she among the multitudes possessed enough mad resolve to have endeavored it—and only she among all others, manifested the bold cunning to have pulled it off. She, who had always possessed an abiding faith in achieving the impossible, had succeeded, yet failed.

Hunter looked up again at his men staring at him, muttered an excuse, and strode to the door. Once on the porch he put his hands on the railing and leaned forward. His breath came fast and hard, so deep and strained that a puff of steam escaped with every gasp. He became so overwhelmed by his remorse that for once his iron will failed him. He sank to the porch, his limbs refusing to support his weight.

I do not ask, 'Can it be done' … but rather, 'Is it worth doing?'" She had laughed when she had spoken these words, as if it explained completely her reckless disregard for danger. She lived by her principles and believed in her logic that anything worth the doing was worth the risk of trying.

Hunter put his head in hands as the memory of that night came back to him with searing clarity. She had not cowered or sobbed or wavered, but that look of utter anguish, that quiet, pathetic despair at his distrust was now far more eloquent than any words. She had endured the insults he had hurled at her like one endures a physical torture, standing her ground like a soldier.

Sweat rolled down his face despite the chill when he remembered her parting words: "I trusted *you* to trust *me*." How ironic that all along she had manifested more trust in him than he had in her ... when all along she had thought it too much to give. She had accepted her banishment, allowed him to believe the worst without a fight, and he understood why. He had broken her trust. And that was not something she would seek to repair, nor something she would ever attempt to gain again.

"Colonel?" Hunter jolted and turned to face the voice.

"Colonel, you all right?" Major Carter looked down at him with concern in his eyes.

Hunter shook his head, and then stood slowly, awkwardly, like one who has imbibed overly much in alcohol, and started to walk away.

Carter followed and grabbed him by the sleeve. "It was her, wasn't it?"

Hunter didn't bother to answer, knowing the pain in his eyes made words unnecessary.

"There was a misunderstanding?"

"I was a fool!"

Carter sighed. "It's the war, sir. It has a way of hurting the ones we care for the most the worst. We judge unjustly in proportion as we feel strongly."

"I thought she—" Hunter choked. "She never told me—"

"I understand, sir. But truth, like water, finds a way to seep through."

A deep groan shook Hunter's frame.

"You can make amends, Colonel," Carter said, sounding fearful for Hunter's well being. "Surely there is naught that cannot be fixed."

"It's too late, Carter," Hunter said, looking straight into the darkness with such despair in his voice it made the elder officer cringe.

"She is lost to me."

Chapter 59

"Fields, roads, trees, and shrubs were alike clothed in the white robes of winter,
and it seemed almost a sacrilege against the beauty and holy stillness of the scene
to stain those pure garments with the life blood of man, be he friend or foe."
– Mosby's Rangers, James Williamson

Winter hit northern Virginia with no warning and little mercy. Snow and sleet fell all day, putting down a cold blanket of discomfort that slowed the horses and froze in the beards of Hunter's men. Although the enemy was in winter quarters, Hunter did not lessen his attacks. Nothing—not sleep, not exhaustion and not the weather—stopped him or even slowed him down.

Hunter walked up and down the tracks in silence inspecting his men's work while Dixie followed diligently behind. His Command had now assumed the size of a full brigade, and his activities had become even more widespread as a result. Many in his ranks were no longer boys, but officers who had resigned their commissions in the regular army for the honor of serving under him.

Satisfied with the job his men had done, Hunter became absorbed for a moment by the shrubs and bushes that glistened like rolling waves of whitecaps under the starlight. He thought how Andrea would enjoy the incredible scenery, then swore under his breath and continued into the pines.

Retreating a small distance from his men, Hunter pulled his buffalo robe from behind his saddle and laid down. The train would be another hour at least in coming. Despite the numbing fatigue that weighed upon his body, he feared he would not be able to rest. Ignoring the strange feeling of dread that had hung over him all day, he put his saddle blanket under his head, closed his eyes, and was asleep before taking another breath.

But sleep did not seem to last long. Hunter heard what sounded like a single horse coming at a trot, its hoofbeats muted on the frozen snow-covered ground. Crawling to the edge of the pines, he listened as the sound grew closer to the bend in the road. He felt the anticipation of his men around him as they too hugged the ground and strained breathlessly. Seconds ticked by slowly, painfully. Sweat trickled down his face, and his heart raced with anticipation. When a nearby branch gave way to the weight of its burden, his nerves reacted with a painful jolt.

Steadying his breathing once again, Hunter watched the shadowy image of a horse and rider appear from around the curve. A full moon shifted in the sky just then, casting a beam of light in front of them like an ethereal pathway. Hunter's pulse quickened at the sight. Somehow he had known, had hoped at least, it would be her. She rode perfectly relaxed, one hand on loose reins, the other on her thigh, seemingly oblivious to any danger.

Hunter watched mesmerized as she glanced up at the moon in all its glory, then reached down and patted the skittish horse on the neck as it shied at the strange shadows created on the crystalline snow. They were nearly in front of him now, so close he could see every detail—the frozen whiskers on her horse's muzzle, the frost-steamed breath pouring forth from its nostrils. He stepped out onto the road to greet her, and thought how beautiful the night star looked shining its light down upon her.

Yet now the scene before him began to blur and move in slow motion.

The sharp crack of a revolver startled him. He saw her lurch to one side, then scramble to right herself. She looked down at her chest, her brow wrinkled in confusion at the redness blossoming there. Then slowly, in disbelief, she raised her head and met his gaze. She appeared bewildered, surprised for a moment. Then her eyes glazed over with the pain of recognition.

Hunter tried to go to her, but his legs remained planted where he stood. He wanted to tell her it was not him, it was not his shot, but he was left voiceless by the utter madness of the scene. She continued to stare at him as she put her hand to her chest, and he stared back in utter confusion when it seemed to disappear inside her. She sighed heavily then, and the pain in her quivering eyes turned to sadness, betrayal, disappointment. But even as she fell forward, she never removed her pitiful eyes from him. She held his gaze with a questioning stare, never blinking, yet seeming to accept the fate that had befallen her.

"Wait! Let me help!" Hunter thought he said the words out loud, but if he did, she did not listen. She slumped off the side of her horse to the crystal earth, almost at his feet. He heard the dull thump when her body hit the ground, stared in awestruck horror at the scarlet-spattered snow all around her. He looked to her face, now devoid of all color, then to the brilliant green eyes that stared blankly at the full moon overhead.

"Andrea! No!" He knelt by her side in frantic horror, blinking in disbelief as he watched the light flicker and go out of those once-expressive eyes, just like a match suddenly extinguished.

"Can you hear me?"

But he knew she couldn't. Couldn't possibly. Not now that the green was gone. Gone! Melted away! Those beautiful windows to the soul were now two gaping, vacant orbs.

Hunter's gaze took in the pure white snow contrasting against the shocking red flow of gore that seemed ever spreading. He looked toward heaven, hoping for some refuge there, but now even the sky had turned to a crimson sea of horror, as if her lifeblood ebbed from her body to saturate the very heavens. Panicking, Hunter looked around for his men, but they had all vanished.

There was no movement. No sound anywhere. It seemed the world had stopped.

"Andrea!" He reached out to touch her, to somehow stop the vital current that continued to spurt like an endless fountain from her motionless form.

That's when he noticed the gun, still smoking, in his hand.

No-o-o!

ℋ ℋ ℋ

"Colonel. You all right?" Carter knelt beside his commander.

Hunter sat straight up, gasping for breath, his hands clenched into fists. "Is she dead?"

"Is who dead?"

Hunter appeared drenched, like he had been caught in a downpour. He rubbed his hand through sweaty hair, and looked over Carter's shoulder apprehensively, as if expecting to find something there.

"You sure you're all right, Colonel?" Carter put a tentative hand on his shoulder. "You kill someone we don't know about?" He tried to make a joke, but he could see it was no laughing matter. He felt Hunter trembling through the heavy woolen coat, and his clothes were so damp with sweat they steamed in the cool night air. Hunter continued to stare into the darkness, breathing heavily, his face solemn.

"Here," Carter instructed, digging through a saddlebag. "Take a swig of this."

Hunter accepted the small flask, but his hand still trembled so violently, he handed it back, exasperated. "I'm all right."

Carter knew differently. The face of the man who had always possessed such extraordinary control over his feelings, expressed perfect despair and hopelessness. Carter waited, hoping Hunter would want to talk, but the sound of a train whistle in the distance brought the Colonel to his feet.

"Get the men ready," was all he said, before walking stiffly toward his horse.

Carter's gaze remained on Hunter as he strode silently across the moonlit field and went through the motions of preparing his mount. War was usually good for taking the mind off things, but Carter could see not even that was sufficient to release his commander from the terrible turmoil within.

Chapter 60

"Love does not die easily."
– Hamlet, *Shakespeare*

A ndrea ignored the unearthly scream of shells. She moved from wounded soldier to wounded soldier, trying to give aid and comfort to those who lay where they fell in the midst of the thunder of guns.

She was not unaware of the chaos or the dreadful suffering and agony around her. She was simply too exhausted and concentrating too much on her duties to take much notice of it. The field on which she worked was a vast plain of wreckage, as if a great storm from a place worse than hell had swept through. Yet she continued her work without pause, refusing to allow brave men to lie in misery while their countrymen continued to slaughter one another.

Lifting her eyes briefly in an attempt to get her bearings through the thick haze of smoke, Andrea caught a glimpse of the seemingly endless sea of writhing humanity strewn around her. The beautiful rolling hills of Virginia were nothing like she had once known them. The paradise she had once considered beautiful was now a living hell. Andrea lowered her eyes again and moved on. She could help but one at a time. There was no use agonizing about it.

Kneeling by a man who lay just within a tree line, Andrea stared at the bloody path he had made by dragging himself there. She ripped open his pants leg and tried to stem the bleeding of the fearfully torn flesh. She knew it was somewhat futile. From what she knew of such injuries he would not have the limb for long, if he lived at all. Still, she was determined to do her best. Concentrating on the wound, she felt a hand grasp her wrist.

"Andrea?"

She blinked at the barely recognizable face staring up at her. The only identifiable features were the eyes—and they portrayed mortal agony. "Yes, Alex. It is me," she whispered.

He stared at her unbelieving, blinking through sweat and blood, apparently trying to decide if she was an illusion or real. Andrea put water on a cloth and wiped his brow, resisting the urge to lay her head upon his chest and weep. She had cried many tears since leaving Hawthorne, more than she thought a human being had within them. Now she wondered what kind of god it was that wished to torture her afresh. Why could he not let her go on with her life and forget?

"I must ..." Hunter swallowed and licked his lips. "I mus ...talk ...to you." He struggled to hold his eyes open, to stay conscious.

"Be still," Andrea commanded, sweeping her eyes across the field. Although she could see none of his men, she knew they must be watching, waiting for the opportunity to extract their leader from this precarious place.

"I made ... terrible mistake." His eyes were eyes glazed with pain. His fevered, bloodshot gaze searched her face.

"I'm sure your men will forgive you." Andrea poured water on his wound.

"No!" He grabbed her again violently. "Nothing to do ... with ... men!"

Hunter seemed to turn somewhat delirious. Although he appeared to be trying to talk, he succeeded in doing little more than muttering incoherently. Still, his voice, his presence, affected Andrea, making her heart throb frantically as she wiped the clammy dew from his brow.

"Andrea ... where are you?"

"I'm right here." She tried to sound calm, while turning her attention back to his mangled leg.

"N-o-o!" His voice sounded agonized. He reached out to her again, grabbing frantically for her wrist, which he held with a strength she could not believe he possessed. "Where *are* you? Take me ... there!"

Andrea looked at his wild, glassy eyes. Sweat ran in torrents down his face. His shirt was soaked. "I cannot take you there ... a field hospital near Winchester," she said, grasping his meaning. "You would be taken prisoner."

"No ... matter. Take me ... there," he said weakly. Do not ... leave me, Andrea! Please!" It seemed to her he was almost sobbing. "I cannot ... *find* you."

Andrea removed his hand and looked down at him. His face was contorted into a blend of physical agony and emotional anguish. "Your men will get you out," she assured him. "You are better off here than in a Union prison."

Hunter whimpered and began talking in a hurried, rambling tone that was frantic and confused. Something was wrong, and it was far more tormenting to him than his injury. Andrea looked again at his leg, an unrecognizable wreck of flesh, and then at his dead horse that lay some rods distant. She sat awestruck at the valor of the man who had faced the obvious superior fire power—no doubt in accordance with orders.

A drink of cool water revived Hunter somewhat, though he was still unable to articulate what he so desperately wanted her to understand. He seemed so distraught, rambling on to her about snow and bloody moons, that Andrea feared the injury affected his senses.

Dressing his leg as best she could on the field, she watched him open his eyes and search for hers once more. "Don't," he commanded her with his tone and his look, "don't . . . leave . . . me!"

Andrea looked away. She had to refuse him. She had no means to move him, and even if she did, she could not bring herself to convey him to a place of certain death. He was safer here.

A movement from the corner of her eye drew Andrea's attention to within the canopy of trees. Shifting her gaze, she saw a single rider on horseback appear from behind a boulder within the dappled depths of the woods. Soon she made out the ghostly figure of another on foot, and then another, crouching in the shadow of the trees. Their eyes and attention were focused solely on the man before her, making it clear she was delaying his rescue.

Leaning over Alex, she wiped again the moisture from his face. "Alex, your men are here. You are safe."

"No." He grabbed her arm. "Don't leave! Take me!"

"It is better this way," she whispered, wiping his brow one last time. Then disregarding her heavy heart, and ignoring his anguished cries and pathetic appeals, she turned her back on him and walked away—though heaven knows it was the hardest thing she'd ever done.

ℋ ℋ ℋ

For weeks Andrea tended the wounded of that horrible battle. Hour after hour in those days immediately following, she hastened to the side of the dying, listening to soldiers plead for mercy while they waited for attention from a surgeon. Her task seemed hopeless—and endless—so she no longer took it personally when she arrived too late to staunch the flow of lifeblood that dripped out while they waited. Yet she could not help but wonder, when she gazed out at the rows of lifeless bodies, if Alexander Hunter, too, had been sacrificed to the insatiable war-god that ruled the land.

Although her mind still reeled at the shock of seeing him, her duties and responsibilities distracted her from her grief. It had been days since she had slept more than a few hours and weeks since she had slept a full night. Yet she had no desire for rest. Lying down and closing her eyes would only cause her to dream of heaping piles of entrails steaming in the morning chill or of some mother's young son holding his leg in bloody arms. The constant cries of "please help me, nurse," kept her body busy and her mind void of any other thoughts.

"*Miss Evans! Wake up!*" She heard the voice, but struggled to clear her weary mind. Had she actually fallen asleep?

Andrea opened her eyes and stared at the patient to whom she had been reading, while another voice spoke harshly from behind her. "Miss Evans, there's a gentleman here to see you."

Knowing that no one knew where she was, Andrea dismissed the nurse's announcement. "They must be mistaken," she said over her shoulder. She leaned forward to wipe the young lad's brow, apologizing to him for falling asleep.

"There's been no mistake."

Andrea swallowed hard at the sound of the voice, straightened slowly in her chair, and turned hesitantly around, afraid she was somehow still dreaming. Hunter seemed to be studying her as he leaned on a single crutch, his left

317

arm in a sling. Although his face was bearded and gaunt, the piercing gray eyes remained unmistakable. Neither war nor wound could diminish his manly strength or vigorous power.

He was still striking.

✿ ✿ ✿

"I've been looking for you." Hunter spoke as if their separation had been one of but a few hours. His eyes did not falter or leave her face. They scrutinized, waiting to see her reaction.

Andrea stood and took a hurried breath, but otherwise successfully concealed any emotion. "Then it appears you've met with success in your endeavor." Her gaze wandered down to his leg, and he could tell she was wondering how he was standing so soon after so serious an injury.

"I feared you would not receive me." Hunter's heart banged so wildly in its cage, he could barely speak. He could not recall ever having been this frightened, never dreamed she would still have this effect on him. Those beautiful green eyes, though sunken and exhausted, had not lost their magic.

Her expression abruptly changed from a look of relief to one of wariness and heartbreaking suspicion once she recovered from the shock of his appearance.

"This is a hospital, sir," she finally answered. "We do not turn away the injured, even if ..."

Her voice trailed off. She did not finish, but stared straight into his eyes with a gaze so penetrating, Hunter knew she would detect any deception if he showed it. She was obviously questioning in her mind the reason for his visit.

"I-I was afraid they would have to amputate," she said, looking at his leg with grave concern.

"It was recommended." He watched Andrea move her gaze to somewhere over his shoulder with a sorrowful expression that appeared to be a part of her now.

"Might I ask what are you doing here?" She returned her gaze and her attention to him.

"I ... need to speak with you." Hunter focused his thoughts back to the task at hand. "Is there some place we can go that's a little more private?"

"I have duties, sir. I cannot just cast them off."

"Pray oblige me," he countered. "I will be leaving in but a few minutes."

Andrea stared at him intently. "Follow me then. I believe I know a place."

When they stepped outside and she turned to her left, Hunter put his hand out to stop her. "I prefer we go this way." The hand in the sling grasped her arm firmly and ushered her toward a wagon holding three injured Confederate soldiers.

Andrea shrugged him off when she saw his intent. "What are you do-ing?"

Hunter's voice became low and lethal. "You must understand," he said, leaning his crutch against the wagon and preparing to help her in. "I've come to talk to you, by force, if necessary."

Andrea took a step back, jerking her arm again from his grasp. "No, *you* must understand, sir. You are in the middle of an enemy camp."

"This camp is surrounded," Hunter replied in an unemotional voice. "My men know their business. If you make a scene, a lot of people could be injured. I hope you will not allow your stubbornness to jeopardize innocent lives."

He watched Andrea's gaze jerk over to the three men in the back of the wagon and observed her jaw tighten as the significance of their presence sank in. Slowly, she lifted her eyes to the tree line behind them, then to the hill that rose beyond the row of tents. He knew she imagined, even if she did not see, the silent, vigilant horsemen gazing down from within its shadows.

"But there are injured men here," she said broodingly, still staring at the tree line. "Surely you would not—"

"We will do what we must," he said gravely, though his pulse raced with violent force through his veins. His stern face masked the agony of anticipation that radiated inside him.

"By thunder, you mean to kidnap me?" She turned back to him with a stamp of her foot. "In broad bloody daylight?"

Hunter's face crinkled into a smile at her predictable reaction. "You could put it that way, I suppose."

Andrea's face bloomed red with rage. She looked at him with wariness and defiance and inflexible determination. "I know no military secrets," she hissed. "Nor possess anything that would be of interest or value to you."

Hunter smiled blankly now, giving her no hint what he was thinking. "I'm afraid I'll have to be the judge of that." He did not allow his voice to betray the offense he took that she would think military information was his purpose.

"But you have no business—"

"I conceive it to be my business, my duty, and, hopefully, my pleasure," he said coolly.

"But you said it would take only a few minutes!"

"I believe you misunderstood. I said I would be *leaving* in a few minutes, and indeed I shall. I beg your pardon if I neglected to mention that you will be with me."

She gasped at his ruse.

Hunter grabbed her arm again. "I regret that there is neither time nor op-portunity to talk here any longer. Please get in." Knowing she would put up an obstinate defense unless he gave her no other choice, Hunter conveyed by his tone that his statement was an order and that it was seriously uttered. Yet he was practically shivering at her proximity. Never upon any battlefield was his self-control threatened more than on this trying occasion.

Andrea climbed into the wagon, shaking off his attempts to help her. "How dare you," she muttered under her breath, though she did not cause a scene. She knew what he, and his men, were capable of.

"You need not be under any alarm." Hunter picked up the reins and moved the horses forward, wondering why he had said the words. The look in her eyes was wild and unearthly, but it was not fright. He was sitting beside a powder keg. And it was giving off sparks.

"What is it you want?"

Hunter did not answer. He remained vigilant now, his eyes intent on the road before them. Only when they met the camp's sentinels did his demeanor change. He smiled casually at the guard and waved, but one of them stepped out in front of them while another grabbed the reins and brought the horses to a stop.

"Miss Evans," one said, looking at Hunter suspiciously, "where might you be off to?"

Hunter slid his hand into his coat pocket when Andrea did not answer.

"You leaving us?" the sentry questioned again.

Andrea's green eyes flicked up to Hunter, expressing once more her displeasure, then she turned to the sentry with a smile. "No need to be alarmed, Corporal," she said with more gaiety than gloom.

Hunter did not see her hand move as she talked, but he felt its pressure. With her fingers wrapped around his, she kept his gun pressed firmly against his thigh. As if by magic, the angry, pouting child beside him had been replaced by a resolute young woman who showed once more her ingenuity when faced with undesirable circumstances.

"There are some injured men at a farmhouse near here that need moved," she continued without pause. "These men have generously offered to help bring them back."

"They have a pass I presume," the sentinel said, glancing at the men in the back doubtfully.

Hunter dared not look at Andrea and she gave him no time to answer. "I would trust my explanation is sufficient, Corporal," she said, sounding offended that he would ask for further documentation. "I asked for volunteers, and these men kindly came forward. Surely you do not wish to humiliate me among men of such generosity."

"It's for your own safety that I ask," the corporal said, trying to defend himself.

"Corporal Jennings." Andrea's tone grew stern and intimidating. "I believe the intentions of these men are honorable and there is no occasion for protection. Are you insinuating I cannot take care of myself?"

"N-o-o, Miss Evans. B-but, you have no escort," he stuttered, quailing visibly before the look of defiance in her eyes.

"I have just told you *these men* are my escort!"

The corporal's face turned instantly red, and his hand dropped to his side as he released the reins. "Pass on!"

Hunter hit the reins against the back of the horses and smiled to himself. Never had he met anyone who could more readily adapt to circumstances beyond her control than the being sitting next to him.

A few miles down the road, Hunter pulled the horses to a stop. The three men in the back jumped off, tearing away their bandages, while eight riders appeared out of nowhere on either side of the road with three extra horses. Without a word, the men went about their business with the precision of a drill team and then disappeared like magic, the shadows of the trees engulfing them instantly and completely.

Hunter ripped the sling off his arm, while Andrea watched the proceedings around her. "See what a skillful nurse you are? Good as new."

Andrea threw him a look of scorn. "You feigned your injuries?"

"That one I did. Wish I could say the same for this one." He ran his hand down his leg and grimaced at the pain. "Still hurts damnably ... begging your pardon."

"You shouldn't be pushing yourself so," Andrea said in a concerned voice, touching his arm before withdrawing it quickly.

"You are worried about me?" Hunter tried hard to make his voice sound unemotional.

Andrea did not answer and stared straight ahead, obviously annoyed that she had allowed him to see her concern.

Hunter tried to act unmoved at her coldness, but he was beginning to wonder if he had made a mistake. He was not sure he was strong enough to endure the ordeal to come.

"Where are we going?" she asked after a few moments silence.

"You'll see." He reached into the back of the wagon and pulled out a woolen cloak. "You may need this."

Andrea looked with cool scrutiny at his offering and accepted it without a word. With the descent of the sun, a chill was back in the air. Pulling the garment on, she put the hood up as if to hide any further emotions. Within moments, the gentle sway of the wagon caused her head to slump, and within a few miles, she was leaning against Hunter's shoulder in a deep, apparently much needed, sleep.

Chapter 61

*"For all sad words of tongue or pen,
The saddest are these, 'it might have been.'"*
— John Greenleaf Whittier

"Andrea, wake up. We're here." Andrea opened her eyes with great effort. "We're where?" She looked around sleepily, though it was now too dark to see any of her surroundings.

"Where we were going." Hunter jumped from the wagon, cursing when his leg hit the ground. Putting his hands around Andrea's waist, he lifted her easily from the seat. Even with his injuries and weariness, he seemed to her like a giant in strength. Yet she thought she felt him trembling once her feet were on the ground. Andrea's eyes went to the back of the wagon where a saddle horse stood tied, munching contentedly on hay. She had no idea where it came from or when it had been acquired.

"You must have been very tired," Hunter said, seeing her questioning stare. He took her hand and led her through the darkness.

They had proceeded but a few steps when Andrea stopped. "What are we doing *here?*"

"I told you. We need to talk. Go inside."

"I'll not!" Andrea crossed her arms and planted her feet

"I insist." Taking her gently but firmly by the arm, Hunter guided her into the cabin. Although Andrea could see every effort had been made to erase any evidence of the past, the crushing weight of memories descended upon her the instant she inhaled its musty smell. "I do not see why you deemed it necessary to bring me *here.*"

"I needed to find a place with privacy," came the steady reply from behind her as he lit a lamp.

She whirled around to face him, her eyes blazing. "I could have found an empty tent for privacy."

"I needed a place where you couldn't get away."

"You will *never* find that!" Andrea watched Hunter wince, and the pain in his eyes made her instantly sorry she had said it.

He swallowed hard as if nerving himself forward in a futile charge. "I-I know I have done you a grave injustice."

Andrea tried to sound nonchalant, as if the pain of the last months had not made her long to die. "Fate and the war have dealt me a number of injustices, Colonel. I've not had the time to contemplate them individually—nor do I care to do so now."

"Andrea, I know I've hurt you deeply."

Andrea threw her hands up in frustration. "Really, Colonel, must we discuss this? I accept being a casualty of war if that is your desire. Nothing more."

"A casualty of war? You think not of the past? Of Hawthorne?"

Hunter stood right behind her now. Andrea moved forward, unable to stand the nearness. All the strength of her spirit rebelled against allowing herself to think about the memories he evoked. "The past is a world to which we cannot return. Hawthorne was a thousand years ago and as far from my mind."

"You cannot mean that." Hunter sounded hurt and confused. "Never for a moment could I force myself to forget you. The thought of you consumes me."

Andrea's insides reeled. *No, I don't mean that.* How many minutes of how many hours and how many weeks and months had she yearned for him—yet dreaded ever seeing him again?

She remained silent, staring at the floor and praying it would open up and swallow her. She could not allow him to know the agony he had caused her, did not want to trust him not to cause that misery again. She must end this here and now. Yet the thought of never seeing him again sent a chill down her spine.

"You say you don't care, yet you are trembling." He put his hand lightly on her shoulder, and she jumped as if a lightning bolt had struck out of a cloudless sky.

"Don't touch me, I implore you." Andrea stepped away. She felt her emotions surging as all of the pain and anguish she had endured over the past few months welled up inside her. Tears formed in her eyes and began running down her cheeks. She put her face in her hands to hide and sobbed like a child. "You bring up things I do not wish to recall. I am not sufficiently strong to banish such memories!"

"Do you think I want to remember what I said to you? What I did to you? I was a fool!"

Andrea tried to hold back the tears, but there were too many now. She no longer had the power to control her emotions like she once had.

"My words should not wound, I seek to heal." Hunter turned her around and encircled her in his arms. "Andrea, I beg of you, please say you'll forgive me!"

Andrea could barely breathe in the tightness of his embrace. She felt his heart pounding wildly against her cheek, felt that manly, prodigious strength she had longed for and never believed she would ever feel again. The sanctuary and strength of his arms felt so good around her—so powerful, yet so gentle, so comforting and so reassuring.

But when she thought of the pain he had caused her, she rallied her strength and pushed him away. "I request not your pity or regret, Colonel Hunter. What's done is done. We cannot return to the past, nor lament over what could or should or might have been."

"But we can begin again."

"We cannot. Too much has happened. Nothing is the same."

"Much has happened. But little has changed. Come back with me to Hawthorne. I will show you."

Andrea struggled to remain strong. "Wish what you will. As for me, I have no way of judging the future but by the past—and it is not a place to which I wish to return." She almost wept afresh when she beheld his expression before he lowered his head.

"You would not say that if you knew what you meant to me." His voice cracked with emotion.

"I believe I learned quite sufficiently what I meant to you in my last few minutes at Hawthorne," Andrea replied unemotionally. "Please do not feel you must reiterate those thoughts for me tonight, for I can assure you my memory serves me overly well in that regard." She angrily wiped fresh tears from her cheeks.

"Andrea, I pray my words have not haunted you as they have haunted me. I hope that you have not hurt as I have hurt!"

"I do not blame you for anything you did," she said. "An officer cannot be expected to trust the enemy. That was a mistake reserved for me alone to make, and a grave one I assure you. Grave enough, indeed, that it shall never be made again."

Hunter put his hands to his head and groaned like a wounded animal. "Please do not deny me the opportunity to explain."

"I just told you I do not blame you," Andrea said, staring at the wall. "I have always respected you for your loyalty and honor and duty to country. You have always been a soldier first. You never tried to deceive me on *that* matter."

"How can you talk like that after what we shared . . . here?"

"What we shared was lust!" Andrea wheeled back to face him. "You loathed me! Despised me for my allegiance! I accept that and do not begrudge you, for you were gentleman enough to have never claimed any different! Thank goodness! At least you never lied and claimed *affection* for me!"

Hunter stared at her incredulously, blinking repeatedly as if her words were blows that were actually making contact. "No. How can you think such a thing?" he choked helplessly. "I did ... I do ... I wanted to ... I tried ... but I thought ... I thought ..."

Hunter stood swaying, opening and closing his fists. He turned pale; his legs began to shake. He looked like he was going to be horribly sick.

"Your wound is painful to you?" Andrea hurriedly pulled a chair over to his shaking form.

Hunter sat down heavily. "Only the one in my heart," he said, his head in his hands, his breath coming heavy under the weight of great suffering. Then he looked up. "You are concerned?"

Andrea kneeled beside him, one hand on the back of the chair the other tenderly on his knee, and studied his ashen features, the beads of sweat on his forehead. "I wish no hurt to you, Alex," she said solemnly and sincerely. "I never have."

"Nor have I. Yet I have hurt you dreadfully." He sucked in a deep, quivering breath. "Please know, Andrea, that it was never my intent."

"I have recovered," she responded mechanically.

"I cannot believe you. Not when I look in your eyes."

Andrea looked up and quickly stood, unwilling to face his expression of desperate hopefulness. "These eyes have seen much, Colonel." She blinked repeatedly in an attempt to stop the images that assailed her vision. "If they do not glow with happiness, rest assured it has nothing to do with you."

Hunter stood and winced with the pain it produced. "Andrea, what can I say to you? What must I do to win your trust again?"

"There is nothing to say, Colonel. The obstacles between us have always been too considerable and are even greater now."

"And my desire even stronger," he said determinedly. "Look into my eyes and test the truth there."

Andrea refused to meet his gaze. "Nothing would change in the end, Colonel. Your distrust of me would lead to the same outcome eventually."

"And that is why you left without explaining the truth to me? Without fighting?"

Andrea gazed into the nothingness beyond his shoulder and spoke the words that had been repeated in her thoughts a thousand times. "I merely submitted to the inevitable. I left because you ordered it. You ordered it because you did not trust me. You did not trust me because we are enemies." She paused and tried to control her trembling voice. "Because we are enemies, I could not stay."

"We are *not* enemies, damn it! Stop saying that!" Hunter grabbed his head in pain. "Can we not be a man and a woman?"

Andrea was not sure if he was asking her or the heavens above, so loud were his words proclaimed.

"Andrea." He grabbed her by the shoulders and shook her. "I will desire you, admire you, cherish you forever, whether our loyalties differ or not, whether our allegiances allow it or not. Can you not look beyond the color of my uniform to the heart that beats beneath it?"

"Release me," she said, her voice and her expression cold.

Hunter's hands fell limply to his side. "Do not make me your enemy, Andrea, for that I shall never be. The enemy is within you and your tormented, tortured soul. If you would only open it to me, I would willingly share your pain."

"Share it? Or *double* it?"

Hunter swallowed hard at her words but did not dispute them. He turned instead to the night that the catastrophic chain of events had begun. "You must know, Andrea, that I ... the Confederacy ... owe you a great debt for your services."

Andrea closed her eyes, trying to shut out the memories. "Pray do not speak of it."

"But why? It was an act of kindness. Of compassion."

"You must realize, that as an ally of the South, I became a traitor to the North, to my country, my flag."

"Showing humanity is not a traitorous act—nor dishonorable. Providing relief will ever be more highly regarded than inflicting misery."

"How can I look in the eyes of those I once stood beside?" She turned away, her chest heaving at the burden she had carried alone these months.

"You cannot blame yourself for doing what is right," he said soothingly. "That cost cannot be measured."

Andrea took a deep breath and shrugged, knowing she had said those same words to him once. But that was long ago. Nothing was the same anymore.

"You told me once your conviction for right and wrong is stronger than that for North and South," Hunter said from directly behind her. "There is no crime in that."

Andrea sighed heavily. "You are wrong. I arrived at Hawthorne with nothing but my honor. And I left with nothing at all."

"Andrea, do not speak this way! Please, I beg of you! It is not true!" When she did not respond, he put his hand on her shoulder. "Andrea, you saved a Confederate officer from drowning in a stream once. Was that traitorous?"

Andrea took a deep breath. "There are some who would say it was."

"Do *you* believe it was?"

She remained silent for a moment, wrestling with conflicting emotions. "I regret it not." She turned around and looked him in the eye. "The *regrets*, I suppose, are all yours, Commander."

Hunter closed his eyes and clenched his fists at the thrust of her words. "I spoke in anger, and I shall carry that burden and regret those words to my dying day."

Andrea realized for the first time that he was trembling. This mountain of a man, this brave and noble soul, stood before her shaky and insecure, his eyes pleading, his countenance one of pain and misery that she knew had nothing to do with his wound. Yet there rested between them an interminable shadow.

"You can't just throw it all away," he finally said. "Not all that we've shared. You cannot deny the sacred ties that bind me to you."

"Apparently you see things differently through the haze of time and distance, Colonel. For you cannot possibly remember our relationship as a harmonious one."

Hunter looked deep into her eyes. "Perhaps not harmonious, yet a more perfect match could not be found. Our wills may run contrary, yet we are always in perfect accord. Even you, Miss Evans, cannot deny the attraction."

"The only attraction I recall is between you and Victoria." Andrea looked at the floor to avoid meeting his gaze. "And she is no doubt waiting for you with open arms at Hawthorne."

"You are mistaken on both counts, Andrea. There was no attraction on my part, and Victoria no longer resides at Hawthorne."

Andrea gazed up at him questioningly.

"Miss Hamilton was a childhood friend—nothing more—as evidenced by the fact that she has tired of Hawthorne and taken up residence at Oakleigh until the war subsides."

Andrea's eyes flicked across his face, but she saw no sign of regret or any indication that he cared one way or the other that Victoria now resided with his nemesis John Paul.

"Tell me, Andrea," he whispered, obviously hoping that what her lips said was in direct contradiction to the emotions of her heart. "Do I really cease to exist to you?"

"I have let go," she said without thinking, "as you asked me to."

"*Asked* you to?"

Andrea looked up and realized that dream and reality were so closely mixed she no longer knew the difference. The warm, compassionate eyes she stared into now were nothing like the ones that still chilled her in her dreams night after night. She watched the steel-gray eyes, usually smoldering with courage and determination, fill with a tenderness that flooded her heart with a feeling she thought was long ago dead.

"Andrea. Don't let this war take any more than it already has. What we have, it's strong enough to survive this war. I know it is."

"No, the war's grip is too tight." Andrea shook her head. "It's too big to think we can overcome it."

"To hell with the war!" Hunter threw his hands in the air in desperation, then took her arms and shook her gently. "I love you," he said huskily. "I love you, Andrea. Desperately. Nothing—not the war—*nothing* can change that!"

"You are wrong. The war had changed everything. And no one and nothing will ever be the same."

Hunter looked blankly at the wall behind her, his lips tightly compressed. All his strength appeared to leave him now. Not a muscle in his countenance moved as he stared into the distance with vacant eyes. "Andrea, I wish to begin again," he said, trying to make a final stand. "I will refuse you nothing in my authority to grant. I will serve you in any way in my power and at any cost to myself."

"Is the offer made out of pity or regret? Because I told you before, Colonel, you need not lament over something that was done honorably as a soldier."

A sigh so deep it sounded like a groan escaped him. "Andrea, must you prove I have a heart by ripping it out?"

Andrea turned from him as she fought for control. She did not want to hurt him, but neither could she allow herself to be hurt again. Every inch of her being, every nerve, every sense, remembered the agony.

"You are in command of this battle, Andrea," he said coming up behind her. "I only ask that you allow me to surrender with honor. Will you grant it?"

Andrea turned her head, startled, knowing that his nature did not allow him to say the words easily.

"No conditions," he said as if reading her mind. "Complete and unconditional."

Andrea felt his hands on her shoulders. "The terms sound satisfactory, but unfortunately I have found it does no good to lodge an objection with fate. And the fate of war has already decided against us."

"Fate cannot deny us what our hearts most crave," he said, turning her around. "I believe our love is sacred! There can be no bond stronger than that which unites enemies—"

"I'm sorry," Andrea interrupted. "I can't."

"*Can't?* Or *won't?* Can't let down your reserve and accept the circumstances that have been thrust upon us? Won't let down that wall you've built thick enough and high enough to keep everyone out?"

"I am enfleshed only by skin, not a coat of armor!"

"Then why won't you allow yourself to feel? Why can't you see that loving someone, needing someone, is not a sign of weakness? What are you so afraid of?"

Andrea turned her back on him, her mind numb and confused. Did he not know she had allowed herself to feel once, and the pain it had caused had been almost more than she could bear? Why could he not see that she was only pretending to be alive now? Of course she could not feel. A part of her had died the day she left Hawthorne. And it would never live again.

"You pretend to be so fearless," Hunter said, interrupting her thoughts. "Yet when it comes to your feelings you are a coward."

Andrea remained silent. He spoke the truth. She turned back to him and asked the one burning question that remained. "Tell me, Colonel, do you come to me now because of the promise?"

"No!" he yelled almost before she had finished the sentence. "This has nothing to do with Daniel! Damnation, your stay at Hawthorne had less to do with that promise than you can possibly know." Hunter let out his breath and leaned against the wall with an outstretched hand. "I am here because my heart ... my soul ... is not whole without you."

"Then I pity you, because I'm sorry, but I have nothing left to give."

Her words were like a deathblow. Andrea watched him let his breath out in a pitiful sigh. She could tell he had finally let go of all hope, given into dreadful despair.

After a few moments to regain his strength he spoke again. "I understand that I have no right to ask anything of you, Andrea, but your forgiveness I will seek before you leave here. Truly, I implore your pardon."

Andrea forgave him all, but she did not form the words. "I blame no one but myself and never have," she said in an unemotional voice. "You are clear, sir, of all liability."

A look of intense regret flashed across Hunter's eyes. "I brought a horse, in case you wished to leave tonight. I assume you would like to do that."

Andrea nodded, her eyes closed tightly. Considerate to the core, generous to a fault, he had envisioned the possibility she would not want to spend the night. He was too chivalrous, too much a gentleman, to force her to do so.

"I-I have the highest regard for you and your wishes, and so will not seek you out again. But live or die, Andrea, my love for you will never end."

Andrea heard the door close behind her as he went out to saddle the horse, and a fresh set of tears spilled down her cheeks. The pain that tore through her was like no other she had ever felt. But she had to send him away—had to get it over with—even if it was going to kill her.

After a few minutes, Andrea put her hand on the doorknob, drew a deep breath, and put her hood up against the cold night air. Hunter stood outside with the horse already saddled, staring at the sky, his face etched with pain. Without words he handed her the reins. Then he pulled back her hood and held her face in tremulous hands, gazing at her as if trying to commit every feature to memory. "I am not the enemy, Andrea," he said, brushing his lips gently against her cheek. "I will wait indefinitely for you to realize that, and will submit to any conditions you impose."

Never had Andrea seen more devotion or affection as she glanced up at him. Never had she looked into eyes such as his and seen a noble soul so tortured by despair. She swallowed hard and blinked back tears as she turned to mount. Strong hands wrapped around her waist and lifted her effortlessly into the saddle.

Hunter put one restraining hand on the bridle and another on her leg as Andrea gathered the reins. "You do understand, do you not, that I have surrendered to you—heart and soul—unconditionally and without hesitation, and swear on all that is dear to me that I shall love you until the end of time."

Andrea nodded, pretending to understand, pretending that she knew anything of the word. For a moment, just a moment, she thought about sliding off the horse, back into the comfort of his arms. But the fear of being hurt again, of hurting him, was too great. She could not allow herself to be weak, for she could never bear the crushing weight of pain like this.

"Andrea, so help me God, with my last breath I shall love you. Please …"

"Goodbye, Colonel." Hunter let go of the bridle and Andrea urged the mare forward. "I'm sorry, Alex."

But her words went unheard. Colonel Hunter sank to his knees and heard nothing over the sobs that raked his body as darkness swallowed the woman he had hoped to never let out of his sight—or his arms—again.

Chapter 62

"Love comes out of heaven, unasked and unsought."
— Pearl Buck

It took Andrea more than a week to track down J.J., thanks to the weather and his constant movements. When she rode into the bustling Union camp, the sound of shouted orders, galloping cavalry, and scrambling orderlies indicated something was afoot.

Her curiosity increased even more when she found that J.J. was not in his tent. A kind orderly allowed her to wait for him there, and after an hour's time, he arrived. Andrea watched his expression change from one of fatigue and worry to shock and surprise when his eyes fell upon her.

"Jehoshaphat, Andrea! Where have you been? How did you get here? Why did you come?"

Andrea forced a smile. "Winchester. Horse. Do I need a reason?"

"I'm sorry," he said, walking over and giving her a hug. "I'm just surprised. It's been a long time. Is something wrong?"

"Does something have to be wrong for me to visit you?" Andrea kept her tone calm while suppressing the urge to remain in his arms and bury her head against his strong chest.

Despite her poker-faced response, J.J. seemed to sense that something *was* wrong. "You've heard." His voice was soft and consoling.

Andrea pulled away and looked up at him. "Heard what?"

"Nothing. Nothing." He waved his hand in air, then picked up some papers on his desk and put them down again.

"Is something wrong with *you?*" she asked, noticing his nervousness.

J.J. looked hard at her, apparently weighing whether or not to divulge something of great importance. "Since you're here, let's take a walk."

Andrea tried to keep up, but J.J. seemed anxious to distance himself from camp. He stopped in a picturesque grove of young trees on the crest of a hill, and took a moment to light his pipe. "We've got him cornered," he said.

"Who?" Andrea's gaze was locked on a squawking blue jay insulting them mercilessly from a limb right over their heads.

J.J. only sighed, resting his foot on a rock and crossing his arms over his knee. His silence told Andrea the obvious.

"Hunter?" She grabbed his arm in alarm.

He nodded but did not turn around.

Andrea's heart stood still, then fell to her feet, then beat tumultuously. Yet her blood seemed stagnate in her veins. "You cannot fight him!"

"It is my sacred duty, Andrea. You know that."

"But how?" she asked, fearing she was somehow to blame.

"They ventured north," he said, "across the Potomac for forage. And now with the rain they cannot re-cross. We've driven them to the water's edge."

Andrea put her hand to her head. The two men she cherished most in the world were going to meet on the battlefield and she was helpless to stop the slaughter that was inevitable and imminent.

"We've given him the opportunity to surrender."

"He will not turn from a fight for his beloved Virginia," Andrea shouted, grabbing his arm again. "It is his lifeblood!"

Andrea knew Hunter better than she knew herself—knew he was a Virginian first, a man second. Surrender would never be an option for him. Even hemmed in by nature and the enemy, he would not consider yielding. She turned away, holding her stomach, gasping for breath.

How much more would she have to endure? She had faced death, anguish, and torment at every hour and at every step in this awful hell of a war. Not this! Please Lord, if you are there—not this!

She took a deep, quivering breath and turned back to J.J. "There is not a cowardly soul among them. They will fight you to the gates of Hell."

J.J. nodded while staring at the tree overhead, seeming to search for the blue jay that had since flown away. "We are ready."

Andrea looked at him, but she did not see. What she saw was two groups of men preparing for mutual slaughter. She turned away and took a deep, agonizing breath, her prophetic gaze fixed on the distance, where the music of the guns would soon commence. "I can take no more of this, J.J.," she said, turning back to him. "For the love of God, I swear to you, I can endure no more!"

J.J. placed his hand on her shoulder and she grabbed fistfuls of his jacket.

"Can we not let them live in peace? They are guided by love of liberty and what they believe to be a just cause. Why must you *fight* them?"

Andrea looked up at him, blinking tears from her lashes, but she already knew his answer. He was too loyal and responsible a general to ignore the enemy and not press the advantage. Drawing a deep, sobbing breath, she stared again at the landscape, thinking of the terrible ending to come from all her suffering and sacrifice. They were going to clash—the Union general who was too conscientious to avert a fight and the Confederate colonel who was too proud to run from one. She would rather be dead than witness the bloodbath to come.

"Andrea, I know your loyalty is with the Union. But it appears your heart lies in the South."

Andrea turned around and looked up at him, confused. "But—"

"He cares for you, deeply. I could see it in his eyes."

Andrea took a rapid breath and averted her gaze, knowing he had figured out her deception about Hunter's identity.

J.J. took her chin in his hand and turned her face up. "You've given enough, Andrea. You've suffered enough. Go to him."

Andrea looked into his eyes, astonished that he would suggest such a thing.

"The South's Cause is not dying, it is dead. Petersburg is about to fall. The end is near and sure. Rely upon it."

"*They* do not believe—will never believe—the Cause is lost!"

J.J. held her by the shoulders and shook her. "Tell *him* it is."

Andrea thought again of Hunter, envisioned him plowing his way through the gates of Hell with nothing but fury, resolve, and strength of will. How could she explain to J.J. that nothing short of annihilation would stop him, that his soul and the soil of Virginia were inseparable?

"This may be your final chance," he said.

Andrea sighed deeply, thinking of everything she had battled for and how confused and distorted it seemed. She looked again at J.J., but her thoughts were miles away. "He's dangerous, you know," she said, as if revealing information new to him. "Too fearless and stubborn and loyal for his own good."

"Perhaps that's why you love him."

Andrea blinked. "*Love* him?"

"You little fool." He shook her gently again, his eyes full of pity. He, more than anyone, knew she had never witnessed love in her childhood, and had certainly not observed it within the midst of the raging war. "You do know you love him, don't you?"

"But I'm— I mean ... he's—"

"My dear, love of country should not exclude you from loving a man. You have sacrificed enough."

"But I don't know if I can." She looked up into his eyes. "How can I love him and be loyal to the Union?"

He pulled her toward him again. "Just let your heart see what your eyes cannot. You love him, and you cannot will it otherwise."

Andrea nodded, staring over his shoulder, thinking back upon the longing, the yearning, the need for him that had never diminished in all their time apart. She smiled and felt something new and elating awakening within her. "How soon will you move? You will give me time? Engage while I am there?"

J.J. gazed into her eyes and smiled, as if he saw in her resolute face the secret that had long lain dormant in her heart. "I will do what I must—as you must do. I will try to give you until tomorrow afternoon, but already Washington is breathing down my neck. You must tell him if he surrenders, he will be preventing the useless effusion of blood."

"I will tell him what will happen," Andrea said, suddenly hopeless again. "But it will do no good."

Chapter 63

"Duty is the most sublime word in our language. Do your duty in all things. You cannot do more. You should never wish to do less."
– General Robert E. Lee

"Kulnel, the boys got someone trying to get through our lines." Hunter looked up at Malone from the map he'd been studying with his officers. "What does he know?"

"Can't get a thing out of him one way or another. Says he wants to speak to you."

"I don't have time for a private consultation with a—" Hunter's gaze drifted to the window where he saw the lone figure being held at gunpoint about twenty yards away. He shifted his focus to Carter and then to the other men in the room. "Excuse me, gentlemen. Perhaps it'd be best if I see what he has to say. Send him in, Lieutenant Malone."

When the other officers had departed and the door opened again, Hunter stared at the figure who stared at the floor. His heart sank and swelled at the sight of the slender form whose boots and trousers were splattered with mud. His nerves quivered and tingled at the danger she had placed herself in by coming, and his mind whirled at what could possibly have been her motive for doing so. He dismissed the escort with an impassive nod, hoping it masked the hurricane of feeling raging within.

Hunter heard the door latch close, but waited for her to speak. He could not help but remember with anguish the torment of their last meeting. And deep down, he possessed little hope there was to be a sudden reconciliation now.

❦ ❦ ❦

"The impending attack," Andrea started, swallowing hard in mid-sentence at the sight of Hunter's stalwart form staring at her. "You cannot—"

There was something in his proud eyes and kingly bearing that took her breath away. Face to face with him again, she could not frame the words she had practiced to say. Andrea averted her eyes and tried to catch her breath, recognizing for the first time she both worshipped and feared this man's size and martial masculinity.

"You did not come to ask me to surrender."

Andrea looked up at the tone of disgust in his voice and noticed his eyes seemed to portray deep annoyance.

"I have never surrendered and it is a little late to be learning the meaning of the word now." His focus moved from the window to her face. "Surely you did not come here thinking to teach it to me."

There was no affection or even friendliness in his voice. His cold and un-caring tone was enough to freeze the blood in Andrea's veins.

"I should not have come." Andrea took another deep, shaky breath. Riding into his heavily armed camp had not been half so hard as facing him thus. "I *would* not have come," she started again, "but you will be facing General Jordan." She exhaled loudly, relieved to have finally finished her sentence.

"And *that* is why you are here?" Hunter threw his hands up in the air. "It is the fate of war. It cannot be helped."

Andrea closed her eyes from his look of scorn, her cheeks burning. So this was to be the conclusion to what she hoped would be a happy ending. Her dream had once again turned to a nightmare. She swallowed hard and looked up at him. "If that is how you feel, then, I'm sorry to have disturbed you, sir." She turned to leave.

"Wait." Hunter walked up behind her and put his hand on her shoulder. "You know that is a sacrifice I cannot make." His voice was softer now.

"Not even for me?" Andrea turned around, imploring him with her eyes.

"You have no right to ask that which I have no right to grant," Hunter said. "It's a matter of duty, not mere inclination, that I must stand."

Andrea stared solemnly out the window at the men talking in small groups outside.

"Andrea, this is not about you and me. It's bigger than you and me. My Command, the Confederacy, demand I fight."

"But the Cause is lost!"

"The Cause is *not* lost!" His voice rose in anger. "And we may yet prove it with another victory."

"Victory?" Andrea threw her hands in the air, forgetting her former fears. "Victory or defeat, the price is the same—a senseless effusion of blood! Tell me, when will it be over?"

"When the last man falls or peace and liberty are restored … whichever comes first. We are willing to sacrifice—and to lose—everything but our honor."

"For heaven's sake! Half a million of the bravest men in the world have already shed their blood for honor! Where did it get *them*? Where has it gotten *you*?"

When she stopped and looked up, Andrea noticed Hunter's countenance for the first time—tired, weary, like he had not slept for days. His eyes looked strained under the weight of responsibility that rested upon him. Yet he bore the burden with the confidence of one who is accustomed to suffering, one who considers it so commonplace as to be unworthy of his contemplation.

"You gamble against great odds." She took a hesitant step toward him.

"I am not good at arithmetic nor accustomed to counting odds." He pulled out one of his revolvers and checked the chamber. "I'm an officer. My duty is to fight, not calculate the capability of the enemy."

"But the size and number of the enemy's guns generally have something to do with the end result, do they not?"

Hunter did not respond other than to raise his eyes to hers and then avert them again. From that look she knew that fear, no matter the odds, never entered his mind, just as the word surrender never entered his thoughts. He was planning to accept an assault he had no chance of surviving, simply in accordance with his habitual policy of withstanding anything placed in his path.

"I do not wish you to come back a corpse."

"I intend to do everything in my power to prevent that," he replied. "The task is difficult, but I trust not entirely impossible."

"You cannot win this battle based on Southern resolve. All your men and your Maker cannot withstand that which is aligned against you!"

"If you are asking why I do not surrender, I'll give you my uncompromising reply. My honor forbids it."

"But it is not up to *you* to vindicate the South's honor!"

"You yourself said honor is the most priceless gift we can have," he said, his piercing gray eyes focusing on her.

Andrea sighed in exasperation at the way he always used her own words against her. Then she looked at him wistfully and bit her lip, wanting to say something more but, for once, not venturing to do so.

H H H

Hunter read the look of private agony and suppressed emotion on her face. "Where will you go?" He took her hand in his and stared at its deceiving size. He knew well the slender figure it belonged to possessed more fire and energy per square inch than anyone he had ever met. Even now, dressed as a boy, she radiated a dignity and nobility that was visible even beneath the low brow of her hat.

She took a deep breath and looked up, distress evident in her troubled eyes. "The general knows I am here. I cannot go back."

"I'll have one of my men take you someplace where you'll be safe."

"I do not wish to leave. With the Colonel's permission, I will share whatever fate awaits him."

Hunter remained silent for a moment, his eyes probing hers. Then he reached for her and pulled her to him, almost melted to tears by the poignant complexity of her affection. Her struggle between devotion to him and duty to country stirred his heart.

"Dear Andrea, I cannot accept such a sacrifice."

"I have come this far. I will share your peril."

"You will stand with Virginia?" He held her at arms length and stared into her eyes.

"I promised you once I would not allow the war to come between us. I did not agree to do one thing to your face, and expect to do another behind your back." Andrea placed her head against his chest, clutching his coat. "I will share in your danger and glory, Alex. I must. I fear you will not come back to me."

"Of course, I will." He rubbed her back. "I have survived worse."

"And we can go home? To Hawthorne?"

Hunter looked down and searched her face, striving to understand the meaning in her words and the promise they contained. Eyes full of devotion stared back at him. "Home?"

"If the offer still stands."

Hunter closed his eyes, smiled, and pulled her back to him. "Oh, Andrea, I told you how I care for you. I do so still." His voice was but a whisper. "I promise. We'll go home."

A knock on the door interrupted them and they parted. "Sir, Gus just got back. Said it's important."

"Send him in."

The scout soon entered, followed by Carter and three other officers, including Captain Pierce. Andrea tried to remain inconspicuous, walking to the back of the room, her hat pulled low.

"What have you?" Hunter took a deep breath and prepared himself for the worst.

"It appears all routes are closed. They are massing in every direction." He pointed on the map. "Looks to be at least a brigade."

Hunter stared at the map, a grave look upon his face.

"Pretty heavy odds," Carter said, "considering we're backed up to the river like this and down supplies."

"If they wish to fight, they will be facing the best the Confederacy has to offer." Hunter walked over to the fireplace, and leaned for a moment in silent meditation against the mantel. "Pierce, I want you to dismount your men as skirmishers at the front. Carter, take your men and place them here." He walked briskly back to the table and pointed to the map. "Jake and Boz, you'll be here and here to protect our flanks. Gus and Hank can hold some men in reserve."

Hunter gazed up at the eager faces of his men and then focused once again on the map and the business at hand. "If only there was a way to bring in reinforcements and supplies, we could handle them easily."

"I've been up and down that river," Gus said. "I have found no ford."

Andrea began to pace back and forth, her spurs clanking loudly on the floor. More than one of the men looked back at her, irritated at the distraction.

"I see no choice but to proceed as planned." The men started for the door at Hunter's words.

"Wait!" The room grew silent as each man turned toward Andrea. Walking to the map, she studied it for a moment, trying to get her bearings. "I know a ford." Her voice was small and weak.

"You don't have to—"

"I know a ford," she said, louder this time. "It's deceiving. Its banks are steep. But the water runs low."

"Do you know this boy, sir?" Pierce stepped forward as if he did not trust what he was hearing.

"Yes. He can be implicitly trusted."

"Capital! We can send for reinforcements. Take me there." Pierce talked excitedly while starting again for the door.

"Wait!" Hunter's voice froze everyone in the room. "Are you sure it is passable?"

Andrea bit her cheek. "It will not be easy, but I've crossed in similar weather."

Again, everyone in the room fell breathlessly quiet. Hunter ran his hand through his hair. "How far?"

"Mayhap a mile, probably less."

Hunter nodded. "Very well. Take some men with you, Pierce. If it's in enemy hands, engage with anything less than twice your number. If you can take it without firing a shot, all the better. I'd rather not alert the Yanks that we are aware of its presence."

Pierce nodded with obvious annoyance, apparently more eager for the opportunity for a fray than to take the ford without a fight.

"Post enough men to keep it in our control. We must command that passage at any cost, whether we chose to stand ..." He paused and looked at Andrea. "Or not."

He sat down to write another hasty dispatch, never raising his eyes, even while giving additional orders. "Get this across as soon as you can get through," he said, handing the message to Gus.

He rattled off more orders with practiced ease and walked to the door with his men as they filed out. He closed the door just as Andrea reached it.

"Are you adequately armed?" His voice was low and strained.

Andrea nodded, but wore a questioning look. "You cannot believe I will use force against *your* enemy."

"Damn it. *Your* enemy is all around you! And if you don't know that then I am reluctant to let you go."

Andrea nodded regretfully, seeming to accept that loyalty and treason had somehow fused. "Still, I will not use my weapon save in my own self-defense."

Hunter put his hands to his temples, trying to decide whether to let her go. The battles fought during four long years of bloody struggle were not half so hard as the decision that confronted him now. "Do you understand the extreme peril you are undertaking?"

"I comprehend both the peril and the necessity. Do not undertake to make a protest about it. I am going."

Hunter looked into eyes that were both uncompromising and decisive. "Return to me here as soon as Pierce is led to the ford. Do you understand?"

He stomped over to the table and drove his pen across another piece of paper furiously. "That means you do not wait for him to engage, or even to see if the ford is guarded. Turn around after showing him the ford's location no matter what you hear. Do you understand?"

"I understand, Colonel." Andrea stood impatiently with her hand on the door latch.

Hunter strode across the room. "Here. Take this pass in case you get stopped by any of my men." Then his voice turned softer. "You've taken enough risks on your own accord. You need not take any more on mine. I understand the sacrifice."

"If you will use the ford to get back to Virginia, it is well worth the sacrifice." Andrea shoved the piece of paper into her pocket.

"I'm not in the habit of choosing routes of retreat. I leave that for the enemy."

"I would hope that you're not in the habit of allowing your men to be needlessly slaughtered either. Your reputation as a brave and gallant soldier is not worth that."

"It's not for my reputation or glory that I fight. It's for the honor of Virginia. You know that."

"There is no honor in fighting a losing battle. I'm showing you the location of the ford so you can retreat with dignity—not get whipped with honor."

"When the ford is in our hands, I will decide our course of action." He frowned when he read the impatience on Andrea's face. "I hope you fully appreciate the risk of the venture. Your hand must be against them, as it has been for them."

"Surely you do not believe I came all this way without appreciating that risk. As for whom I stand with now, I am willing."

One more look in her rebellious eyes caused Hunter to concede. "Very well. Show Captain Pierce the way."

Although he intended to give her a parting kiss, he did not have time. By the time he passed through the door, she had already leaped into the saddle and was holding in her skillful hands a large, spirited, and impatient horse. The massive beast beneath her snorted and pinned its ears when her weight hit the saddle, providing more than a little indication that it intended to try to remove the obstacle from its back at the first opportunity. No need to worry about that, Hunter thought to himself. She would ride a hurricane if someone dared her to, or attempt to jump a mountain if someone told her it could not be done.

He watched in breathless silence as she whirled the horse around, and took off at a gallop with a dozen men following close behind.

Hunter closed his eyes and, for the second time in his life, said a prayer. He could not believe he was entrusting the one he loved with so dangerous an errand on behalf of his Command, nor that she was willing to accept it on behalf of him.

Chapter 64

"So long lost and loved at last, too late."
— "The Three Scouts," J.T. Trowbridge

Colonel Hunter paced impatiently after hearing a few shots in the distance, his heart and eyes weary of watching for her arrival. When the sound of galloping hooves interrupted the silence, he anxiously scanned the lane, waiting for the image of the horse to come into view. But it did not appear where he expected.

The bay, lathered and blowing, came bursting out of the woods not fifty feet away. He watched as she aimed her mount straight for the fence that separated the lane from the pasture, watched men who were lounging nearby scatter, and watched with his experienced eye, a horse that had no intention of attempting flight.

Hunter turned his head when they were but one stride out, seeing in the actions of the horse that it was indeed going to refuse to jump. When he did not hear a crash, he turned back to see the duo sailing over the obstacle with a foot to spare. Andrea's spurs were deeply dug in her charger's flanks, and the horse's eyes still bulged from the shock of the perfectly timed action.

A hellcat on horseback. Hunter stared at her in suppressed amazement as she drew the horse to a jolting stop, spraying clumps of mud upon the porch step where he stood.

"Mission accomplished, Colonel." She saluted him in such a way that he knew it was instinctive rather than planned. "It was occupied but did not appear to be heavily guarded. Gus is through and Captain Pierce should be—"

Andrea sucked in a mouthful of air as she dismounted. Although she made an obvious effort to land on her good leg, she grimaced and cursed under her breath when she hit the ground nonetheless. "...In control." She finished her sentence, and straightened up with gritted teeth. "I await further orders, sir."

"Yes, come with me. I need to talk to you." Hunter turned and clanked noisily up the steps, his gaze falling on Carter who lounged against the wall beside the door as if preparing to stand guard. Hunter nodded in gratitude at the duty being performed with no orders to do so, and Carter nodded back with a kind of contented smile on his face.

"There's going to be a hot fight," Hunter said before Andrea had even closed the door.

Andrea half-nodded and half-shrugged with half a frown on her face, showing as much concern or interest as if he'd just predicted warm weather in the middle of July.

"You need to get away from here."

This caused a bit more of a reaction. First, she blinked in surprise; then her eyes, which had been glowing with satisfaction, narrowed with a grave look of defiance. "But I—"

"After careful reflection, I've decided I don't want you involved in this."

"You mean you've decided you want me out of the way!"

Hunter closed his eyes when he heard the rebelliousness in her voice, knowing there was more to follow when it reached that tone. He braced himself for the fallout. "You've already done more than we can repay, more than we could ask. I want you safely behind the lines."

Although Andrea had stood before him calm and determined before, she now bristled with hostility. "*Which* lines, Colonel? North or South? For I can be felled by a Yankee bullet as easily as Rebel now. It makes no difference to me from where the lead comes!"

He grabbed her by the arm. "I prefer that you return to Hawthorne."

"I'm on the wrong side of the Potomac for that," she spat. "As are you! Though you are apparently too determined to go down in a blaze of glory to care!"

"We have the ford now."

"I did not show you the location of the ford so I could retreat to a place of safety!"

When Hunter spoke, his face was resolute, his tone was stern, and his words were unrelenting. "If you defy me, I will have you arrested and placed there by force."

Andrea's jaw dropped and she blinked in surprise. "You would not dare!"

"Yes. I would," was the calm, but loud, response.

Carter stuck his head in the door at the noisy exchange, and gazed worriedly at the courier and the colonel as they stood face to face—one looking enraged, the other careworn and troubled beyond measure. "Everything all right in here?"

"We're fine, Carter," the latter said, not taking his eyes from Andrea's defiant gaze.

Andrea picked up the conversation where it had left off as soon as the door closed. "If you think for one moment to bend me from my purpose by your threats or command, you will find you are in dreadful error." She took a step closer and pointed her finger at him defiantly. "I will not leave but by force, and you shall not find *that* an easy course! Why, you do not even have enough men to accomplish such a deed!"

"It will take but one man, Andrea," Hunter said in a perfectly calm voice. "Me."

He did not give her time to respond to that. He cupped her face in his hands, bent down and kissed her so tenderly, so longingly, so lovingly that it took her breath—and her anger—away.

"Is it so hard to believe that I want you to be safe?" Hunter whispered in her ear, pulling her into his arms.

"Is it so hard to believe that I want the same for you?" Andrea placed her head on his heart. "Retreat does not indicate defeat when it allows you the opportunity to fight another day."

"When Pierce gets back I will consult the opinions of my officers. I'll yield to their decision on whether the Command fights or crosses into Virginia."

"But there's really no decision to make," Andrea said, trying to keep her voice calm. "Think how the prestige of a victory over you would animate the enemy, Colonel Hunter. I know you worship the sacred soil of Virginia—but would it not be better to fight another day than sleep eternally beneath it? That is the basic premise for your decision, is it not?"

"You make it sound easy." Hunter pushed his hat back off his brow and walked to a window in the back of the room to stare at the horizon.

"It *is* easy." Andrea paced back and forth, her hands flying to accentuate her emotions. "On the one hand, your Command is devoid of every resource for battle including provisions and men. You do not have the choice of ground, or even knowledge of the ground on which you stand, nor do you have the advantage of surprise or the benefit of being the aggressor. You have no time in which to launch a diversion, and even if you did, you possess not the manpower or the ammunition to sustain one. Your horses are jaded, your men are tired, and the enemy outnumbers you five to one. Any attempt to defend this position seems incredibly impractical, unrealistic and, frankly, unattainable due to an uncooperative swollen river. Your only hope of success is a sudden and complete capitulation by the enemy, which we both know is not going to happen. They are well rested and well fed, and are no doubt incensed—nay, infuriated—with your very presence on Northern soil. They carry the added advantage of no longer suffering in fear of ambush or reprisal from you, trapped as you are on a useless piece of land that you cannot afford to hold and from which you do not have the ability to maneuver. The benefit of this to them and the consequences of this to you are nigh impossible to estimate! Tell me Colonel, wherein lies the difficulty of the decision?"

"Gotta couple of pretty good points there," Carter said.

Andrea and Hunter both whirled around at the same time. Neither had heard Carter and Pierce enter the room—Andrea so intent on making her plea, and Hunter intent on listening in bewilderment to her torrent of words. Carter leaned nonchalantly against the door, chewing on his cigar and looking wryly amused. Pierce stood with his head cocked to the side, looking openly shocked at the lengthy expostulation just given by a mere boy.

Hunter cleared his throat. "Thank you for your modest opinion. That will be all."

Hunter watched a stream of sunlight burst into the room and surround her as she opened the door and then disappear as if she were taking it with her when it alternately slammed shut.

"Send in the other officers," Hunter said to Carter, before turning his back and concentrating once again on the map on the table.

Chapter 65

"Yet this inconstancy is such, as you too shall adore,
I could not love thee, dear, so much, loved I not honor more."
— "Off to War," Lovelace

Carter saw Andrea leaning against a tree, her thoughts apparently so absorbed on the men spilling out of the farmhouse behind him that she didn't notice his approach. Her eyes flicked from face to face as men shouted and hurried to obey orders. When her gaze finally met his, he read in her furrowed brow that she sensed the distinctive undercurrent of excitement. She knew without asking that a decision had been made, and it was not hard to see that the men preparing to carry out that decision approached it with enthusiasm.

Carter paused and looked back at the men, too. What he saw on their faces was what he knew was in their minds. They were already thinking of the end result of today's contest and their greatest reward—to see Hunter approach them after the battle, feel his hand on their shoulder, and hear the words from his lips, "Well done."

"Colonel wants to see you," Carter said in a low voice when he reached Andrea.

Her eyes shifted to a point over Carter's shoulder, and the light reflected from them announced the approach of the most dashing and indomitable soldier in the Confederacy. She smiled then, or tried to, her trembling lips revealing the overwhelming emotions she felt at the mere sight of him.

"Ride with me a moment," was all Hunter said when he reached her.

Carter watched the two mount, their legs swinging across the backs of their horses in perfect unison, both settling into their saddles with gentle ease—an act he suspected was more a result of the injuries each had suffered than in deference to the backs of their mounts. Andrea turned toward Carter a moment, obviously trying to wear the same expression of calmness that Hunter so coolly displayed. Before gathering her reins, she saluted in Carter's direction, her lips showing a smile of hopeful optimism, her eyes a look of intolerable dread.

The slender youth and the strong, bronzed officer then swung their horses around to the right and pushed them into a canter in perfect stride and harmony, as if there was but one mind and soul between them. Carter watched them ride away side by side, boot to boot in silence, two opposite forces of energy that had finally found perfect balance.

To a stranger, it might appear they were drawn together by the mysterious relationship of opposites, but Carter knew their affinity to one another was strong likenesses. Both were as stubborn, intrepid, and fiercely independent as any two people could be. He could well imagine the spirited clashes and passion that flickered and flamed between them. On second thought, perhaps he could not. He saw the sparks flying when they but stood in the same room. He could not imagine the meteoric brilliance that flamed when they were in each other's arms—and he felt his face turn scarlet at the thought. In any event, he was glad that a truce had been called, fortifying a bond and creating a union that not even war, hopefully, could separate.

ℋ ℋ ℋ

Hunter rode into a small grove of trees and turned to face Andrea. She cautiously scanned each shadow and silhouette within its depths, her mind obviously alert to any danger that might be hidden within. "You are safe within my lines."

Andrea focused her eyes on him for a moment. "You forget. I am an enemy among your men and a traitor among mine."

"You are not the enemy of this Command, I assure you." He urged his horse a step closer. "My men have decided the battalion shall cross into Virginia. You apparently influenced them no little bit."

"And yet you disagree?"

"I am of the mind it is better to have fought and lost then never to have fought at all."

"It is not rational or logical to gamble all and gain nothing. And," she said, her tone serious as she moved her horse back a step to look at him more fully, "it should worry you, as it worries me, that *I* am being forced to give *you* advice on being rational and logical."

Hunter gazed in awe at the bright smile of humor she wore on her lips despite the desperate situation. She looked perfectly majestic sitting arrow straight, yet relaxed, on her horse, one hand on the reins, the other on the back of her saddle as she twisted to face him. Yet, he felt a sudden stab in his heart

344

when he thought of how few minutes they had now to talk.

"Miss Evans, I rely much on your judgment and hold your opinion sacred, believe me."

"The ford is not easily accessible to a large number of men," Andrea said, her tone serious again. "There is danger in delay."

"Yes, I understand. "I have men moving out as vanguard to help Pierce protect the ford. I want you to go with Carter in the main body. I will move up with the rearguard." Andrea started to shake her head. "That's an order. I'll be right behind you."

"But the rearguard will be the most heavily engaged!"

"So be it." His gaze shifted to a place over her shoulder. "The fault is mine, so must the remedy be. I will not leave until my men are safely in Virginia."

A gust of wind swept down upon them, causing Andrea's horse to rear and, almost in the same instant, buck, while hopping and sidestepping in apparent fear. Hunter watched her bring him back under control, never so much as blinking an eye or changing her relaxed stance in the saddle—or apparently even taking notice that he was attempting to dislodge her.

"Easy, big boy," Andrea said soothingly, bending down to pat him on the neck to calm his quivering. "Nothing but the wind."

The horse stood trembling with alarm, relying on nothing but her voice to keep him from running straight to kingdom come for safety. Andrea appeared surprised when she finally looked up and read the amused amazement on Hunter's countenance. "The boys gave me this horse as a practical joke" she said, patting it on the neck again as if his behavior required an explanation. "Told me if I wanted a broke horse when I requested a mount from government stables then I should have specified as such. They had a jolly good laugh when I got on Buck here the first time."

Hunter winced. "He's not broke and you took that fence earlier?"

"There are only two ways he could have gone—over or through." Andrea shrugged. "My odds were fifty-fifty."

"And you think fifty-fifty makes good odds."

Andrea turned in her saddle again to face him, leaning back and resting one hand on her horse's rump. "Lighten up, Colonel. You said yourself you don't bother to count odds, which is for the better, for I fear yours today are not nearly so high."

Hunter ignored the comment. "The boys, as you call them, that gave you the horse ... they are on the other side of the hill?" He did not say to whom he was referring, merely nodded toward the Union line.

Andrea's expression turned mournful, though she looked down almost immediately to escape his gaze. She nodded, making it perfectly clear that the soldiers in blue whom he considered dire enemies, were friends and comrades by whose side she had shared danger and laughter, peril and mirth. She was one of them. Or had been.

Hunter, who so rarely showed emotion, became clearly overwhelmed by it now. His eyes misted at her commitment and devout loyalty to him. "You have done me and my men a great service today," he said, bringing his horse next to hers. "One that I can never hope to repay."

Andrea grabbed his gauntleted hand, his earlier stinging words apparently forgotten. "But you can." She looked earnestly into his eyes. "I will let you pay it back, slowly, for the rest of your life."

Hunter's mouth curled into a smile, relieved that she was not angry, and now, somehow elated at the prospect of having such an overwhelming debt to pay. "Do not fear, Private Evans, I fully intend to honor my obligations." Leaning forward then, he gave her a long, adoring kiss.

$\mathcal{H}$ $\mathcal{H}$ $\mathcal{H}$

Andrea wrapped her arms around Hunter's neck in obvious desperation and felt herself being lifted with strong arms across his saddle. "Oh, Alex," she said, burying her head in his chest and clutching his manly form. Hunter responded by tightening his embrace, leaving her to wonder how a mortal man could possess such boundless tenderness in such iron muscles.

"Andrea, you will go back to Hawthorne," he said, his voice strangely low. "No matter what."

She lifted her head, not sure if he was stating a fact or asking a question. "No matter what?"

"If anything should happen to me ... I would like to know that you would still go back. That it would be in good hands."

Andrea blinked, trying to hold back the tears that threatened. "If that is your wish."

"It is my most desperate desire."

She looked up in anguish at the businesslike tone of his voice. "There is no need to seal your devotion to the Confederacy with your life, Alex," she said, clutching his coat. "Please, not now."

He did not answer at first, and when he did, his gaze was locked on something over her shoulder. "What I do, I do for my country. You understand, do you not?"

He shifted his attention back to her and remained there in a spellbinding gaze of devotion. "We'd better get back." His tone carried a calmness and determination that terrified Andrea. She pulled her horse close and swung her leg over its back.

"Wait, Andrea." She drew her horse to a halt and looked up at him, a tear breaking loose from where she had willed it to stay. "My love for country, my duty to state, does not mean I love you less. Do you understand?"

Neither spoke for a moment. Even the horses stood perfectly still. "I shall not obstruct the path of your duty, Alex," she said, her chin trembling. "I give you to Virginia and God—if that is what you wish of me."

Andrea caught only a glimpse of his eyes filling with fluid, and then he nodded, turned his head from her, and nudged his horse forward. After riding a short distance, Andrea reached out for his sleeve and stopped him again. Her heart beat tumultuously at the thought that sand was slipping through the hourglass at a speed beyond her control.

"I know it is your right, your privilege to die for the Cause. But Alex, you will be careful?"

Alex turned his attention back to her, but it appeared to Andrea his mind was already elsewhere. "I will see you on the other side of the river, Andrea," he said without concern, his eyes full of a strange brilliancy. "The Virginia side."

Chapter 66

*"Having chosen our course, with guile and with pure purpose, let us
renew our trust in God and go forth without fear and with manly hearts."
— Abraham Lincoln*

The men had already begun to move out by the time Andrea and Hunter galloped back. Andrea pulled her horse into the shadow of some trees while Hunter conferred with Carter in low, whispered tones. When they were finished, Hunter looked up and urged his horse toward her.

"You ready?" He grasped her hand in a final testament of warm regard, his eyes remaining locked on hers during the brief moment they touched as if absorbing her through the contact. "Stay safe, Andrea."

Andrea nodded and forced a smile. "I'll see you in Virginia, Alex." Then she turned, spurred her horse into a gallop, and disappeared into the midst of the Confederacy's most illustrious band of heroes.

Andrea heard only scattered gunfire until she was almost to the river—then all hell broke lose. It seemed the Yankees had been taken by surprise at the sudden departure of the enemy and were now intent on pulverizing them for their own carelessness.

She at once recognized Pierce, riding back and forth like a madman through a shower of lead, directing and strategically deploying his men to meet the coming foe while defending the battalion's crossing. Because of the difficult terrain in reaching the ford, only a few dozen had yet safely reached the southern shore, and it was obvious the enemy was intent on stopping the rest.

"Keep them moving!" Pierce yelled. "Keep that ford open!"

Andrea had every intention of doing just that, but Buck decided he preferred the shore he was on and went madly out of control, sideswiping her leg against a tree.

Unfortunately, he was not the only beast of burden with unenthusiastic thoughts about the crossing. Already horses were plunging into the water, some without riders, many out of control. Andrea rushed into the river as well, slapping horses on their rumps to keep them moving, and holding injured men on their saddles until they could get across.

The fighting came so close to the ford that bullets from both sides whizzed by Andrea's head. Still, she continued riding back and forth across the swollen river, pulling, prodding and poking to keep both injured man and beast from stopping or falling. Once across, the wounded handed her their extra weapons and ammunition to take back to their comrades on the other side. Time after time Andrea crossed, loaded down with carbines, pistols, and powder to be distributed among Pierce's men, who were facing the brunt of the attack.

She had no time to think, no time to process the passage of time. Only once, when sitting on her knees helping reload fresh weapons, did she catch a glimpse of Alex shouting words of encouragement to Pierce's men. Through the smoke, he appeared more spectral than real, raging through the storm of lead like a lion, the lust of battle flashing from his eyes. He did not stop other than to reload or confer with Pierce, then he rode back into battle, appearing to rejoice in the storm.

After losing sight of Alex, Andrea continued her duties, her body numb with exhaustion and her head aching from the incessant gunfire. The crescendo of war reached a feverish pitch, the lead hurling toward the ford seeming never ending. She was halfway back across the river when a man within an arm's length of her blinked with a look of surprise and fell backward into the muddy water. Andrea dove off her mount, pulling him out of the way before he was trampled by a score of frenzied horses.

Standing ankle deep in mud and knee deep in water, she saw the man had been hit in the upper leg and was bleeding profusely from the gaping wound. Springing to his assistance, she took off her coat and bound his injury, speaking words of encouragement to rally him.

When she was all but through, Andrea felt a tingling sensation on the back of her neck. She turned, seeking Alex through the smoke and confusion on the other side of the river. It did not take her long to find him sitting on his frothing steed, silently watching her with a resolute stare. Enshrouded by the light from above and backlit with the smoke of battle, he appeared to be something other than mortal.

The world stopped for Andrea. Slowly, deliberately he raised his hand in a poignant, heartfelt salute. Andrea rose to her feet and returned the salute, her eyes searching his from across the wide expanse. She was afraid to blink, afraid he would disappear—and all too soon he did, wheeling his horse back toward the field and the fury, vanishing like a dream vaporizes upon awakening.

Andrea felt a strange, sinking feeling in the pit of her stomach. She knew he had sought her out, and feared to the very depths of her soul she had just witnessed a final goodbye.

Within a few moments, the firing on the other side of the river diminished in its intensity indicating the enemy was maneuvering for some new assault.

The men around her began maneuvering as well, most preparing to make a stand at the ford while others, like Pierce's company, rushed forward to check the advancing forces before a new attack could be made. Andrea glanced around at the picture of vigorous martial splendor. She knew she would remember those grimy faces lit with battle fire for the rest of her life.

On both sides of the river now, exhausted and desperate men summoned all their strength for a final convulsive effort to repel the enemy long enough to get the remainder of the battalion through the perilous passage. To Andrea, the hazardous situation only rendered the men more fearless. It seemed their commander had instilled in them the idea that they were unconquerable, and they therefore did not know they were not.

All too soon the onslaught began again, the guns of the enemy pouring death and destruction in a storm of lead. The barrage was of a character more desperate and determined than Andrea had ever seen, but the ranks held, and the stream of gray kept moving to safety, despite the shelling that seemed to come from every direction.

"What's your name?" Andrea kneeled by an older man she knew was one of Hunter's officers.

"Boz," he said grumpily. "Got me in my darn shooting arm."

Andrea began tying a large handkerchief around his arm to help stem the flow of blood, when he struggled to his feet, almost pushing her down.

"Captain!" he yelled at the top of his lungs. "To your right!"

Captain Pierce, sitting on his horse on the opposite bank, wheeled his horse around and shot a man in blue who had apparently crawled to the riverbank to pick off those who were crossing.

The Yankee, shot in the stomach or lower chest, went down, but Andrea and the man beside her watched in horror when the gun rose again. What only took a few seconds seemed to play in slow motion to Andrea. The sharpshooter, struggling for his life, propped his back against a tree for support. Slowly and deliberately, he lifted the gun to his eye and again took aim at Pierce, who by now was too far away to hear any shouts of warning from Andrea or Boz. They looked around to see who could help, but everything was in a state of chaos with horses whinnying, water splashing, and guns firing in rapid succession.

Andrea did not remember thinking or reacting or planning a response. Without warning there appeared on the side of the Yankee's head a horrid red fountain, and at the same instant, he fell a corpse. She looked at Boz in relief, for the danger, it seemed, had been averted.

Boz's eyes were not on the fallen Yankee. They were on her. Andrea followed the line of his gaze to her outstretched hand, to the barrel of the still-smoking gun pointed toward the opposite bank.

She blinked, as if by doing so the gun would vanish. Then she glanced behind her, thinking surely someone else had taken the shot. But as for the former, the gun did not disappear, and as for the latter, there was no one in sight to assume the blame or accept the honor.

The cold reality of the situation rushed over her. With a shiver of revulsion that shook her body, Andrea threw the dreadful instrument of death into the river. "It was just a Yankee," Boz said, watching a perfectly good weapon disappear. "And he was dead before you shot him. You just hurried him up a little."

Andrea took no comfort in his words. She continued to stare at her hand as though it belonged to someone else, then turned away, unable to endure the sight of the opposite bank. Stumbling into some bushes, she bent over, and with her hands on her knees, gagged and heaved. She turned back toward Boz, but took only a few steps before sinking to the ground at the thought she had sent a human soul, fighting for his country, into eternity.

"Don't see why you're so upset, but look at it this way, kid," Boz said, walking to her and patting her on her shoulder. "You saved a life today. One man was already on his way out. If you hadn't shot, there woulda been two."

Andrea nodded, but it was plain to see his words did not ease her anguish nor console her mental torture. Boz had no way of knowing that she had not just killed a Yank, she had killed a comrade—in order to save a Rebel, no less.

Andrea's mind whirled with pain and confusion, but she had little time to lament. Hearing heavier gunfire, she caught a horse and rode to a small eminence a short distance away. What she saw filled her with dismay and horror. Union troops, attacking the rearguard with furious determination, had almost surrounded those remaining, cutting them off from the river and safety. Although holding their ground tenaciously, there was only a small force to meet the shock of the advancing hosts. And Alex was likely among them.

Andrea watched the two forces move closer and closer to hand-to-hand combat. Her soul froze at the sight of the Confederate banner waving defiantly within the chaos. This was not war, it was slaughter. A useless sacrifice. She spurred her horse up to Carter.

"Major, you must do something," Andrea yelled above the din. "They are almost surrounded!"

"My orders are to move forward, not to look back." He continued to wave on the men.

"But they shall all perish!" Andrea tried to remain calm, but it was useless. Pure and complete panic prevailed, to the extent that she was unable to think rationally. She looked Carter dead in the eye when he refused to budge or respond.

"I have no such orders," she yelled.

Whirling her horse back to the river in desperation, Andrea had no idea what she could do. But she had a feeling Carter would follow to stop her—and he did. And she had a feeling the rest of the men would follow him—and they did. Dozens of those from the main body, apparently thinking there was to be a renewed fight, advanced at a full charge toward the river where their companions stood firm against the enemy's fire. Some of Carter's men charged undaunted back across without orders, willing to sacrifice all in defense of their comrades who they knew were in serious trouble.

Carter joined forces with Pierce, who split the command to attack the flanking parties, hoping to keep them back long enough to get the final seventy-five across.

More heavy firing a half-mile to the east, and a lessening of fire where the rearguard had been fighting, caused Andrea to cast her eyes in that direction. Seeing Carter again, she rode up beside him. "What could that be?" she yelled. "Have some of the men gotten separated?"

"Probably the Colonel creating a diversion," Carter said with forced calmness, continuing to wave his men forward.

Andrea felt her heart do a summersault as she stared at him in horrified astonishment. "A diversion?" She grabbed him by the arm when he started to ride away. "He told me he was serving in the rearguard!"

"That too ... but if I know him, he's engaging the enemy to the east." He nodded toward the sound of gunfire. "Giving time for more men to cross. Then he'll cross over with ... er-r, *after* ... the rearguard." Carter took a deep breath, and then added, "If all goes as planned."

"But the diversion—" Andrea shook her head, trying to allow her brain to catch up to what her heart already knew. "How many men has he with him?"

She suddenly found it hard to concentrate with the whooshing in her ears that had nothing to do with the lead flying around her.

Carter shrugged. "The object is to draw their attention from the ford—"

"I know what a bloody diversion is," she screamed, standing in her stirrups.

"How many men has he with him?

Carter gazed at her intently, looking like he did not wish to answer. "There is but one man popular enough to distract the Yanks."

He did not finish. He did not need to. A thunderous explosion of gunfire in that direction caused Andrea's jaw to drop. Hunter was facing the enemy alone. She remained motionless, watching the scene play in slow motion before her eyes.

"Is it a diversion?" she cried out like a terrified child. "Or a sacrifice?"

"It's his duty," Carter said, more brusquely now, apparently afraid he was going to have a bawling woman on his hands. "And he is not one to evade it—not at any cost."

Andrea looked back toward the sound of gunfire. It grew quiet for a moment, the enemy apparently checking to see if the target still stood. Then it began again with renewed and more violent intensity. *Damn him! Damn him!*

His words came back to her. He never said he was going to retreat. He had said he would allow the officers to decide what the *Command* would do. He knew all along he was going to stand and fight while securing his men's safe passage. His instinct to protect his country's honor was stronger than his instinct for personal safety—even in so desperate and unequal a struggle. His own personal gallantry would not allow him to quit the field and retreat, even when solid military prudence made it clearly advisable

Andrea blinked hard, fighting back tears that were stinging her eyes. She looked at Carter with brimming lashes.

"He'll come out all right, darlin'," he said in a reassuring tone. "He always does." Then he turned his horse and galloped back into the fray.

It seemed like only minutes later, but was certainly much more, when Carter and a dozen other riders splashed through the river now red with blood. "Move out!" he ordered to all those who remained on the river's bank. The firing behind them continued and the water around them gurgled with gunfire as his remaining men galloped through. The rearguard, cut and slashed and war beaten, followed across beneath a hail of suppressing fire from some reinforcements Gus had brought up to cover their passage.

Andrea, who had been helping load men into wagons that had come with the reinforcements, caught a horse, and with great difficulty in the excitement, mounted. She tried to find Carter again, but could not in the rush. All around her were battered and beaten, yet living men. Almost all suffered a wound of one kind or another, but she knew few had been killed outright.

Glancing back at the far riverbank, which was now filled with blue, Andrea watched the fresh troops move forward, ready to shell anyone who ventured any closer than the northern bank. She swept her eyes over the faces of those around her, searching desperately for Alex or any sign of his fate, as a vague uneasiness began to gnaw at her spine.

Dripping wet and stiff with cold, Andrea blew on her fingers to keep them warm in the cool evening air. The only sounds now were that of distant and sporadic gunfire to the rear, the men being either too exhausted or too injured to speak. Someone apparently noticed her shivering and dropped a coat over her shoulders. Too exhausted to turn and see who it was, Andrea slipped her arms into the garment, thankful for the warmth.

Dozing in her saddle as the horses walked single file down a narrow path, Andrea awoke when the rider in front of her struck a match. For just a moment in that flash of light, she saw the color of the coat she now wore. Odd, it was lined in scarlet, just like the one Alex often wore. Trying to suppress the strange feeling in the pit of her stomach, Andrea reached up and ran her fingers across the collar. Three stars. She pulled the coat more tightly around her, reveling in the comfort it provided both to her body and her soul. When she did, her hand passed over a damp spot, and then a large hole in the fabric. She stifled a scream. The sickening realization hit her with such force that she unknowingly spurred her horse forward, causing it to run into the next horse and creating a general bunch-up and swearing match ahead.

Andrea looked frantically around for Carter just as the road opened up on both sides. The men fanned out into a field to rest their mounts as Andrea rode up the line, searching the faces for someone she knew. She spotted Carter in a circle of men, but when he saw her approaching, he put his hand in the air to stop the conversation. With a nod, he gestured for Andrea to follow him into the woods.

"He's still alive," Carter said, turning his horse to face hers. "Or he was when I saw him."

Andrea stared at him in stunned silence, her trembling lips the only sign she had heard him. "But where is he? I need to see him."

"It's too dangerous." Carter shifted his gaze away from her. "We got Yanks crawling everywhere. They know he's been wounded. They're looking for him."

Andrea kicked her horse and moved him to within inches of Carter's mount. She leaned over and looked straight into his eyes. "Where is he?"

He shrugged and looked down. "It's the Colonel's orders. No one is to know where he is, or go there, in case ... you know, they're being followed."

Andrea tried to suppress her tongue, but her emotions got the best of her. She unleashed a cavalcade of curses, pointing out that Major Carter was no judge of whether or not she could successfully evade the enemy, followed by the general proclamation that he had no right, jurisdiction, or authority to stop her. "I'll not remain in suspense as to his fate," Andrea said defiantly.

"He'd have me court-martialed if I told you."

"He'd do no such thing," Andrea shot back.

Carter squinted and rubbed his chin, but still hesitated.

"Have it your way, Major Carter." Andrea picked up her reins. "It would be easier to dodge the enemy if I knew where I was going. But I will find him with or without you."

A low rumble of angry thunder growled in the distance, sounding heavy and threatening. Andrea glanced toward the sky where lightening stabbed the horizon to the west.

Carter followed her gaze, then looked at her long and hard. "They took him to a farm about a mile due south. Whether he's been moved—"

Before he could finish the sentence, she had disappeared.

"I hope to God you have a pass to get through our men," he said to nothing but the night.

Chapter 67

"Honor has caused more deaths than the plague."
— Julian Pitt Rivers

"At ease, men." Andrea spoke in the lowest voice she could muster as three heavily armed soldiers stepped in front of her horse. "I'm here to see Colonel Hunter."

The click of another half dozen guns being cocked at close range was the reply that greeted her.

"Dismount or we'll shoot," a threatening voice in the darkness drawled.

"I'm here to see the Colonel," Andrea said again.

"We heer'd what you said." The man nearest her horse grabbed the reins. "And if you don't soon hear what I said, you ain't gonna live long enough to tell about it."

Andrea dismounted at gunpoint, while another man helped himself to her horse. Since none of the men surrounding her appeared to be in particularly amiable frames of mind, she did not dispute their authority. "I have a pass," she said, suddenly remembering the one Alex had given her. "I'm here to see the Colonel."

"Shur you is. Too bad the Kulnel ain't heah."

"I know he's here, and he will see me if you'll just tell him I've arrived."

"Zat so?" The soldier sounded skeptical. "Little young to be out after dark, ain't ya?"

The soldier nearest her then yelled to someone in the darkness. Andrea felt the cold metal of a Colt pushing into her back, which she suspected meant that someone wanted her to move forward. "Now walk real slow, boy soldier. Don't do nothing stupid." The man pushed her in the opposite direction of the farmhouse she had hoped to find Hunter, toward a barn.

"No!" Andrea stopped. "You don't understand. I need to see the Colonel!"

"It's *you* that don't understand. You ain't getting nowhere near the Kulnel—if he was heah—which I ain't sayin' he is. You can show your pass to the officer in charge."

"But I must see him." Andrea stopped again and turned so abruptly that the gun caught her in the ribs and almost knocked the wind out of her.

At the same time, another man came up from behind her and grabbed her arm. His iron grip held her with one hand, while his other continued pointing his gun at her head. Andrea kicked and struggled but to no avail. The man did not even flinch as he continued dragging her toward the barn.

"At ease men," a deep voice drawled from out of the darkness.

"You know this kid?" one of the men asked the solitary soldier on horseback who rode out of the shadows by the barn. "Says he's here to see the Kulnel."

Captain Pierce leaned forward in his saddle and squinted, either deciding if he did or not—or deciding if he wanted to say or not. "Yea. Let him go," he said gruffly. "He's the kid from earlier today."

Nursing an injury of his own, he dismounted, then grabbed Andrea none too gently by the arm and turned her face toward a lantern. He wore a perplexed look on his countenance. "How'd you get here? An owl couldn't find that road in the dark."

"I have a duty to perform," was all she said in response.

"Follow me." Pierce began walking, or rather limping, toward a small outbuilding around which a number of men were standing. "Who sent for you?" he asked over his shoulder. "Why didn't they send an escort with you? These men were ordered—by me—to shoot anything that moves."

"Major Carter told me where to find the Colonel." Andrea thought it best not to lie to him. He seemed to be highly agitated.

"What for?" he barked. "No one can see him."

Andrea noticed Pierce's limping grew steadily worse, and that a shirtsleeve, dripping scarlet, had been tied around a serious wound to his thigh. From the amount of blood flowing forth, it appeared a bullet had plowed clean to the bone, causing her to wonder why he was still walking on it. With her thoughts and eyes focused on the trail of blood spilling in her path, she ran straight into him when his massive form stopped and whirled around. "It's *you*!"

Andrea's breath caught in her throat. She did not respond. If he had figured out who she was, he needed no further information from her. If he had not, she was not going to help him. Anyway, what had he figured out? That she was Andrea Evans? Or that Andrea Evans was a long-sought enemy? It did not take her long to find out.

It was both.

"Your expertise on a horse is conspicuous," Pierce said, his voice now cold and cruel. "One might even say—memorable."

Andrea stood before him, looking at the ground, trying to appear confidant and calm beneath his inscrutable gaze. In her mind she was neither. Glancing at the house, she saw it was but fifteen yards away. Yet the officer in command stood between her and the door, and it looked like the ruthless reputation of which she had been warned was going to make an appearance tonight. From the look on Pierce's face, and from the stance of the sentries posted on the porch, Andrea knew permission had been granted to fire first and ask questions later.

"Almost as memorable as your eyes." He leaned down closer. "You had to have known I would recognize those bloody, bewitching eyes."

For the first time, Andrea looked up and met his gaze, an action that seemed to infuriate him greatly. He twisted her arm behind her back with savage strength, shoved her face against the side of the small building, and placed his revolver against her head. Andrea heard the familiar *click* of the hammer being pulled and felt the cold steel press directly behind her ear.

"What are you doing here?" he asked through gritted teeth. "I know who you are."

Andrea would have answered if she could have breathed. Pierce leaned against her so heavily and bent her arm so far back that she feared she would pass out from the effect of one or the pain of the other.

"Do you take me for a fool?" he growled. "Believe me, I remember well the blasted rider on the black horse. The resemblance you share is uncanny. I watched you all day."

Pierce shifted his weight and Andrea grabbed one quick breath before he leaned into her again.

"It all makes sense now. What better place for a spy to lodge than with the Colonel? He may have fallen for your treachery, but I have not."

Andrea felt the steel of the gun press more firmly against her neck and had no doubt she would be black and blue as a result.

"Are you alone?"

The most she could do was nod her head.

"Captain?"

"What is it?" Pierce sounded exasperated at the intrusion.

"Sorry, sir, I don't mean to interrupt whatever is going on, but this here boy did save your life today."

Andrea closed her eyes tighter.

"What are you talking about?"

"That sharpshooter you shot on the river bank," Boz said. "You didn't kill him right off. He had you dead in his sights."

Andrea felt Pierce pull off just a little and she grabbed another breath.

"I seen it with my own two eyes," Boz added for emphasis.

"That true?" Pierce apparently felt her struggling for air and slammed her head against the wall again.

Andrea remained silent, too proud to defend her life based on the fact that she had saved his.

"That true?" He spun her around and stuck his gun none to gently under her chin to lift her head. Andrea found herself gazing into the eyes of a soldier with whom she knew there would be no trifling. Pierce seemed overly eager to dispatch her to the place from which she had saved him.

"Will you not take the word of one of your men?" Andrea's voice was hoarse, and she gasped for breath. The top of her head began to throb, while the left side of her face was nothing but numb.

"Show me your weapon," Pierce said, as if that would prove the case once and for all.

"He throwed it in the river, right after," Boz answered for her. "That ain't all he throwed," he added under his breath.

Pierce accepted that with a grin, understood without further explanation the torment the action had caused her. "Killed one of your own for me, did you?"

Andrea closed her eyes and swallowed hard to keep from gagging again. Her legs began to shake at the thought, and she knew Pierce was standing close enough to feel it.

He let the hammer of his gun back slowly. "This is a little ironic, is it not?" He laughed. "You save my life, and I threaten to take yours."

"Quite a good joke," Andrea said, her voice shaky and gravelly.

"My reaction was based purely on beholding a spy in our midst. You cannot blame me for trying to protect the Colonel."

Andrea did not know if his words were meant as an apology and did not really care. The skies had finally opened up, soaking her hat and dripping off her lashes. Pierce seemed to take no notice of the drenching, and was, she decided, not even conscious of it.

"Why are you here?" He looked away to return his gun to its holster.

"My heart demands it."

Pierce looked up slowly, as if all the other parts of the puzzle were now falling into place. His gaze drifted down to the oversized coat she wore. He reached out and roughly fixed the collar she had turned under, making the three stars visible once again.

"I see."

Andrea thought she saw a hint of regret flash across his eyes.

The rain started coming down even more furiously, which brought it to his attention. Without a word, he grabbed Andrea by the arm, and led her past three sentries to the shelter of the farmhouse's back porch. He stopped again. "You believe he will wish to see you?" He did not try to hide the disgust in his voice.

"He will."

"It is folly to fall in love with the enemy. I would think one of you would have more sense." He looked at her in such a way that Andrea knew he was inferring he expected more self-restraint from his leader, not from her, though whether because she was a Yankee or a female she could not tell.

"It is folly to look for logic in the chambers of the heart." Andrea spoke as if it was a lesson she had always known—not learned through months of torturous pain.

Pierce stared at her long and hard with a mixture, she thought, of curiosity and disbelief. "You have forsaken the Union cause for this?"

Andrea looked down, closed her eyes, and exhaled loudly. Hearing the words spoken aloud was a damaging blow. "There are other sacred claims," she said, her eyes filling with tears in spite of her best efforts to stop them, "that touch as deeply as patriotism."

Pierce's gaze locked on hers again. Perhaps he saw the devotion shining there for the Colonel. Perhaps he thought of the peril and the sacrifice she had made in getting there. Or perhaps he thought of the bullet from which his life had been spared. In any event, he reached toward her cheek with the back of his hand, an impulse that appeared to be partly of pity and partly of apology.

"I hope I did not hurt you overly much," he said. "I do apologize."

Andrea reacted by wincing at the nearness of his strong hand, causing him to withdraw and drop it dejectedly to his side.

"Wait here," he ordered. "I need to speak to the doctor."

After counting to ten, Andrea let herself in, just as a burst of thunder shook the house, covering the sound of the creaking door. She heard muffled voices in a room to her left and noticed stairs off to her right. Taking them two at a time, she saw an open bedroom door and entered, ignoring Pierce's orders from downstairs to halt.

Hunter lay in a bed, seemingly asleep, yet so pale Andrea barely recognized him as living. Approaching slowly, fearing she was too late, she tentatively put her hand on his forehead. The soldier who had appeared just hours earlier the essence of magnificent manhood and muscle, now appeared drained of all vitality. She gazed at a life hanging by a thread.

Feeling her touch, he opened his eyes. Andrea watched him try to focus, his gaze moving from her face, down to the stars on her collar. "Howdy, Kulnel," he said hoarsely.

Andrea smiled in relief, and knelt beside him. "It appears I've received a promotion."

"Well deserved," he said closing his eyes.

Andrea held his hand in both of hers. "I yield, sir, to your wisdom and authority," she whispered, leaning near him. "And accept any orders you are inclined to give."

"Stay ...with me ...Andrea."

"I'll never leave you, Alex." She threw her arm across his chest. "Never, never again!"

Kissing his forehead and then his cheek, Andrea stared at his strained face. "Alex, how do you feel?"

He was quiet for a long moment, as if trying to find the energy to speak. "Like I've been . . . humbled." He winced and then opened his eyes. "You look like—" He paused and licked his lips. "Hell."

Andrea brought her hand up to her face and felt the puffiness in her cheek where it had been rammed against the building. "Just a little disagreement."

Alex let out a long, deep sigh as if agitated he could not come to her defense, could not move, could not find the strength to keep his eyes open. He gazed vacantly at the ceiling with livid lips and contorted features as a wave of pain overcame him. And then his eyes glazed over with agony.

Andrea could see strength was failing him, and so could the doctor, who walked briskly to the bed. "That's enough. He needs rest."

Andrea nodded in response. Alex did not respond at all. "Fight, Alex," she whispered, laying her head on his chest for a brief moment to soak in the essence of him. "Please fight like you've never fought before. You cannot leave me now."

There was still no response. His eyes were slightly open, but they were not seeing. He had fallen back into the darkness Andrea knew so well.

℀ ℀ ℀

Doctor Hobbs stood in the hallway with Pierce, eyeing Andrea from head to toe with a disapproving look. "You are a mess," he said gruffly, squinting at her. "I don't know why you are dressed like that and what you are doing here, but you cannot be permitted to continue this charade any longer."

Andrea looked at him defiantly. "I'm not—" But catching a look at herself in a hall mirror made her lose her train of thought. Black, sooty streaks marred her face, but did not conceal the red, swollen cheek or dirty, stringy hair. She could barely even recognize herself. She wondered how Pierce had.

"I need to get back to my duties." Pierce gave Andrea one more backward glance of disgust or bewilderment, then hobbled down the stairs, his leg obviously causing him great pain.

Hobbs did not even wait for his footsteps to fade away. "I shall order a bath drawn for you. There is a lady in the house about your size. You should be able to find something appropriate to wear."

Andrea stared at him, her eyes blank. Exhaustion and worry left her too tired to argue—almost. She gathered her strength for one final skirmish. "I have ridden all night to find out the Colonel's condition, not to take a bath and change my clothes.

Hobbs led her by the arm a short way down the hall. "He's got a good chance." He gazed down the stairs, avoiding Andrea's eyes.

"That's all? A good chance?" When he did not respond, Andrea grabbed him by the arm. "In mercy, speak! Tell me the truth!"

"He was hit on the left side, near the stomach," Hobbs answered in a low voice. "I took the bullet out of his back. We have no way of knowing what damage was done in—"

Andrea swayed and grasped the banister for support. It was worse than she had expected. "Like Stuart," she said in a whispered voice.

"The fact that he's still alive is encouraging." Hobbs ignored her reference to the fatal wound. "That makes it appear the bullet missed all his organs."

Andrea nodded, but her mind was miles away, stuck on that night in the cabin. She thought of all the terrible things she had said—and all the heartfelt things she had not. Her hand and her eyes dropped to the torn fabric of the coat she still wore. Running her fingers over the wool, she found it was no longer damp. But a dark stain around the gaping hole showed where the bullet had penetrated.

Feeling that cavernous hole was more than Andrea could take. She felt sick, like she was going to faint or vomit, or both. Her legs began to tremble. She looked helplessly into the eyes of the physician and tried to speak, but could find no words.

He grabbed her by the arms and shook her. "You've got to be strong. Do you understand me? And that is an order!"

Andrea blinked back tears that hopelessness and fatigue forced into her eyes. She nodded, and in a quivering voice responded in a way that Hunter would not have believed if he had heard it. "Yes, sir ... I'll do whatever you say."

H H H

A warm bath and clean clothes served only to make Andrea's eyes heavy as she sat by Alex's side, fighting to stay awake.

"Go get some sleep," Hobbs said with a commanding hand on her shoulder. "I'll stay with him the rest of the night."

When Andrea started to protest, Hobbs pointed his finger in her face. "I'm not prepared to handle two patients. Go to bed. And that's an order."

Andrea came close to reminding the cantankerous doctor in no certain terms that she did not take orders. But upon reflection, she bent down and kissed Alex on the cheek. After exiting the room, she ran into Pierce talking in low tones to a private at the head of the stairs.

"Captain." She nodded curtly.

"Miss Evans."

Pierce quickly removed his hat and elbowed the private beside him to do the same.

"The apology I offered yesterday was most sincere," he said, his eyes cast on the floor.

"In that case," Andrea said, holding out her hand, "it is sincerely accepted."

Pierce looked into her eyes to test her sincerity, then grasped her hand firmly.

"No hard feelings I hope." Andrea stared straight up at him, conveying her desire for reconciliation.

"None here, Miss Evans." Pierce finally released her hand, but did not unlock his gaze from hers. "Boz told me again what you did yesterday. Words cannot express—"

Andrea held both hands in the air to stop him and closed her eyes to shut out the memory. "I beg of you, if you value the service, do not pain me with mention of it again, Captain Pierce. Ever."

"Of course. I'm sorry. I understand." Pierce touched his hat and headed down the stairs, leaning heavily on the handrail, but limping slightly less than before.

"Captain?"

He turned. "Yes?"

"You've had your leg properly cleaned and dressed?"

Pierce cocked his head, seeming to be surprised that Andrea had noticed or that she cared enough to ask. "Yes, ma'am. Doc worked on it."

"Very well. Please continue to see it is properly taken care of. I would like to have the Colonel's best officers stay healthy during his convalescence." Andrea did not give him time to respond to the compliment before turning and walking away.

From the hallway, she heard Gus Dorsey greet Pierce at the bottom of the stairs. "Captain Pierce. How goes it with the Colonel?"

"Tell the men not to worry overly much," Pierce said. "The lady up there has will enough for both of them." The words sounded sarcastic, but Andrea thought his tone revealed a hint of respect.

She heard the door below creak open and the sound of Gus's voice with a touch of humor in it. "But what shall become of us when they are both at full strength at the same time?"

To this, she did not hear Pierce's reply.

ℋ ℋ ℋ

When Andrea awoke again, light was pouring in the window. She had no idea how long she had slept. An afternoon? A day? More? Although her eyes were still blurry with sleep when she entered Hunter's room, it took only a moment to realize it was full of people. Her heart lurched hard against its cage.

But the sight of Mrs. Duncan sitting by the bed dispelled any gloomy illusions of death. "Ah, there you are, dear," she said, leaning over Alex and feeding him a spoonful of soup. "The Colonel was just telling me a secret."

Andrea's heart slowed its violent hammering when she realized Alex was not only alive, but apparently had the strength to flirt with the hostess of the house.

"He said he needs to get back to Hawthorne for a wedding," Mrs. Duncan announced.

"A wedding?" Andrea pretended to be surprised as she walked toward the bed.

"Most decidedly," Alex answered, taking her hand, his eyes sweeping her appreciatively. "Don't tell me no one informed you."

"Perhaps it was an oversight." Andrea sat down and Alex motioned for her to come closer.

"It appears you are out of uniform."

"If I'm to be a wife," Andrea responded, "I have no more plans to be a soldier."

"If you are half as good at the former as you were at the later, I'll be the luckiest man in Virginia."

"Just Virginia?" Andrea bent down and kissed him on the forehead. His color looked better, she thought, but he still felt warm.

"Oh, all right, the world." He grabbed her weakly and pulled her down for another kiss.

The lines and the tension on his face revealed his pain, and Andrea knew he was only pretending to be stronger—for her sake.

"All right you two, break it up," Hobbs said gruffly, walking to the bed. "I want no more talk of moving back to Hawthorne. Not yet."

"It's not that far. I can—"

Alex looked instinctively to Andrea for backup, apparently assuming she would agree with him wholeheartedly. But she remained silent, her gaze instead going to the doctor. "I believe, perhaps, Doc knows what's best, Alex."

Hobbs looked at her appreciatively. "You are weak. There's still a chance of

362

infection. The stronger you are the better chance you'll have to fight it."

The sound of hoof beats thundering into the yard below interrupted the conversation. Andrea ran to the window. "It's Carter and some of your men." She tried to sound calm, but she could see by the look on all of the faces in the room that Carter would not have come if there was not trouble. By the time Andrea turned around, his spurs were jangling up the steps and he burst into the room.

"'Scuse me, sir," he said, relief evident in his eyes at seeing Hunter sitting up. "We got trouble in blue coming down the pike. I'm afraid you're gonna have to move."

Andrea's gaze went to the doctor, but he looked away. "But where? Where is safe?"

They're searching every house within fifty miles," Carter reported. "We got two choices. We can go to the Carvers, about five miles, and then move again, or we can go to Hawthorne. The Yanks have already been there. Searched it up and down. Chances are they won't be back. We got townspeople out spreading rumors that you've already been taken south."

Alex looked at Andrea. "Got a wedding to go to. Let's go to Hawthorne."

A smile flashed across Carter's face, but he quickly became all business again. "They're hitching a wagon now," he said. "Loading it with vegetables. Might be a bit uncomfortable."

"I'll drive it." Andrea stepped forward.

She saw Carter look questioningly at Alex. "Give her a gun," was all Alex said. Then he looked at Andrea. "You spoke too soon. Your soldiering days are not yet over."

Before Andrea had time to think another thought Alex was loaded and an advance guard had been sent forward. Twelve more riders waited nearby to serve as rearguard and flankers. She tried to appear calm as her gaze landed on Pierce, but when their eyes met, she knew he saw the panic there. He smiled and nodded in a reassuring gesture, and she nodded back in acknowledgment and appreciation. It somewhat unnerved her to see his confident gaze, a look that told her he would defend both lives in the wagon, unhesitatingly, with his own.

Before she picked up the reins, Andrea jumped back out of the wagon and grabbed Carter by the arm as he walked to his horse. "I have no one to give me away. You will come to the wedding?"

Carter looked at her with surprise and then shook his head in feigned annoyance. "Just like a woman, thinking about her weddin' instead of her life. Now git!"

Before she could turn, he grabbed her and kissed her on the cheek. "Wouldn't miss it for the world, darlin'," he whispered. "That man's like a son to me."

Chapter 68

Amor de mi alma.
"You are the love of my soul."

Andrea tried to control the racing of her pulse as she guided the horses toward Hawthorne. When the majestic house appeared beyond the trees, she could not keep her hands from shaking, nor stop the memories that besieged her mind. There it stood, the beautiful, magnificent shrine, just as she remembered it. She knew as never before that this is where she belonged.

By the time she was able to pull the horses to a stop in front of the porch, four men had already dismounted and hopped into the wagon, removing the covering they had placed over their leader. Andrea jumped down and leaned over the side. Finding Alex's hand, she gave it a squeeze. "You're home."

He weakly squeezed it in return. "*We're* home." He took a deep breath of Hawthorne air as if having it inside him again was all he needed to heal.

Andrea watched the men unload Alex and carry him into the house. Then she paused on the porch long enough to give a hurried hug to an excited Mattie, Izzie, Gabriella and Zach.

"Where's Andrea?" Alex was already asking for her by the time she arrived in his room.

"I'm here, Alex." He took her hand when she sat on the side of the bed and brought it to his lips. "Two days," he said, with unopened eyes.

"What is two days?"

Alex opened his eyes, long enough to say two words. "Our wedding."

"You must have a fever." Andrea placed her hand on his forehead. "We cannot possibly be married in two days."

"Don't worry," he replied weakly. "Everything is taken care of."

He sounded convinced—and tired—so Andrea did not argue. "Get some sleep. We'll talk when you wake." After kissing him on the cheek, Andrea headed toward the kitchen, where she found Mattie and Izzie in a state of complete pandemonium.

"Gal, I gonna wup you from here until Sunday if you don't stop that clatternation." Mattie scolded Izzie when she knocked a dish off the table, causing little Angelina to cry.

Andrea ran over and picked up the baby. "Look at you, you little darling! Oh, how you've grown!"

The women barely looked up from their work. "What's the rush here?" Andrea asked, rocking the child in her arms.

Now the heads of both women jerked up at once. "Why, there's to be a weddin' drekly."

Andrea' drew her brows together. "I was somewhat aware of a wedding, but I did not know date had been set."

They both went back to work, ignoring her. "Two days," Izzie said. "Ole Him gived us two days." She paused. "And den the dinner party."

"Such jollifications as ain't neber before been seed," Mattie added.

"Dinner party? Whatever are you talking about? Has everyone at Hawthorne gone mad? There is not possibly time."

"Now, Miz Andrea," Mattie said, taking her by the arm and leading her from the room like she was a misbehaving child. "Why you gotta be all worriment and act so confuzzled? Ain't no botheration at all."

"No botheration?" Andrea shrieked. "Why, for heaven's sakes, I don't even have a proper gown."

"Natchelly Ole Him took care of dat."

"Ole Him took care of it?" Andrea stood blinking in complete bewilderment.

"He done sent a courier. Zach got the material and Gabriella, she workin' sun to sun on a gown. Why such amazinations as you never before sawed been going on around heah. Wait and see if she don't make you the most splendiferous gown you ever sawed!"

Andrea cocked her head, trying to figure out how a brilliant military leader would think of such a thing as material for a gown at such a time as on the battlefield. Then she wondered if the entire household had indeed gone mad if they believed there was actually going to be a wedding in two days.

"Don't matta about all the extra work," Mattie said interrupting her thoughts. "Ole Him say he pay extra."

Now Andrea became even more bewildered. "Pay you extra? Whatever do you mean?"

The servants looked at each and rolled their eyes. "We done been abolished since befoe last frost time." Izzie leaned over the table, "Don' tell no one, though."

"But," Andrea said, trying to think back. "I was here until September."

"Prezactly," Mattie said. "I dismember the exactified day, but Ole Him proclaimated us free right after you lef'. Now you go gets some rest." She looked at Andrea sternly. "You looks like you need it. The boys start coming and jubilatin' day after 'morrow. Natchelly, they out gettin' them Yankees off the scent fust."

A hurried knock and the sound of the door opening interrupted Andrea's confused thoughts. Carter walked into the house with a simple nod in her direction when she went to see who it was.

"Gotta see the Colonel," he said.

"Wait!" Andrea grabbed his arm. "He's resting."

"That's all right. I won't disturb him."

Andrea put her hands to her temples.

"Just gotta leave something for him," Carter said over his shoulder as he took the steps two at a time.

♫ ♫ ♫

Hunter slept all that afternoon and completely through the night, just as the doctor said he might. When his eyes finally opened, his first words, to Andrea's surprise, were, "Did Carter come?"

She looked at him in complete confusion. "Yes ... he said he had to leave something for you. Alex, what—"

"Can you hand me that?" He ignored her words and nodded toward a small package on the stand beside his bed. Andrea walked over and handed him the box she had not even noticed, while he struggled to sit up. "Sit down, please," he commanded, opening the package.

Andrea lowered herself onto the edge of the bed, so confused she did not know what to do or say.

"Andrea Evans, I wish at last to claim you as my bride. Will you accept this as evidence of my desire to give you my name and my loving protection and esteem?" He paused for a moment and seemed almost worried of her answer, because his voice got low. "Will you do me the honor of becoming my wife?"

Shrieking with mad joy and surprise at the sight of the beautiful band, Andrea laughed and cried at the same time. "Alex, it's the most beautiful thing I've ever seen!" She took the ring in shaking hands.

"Does that mean yes?" he asked innocently.

"Yes! Yes! Yes!" She handed him the ring and watched him slide it on her finger. "I shall cling to you for life! You shall never be able to get rid of me!"

Alex held both of her hands in his and looked her directly in the eyes. "My darling, I shall never wish to be rid of you."

The door burst open and Mattie, Izzie and Gabriella came rushing in. "What's all the screaminations up heah?" Mattie asked breathlessly.

"Look!" Andrea stood and held up her hand.

The three women nodded and shrugged, making it clear the news was not unexpected. "I done told you everything was takin' care of," Mattie said, shaking her head, before ushering the other two servants out the door.

Andrea sat down again on the side of the bed, and Alex pulled her to him in a loving kiss. She cupped his face in her hands, and spoke in a serious tone. "You need not treat me like a princess, Alex. All I need is this." She moved one hand to his heart.

Alex took a deep breath and his eyes instantly moistened. "Oh, Andrea, my love," he said, kissing her hand tenderly. "That is yours. Above all else, I give my heart—and my soul—to you for all time." He gazed down at her right hand then, at the other ring that to this day she had not removed.

Andrea saw the look and her eyes went up to meet his. "I can remove it, if you wish."

"No, my darling. His memory is part of both of us. It pleases me to see you wear it. But I would be pleased if you would wear this as well."

He carefully opened another small box and pulled out a silver necklace. After inspecting the engraving carefully, he held it in his hand for her to see. "My grandfather started a practice that I wish to continue," he said. "And so I present this to you, my bride, as a way to welcome you to Hawthorne."

Andrea looked at the medallion that closely resembled the rings that both she and Alex wore. In the center was a large *H* surrounded by the words *"Armed With Honor No Battle Can Be Lost."*

"It's the most magnificent thing I've ever seen," she whispered. "I shall cherish it forever."

"And I shall cherish you," Alex said, pulling her into his arms. "Forever."

Andrea took a deep breath, inhaling the scent of him. "Promise you'll never leave me, Alex," she whispered. "I could not bear it."

He grew quiet and she lifted her head. "I can promise I will not leave willingly," he said, forcing a smile. He sighed deeply and closed his eyes.

"Would you like me to change your dressing before you rest?" Andrea tried to keep the concern from her voice. With his eyes closed, Alex looked pale and strained. She could see he was in much more pain than he pretended to be.

"No, Doc will do it later." His voice sounded casual and indifferent.

"You do not trust me?" she asked, half-jokingly.

"I trust you, Andrea." He took her hand and kissed it, though his eyes remained closed. "With my life. Forever."

"But you wish Doc to do it."

He turned his head away and drew a deep breath. "Yes, I wish Doc to do it."

Andrea struggled to keep her voice from trembling as a wave of unreasoning alarm swept over her. She studied his face and suddenly found it difficult to speak. "Now that we are betrothed, you wouldn't keep anything from me, would you, Alex?"

Alex opened his eyes and gazed intently at her a moment before answering. "There is no reason to panic, Andrea."

Andrea let out her breath as an unexpected whooshing sound in her ears made it difficult to hear. "About what?"

Alex closed his eyes again and sighed deeply. "Doc says I have a fever—"

Andrea sat blinking, trying to erase from her mind the image of the men she had nursed at the hospital. Once infection set in they would linger in agony for days, weeks ... longer—but they rarely survived. Like a mighty warrior, the infection would stalk them, overtaking them no matter how hard they fought. Andrea moved her hand to the bandage under the covers, and felt the warmth pulsing against her fingers. Her eyes grew moist as she consumed the information.

Alex reached put his hand on hers. "It's probably nothing, Andrea. I will fight it."

Andrea dared not move her lips nor try to speak lest she should give away her despair. But the enormity of the situation overcame her, and she sobbed out her feelings of unutterable anguish.

H H H

Carter, who had started up the stairs to check on the Colonel's condition, heard the unearthly sound of Andrea's cry and retreated, his own heart immersed in similar misery. He shivered at the thought of facing her, of trying to console one whose distress would be too profound for comfort of any kind.

After pacing restlessly, he heard the closing of the chamber door above and watched as she descended the stairs slowly and gracefully. Her eyes, swollen and red from grief, appeared dry now, and he sighed with relief. She seemed to have gotten over the initial shock, had accepted the news with a courage and strength typical of her nature. This was a young lady capable of handling her future husband's illness with the deportment and distinguished character of one thrice her years.

"Miss Evans," Carter said when she reached the bottom stair. "You must not be overly alarmed at the news."

When she did not answer or acknowledge his presence, he touched her arm, though he knew his words would be useless. "Andrea, I am here for you. I will help you bear this."

Carter knew she heard him because her head rose a little higher and her hand tightened somewhat frantically on the banister post. She still refused to meet his gaze, continued to look beyond him in an effort to hide her feelings of helplessness.

The fight was an admirable one, but the battle raging within her to maintain her self-control caused her body to tremble violently. Carter watched her swallow forcefully, as if trying to conquer the feelings that threatened to overpower her.

"His loss would be death to me," she whispered. "I would not care to bear it." She had scarcely uttered the final word when her body gave into the anguish. She crumpled to the floor like a soldier who had been suddenly struck down by an unseen bullet.

As Carter gathered the small, unmoving frame into his arms and yelled panic-stricken for the doctor in the next room, he knew his worst fear was coming true. A single bullet was going to come precariously close to extinguishing two lives: one of whom had devoted his all to his country, the other who had devoted her all to him.

Chapter 69

"That love which breaks the heart that was whole,
shall join together, and make whole the heart that is broken."
— *Francis Warrenton Dawson to Sarah Morgan Dawson, 1873*

Andrea stood in the shadows on the balcony and watched the men riding in, her stomach churning with anxiety at the thought of meeting them. Though the wedding celebration had been delayed a week, the marriage had not. Despite Alex's weakened condition the vows had taken place, and his health now seemed to be improving steadily. The fever that had threatened to overtake him had been replaced by increasing vitality and an impatience to return to the field.

"You lost, young lady?" Carter came up behind her. "The Colonel's beginning to think he's been stood up by his bride."

Andrea stared at her feet. "I-I do not know how to face them, Major. How can I?" She turned to face him. "Those I stood against."

Carter put his hand on her shoulder. "You need not fear them."

"But they know, do they not?" Andrea whispered the words. "Who I am? Who I was?"

"I believe it is common knowledge among them. But you have fairly won their regard and their esteem."

Andrea looked into his eyes to see if he told the truth. "Come," he said, holding out his arm. "You've been out of your husband's sight for too long."

Andrea nodded and allowed herself to be escorted down the stairs. When they entered the dining room doorway, there was a sudden hush, and then three-dozen chairs scooted across the floor as everyone stood.

Andrea swept her eyes over the room. When they at last fell upon the bold gaze of her husband, she found herself blushing like a schoolgirl rather than feeling any apprehension about his men. Dressed in his finest military uniform, he appeared every inch the stalwart, intrepid officer he was reputed to be. Her heart skipped a beat at the sight of his imposing form.

Carter escorted Andrea to his side, while Alex continued to devour her with his eyes. After bending down and placing a reverential kiss upon her brow, he put his hand gently on the small of her back and turned toward his men.

"Gentlemen, we are gathered here to celebrate my newest promotion, to a place and title of honor of which I feel I am unworthy—husband. Allow me to introduce my wife, Mrs. Andrea Hunter."

The men clapped and raised their glasses in toast to their leader who, for the first time in a long time, wore a wide and contented smile.

"To love," one of his men said, causing glasses to tinkle up and down the long, glittering candlelit table.

Andrea's heart began to beat at a normal pace while she half-listened to the conversations going on around her. Dropping her eyes to the table, her gaze came to rest on the strong hand that rested upon hers. That hand, she mused, which in time of battle wielded the terrible power of death in but one finger, now wore a band of gold that pledged his life to her.

Alex must have noticed the contemplative look upon her face. He squeezed her hand, leaned over and whispered so only she could hear. "Dear wife, my heart and soul are wrapped around that finger."

Andrea looked up at him, eyes suffused with a mist she quickly blinked away. It seemed to her incredible, and frankly unbelievable, that a man so strong and powerful as the one who sat beside her should wish to call her by that title.

With conversation and drinks now flowing freely, Andrea barely noticed the passing of the hours. Only once, when she happened to glance at Alex and see him reading a dispatch, did her heart flutter with apprehension. Not a shadow crossed his face as his eyes moved across the missive, yet Andrea sensed its importance. When he looked up and his eyes sought Carter's, she prayed it did not mean the enemy was near. If they were in striking distance, she knew her husband would not remain idle, no matter how weak and precarious his physical condition.

But after seeing no change in the joyful, carefree attitudes of the men, she began to relax again. Not until she glanced at Alex and noticed him holding his side painfully did she hurriedly call an end to the evening.

With a strained smile on his face, Alex led her to the door, where one by one they bid each guest goodbye. When Andrea got to the last man, Carter, she threw her arms around his neck. The embrace he gave her was heartfelt, but while in his arms she felt him gesture in a signal to Alex behind her. When he released her and she looked at her husband, she could read nothing on his face, yet she knew the communication had meant something of significance.

Taking Alex's hand she turned toward the stairs, dismissing the scene. It was too late to begin trying to decipher the secret language between her husband and his second-in-command, and she was too tired to try.

"Ah, one more minute," Alex said. "I've ... asked the men to wait outside. There's something I need to tell them. I'll be right up."

"Are you sure? You look so tired. Do you wish me to wait?"

"No. No." He waved his hand. "Carter will help me up the stairs. Go on."

Andrea obeyed, but looked back, confused, when the door closed again. There was something wrong, something she felt now more so than could identify. And when she heard the front door close a half hour later and walked out on the balcony to watch the men ride off, her suspicions were confirmed. Gone was the festive attitude of just an hour before. Although she waved cheerfully at those passing beneath her, they seemed intent on avoiding her gaze. Some nodded sadly in her direction, while others stared straight ahead as they rode silently toward the bridge and into the night. Every countenance reflected a calamity that thus far she had no knowledge.

Andrea tried to push away any thoughts of foreboding. The night had been too magical, her life too wonderful, her future too incredible to worry about such mysteries now.

Chapter 70

"I sometimes feel sure that, if we had known it was to be the last fight of our career, every man of us would have died rather than suffer the defeat that followed."
— *John Munson, Mosby Ranger*

Andrea continued to stand on the balcony and breathe in the cool evening air, even after hearing movement in the room behind her. Shrugging away the shadow of apprehension that continued to pursue her, she concluded that the men were just tired. Now that she thought about it, so was she.

Stepping back inside, she found Alex with his back to her, one hand pressed against the wall, his head bowed as if he had no strength to stand on his own.

"Darling, is something wrong?" Andrea ran to him. "Is it your wound? Come, let me help you to bed."

Alex turned slowly, his face looking serious and stricken. Yet with his usual composed calmness he glanced down at the hand that clutched his arm and spoke casually. "No. It's the war, dear. Lee has surrendered." His voice grew low then, like he was speaking at a funeral. "It is over."

Andrea stood gazing up at him, gasping for the breath she could not catch.

Oh how she had prayed for this day! Yet now as she stared at her husband's tall form arrayed in the splendor of his uniform, the news filled her with distress rather than bliss. She could think only of the pain and sacrifice the man before her—and thousands like him—had endured.

"Oh, Alex, you have served your country with honor," Andrea said, trying to comfort him. "Think of it! There is peace for the living at last."

Alex paced for a moment, the heels of his boots clacking so loudly, each step sounded like gunfire. He paused and took a ragged breath, his countenance reflecting deep and agonizing despair. "But what of the dead?" He turned toward the fire, and for a moment seemed to be reliving the battles and hearing the gunshots of the gallant men who had dashed so freely to the front. "What of the dead?" he murmured.

Andrea stared at the gray cloth stretched across his broad shoulders and felt strangely guilty for not thinking of the heroic departed that had sacrificed all for their beliefs. That he had survived the awful perils of the war—that was her thought beyond all other thoughts.

"If I had only known it was my last battle ..." he muttered, his hands clenched as he stared into the fire. His body heaved, and Andrea felt as if she were gazing upon someone whose life was ebbing out. The fact that he did not die in battle or succumb to his wound did not lessen her fear that he would somehow perish from this loss.

"Do not say it!" Andrea ran to him and wrapped her arms around his waist. "Dear husband, do not think it!" Placing her cheek against his back she wept, knowing that submitting to surrender was a far more intolerable fate to this man than death. The graves of his friends, and those of his men, were scattered all over the blood soaked soil of the Old Dominion. She knew he would rather be nestled with his brother in the bosom of his native Virginia than witness this day—yet Andrea could not help but thank God she was holding him in her arms.

"'Tis the Cause, not the fate of the Cause, that is glorious," she said, turning him around, and grasping his coat with both hands. "You and your men ... you can ..."

"I have disbanded my men."

His voice came to Andrea like waves of sound rolling muffled and indistinct through a thick, impenetrable fog, as her mind drifted back to the dispatch he had received earlier. To neither she nor anyone else had he given a sign of the significance of its contents, in deference no doubt to the joyous occasion. Even now he spoke calmly, though just moments earlier he had severed forever the cords which had so long bound the destinies of his men in one common cause. Tonight, with little warning, the members of his Command had been given the choice to cut the ties forged in the deep heat of battle—or surrender. The gloom on their faces had revealed with what awful force the news had hit them. She pictured them standing with unshaken fidelity until he told them to go, and understood now the tears on the cheeks of those who had dared death for so long.

"This is what is left of my Command." Hunter opened his hand to reveal a red, ragged piece of cloth. "Each man has a piece."

Andrea stared at the last remnants of the flag that had been carried through so many fields of battle and had waved above so many victories; a small piece of faded fabric whose bloodied threads were woven with the noble doctrines of unselfish patriotism and devotion, hope and determination, courage and unwavering resolve. She drew some consolation in knowing that the banner from which it had come—and others like it—would stand as a symbol to future generations of the honor and faithfulness of those who had struggled and died beneath its folds.

"I don't know what to say, Alex," she whispered. "I take no joy in the victory, but I cannot deny I am thankful I have my husband back."

A spattering of celebratory gunfire from a far-off Union camp fell upon their ears, luring them onto the balcony. Both stared silently at the myriad of stars gazing down with peaceful radiance overhead, as if recalling scenes from times past and trying to see what hardships and triumphs the future might hold. It seemed strange to each that on the surface the world looked the same—when they both knew everything was completely and profoundly different.

We will bear the burdens of the future together," Andrea said, leaning against Alex as he wrapped her in his arms. "However great they be. Think of what we have ... of what we can never lose. "

Alex nodded, sorrowful for the loss of his country, yet rejoicing in what he had gained. With Andrea in his arms, all worries about the future vanished. With her by his side the world was full of possibilities.

"I was wrong all along about God not having his hand in the fate of war," he said, staring at the moon rising over the treetops contemplatively.

"What do you mean?" Andrea turned her head and rested her cheek against his heart.

"I would not trade having you in my arms for a thousand battlefield victories, Mrs. Hunter."

Andrea smiled as the gunfire suddenly stopped, enveloping them in a strange and peaceful silence. Even the wind in the trees ceased for a moment, replaced by the faint sound of bells that seemed to move and swell among the hills. "Yes, God had a plan all along," she said, rejoicing in his strong arms around her. "He gave us nothing that we asked for ... yet everything we could hope for."

Alex bent down and kissed the top of her head. "United hearts. United country."

Andrea blinked back tears as she stared out over the moonlit fields of Hawthorne, and whispered the words they both were thinking: *"Neither to be severed, ever again."*

Note to Readers

Though he may seem an exceptional and iconic character, Colonel Alexander Hunter is no more remarkable than thousands of other citizen-soldiers who fought for the Confederacy during the War For Southern Independence. In fact, the inspiration for his character came from the real life exploits of Colonel John S. Mosby of the 43rd Virginia Cavalry—Mosby's Rangers.

Mosby and his band of recruits terrorized the Federal army in northern Virginia from 1863 to 1865. Like the fictional Hunter, Mosby grew into a myth, effectively using terror as his weapon of choice and surprise as his watchword. The Yankees believed that Mosby and his band of outlaws appeared and disappeared with the mist, that when they arrived they made no sound, and when they departed they left no tracks.

Today, travelers on Route 50 (the John Mosby Highway) in northern Virginia can still enjoy the beautiful vistas and quaint towns and villages where Mosby and his famous Rangers once roamed.

I hope you enjoyed this story, and more importantly, that you will want to read more about the brave men and women who believed that honor and principles were worth defending at all costs.

Surely there is something in all of us that longs to return to a time when faith in God and duty to country were noble ambitions, and when love endured as long as the spirit of life remained.

Jessica James

To learn more about John S. Mosby, visit www.mosbyheritagearea.org

Excerpt from the Richmond Whig, October 18, 1864

"The indomitable and irrepressible Mosby is again in the saddle carrying destruction and consternation in his path. One day in Richmond wounded and eliciting the sympathy of everyone capable of appreciating the daring deeds of the boldest and most successful partisan leader the war has produced—three days afterwards surprising and scattering a Yankee force at Salem as if they were frightened sheep fleeing before a hungry wolf—and then, before the great mass of the people are made aware of the particulars of this dashing achievement, he has swooped around and cut the Baltimore and Ohio road—the great artery of communication between East and West, capturing a mail train and contents, and constituting himself, by virtue of the strength of his own right arm, and the keen blade it wields, a receiver of army funds for the United States ...

If he has not yet won a Brigadier's wreath upon his collar, the people have placed upon his brow one far more enduring."

To find out what happens to the characters
of *Noble Cause* after the war,
visit www.jessicajamesbooks.com
and download the Epilogue.

Patriot Press offers a discount for the purchase of 10 or more books. Contact the publisher at www.patriotpressbooks.com or e-mail: patriotpress@live.com

CPSIA information can be obtained at www.ICGtesting.com
Printed in the USA
LVOW11*0311170815

450385LV00004B/14/P